ALISSA CALLEN

Snowy Mountains Dawn

D1653028

SNOWY MOUNTAINS DAWN
© 2024 by Alissa Callen
ISBN 9781867215875

First published on Gadigal Country in Australia in 2024
by HQ Fiction
an imprint of HQBooks (ABN 47 001 180 918), a subsidiary of HarperCollins Publishers Australia Pty Limited (ABN 36 009 913 517)

HarperCollins acknowledges the Traditional Custodians of the land upon which we live and work, and pays respect to Elders past and present.

The moral right of the author has been asserted in accordance with the *Copyright Amendment (Moral Rights) Act 2000.*

This work is copyright. Apart from any use as permitted under the *Copyright Act 1968,* no part may be reproduced, copied, scanned, stored in a retrieval system, recorded, or transmitted, in any form or by any means, without the prior written permission of the publisher.

This is a work of fiction. Names, characters, places, and incidents are either the product of the author's imagination or are used fictitiously, and any resemblance to actual persons, living or dead, business establishments, events, or locales is entirely coincidental.

A catalogue record for this book is available from the National Library of Australia
www.librariesaustralia.nla.gov.au

Printed and bound in Australia by McPherson's Printing Group

To Luke

CHAPTER 1

Brenna Lancaster was a breath away from doing the unthinkable.

The familiar timber and iron facade of the historic stables surrounding her never failed to wrap her in comfort and peace. Yet, in that moment, being in her favourite place wasn't enough.

She was livid. Not just frustrated and cranky because she'd tried to follow a recipe that had yet again ended in a cooking disaster. And not just stir-crazy mad like when she was stuck inside on a rainy day doing bookwork. No, she was steam-out-the-ears incensed. She clenched her hands.

She would *not* swear.

The stables were her sanctuary. Her strategy of leaving her emotions outside and thinking only positive thoughts within had helped her through the loss of her parents. First, when a brain tumour had robbed her and her twin, Taite, of their loving mother and next when a tractor accident had stolen their father.

But right now, as she stood in the tack room and out of sight from the three city boys drinking their soy lattes in the kitchenette, she felt far from serene.

As much as she loved running her horse treks into the high country of her home at Glenwood Station, the months of wet weather had taken its toll. She prided herself on being organised and prepared for anything, but there were some things she couldn't plan for. The tree that had fallen across the track on her first trek of the summer had only been the beginning of what Mother Nature had thrown at her. And don't get her started on the mud. Or, more to the point, the aversion any city person had to getting their new boots mucky.

Her jaw ached from her tightly gritted teeth. And this morning, she had the fourth member of her corporate retreat party still sitting in his fancy four-wheel drive that wouldn't know a proper dirt road if a neon sign pointed towards it. Not only was the man on his phone, but he wasn't just making a quick call. His talk fest was forty-five minutes long and eating into the small window she had to get her clients to shelter before the forecasted deluge arrived.

She glanced through the window at the swollen clouds clustered around the mountain tops and strove for calm. She'd already made three trips outside to deal with the tardy trekker and if she had to go out again, she would at least need to appear professional.

The first time, surely, he couldn't have missed her standing at the stable door or that her hands were on her hips. The second time, he'd left his car and stood with his back to her, his dark head angled as he listened to his phone. As irritated as she'd been, she'd noted the width of his shoulders beneath his blue-and-white checked shirt and the way his designer jeans hung on his lean hips. Usually her city-boy clients didn't look as though they could do a day's work outdoors.

The third time, the man had again been in his car. She'd marched over to tap on the tinted windows. As she couldn't see inside, she had no idea what his response was, but it obviously hadn't been to end the call.

She forced her hands to uncurl. Despite her polite request for the others to get their colleague off his phone, they'd refused. Even the cocky blond who was yet to stop giving her the once-over followed by what he apparently thought was a winning smile. Unfortunately for him she'd seen more charm in a dingo.

The tense glances the three exchanged warned her that the final member of their group could earn the title of her most pain-in-the-butt client yet. Which was saying something, as she'd had some doozies over the years. The final two weeks of her summer trekking season couldn't end soon enough.

She left the tack room and channelled her inner optimism. Maybe she'd have four pampered city slickers in her kitchenette. A tan-and-black kelpie came to lean against her legs, and she ruffled his neck. Bundy called the small town of Bundilla home and had jumped onto the farm ute to stay with her when she'd been in town yesterday.

'He's not in there, is he, Bundy?'

The kelpie gave a soft whine.

Long ago whispers of her mother's voice echoed in her head. *Brenna, just breathe.*

She briefly closed her eyes and did exactly that. Her anger dialled down a notch.

'Okay, Bundy, here's the plan. We check on the others and if that …' She stopped to make sure she kept to her non-swearing policy whenever in the stables. 'That *person* isn't out of his car, we're leaving without him.'

Bundy wagged his tail. She gave him a pat. 'Don't forget my front door is open so you can hang out there until Wedge arrives. Trust me, this is one trek you don't want to come on.'

She didn't know how the kelpie knew but he sometimes turned up to accompany her into the high country when her brother couldn't. If she was ever on her own, she'd sleep with her trusty stockwhip by her swag.

She made her way into the kitchenette. When she'd renovated the stables after her third year of running her trekking business, she'd made sure she included a shiny new coffee machine in the small kitchen and a shower and bedroom next door for her luxury-liking clients.

As soon as she entered, all three men stopped what they were doing on their phones. She'd never understood the attraction of technology. She did admit she was partial to viral goat videos because Grace had a tiny goat called Rebel who terrorised her twin, but otherwise she mainly used her mobile for calls. There was a reason why she had a box in her safe for her clients' phones. The whole idea of the trek was to unplug, get back to nature and reconnect.

'Right.' She kept her voice businesslike. It was a constant mission to prove that despite her lack of height, she was a force to be reckoned with. 'We leave in twenty-five minutes, with or without your colleague.'

Jim, a redhead with pale skin, swallowed. 'Wyatt won't like that.'

'I don't like having to wait.'

The blond smirked. 'I vote for leaving him behind.' His gaze slid over her, the message clear. The less competition there would be for him.

She stopped herself from rolling her eyes. Just. If it wasn't enough that men usually thought she needed help, they assumed she was available.

'Dean, you look anywhere except at my face and I'm leaving *you* behind.'

Disbelief caused his brows to shoot upwards. 'You can't.'

'Yes, I can. You are my guest and as such the rules of common decency and respect apply. The money your employer paid is non-refundable if I kick you off the trek for sexual harassment.' She narrowed her eyes. 'It's your call. You know where the door is.'

Dean gave a stiff nod. His reaction wasn't a surprise. Despite the amount of urban swagger she dealt with, she didn't often encounter resistance. If she did, and it pointed to an iota of aggression, she used the out clause in her contract to send the client packing.

She glanced at the room's third occupant whose attention was focused on where Bundy sat beside her.

'Is he a wild dog?' Steve asked, voice thin. 'I heard there were dog attacks in the mountains.'

She summoned the acting skills she always professed to have after a starring role in her kindergarten play and offered a reassuring smile. Usually, she didn't mind answering questions and bridging the information gap between her world and the one her riders were from. She wanted her guests to leave loving the high country as much as she did. But thanks to the no show client, her well of patience was a little shallow.

'Bundy's a kelpie. You'll find he's a local celebrity.' She cast Dean a saccharine sweet glance. 'Out of the two us, my bite is far worse.'

Dean glowered but wisely didn't say another word.

She checked the weather through the window beside her. The clouds had darkened to a dull pewter. 'Okay, it's twenty minutes until we ride out. You lose your phones in fifteen.'

She spun on her boot heel and left to deal with the thorn in her side that had grown to the size of a blackberry thicket. Whoever this Wyatt was, his total disregard and lack of awareness would only cause further disruptions. There was no way he was coming on this trek. Taite wouldn't be there to play peacemaker and hand beers out around the campfire to smooth any feathers ruffled over her necessary rules.

She squared her shoulders as a deep-seated fatigue dragged at her. As independent and self-sufficient as she was, if she was honest, she was becoming weary of being a one-person team. She only had to see the smile on Taite's face now he was engaged to Hettie and feel his joy through the twintuition she hoped he didn't share, to know how empty her life was.

If that wasn't enough, they weren't the only loved-up couple she had to contend with. Clancy, Rowan and now Trent all had someone special in their lives, making her one of the last singletons in their closeknit group. As much as she loved Bundilla, the small town didn't exactly offer a smorgasbord of dating prospects, let alone anyone who met her non-negotiable criteria. Unless a man looked good on a horse and let her call the shots she wasn't interested.

She'd seen what the world beyond the mountains offered and there'd been even slimmer pickings there. Her steps slowed as the darkness of what had happened a few years ago while she'd been away from her beloved high country overshadowed her anger. Never again would someone else have power over her life. The only silver lining to her secrets was that Taite wouldn't ever know what she'd been through. She couldn't have ever added to the burdens he'd carried after the death of their parents.

She left the stables, the brisk wind toying with her loose hair. Wyatt was again out of his car. All she could see of his face was his carved profile as he stared out at the granite peaks, hip propped against the wooden fence. One large hand pressed his phone to his ear and his other hand was casually shoved into his jeans pocket. Despite the high-end cut of his clothes, his boots were worn. No doubt he was a city boy who'd adopted the trend to wear boots with his suits. Just like his fancy four-wheel drive, his traditional rural footwear wouldn't have seen a speck of real dust.

She swapped an exasperated look with Bundy. She could forgive Wyatt if this was some sort of emergency, but she was yet to hear him talk. It was as though all his focus was on letting the other person have their say.

Wyatt may have listed a work colleague as his contact person but that didn't mean he wasn't in a relationship and this wasn't some sort of long lovers' goodbye. She was far from an expert on such things, but if so, wouldn't he at least appear as though he felt something, let alone speak? No, this had to be a work call. There wasn't any other reason why Wyatt would look as though he had all the time in the world to chat. Unluckily for him, she didn't.

She stalked over. He finally appeared to speak before he casually lowered his arm and slid his mobile into his shirtfront pocket.

Brenna stopped a body length away. As she was out of her happy place she technically could swear, at least in her head. She pressed her lips together and mentally ran through every word in her venting repertoire before making up some more.

Wyatt pushed himself away from the fence and turned. Alarm ricocheted through her. He was gorgeous. Not just stop-and-stare gorgeous but to-die-for gorgeous. And he wasn't even smiling. His flint-grey eyes locked with hers and she felt the impact to the bottom of her scuffed soles.

The functioning part of her brain immediately crossed the let-her-call-the-shots item off her potential partner list. Even if Wyatt was unattached, there was no way he'd meet such a criterion. He was no mollycoddled city boy. The hard, strong lines of his body and his piercing gaze said he'd never concede control to anyone. Beneath his polished veneer was a man as tempered and immovable as the mountains surrounding them.

The silence lengthened and something indecipherable skated across his features before a muscle worked in his cheek. As unemotional as he'd seemed earlier, she now sensed a don't-mess-with-me edge.

If he thought she'd duck and run, he was mistaken. Her tough guy wrangling skills were top notch. After all, she'd been bossing around her twin since the day she was born. His colleagues might not be game to take him on, but she was.

She kept her tone polite, despite the message she was about to deliver.

'I'm Brenna. I usually try to give people the benefit of the doubt, but you have been on your phone for almost an hour, keeping everyone waiting. This corporate retreat will only involve three members of your team. I will no longer accept your booking. If you need a place to stay, I recommend The Bushranger in town.'

Wyatt studied her before scrubbing a hand across his clean-shaven chin. A weariness that almost matched her own dulled his eyes and left lines of strain bracketing his mouth. If anyone needed a corporate retreat and a break, this man did.

She pushed aside her sympathy—plus the thought of how his jaw would look with three days' worth of trekking stubble.

'Dean give you any trouble?'

She frowned at the conversational U-turn as well as the way his low deep voice skittered over her skin like a physical touch. 'Nothing I can't handle.'

An almost smile shaped his lips before he assessed the sky like any country boy would. 'Sorry I didn't keep a closer watch on the weather.'

Brenna raised a brow. That was unexpected, but she needed more than a half apology.

'And,' Wyatt moved to pat Bundy, 'I'm truly sorry I've held up the trek. My call was unfortunately necessary and unavoidable.'

She hesitated. He'd not only apologised and with a sincerity that surprised her, but Bundy greeted Wyatt like a long-lost friend. Even as she watched, the kelpie rolled over to have his stomach scratched.

An unwelcome suspicion unfurled.

Bundilla had a local quilting group who filled their days with as much matchmaking as they did patchworking. But Bundy was gaining his own reputation as a master at bringing couples together. She'd thought the kelpie had either popped out to see Taite's cream kelpie puppy, Waffles, or had known Taite wasn't accompanying her on this trek. He'd better not have turned up to work a little Cupid's magic because all four of the city boys would not pass muster.

She snuck a quick glance at Wyatt. He'd already failed to meet the first item on her list. As for the second, it was a given he'd look good on a horse. He'd look good riding a go-kart. But her stipulation was about more than aesthetics. Nothing moved her more than seeing the depth of a true bond between a horse and their rider.

Horses were a discerning judge of character. Considering Wyatt had indicated on his form that he hadn't ridden in fifteen years, his challenge would be to simply stay in the saddle.

Wyatt gave Bundy another belly rub and straightened. She'd thought his eyes were a pure grey but now glimpsed flecks of steel blue. She ignored the trip in her pulse as he turned his full attention on her. A raindrop had splashed onto her cheek, reminding her of the urgency to get going. She was just twitchy thanks to how the morning had started.

'I better not regret this,' she said, tone firm. 'But if you're ready to go in fifteen minutes, you're back on the trek.'

CHAPTER 2

Wyatt Killion's grandmother used to say that life was made up of moments and to value each one. Except there were some moments he wished he could reset.

One would be his mother driving on bald tyres in the rain to buy another carton of beer for his father. If he could rewrite that moment, his five-year-old self would have hidden the car keys. Then his mother wouldn't have had a tyre blow, lost control and left him without giving him the chance to say goodbye.

The second would be when he accompanied Nick, who had been like a brother to him, into the grave-faced specialist's office. On this occasion he'd have made sure he was the one to be diagnosed with pancreatic cancer. Then Mia wouldn't be alone in raising the newborn daughter Nick had never met. Wyatt had no one to miss him if he were gone.

And the third would be agreeing to Mia's plea to take Nick's place on the corporate retreat. Riding in the high country had been a bucket-list item that Nick hadn't been able to complete. Mia was convinced that a part of him would be doing the trek with Wyatt. If Mia hadn't made such a request, then she wouldn't have had to sob out her despair over the phone—he would have been there in person to support her.

Wyatt's gaze centred on the country girl dressed in jeans, a pink shirt and muddy boots striding through the stable door ahead of him. And he'd have not met a woman who his gut told him was a threat even before his mind had done a risk assessment.

His jaw hardened. Some childhood lessons were as instinctive as breathing. To survive, know your adversary. He'd learned the critical moment to back off before his father turned into a mean drunk. When surrounded by bullies in the playground of yet another new school, he'd worked out when to strike first.

Brenna turned to smile at the kelpie trotting beside her. With her shoulder-length blonde hair, pale blue eyes and fine-boned features, she wasn't only stunning but gave the illusion of fragility. An impression that had been dispelled within seconds of her rapping on his car window. The fierceness of her frown left him in no doubt she was as formidable as any seasoned CEO.

But only when they'd stood face to face had he realised the true extent of how much she tripped his internal switches. If this corporate retreat were a business deal, he'd walk away.

Brenna seemed to be everything he wasn't. She changed emotional gears with an expertise he could only dream of. Despite the glare she'd scorched him with, she'd reined in her anger and with a level-headed rationality reversed her decision to kick him off the trek. She was in control of her feelings; they weren't in control of her.

He swapped his monogrammed leather duffle bag to his other hand to ease the tension in his shoulders. There were two things he'd cauterized from his life: feelings and failure.

Emotions had only ever rendered him weak or been turned into weapons to use against him. So, he'd taught himself to feel nothing. If he was numb, then he couldn't be hurt. He was indifferent, unemotional. His laser work focus left zero room for diversions or downtime.

His attention solely on Brenna, he barely registered the horses sticking their heads over the half doors of their stalls as he walked by. When a chestnut gave Brenna a side eye and a loud whinny, she stopped.

'Major, you've already had extra molasses. I'm not giving you morning smoko just because Hettie does. We both know she's far nicer than I am.'

The pair appeared to engage in a battle of wills before the chestnut gave a disgruntled huff and vanished into his stall. Despite Brenna's words, there'd been affection in her tone.

The kelpie looked back at Wyatt and he met his amber stare. It was almost as though the dog knew why he was dragging his heels. Not only was he about to spend days with a woman who clearly handled her feelings as well as her horses, he had no doubt she'd shine a spotlight on how he was failing both Mia and Nick.

It didn't matter that Wyatt had structured his life to guarantee success in every facet that didn't involve personal relationships. Or that he'd vowed to never again allow failure to make him feel worthless or inadequate. To fulfill his promise to Nick and be there for Mia, he needed to be the exact opposite of who he was. He didn't have a clue about what to do to help her, let alone the right thing to say. The truth was he wasn't only failing, he was freefalling. And he had to find a way to stop.

Resolve tightened his grip on the bag. By the end of the trek, he had to have the answer on how to deal with the emotional wrecking ball inside him. He couldn't keep letting Mia and baby Emily down.

When Brenna and the kelpie disappeared into what Wyatt assumed was a guest area, he didn't follow. He hadn't come to socialise and was in even less of a mood for company than usual. He'd head outside to where a group of saddled horses were tied to a hitching rail.

At the kitchen doorway, he dropped his leather bag beside the others and glanced inside the room. Tim and Steve gave him a nod. He'd only met the men that morning when he'd collected them as per Nick's PA's instructions from Glenwood Station's airstrip when they'd landed by helicopter. He'd chosen to drive on his own from Sydney.

All three men had been Nick's colleagues from his finance firm. Nick had spoken about Tim and Steve but barely mentioned Dean. Wyatt had heard enough from the opinionated blond on the short drive from the airstrip to know why.

Dean glanced at Wyatt before giving Brenna a million-watt smile. Brenna's only response was to tap her foot and hold out her hand for Dean's phone. When he felt sure Dean wouldn't cause Brenna any problems, Wyatt continued towards the horses. The open stable door framed the sweep of the valley that rolled into gentle hills and rugged mountains. A pair of galahs perched on a trough, dipping their beaks into the water. A fresh breeze, untainted by city fumes, washed over him.

He snapped a photo for Mia and typed off a quick message to say he'd call as soon as the trek ended. Nick's parents were due in Sydney that afternoon and would stay at least a week. As guilty as he felt for being away, at least Mia would be well supported while he was off-grid.

Wyatt returned his phone to his pocket. He'd use the minutes alone to regroup. But as the once familiar smell of horses and hay filled his lungs, memories he'd carefully filed away flew open.

The quietly spoken words of his grandfather as they worked with the draft horses he'd loved. The tears in his grandmother's eyes when he'd felt comfortable enough to accept her hug. And the bleak emptiness when he'd lost them both.

He focused on the horses in front of him to keep himself in the here and now. He'd known coming on the trek would heighten his grief at losing Nick and also return him to a part of his past he couldn't bring himself to face. Naively he'd thought he'd have been in a better position to deal with everything. Yet, here he was, not even in the saddle, and his thoughts were as turbulent as the approaching storm clouds.

He forced himself to study a stocky bay who had his head lowered as though asleep. He was the tallest of the four trekkers so the bay would be for him. While he was sure the horse would be safe and reliable, it wasn't what he needed. His attention swung towards the herd grazing in the adjacent paddock.

A blue roan had his head flung high as his ears flickered and his mane rippled in the wind. Something about the horse's restless energy spoke to him. Without his phone it would prove a struggle to keep his always-switched-on brain busy unless he rode a horse that would challenge him.

He sensed rather than heard the kelpie come to sit beside him. Then Brenna's boots sounded. As he turned, she held out a box for his phone. Her brow was slightly raised as though expecting opposition.

He dug into his pocket to add his mobile to the other three, then looked back at the blue roan.

Brenna followed his gaze. 'His name's Outlaw. He's a brumby.'

The horse spun around as though trying to catch whatever scent carried on the wind.

'I'm guessing the saddled bay on the left is mine?' Wyatt said.

'Yes.'

He glanced at Brenna and found her watching him. 'Am I pushing my luck if I ask for a change?'

'I matched you with Sonny because you indicated on your form you haven't ridden in years. Outlaw's a seasoned trekking horse but he's only suitable for my most experienced clients or my brother.'

Wyatt broke eye contact before she could glimpse the anguish he couldn't contain. 'As a teenager I lived on my grandparents' farm. I rode anything and everything.'

Brenna didn't immediately reply and then she turned to collect a black riding helmet from a nearby stand. 'Humour me. Jump on Sonny.'

She passed Wyatt the helmet and went to tighten the bay's girth before leading the gelding towards the round yard.

Wyatt followed, adjusting the chin strap of the helmet as he walked. Once inside the yard, Brenna cast him an assessing glance before lengthening the stirrups. With a slight smile, she handed him the reins.

He gave a nod and concentrated on making sure he wasn't going to fail at anything else today. Mia's tears continued to make his jaw ache. He should have been able to help ease her sorrow more.

He ran a palm over the white stripe on Sonny's nose before gathering the reins in his left hand and swinging into the saddle. He'd already held the trek up long enough. Brenna needed to see he could manage Outlaw. He nudged Sonny forwards as muscle memory and his grandfather's long-ago instructions replayed in his head. Heels down. Shoulders back. Look where you want to go.

As soon as Sonny responded to the shortening of the reins and a leg squeeze to break into a trot and then a canter, it was as though the real world ceased to exist. It was just Wyatt and the bay and the rightness of the connection he'd felt the first time he'd sat on his grandfather's old grey gelding.

On the third pass around the circular yard, Wyatt realised Brenna no longer stood at the gate. Instead, with a lead rope and halter in her hand, she strode into the paddock to catch the blue roan.

Wyatt slowed Sonny to a walk and rubbed his neck. 'Thanks, mate. I owe you.'

He dismounted and led the bay to the hitching post where he unsaddled him. Brenna tied up the blue roan nearby. At Wyatt's questioning look, she took a second to nod that yes, he could take Sonny to his paddock. She was either surprised by his offer or didn't like accepting help. As unreadable as her expression was, he sensed a new wariness that hadn't been there before.

When he returned, the blue roan was saddled and Brenna had passed around helmets to the other trekkers.

She collected oilskins from off the pegs set into a knotted log attached to the wall. 'For obvious reasons,' she said with a tilt of her head towards the moody sky, 'our rolling up an oilskin lesson will need to wait until we get to camp.'

Wyatt shrugged on the stiff coat. The distinctive smell of waxed cotton further stirred the memories of feeling content on his grandparents' New England farm.

Tim came to his side, every button on his oilskin done up and the polish on his new boots gleaming. The kelpie too approached.

'His name's Bundy,' Tim said, taking a cautious step away from the kelpie. 'He's not a wild dog, in case you were wondering.'

Wyatt ruffled Bundy's neck. 'Thanks.' He hesitated and gave what he hoped passed as a friendly smile to the redhead. When Nick was ill, Tim had taken on extra work to make sure he hadn't overdone things, and Wyatt appreciated it.

Tim's eyes rounded and then he too smiled.

Feeling Brenna's gaze on him, Wyatt glanced over to find her brow furrowed. She looked away and didn't pay him any further attention as she took the men and their horses to the round yard.

Wyatt went over to Outlaw. Even without the saddle bags attached to the black mare beside the brumby, Wyatt knew she was Brenna's. The horse gave him a glare as if to say, *don't even think about befriending her*.

The blue roan gave a quiet whicker and Wyatt smoothed a hand down his shoulder. 'I'm happy to see you too. I'll be a little rusty so bear with me.'

Over in the round yard Brenna helped the final member of the trekking party use the mounting block to climb into his saddle. The group walked around the fence perimeter to become used to their horses.

Brenna returned to slip on an oilskin and a battered felt hat. When she approached her mare and the horse nuzzled Brenna's cheek, Brenna's expression softened. As she turned and saw Wyatt looking across at her, she shot him a sharp glance. He held her gaze before going back to adjusting the stirrups on his new saddle. If he hadn't already felt on edge, it had taken more effort than it should have to look away from the country girl.

Makeup free, Brenna's lightly tanned skin had been smooth and her full lips a natural pink. When she'd used her hand to flip her pale blonde hair out from beneath the oilskin collar, he'd caught a faint scent of roses. A fragrance that reminded him of summer and his grandmother's garden.

He went to lengthen the second stirrup. To keep his life as uncomplicated as possible, his relationships were always brief and casual. He'd be upfront with whoever he was involved with about his expectations, even if they later decided to change the rules. He'd never had a woman distract him. Until several minutes ago.

He swung onto Outlaw's back. The trek hadn't even begun and he was off to a bad start. The key to achieving what he needed to over the upcoming days would be to stay away from Brenna. He hid a frown as she led her mare to where Bundy sat nearby. The pulled-low brim of Brenna's hat shaded her eyes, making it impossible to ignore the delicate curve of her jaw.

Brenna bent to give the kelpie a farewell pat. 'See you later. Enjoy Hettie's baking.'

Except once she too was in the saddle, Bundy moved as if to follow her.

Brenna's shoulders lifted on a sigh. '*Of course* you're coming.' When a gust of wind swept by, Wyatt wasn't sure but he thought she then said, 'If there's any nonsense, your days of being snuck bacon under the breakfast table will be over.'

The kelpie tilted his head and gave a grin before wagging his tail.

CHAPTER 3

Do. Not. Look.

Brenna reprimanded herself for the umpteenth time since they'd ridden away from the stables. But still her head turned to where Wyatt rode several horse lengths away on her right. What was wrong with her?

She looked forwards and directed her stare at the wide track that wound its way alongside the creek. They'd left the paddocks filled with Taite's red deer behind and were riding towards the valley edge before climbing into the hills.

There was still at least a twenty-minute journey to where she'd planned to stop for lunch. So far the sullen clouds had only delivered a smattering of rain that had barely made a sound on their oilskins. But going off the ink-dark sky they would soon encounter the forecasted storm. All her focus should be on making sure they reached shelter as soon as possible. Instead, it was fixated on Wyatt.

She'd grown up surrounded by people who looked good on a horse so there was no excuse for being so enthralled by him. But there was something about Wyatt that said he was more than a skilled and confident rider. When he'd settled deep into Sonny's saddle, his long legs in the stirrups and hands soft on the reins, she'd known she'd be catching Outlaw. She hadn't been the only one to recognise Wyatt for the gifted horseman he was. Sonny's ears had pricked, his neck had arched and he'd cantered around the round yard as if he'd been in a showring.

As for Outlaw ... She lost the battle to not sneak another sideways glance. She'd never seen the brumby so in tune with anyone, even her twin. Outlaw was the perfect barometer of a rider's mood. The gelding didn't do well with anyone who wasn't relaxed or present. While Wyatt's face was unreadable, his intelligent grey gaze took in everything around him. It was as though being on horseback put his soul at ease and his demons to rest. A feeling she knew all too well.

She made a point of looking straight ahead. She'd had a lifetime of reading her gruff twin so when it came to tough guys and what they could be hiding, her intuition was finely honed. When Wyatt had stared at Outlaw, she'd glimpsed longing but also profound pain. His jaw had been set so hard it was as though it had been carved out of high-country granite. A man like Wyatt wouldn't have asked for a horse change unless it had been important.

Which brought her to the other reason why she couldn't stop thinking about him. He didn't just surprise her, he confused her. And she hated not knowing exactly who she was dealing with. Never again would she allow a man to catch her unawares. Still waters ran deep and she was certain there was far more to Wyatt than the snapshot he allowed people to see. He was as complex and multilayered as the rescue horses she worked with, the ones that others had given up on.

Ever since she was a child, she'd looked for patterns or connections to make sense of the world. This usually ended up with her having a theory about something or someone. But her theory about Wyatt being arrogant and self-centred, even if he had kept them waiting, felt more and more wrong. It was proving difficult to reconcile the man she'd believed him to be with the person who had ridden by Tim's side when they'd left to make sure he was okay.

Then there had been Wyatt's offer to put Sonny in his paddock. When Taite discovered that she'd let someone do something for her he'd have a field day. There wasn't anything she detested more than being perceived as weak or helpless, apart from being called *little lady*. Except Wyatt hadn't been patronising or trying to curry favour. He'd seemed genuine in wanting to be of use.

Bundy came to walk beside her, his tongue lolling.

She threw the kelpie a pointed glance and kept her voice low so only he could hear. 'Just to be clear, a certain someone only ticks one box. And I meant what I said. Any matchmaking shenanigans and there'll be no more sneaky breakfast bacon.'

Bundy gave her an innocent look before dashing off, nose down, along an animal trail.

She turned again but this time it was to check on the three novice riders. Tim still had his hands high, but his shoulders were relaxed. Steve continued to push his boots too far into his stirrups, but after they'd seen their first wallaby, he hadn't stopped grinning. As for Dean, he gave her what she guessed he believed was his most winning smile.

Predictably, he thought that since they were on the trek she couldn't kick him off. While her clients mightn't have their phones, she had hers. In a saddle bag she had a two-way radio along with a first-aid kit, emergency beacon and other essentials like farrier tools. She was prepared for any eventuality, especially sending someone home.

She met Dean's overly interested gaze. 'For the record, my rules still apply. We might have ridden for an hour, but Wedge can be here in fifteen minutes. He doesn't take kindly to anyone ruining my day. So, if I ask him to take you back, I'd count on having to walk at least half the way.'

Dean stiffened and pulled on his outside rein to put more distance between them.

Just like earlier at the stables Brenna felt Wyatt's gaze on her, but she refused to meet his eye. She could fight her own battles.

A flurry of raindrops on her oilskin had her increasing Ebony's pace to a fast walk. The other horses would follow the mare's lead.

It wasn't long until a weathered boulder came into view. She led the way along a bridle track to where the timber opened up into a small clearing. The leaves on a lone poplar rippled in the strong wind, while beyond a stand of candle barks a ribbon of water gleamed. A pitched corrugated iron roofline soon appeared along with a stone chimney.

The horses, sensing that the sky was about to rip open, headed for the open-sided shed. All five were inside, their riders dismounted, when thunder rumbled and rain pounded on the roof.

Raising her voice to be heard, Brenna ran through how to clip the lead ropes on the hitching post to the rope halters that the horses wore beneath their bridles. She then showed the group how to loop the reins onto the saddle, run up the stirrups and loosen the girth.

When the horses were settled, she took off her oilskin and hat before making sure each man had a lunchtime job to do. Part of the experience was for trekkers to get their hands dirty. Plus there was no way she was waiting on anyone, particularly city boys used to having everything done for them. Just as she had been when riding, Brenna was acutely aware of where Wyatt was and what he was doing.

It wasn't long until Tim had lit the fire in the stone fireplace that Brenna had set earlier that morning when she'd dropped off an esky full of fresh food. When Tim didn't seem sure about what to do next, Wyatt added logs from the circular wood stacker Taite had welded out of rusted metal.

By the time the billy had boiled and steam curled from mugs of tea and coffee, the rain had slowed enough so that the group could speak at a normal volume. Everyone tucked into the salad rolls, wraps and assorted sandwiches as the rain continued to fall in a curtain of silver-grey. Brenna hadn't missed how Wyatt seated himself at the second wooden picnic table away from the others.

'What is this place?' Tim asked as he took another roast beef roll.

Brenna glanced at the overhead beams sawn from alpine ash that Taite had salvaged from a derelict stockman's hut.

'The stone chimney is all that's left of an old miner's hut. Not that you can see it, but across the clearing and through the candle bark trees there's a creek where platypuses live.'

She stopped to share her ham and cheese sandwich with Bundy. There was no way she was going into how the summer after they'd lost their mother, she and Taite had built this shed in her memory. Platypus Hollow had been one of their favourite picnic and camping spots as children. Wyatt's gaze caught hers as though he knew the place held sentimental value. She looked away. She could add perceptiveness to the new theory she was building around him.

Steve sighed. 'Nick would have liked it here.'

If Brenna hadn't been watching Wyatt all day and knew some of his tells, she'd have missed the subtle tightening of his shoulders. He gave a single nod.

As the mood shifted, she studied the men at her table. Steve and Tim wore solemn expressions while Dean appeared disinterested. Months ago, there had been a Nick scheduled for the trek, but an email had arrived to change the name to Wyatt's.

Tim cleared his throat before saying to Wyatt, 'Was Mia okay when you spoke to her?'

Wyatt pushed his unfinished roll away. 'No.'

Tim and Steve gave slow nods.

Wyatt came to his feet and without a word strode over to the horses.

Brenna didn't want to pry but if there was anything going on that might affect the members of her trekking party, like losing a colleague, it would be helpful to know. There was something not quite right between the four men. Tim and Steve treated Wyatt with a nervous deference, while Dean would scowl at Wyatt when his back was turned.

At Brenna's questioning look, Tim and Steve exchanged a glance before Tim spoke. 'Nick worked with the three of us. He passed away from cancer.'

'I'm so sorry.'

The two men nodded while Dean reached for another sandwich.

'Three of you?' she asked. 'I'm guessing not Wyatt.'

'We only met him today,' Steve answered. 'He and Nick were close.'

Brenna finished her tea. No wonder the group dynamics were off. At least two of the men were grieving and instead of a cohesive group, she had one member who was a stranger to the others.

Deep in thought, she collected the empty lunch containers and put out a selection of Hettie's salted caramel brownies, shortbread and carrot cake. While the downpour continued, they weren't going anywhere.

'I could get used to this,' Tim said, taking a brownie while Steve deliberated over which of the delicious home-baked goods to try first.

Dean's fingers drummed on the wooden tabletop.

She'd double-checked that none of her trekkers were smokers. Thanks to the wet summer there was an abundance of grass that could pose a fire risk once things dried off. But not all her clients were truthful. She left her seat to reach into the bottom of the tub for the gum she always included.

She tossed Dean the small packet. It would help keep his mind off needing a nicotine hit. He gave her a smile that was close to being genuine.

Even after a second round of fresh tea and coffee, Wyatt stayed over with the horses. The tank to fill the water buckets was attached to the modular amenities unit out in the rain, so they'd filled the buckets using the roof run-off. Wyatt stared into the storm while he waited for another container to refill.

Brenna picked up the plate of carrot cake and headed over. Arms crossed, Wyatt leaned against a wooden pole. The cotton of his blue-and-white checked shirt pulled tight across his shoulders. She advised her clients to wear long-sleeved shirts, but none had ever made her take a second look let alone cause her attention to linger.

He half turned before she reached him and she caught a subtle hint of sandalwood. The scent wasn't something country boys usually wore but she recognised it from some of the candles in Ruth's shop.

Wyatt's exhaustion appeared to seep through his rigid control, causing the lines bracketing his mouth to deepen.

'Cake?' she asked, resisting the urge to step back. She needed to work on being better prepared for the whirlpool in her stomach whenever their gazes met. 'Before you ask, I didn't make it. I'm more of a camp oven cook.'

He hesitated before selecting a piece.

When he didn't continue the conversation, she spoke again. Thanks to her twin, another thing she excelled at was making uncommunicative men talk. Except with Taite it usually involved having him seated in a moving vehicle so he had no means of escape. 'I'll wait until the bucket's filled if you'd like to finish your coffee.'

'I held you up earlier. It's the least I can do.'

'Which brings me to why I've come over.'

A gleam of amusement shifted the darkness from his eyes. 'It wasn't to bribe me with cake so I'll forget about how saddle sore I'll be tomorrow?'

Her lips twitched. 'I'm nothing but a consummate hostess.' Her tone sobered. 'It's my turn to apologise. I assumed you were making a work call. If I'd known why you were on your phone, I wouldn't have been so hard on you.'

'There was no way you could have known. Besides, if I'd done a better job of helping Mia, the call wouldn't have gone on for as long as it did.'

There was no missing the self-criticism in his voice or the way his slice of carrot cake now seemed forgotten in his hand.

'Take it from me, there isn't any rule book on how to deal with grief. Whatever worked to help Mia yesterday might not work today.'

She answered the unspoken question in his eyes. 'My parents. Just being there to listen to Mia, even if you don't think you did much, would have been a huge help. If you need to call her, please feel free to use my phone.'

'Thank you.'

She nodded and turned to walk away, heeding the urge to put distance between them. She didn't usually reveal so much personal information and especially not to someone she'd just met.

She had a new theory, except it wasn't about Wyatt, it was about herself. As it turned out, having just two requirements for her future partner wasn't going to be enough. She needed a third.

She'd always thought of herself as being self-aware, but she'd learned something today. Her judgement couldn't be trusted.

Just because Wyatt had grey eyes she could get lost in and a jaw she couldn't stop sneaking glances at was no excuse for forgetting he'd never pass her first condition. As good as he might look on a horse, he'd never let her call the shots, and that was assuming he was available.

Dean looked across at her and she kept her thoughts from showing on her face.

Her third non-negotiable had to be that on a chemistry spectrum the heat metre was set to mild, not high. It didn't matter if every couple she knew couldn't keep their hands off each other, she refused to allow attraction to cloud her judgement.

If her time away from the mountains had taught her anything, it was that never again would she allow someone else to sit in the driver's seat of her own life.

CHAPTER 4

There was no doubt Wyatt wasn't in the city anymore.

Instead of the glow of an urban skyline lighting up the night sky, campfire flames flickered in front of him. Instead of conditioned air cooling his skin, a crisp evening breeze drifted by, carrying with it the scent of woodsmoke. And instead of a vaulted ceiling above him, a blanket of stars shimmered with pinpricks of muted light. But most of all his end-of-day exhaustion stemmed from physical exertion and not solely from struggling to make sense of his emotions.

A warm weight moved against his leg and he bent in his camp chair to pat Bundy. Brenna had gone to have a shower and the kelpie had joined him.

'You have a hard life, Mr Bundy.'

The kelpie's tail thumped his ankle.

'As sore as my muscles are,' Tim said from where he sat nearby, 'if this is country life, sign me up.'

Steve nodded. 'How did I not know hot showers could feel so good? And as for that dinner, I'm never eating apple pie again unless it's cooked in a camp oven.'

Across from Wyatt, Dean remained silent as he took a swig of beer. If he wasn't staring into the fire, expression moody, Wyatt noticed he was keeping tabs on when Brenna finished her shower.

The conversation lapsed and the only sounds were the crackle of burning wood and the call of an owl. Wyatt allowed himself to relax into the simplicity and peace.

The rustic but comfortable shelter where they'd had lunch was only a taste of what was to come when they'd arrived late afternoon at their base for the next two nights. The permanent camp was nestled in a picturesque valley by a river and boasted eco-friendly bathrooms, a solar power generator and another huge open-walled shed with a pitched roof.

At one end of the shed, hessian walls divided off rooms containing double-sized iron camp beds with intricate headboards welded out of old tools. The other end contained a large table and chairs and a side table that doubled as a bar. Whoever Wedge was, he'd delivered swags, their bags and whatever food and supplies they and the horses would need.

Wyatt took a mouthful of beer as Dean again glanced over to the shower block. The camp had been designed with Brenna's privacy in mind. A small lockable building, which she'd explained was a relocated shearer's hut, doubled as her sleeping quarters plus storage. After they'd arrived, she'd produced fishing rods, beach towels for swimming, a chess board, books and an assortment of games.

While Tim and Steve had attempted to go fishing, Wyatt had read a book.

Even if he hadn't planned to keep to himself, when Dean had lounged in a camp chair tracking Brenna's every move, Wyatt hadn't felt comfortable leaving. He looked to where Bundy had his head on his paws, his gaze trained on the blond. He had no doubt Brenna could deal with Dean, but he shared the kelpie's view that Dean was paying too much close attention to Brenna.

When a door closed from over in the amenities block, Dean sat taller to gain a better view of Brenna walking along the solar-lit path. Dressed once more in jeans and a pink shirt, her tousled hair fell in a blonde cloud around her shoulders. Bundy disappeared into the shadows and reappeared by her side.

Tim and Steve left their chairs, one to get another beer and the other to head to his sleeping quarters.

When Wyatt was sure his words wouldn't be heard by anyone but Dean, he spoke. 'You make one wrong move towards Brenna and that kelpie will not be happy.'

Dean threw him an unfriendly look. 'I can handle a pet dog.'

Wyatt shook his head at the man's ignorance and arrogance. 'Brenna wasn't joking about kicking you off. As for how this Wedge would feel if he and Brenna were involved, I hope those new boots of yours are broken in. You'll have a long hike back.'

'There was a photo of Wedge on her website. He looks old enough to be her grandfather.'

'That doesn't mean she doesn't have someone in her life.'

Dean shrugged. 'There's no ring on her finger. In two days the trek will be over. I think I'll hang around.'

'You'd better be certain you'll be welcome. That stockwhip Brenna carries is not for show.'

Dean's lip curled. 'I haven't met a woman I couldn't win over.' He turned for a last look as Brenna disappeared into the shearer's hut. 'She's different. Plus she's hot, the way she fills ou—'

'Enough.' Wyatt's growl cut him off. 'Show some respect.'

He ignored Dean's glare as Tim returned.

Dean wasn't saying anything Wyatt didn't already know. Brenna was stunning and unlike any woman he'd met in his city world. But should Dean put one foot out of line with her, either on or off the trek, it wouldn't only be Bundy he'd have to deal with. Even if Brenna had made it clear she didn't appreciate anyone coming to her defence.

He'd have any woman's back if they were faced with unwanted attention. Except for some reason this felt personal. It mattered more than it usually would that it was Brenna Dean was interested in. Which didn't make sense. He'd only just met the country girl and even if he had known her for longer, he didn't form emotional connections. That was how he kept himself focused.

He stared at the fire as an ember flared and disintegrated into a shower of sparks. The only logical explanation for his strange mood was that between his grief and being away from work, his feelings were running riot.

Despite his fatigue and the ache of long unused muscles, Wyatt woke the next morning before even the birds had stirred. Through the open shed wall he could make out the glow of stars and the faint silhouette of the mountains as dawn seeped across the coal-black sky. If he had been in Sydney, he'd reach for his laptop to deal with the latest flood of work emails. But without such a distraction, or his phone, he had no choice but to brace himself. He didn't have to wait long for the loss at no longer having Nick around to take hold.

As sore as Wyatt was, a new tension bled through him. The effort it took to accept his emotions and not fight them fisted his hands and left his body rigid. Here, in the high country cloaked in darkness, where the sky felt so close he could touch it, Nick didn't feel so far away.

Miss you, mate.

He and Nick had been in the same first year economics class at Sydney University. Busy working two jobs and leaving his past behind, Wyatt hadn't been concerned with making friends. Just as well gregarious and social Nick had been. As different as they were, and as long as it had taken for Wyatt to drop his guard, they'd shared a mutual respect and unwavering loyalty. Wyatt had been Nick's best man and was now baby Emily's godfather.

He speared a hand through his hair.

I'll do better at taking care of them. I promise.

In the room beside him, Dean snored. Wyatt flipped off his blankets. It was bad enough their conversation last night about Brenna had kept him awake until the fire had turned to ash. He didn't now need to listen to Dean rattling the tin roof.

He silenced a groan and forced himself to leave his swag. He'd need a hot shower, otherwise he'd spend the day hobbling on bowed cowboy legs. The predawn chill curled around his bare arms and chest. He flicked on the torch Brenna had provided and grabbed a towel, leather washbag, clean jeans and a shirt. After his shower, he'd light the campfire, make a coffee and watch the sunrise. With any luck, he'd still be the only one awake.

Just before he reached the showers, he stopped on the solar-lit gravel path. A prickle of warning rippled across his nape. It was as though he was being watched. He swept his torch over the dark voids either side of him before looking over his shoulder at the camp. Nothing moved and the only sound was Dean's snoring. When Wyatt was certain everything was as it should be, he continued towards the small building.

Thanks to the pummel of piping hot water, when he emerged he could walk without his every muscle protesting. Needing to cool down after the shower, he rolled up the cuffs of his navy shirt and left it unbuttoned. A cool breeze stripped the heat from his skin.

The sky was now a pallid grey and he didn't bother using his torch. He could see enough to avoid any obstacles. He'd almost reached the point where he'd stopped earlier when a rustle and low growl to his right had him pause. He scanned what he could see of the nearby trees before turning towards the horses. If there was one wild dog, there could be more.

He wasn't the only person awake. Light bobbed from near the shearer's hut as Brenna made her way to the horse yard. He strode in her direction. Not seeing any sign of Bundy, he increased his pace as he walked up behind her. Before he could say her name, Brenna gave a gasp and whirled around. The torch light wavered in her unsteady grasp, while her other hand pulled back into a tight fist.

His mouth dried. The action was defensive, instinctive, and one he'd used as a child.

'Brenna.' He kept his voice quiet and gentle. 'It's Wyatt. I'm not coming any closer.'

For a stretched second she didn't speak. All he heard were her rapid breaths. Then her fist lowered. She angled the torch light so the shadows concealed her expression.

'You startled me.'

As flat as her tone was, the steel beneath her words warned him to never approach her unawares again.

'I'm sorry.'

Her breathing quietened and she lifted the torch until the soft glow illuminated him.

'Why are you awake and skulking around anyway?' She paused as though to take in his unbuttoned shirt. 'The shower block is in the opposite direction.'

'We have a visitor of the growling kind.'

She spun around to shine her torch over the horse yard. 'Just one?'

'That I could hear.'

'We've never had wild dogs in this part of the station before, but they're the only thing that would make Bundy act like he did. I left him inside where he'd be safe.' She paused as the beam of light revealed Outlaw in the corner of the yard, his head high and ears pricked as he stared at the shower block. 'The dog must have been on its own. Otherwise Outlaw would be more agitated.'

By now the sky had lightened and the shapes of trees and grass tussocks materialised out of the gloom. Instead of jeans, Brenna wore shorts with her pink shirt and cowgirl boots. As sassy as she was, the slender outline of her legs made her appear delicate and vulnerable.

His gut told him a man had to be behind why she'd acted like she had. She'd automatically assumed he was the threat even though she'd suspected wild dogs were around. The knowledge caused a burn of anger. Brenna, or any woman, should never be put in a position where they felt they had to defend themselves.

Brenna shone her torch away from the horses. 'There was a rumour that wild dogs attacked two of our neighbour's calves. I'd have confirmed this, except he's rather fond of his shotgun and our families haven't exactly been friends.' She took a step towards the shearer's hut. 'My brother's back. I'll get him to have a look around.'

Brenna's intention was clear. She wanted to wrap up their conversation.

Wyatt knew he needed to leave too. The start of the birdsong chorus signalled dawn would soon arrive. With every degree that the sky lightened, more of Brenna would be revealed. The pale lustre of her heavy hair. The force of her thick-lashed stare. The full curve of her bottom lip.

But the image of her fisted hand refused to leave him. It wasn't his place to ask questions, but he needed to reassure her she'd always be safe with him.

'Is your brother another person who doesn't appreciate people ruining your day?'

As he'd hoped, she faced him. 'Absolutely. Wyatt …' Something close to uncertainty edged her voice. 'About you startling me …'

'It's my fault. As I said before, it won't happen again.'

She gave a small nod before her shoulders relaxed. 'The others won't be awake for hours so help yourself to breakfast. I'll get some more sleep. Bundy will want to come out with you, if that's okay?'

He nodded. He respected her need to shut down their conversation. She also didn't owe him any further explanation.

She hesitated before giving him a smile. Even though the effect was dulled by the poor light, he felt the beauty and warmth touch parts of him that had never felt anything but cold.

Without another look in his direction, Brenna headed for the shearer's hut. As soon as she opened the door a black-and-tan shadow bolted towards the shower block. Once Bundy had investigated where the wild dog had lurked, he joined Wyatt by the fire. By the time he'd cooked bacon and eggs, the vivid brushstrokes of amber and ochre across the horizon had faded.

With the start of a new day, the bush came alive. A magpie perched on the top rail of the horse yard carolled while at the edge of the clearing grey kangaroos grazed. Still, no one in the shed stirred.

Wyatt finished his coffee and went to groom the horses. The crisp air and solitude failed to extinguish the emotions smouldering within him. As fearless and in control as Brenna was, he suspected someone hadn't always treated her with care. Again, just like when Dean had made his interest in her obvious, Wyatt's reaction felt personal.

Which still didn't make sense. Brenna was far from defenceless and could take care of herself. He had no doubt that had he acted differently after she'd swung around to confront him, he'd be nursing a bruised jaw.

Another thing his grandmother had always said was to pay it forward. His grandparents and their horses had saved him and where he could he helped others in return. He made regular large donations to charities and had set up an education scholarship to his old university. He'd try to help Brenna somehow too.

He stopped brushing the mud out of Outlaw's roan coat to glance over at the shearer's hut. He'd start by proving that not all men were like Dean and whoever had set her default setting to fight mode.

CHAPTER 5

'What does Taite want this time?' Brenna muttered to Bundy where he sat beside her on a slab of granite after they'd stopped riding to have lunch.

She scooped her vibrating phone from out of her shirtfront pocket. Luckily for her twin, and unluckily for her, they were at a spot where there was phone reception. She'd known that the news about the morning's wild dog visit would have got Taite's attention, but his texts continued to whoosh in. It was as though his brain was on overdrive after eating too many red frogs.

Conscious of her trekkers watching from where they sat in the shade of the snow gums enjoying their salad rolls, she read Taite's message. The desperate look Dean fixed on her mobile suggested he was having technology withdrawal symptoms.

Everything still okay?

Taite should have finished scouting around the camp by now. Perhaps his frequent texting was a sign he'd discovered that more than one dog had visited and maybe he hadn't told her because he didn't want her to worry. She tapped out a reply.

Yes. Why? What have you found?

She glanced up while waiting for his answer. Tim and Steve had their heads tilted as an eagle soared high above them. Dean, as usual, stared at her, and Wyatt's gaze rested on Dean. She turned away to look out over the mountains that rolled in a haze of gentle blue waves.

The second day of trying to ignore Wyatt was going as well as it had yesterday. It was as though the early morning image of the torchlit hollows and ridges revealed by his open shirt was seared into her brain. There wasn't a summer when she hadn't been surrounded by fit male bodies whenever swimming in the river. But unlike Hettie, who'd be sneaking glances at Taite, or Clancy at Heath, she'd never been affected. Until now.

One shadowed glimpse of Wyatt's chest and abs and her lungs had forgotten how to inflate. She just hoped he hadn't noticed she'd been so busy gawking she'd lost her train of thought. If the way she'd reacted wasn't enough, she'd revealed too much.

Someone else might have not registered the significance of her raised fist. But Wyatt had. She'd heard it in his calm and careful tone and how he'd reassured her he wouldn't come any closer. He knew full well she'd been more than startled and how much anger and adrenaline had surged through her.

No longer hungry, she fed Bundy the last of her roll. There was no excuse for being so unguarded. As much as she knew she could handle Dean, his constant scrutiny must have left her feeling more on edge than she'd thought. Her concern was, especially considering how dark it had been that morning, how Wyatt had read her so well. He didn't know her, or her history.

When her phone whooshed again she released a silent breath. She'd been about to glance at Wyatt as if the answer was written on his unreadable face.

No sign of any more dogs.

She reread Taite's message, brow furrowing. If that was the case, why was he still checking on her? Even though they were twins they'd never done the whole finishing-each-other's-sentences thing. They were their own people and operated independently to each other. So much so they'd never talked about any possible 'twintuition'. The truth was, she could feel some of the things that Taite did. Not exact emotions, just an echo of his most powerful feelings.

She'd always known Taite loved Hettie and she'd been able to sense when he did something that was emotionally bad for him, like when he pushed her away. She could only hope he didn't experience her emotions too. Not only would he have felt her alarm that morning but he wouldn't have missed that something had happened to her while she'd been away at a residential school for her online business degree.

'Lover's tiff?' Dean asked.

She shot him a chilly look that said she didn't appreciate his comment. 'My brother's found no further sign of any wild dogs.'

In the interest of transparency and safety she'd explained to the others about their dawn trespasser.

'So, the dog has gone?' Steve asked, his voice matter of fact.

It never failed to surprise her the difference a day could make. Yesterday Steve couldn't be within a body's length of Bundy and now he was taking the presence of their unplanned visitor in his stride. Seeing such changes and the way being out in nature helped people to relax and unwind made her appreciate her home as well as her job all the more.

She nodded. 'But like with anything in the country, it pays to stay alert. A lone dog visiting makes me suspect it could have been a pet that has been lost or dumped. At some point in its life, it associated humans with food and shelter.' She looked around the group, making sure her attention didn't rest on Wyatt. 'Everyone had enough to eat?'

Tim and Steve reached for more Anzac biscuits while Wyatt left to do up the horses' girths. Just as he'd done since the trek started, he anticipated what tasks needed to be completed and quietly set about seeing to them.

The other three helped her pack away the remains of lunch into her saddle bags. While their high elevation ensured that the temperature was cooler in the mountains than in the valley, it still felt like the start, and not the end, of summer. They left the shaded clearing at a walk. When the stands of mountain ash opened up into a flat area carpeted in yellow and white everlasting daisies, they set off in a slow trot.

Even Dean was smiling when they stopped. Despite her best intentions Brenna snuck a look at Wyatt. He was proving to be a model trekker as well as a good sport. He must be bored witless with the occasional trot but so far he hadn't shown any frustration. His eyes briefly met hers. She blamed the flare of warmth in her face on the hot sun.

For the next three hours they rode the long way back to camp. The trekkers were now adept at avoiding wombat holes that could swallow a horse's hoof. They also remained relaxed when their horses waded into crystal-clear streams and pawed at the water before lowering their heads to drink.

As they approached their destination, Wyatt came up to ride alongside Brenna. For the first time she noticed a pale scar on the back of his left hand. She tried to blank out how broad his shoulders were and how his stubble looked exactly as she'd pictured. He really was ridiculously gorgeous.

'Expecting any visitors of the two-legged kind?' he asked, voice serious.

She quickly surveyed the camp. He wasn't only perceptive but far too observant. He'd registered the white dual cab ute parked near the shearer's hut even before she had.

'No. But considering my twin has blown up my phone with texts I'm not surprised he's still here.'

Something indefinable flittered across Wyatt's eyes, prompting her to ask, 'Were you expecting a different answer?'

'Possibly.' He didn't shy away from the challenge in her tone. 'I thought maybe someone could be missing you.'

'I run a professional business. As if I'd allow anyone, even if they *missed* me, to suddenly turn up.'

Amusement ticked the corner of his mouth upwards.

She wasn't sure why, but she had a peculiar need to add, 'For the record, there's no one to miss me let alone think they couldn't live without me for three days.'

This time his whole mouth curved. Before she could register the change even just a small smile made to Wyatt's face, Dean rode up on her far side.

'So, Brenna,' he said, his grin straight out of a how-to-look-like-a-prat-when-trying-to-be-charming book. 'Fancy a swim to cool down?'

'No.' She worked hard to keep her tone professionally polite. 'But I'm sure my brother would.'

'Your brother?'

She nodded towards the figure standing with his arms folded while he waited for them. Taite had a heart as vast as the high country but between his formidable size and current stance, anyone would be justified in thinking he was intimidating. There was a reason why he was the town's star rugby player.

Dean swallowed.

'My twin actually,' she said, voice saccharine sweet.

As they approached, Taite's hard blue gaze raked over Dean before sweeping over Wyatt. Brenna didn't need to state the obvious that Taite was a protective brother. Dean urged his horse away from her. Wyatt remained where he was by her side. Something passed between him and Taite. Not so much a greeting as a tacit acknowledgement that they'd summed each other up and recognised similarities that they respected.

She left her saddle to give Taite a hug. 'What are you doing here?'

'Can't I come and say hello to my sister who I haven't seen in a week?'

Despite his playful words, as his arms enfolded her, his tension was unmistakable. He released her to study Tim and Steve as they arrived.

When the group had dismounted and Brenna had made the introductions, Taite shook each man's hand. She didn't miss Dean's flinch.

'I have a ute full of beer and banana cake.' Taite looped an arm around Brenna's shoulders. 'And I'm keen to go fishing if anyone wanted to throw a line in.'

Tim and Steve's heads bobbed before the group went to unsaddle their horses.

After they left, Taite pulled Brenna close to say in her ear, 'That Wyatt … I'd have him on my rugby team any day.' When he paused to grin, Brenna hissed, 'Don't say it. I know he looks good on a horse. But he'll never let me call the shots. Besides, I have no idea if he's single, plus I have another thing on my list.'

Taite's brows lifted.

'I am not telling you.' She patted his chest. 'Now be a nice twin and make me a coffee.'

She went to unsaddle Ebony and check the other horses. The trekkers wandered away to have showers, except for Wyatt who stayed to brush Outlaw. Bundy flopped in the shade by the yards to sleep.

After Taite brought Brenna a coffee and a slice of Hettie's fresh banana bread, she went to make damper. Taite had already put the lamb roast for dinner into the camp oven.

Hearing the rumble of Taite's voice, she looked up to see her brother at the yards talking to Wyatt. As reserved as Wyatt was, he'd had no trouble connecting with her gruff twin. Both men had their backs to her but from the angle of their heads it was obvious they were having a conversation about more than the weather. She gave a deep sigh before heading over to them. Odds were it was about her.

She didn't need to walk very far to catch Taite's words.

'This Dean … did he cause Brenna any grief?'

Wyatt didn't answer, just half turned his head. Somehow he knew she was walking towards them. She stopped, hands on her hips, and waited for Taite to realise where she was.

'Brenna's behind me, isn't she?' he said.

Wyatt nodded. Both men shared a look before facing her.

She pinned Taite with her best what-are-you-doing stare. 'Haven't you got better things to do than to discuss me … like running up a hill of death or wrestling a grumpy stag?'

'I do but not until I've gone fishing.' Taite winked at Wyatt as he linked his arm with Brenna's. 'As bossy as my sister is, she does love me. She even says thank you when I save her from burning tea towels.'

While Wyatt's mouth didn't move, his eyes smiled.

Taite guided her away and when they were out of earshot, he murmured, 'We need to talk.'

'About what?'

Usually, she was the one to instigate their deep-and-meaningful conversations that Taite couldn't end quick enough.

Instead of replying, Taite slanted her an assessing look. There was something in his expression she didn't want to see. Speculation. She couldn't have him even come close to discovering her secrets. He'd already paid enough of a price for the crummy hand that life had dealt them.

To her relief Tim and Steve approached holding fishing rods. Taite gave her a quirk of the eyebrow that told her this wasn't over. Normally she was the person giving such a look. She wasn't sure when their roles had reversed. All she knew was that Taite was as stubborn as she was, so there was no chance of avoiding their talk. She kept well out of his way as she prepared for the final day of the trek.

By the time dusk cloaked the camp in a soft grey light, Taite's roast lamb and berry crumble had been polished off. Laughter echoed around the fire as Taite recounted stories about growing up in the mountains. After he'd handed out another round of beers and bid the group farewell, Brenna walked with him to the farm ute.

They exchanged a hug. A rush of gratitude had her tighten her hold. He was so much more than her brother. He'd been her rock when the world around her had crumbled.

'You'd tell me if you weren't okay, right?' he said, gaze intent as he eased himself away.

She managed a nod. There never were any lies between them but they did keep some things from each other. While she now knew what Taite had hidden about their father to protect her, he didn't need to learn how she was still protecting him.

'I'm more than okay. Dean's all hat and no cattle.'

'And Wyatt?'

She blinked. She'd expected more teasing about how good Wyatt looked on a horse, not his name uttered in such a solemn tone.

'He's been the perfect gentleman. I thought you two bonded over being strong-and-silent tough guys.'

Taite gave her a long look. 'Yes. I liked him.'

'After tomorrow I won't see him again.'

She ignored the pitch in her stomach at the thought.

'Brenna …' Taite rubbed a hand behind his neck. 'Never mind … our talk can wait.' He pulled her close for another hug. 'Sleep tight.'

'Night.'

She stayed where she was until she could no longer see the red of the ute's tail-lights. All her twin senses tingled. The sooner Hettie was home from the city, the better. Taite was behaving very strangely. Restless, she spun on her boot heel. Only three chairs were occupied around the campfire. In the moonlight she could see Wyatt standing by the horse yard. Even though she knew she shouldn't, she walked over.

This might be her last chance to talk with him alone. For an irrational reason it felt important to have some sort of closure. As much as he didn't meet her criteria and was all kinds of wrong for her, she'd be lying if she didn't acknowledge that he'd made an impact. She'd never been so aware of a man before.

Just like earlier, Wyatt heard her while she was still a distance away and turned. The realisation slowed her steps. He was as hypervigilant as she was. Empathy flowed through her. Wyatt too had things in his past that had shaped him. No wonder he'd been able to read her reaction so accurately when he'd surprised her. He'd seen something in her response that he recognised or understood.

But the realisation also made her wary. His astute gaze already saw too much. She couldn't have him uncover any of the things she kept hidden.

She gave what she hoped passed as a relaxed smile. 'Tomorrow will be busy, so I wanted to say thank you for your help.'

'It was the least I could do after holding you up.'

'Did you enjoy being in a saddle again?'

'I did. I'm hoping to bring Mia next summer as this retreat had been Nick's idea.'

'I can take the two of you on your own, if that would help.'

'I'm sure it would.'

Brenna shifted her weight, readying to leave. She'd said what she'd needed to say. The longer she stayed, the harder it became to make small talk. For someone who never became tongue-tied or lacked confidence, somehow when she was around Wyatt she turned into a person she didn't recognise.

Before she could go, Wyatt spoke, his voice low. 'What's wrong with these country boys?'

'Sorry?'

'Why don't you have someone to miss you?'

Usually she wouldn't answer such a personal question, but there was something about his tone that suggested the query was sincere. 'Let's just say I'm fussy. I do fine on my own.'

Wyatt's white smile flashed.

'How about you?' she asked. It was only fair he answered a private question too. Plus, if she was being honest, a part of her wanted to know. Even if it was just to reaffirm that they could never be a couple. She'd never involve herself with someone who was in a relationship. 'Is there anyone besides your work colleague I should contact if you come a cropper?'

'No.' His reply was instant. 'I do fine on my own too.'

She nodded. The knowledge he was single started a whirlpool in her stomach and she wasn't even looking into his eyes. It would be wise to wrap up their conversation.

'Well, it's been nice meeting you, Wyatt Killion. I hope to see you and Mia next summer.'

She went to turn.

'Brenna … about this morning.'

'Don't go there.' She didn't try to soften her terse words.

'I've been where you've been, as a child.'

The admission confirmed her suspicions about his past and held her silent. Her throat ached. No child should ever live with the constant need to look over their shoulder.

Wyatt spoke again, voice deep. 'Does your brother know?'

'I'm *fine*.'

Wyatt's jaw flexed. 'My contact details are on my form, if you ever want to talk.'

She was shaking her head even before he finished. 'Thanks but there won't be any need.'

Silence swelled between them. Then she felt a touch so light on her hand she could have imagined it, except she'd caught the scent of sandalwood.

'Nice to meet you too, Brenna Lancaster.'

Wyatt slipped into the shadows.

She stayed where she was, focusing on the shuffle of horse hooves and the breeze ruffling her hair and not on the thumping of her heart. In about five minutes she'd thank her lucky stars that she'd probably never see Wyatt Killion again. But all she felt was an unaccountable sense of emptiness.

CHAPTER 6

If Wyatt thought his goodbye to Brenna would cure him of thinking about her, he was wrong.

After another night of poor sleep he'd woken early with their conversation on his mind. And now, hours later, his laser focus was yet to shift onto something else. What had possessed him to delve into Brenna's personal life, let alone divulge information about his past? He glanced at the faded scar on his hand as Outlaw followed the other horses along a trail that led out of the high country.

Apart from his grandparents, Nick, and a teacher at a long-ago outback school, he'd never admitted how bad things had been with his father. It was just that he'd felt he needed to let Brenna know he understood. As for his offer to talk, he knew she'd refuse.

The only silver lining of having Brenna occupy his thoughts was that his grief for Nick seemed to have been pushed into the background. When memories of Nick filled his head, he could revisit them without the usual intense pain. As for Mia, Brenna's reassurance that listening did help gave him hope he hadn't totally dropped the ball on supporting her.

He looked ahead to where Brenna rode chatting to Tim. Today she wore her customary pink shirt, jeans and hat but her hair was in a loose braid that fell down her back. Slender and graceful, she sat in the saddle as though born there. When she smiled at something Tim said, Wyatt felt the warmth as though her grin had been directed at him.

Yesterday's confirmation that she wasn't with anyone had lodged in his brain like the stone he'd removed from Outlaw's hoof. It wasn't only Brenna's appearance that stirred something within him—she had a natural beauty that would turn any man's head—it was the tenacity of her spirit. As fragile as she looked, she had an inner strength that he admired and respected.

He'd never met a woman so comfortable in who she was and how she lived. She was as real and as authentic as the landscape she loved and called home. The prospect of not seeing her until next summer already left him feeling unsettled and the trek hadn't even ended.

Dean came over to ride by his side. With his three-day stubble and wrinkled clothes, he no longer looked like a suave city boy.

'Still thinking of staying?' Wyatt asked, in case he had to give Taite a heads up.

'No way.'

Taite didn't conceal his surprise.

Dean grimaced. 'When I mentioned the idea to Brenna, she was all for it. Except it turns out Bundilla has a matchmaking quilting club. Seeing as I'm single and as Brenna said, *quite a catch*, she warned me to prepare to be mobbed.' Dean's expression morphed into one of horror. 'Which would be any man's dream … except all the women would have *marriage* on their minds.'

'Ah.'

'Yes.' Dean shuddered. 'There's no way I'm staying a minute longer, even for a woman like Brenna.' Dean directed a scowl to where Bundy loped beside Brenna. 'As for that dog, he's also supposedly a matchmaker. Just as well he didn't like me.'

Without waiting for a reply, Dean nudged his horse to walk faster so he could lead the group and be the first to arrive at the stables.

Brenna turned to look at Wyatt. He gave her a little salute. She'd more than handled Dean. She dipped her head in silent acknowledgement.

The sun warm on his shoulders and the sky an unblemished blue above him, Wyatt relaxed into the saddle. Outlaw lengthened his stride as they descended into the valley. Behind high fences, stags milled, their antlers lethal and wide. In other paddocks red deer grazed, their fawns sleeping close by. White wings glinted as cockatoos soared overhead before landing in silver-tipped gum trees. All too soon, the stables came into view.

Once at the hitching rail, Wyatt unsaddled Outlaw. He gave the gelding an extra brush before leading him to his paddock.

'Thanks, mate.' Taite slipped off the brumby's halter. 'See you next summer.'

Outlaw nuzzled his hand.

Wyatt watched the blue roan amble away. While the trek hadn't delivered any answers on how to deal with his inner wrecking ball, it had unlocked a part of himself that he hadn't been ready to face. Being around horses had catapulted him back to living on his grandparents' farm and in doing so had led to an unexpected peace. He still had memories and emotions to unpack, but this didn't seem as daunting as it had before. Moving forward, he'd find a way to have horses in his life.

When he headed into the stables, the other three trekkers didn't look up from their phones. A pile of duffle bags sat beside a stack of hay bales. Taite had arrived at camp early to collect their luggage. He'd also asked for Wyatt's four-wheel drive keys. One of the front tyres had gone flat and Taite wanted to pump it up from the air compressor he had in the shed.

Taite and Brenna walked out of the guest area. As usual Bundy was by Brenna's side.

She handed Wyatt his phone with a smile. 'Lucky last.'

When his fingers brushed Brenna's, the touch hadn't been intentional. Yet the brief contact was enough to send a spark of need through him. If Brenna experienced the same reaction it didn't show in her expression, even if her gaze slid away from his.

His hand curled around his mobile, but he didn't turn it on. Despite the desperation of his busy brain to return to work, the instant he connected to the life he'd stepped out of three days ago, the door would shut on his one here.

'Bad news about your tyre,' Taite said, his tone upbeat despite the news he was delivering. 'It's not a slow leak. The rim's damaged. After the rain, the roads are a mess. The tyre shop's had to put another bloke on to deal with all the repairs.'

Busy tracking the frown that creased Brenna's brow, Wyatt nodded. He'd hit multiple ruts and potholes on the drive here.

Taite continued. 'I've called Joe, and as your car isn't a model he usually deals with, it'll take a few days for a new rim to arrive. I could drop you with the others at the airfield? Hettie has to fly to Sydney next week, so she could bring you back then.'

Wyatt glanced at his phone and then out the wide door to the mountains drenched in the golden afternoon light.

As much as he belonged in the city, he was tired of moving around. His nomadic childhood had ensured he'd never had the luxury of staying put, especially not in a place that made him feel grounded. An extra few days away would allow him to sit with his emotions a little longer. There was then the obvious advantage of buying more time with the woman standing still and silent in front of him.

He ignored the warning voice in his head.

'Or I could stay.' His gaze flicked to Brenna and her eyes widened. 'You recommended The Bushranger.'

'I did.'

'Great,' Taite said, tone pleased, earning a pointed glare from Brenna. 'I'll top up your tyre with air so you can make it to town.' Taite clapped Wyatt's back. 'Don't be a stranger. Come for dinner. We can eat over at Brenna's. No tea towels will be harmed, I promise.'

'Taite, can I have a *word*,' Brenna said through gritted teeth before marching out the stable door, dragging her twin by the arm as she went.

Taite gave Wyatt a grin over his shoulder.

Wyatt powered up his phone and went to find a quiet corner to talk to Mia. If she'd had a bad few days he'd head home as planned. After Mia had reassured him she would be okay as Nick's parents were staying another week, he ended the call.

He went to join Brenna as she farewelled the other trekkers as they loaded their bags into Taite's ute. Once Taite had driven away, Brenna disappeared into the stables. Wyatt followed. He found her over with the chestnut she'd had a power struggle with on the day he'd arrived.

'All set to go?' she asked him over her shoulder as the gelding munched on something Wyatt suspected was an apple.

'I will be when I have my keys.'

She slowly turned. 'Let me guess, Taite said I had them.' Under her breath she muttered, 'I will make him eat every one of my rock cakes.'

Before Wyatt could accompany her into the guest area she strode ahead. Metal jingled as she quickly returned.

She tossed him his keys. 'When you meet the old publican Roy, don't mention my name. It's a long story and involves pool and salt and vinegar chips.'

Wisps of hair had escaped her braid and he closed his fingers around his keys to stop himself from tucking them behind her ear.

'No burning tea towels?'

Amusement gleamed in her eyes as she shook her head. 'Bundy's waiting by your four-wheel drive. If it's okay, can you give him a lift to town? He's a story dog at the local school tomorrow. He'll find somewhere to stay tonight.'

'No problem. See you around, Brenna Lancaster.'

'Possibly, Wyatt Killion.'

The arch of her eyebrow and her sassy tone kept him smiling as he left the stables and went to open the passenger door for Bundy to jump inside.

The journey to Bundilla involved yet more potholes and rain-gouged roads. Not that Bundy seemed to mind the bumpy ride. Wyatt could hear the kelpie's soft snores from the back seat.

When Wyatt reached a wooden bridge on the edge of town, the rattle of the boards beneath his tyres gave him a momentary sense of familiarity. Except when he drove along the wide main street lined with Manchurian pears the small town resembled every other place his father had dragged him to. In each one his father would run up debts. Then, weeks later, they'd do another runner in the middle of the night. In the end all the streetscapes blurred together.

Wyatt parked outside The Bushranger. Bundy jumped out and after a quick pat melted into the evening shadows. Wyatt surveyed the front facade of the wrought-iron double-storey pub and again had a sense of having been there before. He pushed open the door and went into the front bar. A few locals gave him the once-over before a white-haired man pushed himself to his feet.

His shrewd gaze swept over Wyatt. 'I'm Roy. Taite said you'd be in.'

Wyatt shook the older man's hand. His grip was strong. As their fingers unclasped, the publican's attention dropped to the faint scar on Wyatt's hand.

He motioned for Wyatt to follow him as he shuffled into the hallway and then an office. After he took a key out of the drawer, instead of passing it to Wyatt, he waved at a chair. Wyatt sat, his senses alert. There was a niggle at the back of his brain. He tried to picture the publican in his younger days. If he had met him before, it would have been almost twenty-five years ago.

Roy took a seat behind the desk, his grey brows drawing together. 'Did Brenna say not to mention her name?'

Wyatt kept his expression deadpan.

Roy gave a quiet chuckle. 'I thought so. She'd appreciate your loyalty.'

When Wyatt didn't react, the publican shook his head. 'After all these years, you're still as inscrutable as ever.'

Wyatt hadn't realised his hands had clenched into fists on his thighs until Roy nodded towards them. 'And you're still wound tighter than a beer cap. Relax, son. I'm glad to see you. I always wondered where you ended up and how you were doing. So did Patty.'

Wyatt frowned as fragmented memories formed but refused to fit into a complete picture.

Roy continued. 'I'm guessing there are things you'd rather forget.'

Wyatt forced words past his dry throat. 'Did Patty have red hair?'

'She did.' Sadness clouded Roy's gaze. 'She's not with us now but she sure did miss you when you went. She enjoyed trying to fatten you up.'

'I'm sorry I didn't get to say goodbye.'

There were so many unsaid goodbyes bottled up inside him.

'She didn't like it, but she understood why you had to go.' Roy glanced at the scar on his hand. 'She was worried that wouldn't heal but it looks like it did.'

Memories returned of a woman's kind touch as she held his arm while his wound was cleaned and stitched. In a fit of fury, his father had thrown a bottle at him.

Roy spoke again. 'Besides, you did say goodbye. You left a thank-you note and told me to watch that new guy as he was putting more money in his pocket than the till. I seem to remember you had a fascination with numbers.'

'Still do.'

'I don't doubt it. Even then, you were whip smart and a decent kid.'

The unspoken words, *unlike your father*, hovered in the room.

'Giving us a place to stay, it meant a lot.'

'I did it for you. The minute I found you in the kitchen washing up because you knew you had to pay for whatever your father was drinking, you earned my respect.' Roy's tone soured. 'Is he still around?'

'He drank himself to death.'

Roy stayed silent. 'Your grandfather … he came looking for you. I could see lots of you in him.'

Wyatt had been ten when he'd been here, he remembered now. Patty had made him the only childhood birthday cake he'd ever had. It had taken another two years before his grandfather had tracked him down.

Roy stood and moved around the table to hand Wyatt his key. When Wyatt came to his feet, Roy pulled him in for a hug. Wyatt remained stiff.

'I mean it, son. It's great to see you.' Roy drew away with a smile. 'As for Brenna … three days together and she's still talking to you. No wonder Taite said to give you the VIP treatment.'

CHAPTER 7

She had to be coming down with something.

Brenna placed a hand on her brow. It felt cool and not at all clammy, but there was no other explanation for feeling out of sorts.

On the day after a trek, she usually powered through the jobs she needed to do to prepare for the next group. Instead, here it was mid-morning and all she'd done was check how many clients she had coming.

She leaned back in her pink office chair to glare at the blinking cursor on her laptop. She was agitated, fidgety and stir crazy and she wasn't even doing bookwork. Even country music had irritated her, so she sat in silence.

It would have been so much easier had Wyatt simply left. He'd be long gone and out of her life by now. But no, not only was he still in town but her brother had turned into a not-so-subtle matchmaker. She bent to rest her chin on her palm.

Sure, last winter she'd given her twin a *teeny* shove to face up to his feelings for Hettie, but at least her meddling had been executed with finesse. Taite's open dinner invitation to Wyatt had been about as obvious as a city slicker in a cattle yard. She should never have told her brother about any of her relationship criteria. He'd forgotten the obvious, that Wyatt only matched one of the three. At least Wyatt wouldn't have any idea about Taite's hidden agenda.

She straightened and swivelled in her chair to gaze out the window. She'd cut her losses and revisit her trek preparation later. She still had five days until she needed to be ready for the bridal party. If they were hoping to see the man from Snowy River, she was going to have to bribe Taite with red frogs to put in an appearance. He'd rather beer, but his shed fridge was already full from the last favour he'd done for her.

Her attention went to what she could see of the neighbouring farmhouse through the trees. She'd taken to staring at the old home. As much as she loved the Glenwood Station homestead that had provided her with a sense of security after losing her parents, she increasingly felt guilty living there. Taite and Hettie had settled in a small stone cottage near the creek. While they were deliriously content, one day when they started a family they would need and deserve the main house.

She hadn't been exaggerating when she'd explained to Wyatt that her neighbour Arthur was fond of his shotgun or that their families had never been on speaking terms. She wasn't sure how the feud started but it stretched back generations. Whatever the cause, a deep animosity had been embedded in the fabric of both families.

The trouble was, Arthur was a crochety bachelor who according to the rumour mill only had a distant relative, with whom he was at odds, to leave the farm to. In a perfect world she'd be able to waltz up his driveway, knock on his front door and make him an offer he couldn't refuse. Not only would Strathdale's river flats enable her and Taite to grow their own hay, the house would give her somewhere nearby to live.

She couldn't bear the thought of not being close to her future nieces and nephews. She was going to have such fun being the favourite aunt and teaching them to ride. She ignored a pang of longing to have little whippersnappers of her own. At the rate she was going it would take light years just to find someone to go on a second date with.

Footsteps sounded on the polished floorboards in the hallway before Hettie appeared in the doorway.

'There you are.' Hettie smiled as her vivid blue gaze swept over Brenna and then her laptop. 'It's very quiet in here.'

Brenna went to hug her old boarding school friend. 'It feels like forever since you've been home.'

Hettie was a chiropractor but thanks to her hobby of photographing farmers she was now a published author of a beautiful coffee table book. She'd been away in Sydney doing promotional activities and Taite had joined her for her last event.

'It does.' With her striking red hair and porcelain skin, Hettie was as lovely on the outside as she was on the inside. It warmed Brenna's heart to see Hettie and Taite together after all the years they'd loved each other from afar. 'Taite's filled me in on the news.'

'I bet he has.' Brenna's voice was deliberately wry. 'No doubt he left out the part where he has a bromance going with one of my trekkers and invited him for dinner at *my* place like he was setting up a *date*.'

Hettie failed to hide a grin. 'He mentioned something along those lines, but he put a different spin on it.'

'Of course he did.' Brenna glanced at the pretty floral dress Hettie was wearing. 'Off to town?'

'The gift shop has some books they'd like me to sign. Fancy a road trip?'

Brenna hesitated. She did need to do a grocery shop. A full fridge would at least make her feel like she'd achieved something today. Except town was where Wyatt was. She bit the inside of her cheek. It would be fine. He wouldn't be strolling around the shops or sitting outside The Book Nook Café people watching. He'd most likely be working in his room at the pub.

'Sure.'

But no sooner had she clipped in her seatbelt than she regretted her decision. She should have gone for a ride instead. Until now Wyatt had been on her territory. If they met again, it would be on neutral ground. She didn't own a dress, heels or a hair dryer. It would be obvious she was a no-frills country girl and very different from the women Wyatt associated with.

Her right knee started a restless bounce. Normally she'd never worry about her appearance but for some reason it mattered what he thought of her.

Hettie glanced across from where she sat behind the steering wheel. 'Everything okay?'

Brenna summoned a smile. From the days of sitting next to each other in school assemblies Hettie knew Brenna's telltale signs of when something bothered her. 'Just thinking.'

'About Wyatt?'

She pulled a face. 'Please don't tell me it's obvious.'

'Only to me.'

'It's so annoying ... why can't I get him out of my head? He only ticks one box and I'm not bending my rules.'

'Taite said you added something to your list?'

Brenna blew hair out of her eyes. 'I am not trusting my hormones with who I let get close to me. My attraction has to be ... mild.'

'As opposed to ...'

Knowing she didn't have the words to explain how much her senses responded to Wyatt, she searched on her phone for an online picture. When Hettie stopped at the crossroads, Brenna showed her the photo of Wyatt featured on a business profile page.

'Brenna ... he's gorgeous.'

She frowned. 'And that's him without three days' worth of stubble.'

'Apart from Reece at school, you don't usually get distracted by a handsome face.'

'Reece might have put stars in my teenage eyes with his dark hair and high cheekbones, but when he left me to change his ute tyre, I learned my lesson. Never judge a guy by his appearance.'

Hettie laughed softly. 'As much as that turned you off Reece, it had the opposite effect on him. He became obsessed with you.'

Brenna forced her hands to keep a relaxed grip on her phone. Reece following her around like a puppy didn't come close to an obsession. Life had taught her exactly what lengths someone could take to ensure that she was a part of their world.

'Brenna.' Hettie's voice was gentle. 'You're not someone who gives any guy a second thought. I can understand why Wyatt being on your mind bothers you.'

'I don't like the unexpected.' Brenna cast Hettie a serious look. 'I might love my theories, but you love your plans. If I see Wyatt, please come up with a strategy to get me away from him.'

'I will. I promise.'

Their conversation changed to Taite's upcoming sculpture exhibition that was being held in Glenwood Station's garden and for which there was a sizable to-do list.

Once in town, Hettie parked in the shade near the sandstone church around the corner from the red brick clock tower. In another month the leafy green of the Manchurian pears along the main street would turn into a kaleidoscope of crimson and amber.

When Hettie headed into the gift store, Brenna continued to the candle shop. Ruth gave her a smile from behind the counter where she was helping another customer. Telling herself to avoid the sandalwood section, Brenna browsed the shelves on the opposite side of the room. She'd only come to look for a birthday present for Clancy. Thoughts of Wyatt were not going to keep sabotaging her day.

But it was as though her feet didn't receive the memo. Not only did she find herself near the sandalwood display, she picked up a candle to breathe in the distinctive aroma. Too late she registered the jingle of the doorbell and the arrival of two elderly ladies. Vernette and Mrs Moore's smiles grew as they made a beeline for her.

Brenna pressed her lips together to make sure she didn't revisit any of the colourful words she'd used the day Wyatt had arrived. Vernette was a master lip-reader and she'd been caught before voicing thoughts that had best remain private. Mrs Moore's goose Horatio really had looked ridiculous when she'd dressed him up in a pumpkin costume to enter the most well-dressed pet section at the local show. She'd only been saying, and in a private conversation to Clancy, what everyone else had been thinking.

'Brenna,' Mrs Moore gushed. 'What a coincidence. You're just the person we've been hoping to bump into.'

Brenna didn't buy either woman's wide-eyed innocence. Both were members of the notorious quilting club. As Brenna too was a member, she knew exactly how their matchmaking minds worked.

'Why?'

Vernette wasn't at all fazed by Brenna's blunt tone. If anything, the delight in her expression intensified. 'As you've been away *trekking*, we've missed seeing you at quilting club.'

During the summer it was given that she'd be away leading rides into the high country; there was no reason for Vernette to place emphasis on the word *trekking*. Unless they knew she'd had a single and very easy-on-the-eyes Wyatt as a client.

Before she could reply, Mrs Moore leaned forwards to sniff the candle Brenna held. 'Shopping for Clancy's birthday?'

She nodded.

Vernette read the label. 'Sandalwood? Silly me, I thought Clancy being a flower farmer would have been more of a floral girl.'

The trouble with small towns and quilting ladies with very long memories was that they knew everyone's birth date as well as their personal tastes.

'Well, they say a change is as good as a holiday.' She put the sandalwood candle back on the shelf. 'Or there's this option.' She held up a bergamot candle for Vernette and Mrs Moore to smell.

Both shook their grey heads before Vernette picked up the sandalwood candle once more.

'I like this fragrance better and so will Clancy.' Vernette plucked the bergamot candle out of Brenna's hand and replaced it with the sandalwood. 'It reminds me of something.' Despite the vagueness of her tone, behind her thick glasses her eyes sparkled. 'I'm sure that nice young man staying here while his tyre gets fixed smelled like sandalwood. Didn't you just spend *three* days with him?'

Brenna gritted her teeth. Not only did Vernette and Mrs Moore know about Wyatt being on her trek, they'd met him as well. She sat the sandalwood candle on the shelf with a thud and picked up a nearby candle, not reading the label.

'I'll get this one.'

She went to spin around to head to the counter when Vernette's surprisingly strong hand caught her elbow. 'Brenna, be a dear and take two of those sandalwood candles to the counter for me. I've decided I quite like the fragrance. I'll also need help carrying them to my car. My old bones …'

Brenna hid a sigh. She'd never refuse anyone assistance even if her gut told her Vernette was up to something. Last week when she'd offered to carry Vernette's heavy bag of groceries, the older woman had waved her away with a scoff. As for Mrs Moore … Brenna slanted her a look and received a smile in return. Mrs Moore had no trouble carrying her very well-fed geese whenever their legs were too tired to walk.

Brenna collected the sandalwood candles. With any luck she'd find someone outside to deliver them to where Vernette was parked. Whatever plans the wily matchmakers had hatched, she was determined to thwart them.

With her hands filled with carry bags, Brenna shared a resigned glance with Ruth before opening the door for Vernette and Mrs Moore. When she followed the women out onto the street, she scanned right and then left. First, to check there was no sign of Wyatt. Second, to look for someone to carry Vernette's candles. Dr Davis was heading in their direction. Perfect. He wouldn't hesitate to help. Except instead of continuing towards them, he turned into the post office.

Brenna glanced up at the blue sky and channelled her inner calm. Even bookwork was preferable to trying to outsmart two crafty old women determined to snowplough her and Wyatt together. She set off after Vernette and Mrs Moore who were walking slower than a snail past the bakery.

Brenna searched the line of parked cars for Vernette's small white sedan. When she couldn't see it, on a hunch, she glanced over her shoulder. Vernette's car was parked in the opposite direction near the grocery store.

Brenna stopped. '*Vernette.*'

'Yes, dear?'

'Your car is that way.'

Both women halted, appearing unconcerned.

'Is it?' Vernette said, not even attempting to look for her vehicle. 'How silly of me to forget.'

Brenna didn't immediately answer as behind the two women she saw Hettie exit the gift shop and give her a wave. She didn't have a chance to ponder why Hettie's greeting seemed more vigorous than usual. From the corner of her eye, she caught sight of a broad-shouldered figure stepping out of the bakery.

'Why hello there, Wyatt,' Vernette said with what Brenna was sure was a flutter of her eyelashes. 'What a coincidence bumping into you again.'

CHAPTER 8

It took one swift glance for Wyatt to sum up the tableau filling the main street footpath.

Brenna stood stock still with her back to him. If she held the bags she carried any tighter, the thin paper handles would tear. The two grey-haired women who he'd suspected had been waiting for him outside the pub wore wide smiles. There was something about their delight that was a little too gleeful. Then further along the street, a redhead sped towards them.

He gave the older women a nod. Brenna was yet to look at him.

The elderly pair had stared at him earlier with such interest, he'd thought they'd recognised him like Roy had. But apparently a friend had seen him leave the tyre shop and they'd wanted to welcome him to Bundilla. He wasn't sure what it was that he'd said, he'd only given noncommittal replies, but he hadn't missed the excitement sparking in their eyes. Now here he was bumping into them fifteen minutes later.

As thrilled as the women were to see him, Brenna didn't share their pleasure. She took a step away.

'I'm so glad you found something you liked in our little bakery,' Vernette said, referencing the paper bags he carried. Her focus flipped between him and Brenna. 'We're not the city, but small-town life has so much to offer.'

Exasperation crossed Brenna's face before she threw a glance at the fast-approaching redhead. He didn't know what quilting club matchmakers looked like, but he'd hazard a guess these two were members. Brenna hadn't been joking when she'd warned Dean about the favourite local pastime.

'I'm sure it does. This isn't all for me. I've grabbed morning tea for Roy and Elsie.'

'That's so kind of you, don't you think, Brenna?' Mrs Moore piped up.

'Do you *really* want me to say what I think?'

Wyatt couldn't stop amusement twitching at the corner of his mouth. Brenna's honesty was refreshing and appealing. But as much as she glared at her two companions, they appeared unfazed.

The redhead reached them. Not stopping, she came to his side, tucked her arm in his and with a bright smile said, 'What perfect timing. Wyatt, I promised Taite I'd give you a tour of the ...'

'Bookshops,' Wyatt finished smoothly. 'I collect old books.'

His willingness to go along with what was obviously a rescue mission earned him a quick glance from Brenna.

'Ladies.' He dipped his head at the two quilting club members. 'Enjoy the rest of your day.'

Before he could say anything to Brenna, she strode off in the opposite direction.

The redhead kept hold of his arm while they walked away. 'I'm Hettie. Thanks for the bookshop suggestion.'

Taite had mentioned a Hettie and the way he'd said her name left Wyatt in no doubt of the deer farmer's feelings for her. The redhead also wore an elegant diamond ring on her left hand.

'Anytime.' Several cars drove at a crawl beside them, the drivers' and passengers' heads swivelling in his direction. 'Is the matchmaking welcoming committee still watching?'

'Unfortunately for you and Brenna they'll always be watching.'

At the second-hand bookshop Hettie let go of his arm and after opening the door for her, he followed her inside. They stopped in an alcove of fiction titles that afforded a clear view of the main street. The smell of the cinnamon donuts he'd bought for Roy's granddaughter, Elsie, filled the cosy space.

He stared through the large front window for a last glimpse of Brenna. She'd stopped further along the street at a white car to wait for the other women.

Feeling Hettie's attention on him, he met her gaze.

The redhead studied him before saying, 'Thanks to your welcoming committee, you won't see Brenna again.' She paused. 'Unless you want to.'

While Hettie's question appeared simple on the surface, it felt loaded with meaning. Whatever he said in the next few seconds would be important. The rational part of his brain said the correct answer would be no, he didn't want to see Brenna. He didn't do relationships, let alone failure, and there was no way a city and country liaison could work. But it would be a lie.

'I do.'

He hadn't meant for his reply to sound so deep or low.

'In that case, you're going to need a hand. Once Brenna makes up her mind, she can be unmovable.' Hettie's voice grew soft. 'Taite likes you, and so do I. The town already has enough matchmakers, but I owe Brenna, so consider me more like a fairy godmother. Once you see Brenna, though, the rest will be up to you.'

He dipped his head in acknowledgement. He didn't usually accept help but since he'd arrived in the mountains the normal rules of his city life seemed to no longer apply.

The conversation lapsed while they watched the two seasoned matchmakers reach Brenna. Whatever the older women said to her, it caused her to tilt her head up to the sky as if striving for patience while they climbed into their car. She passed them their bags before stepping onto the footpath to wave goodbye. As soon as the white sedan pulled away from the kerb, Brenna disappeared into what looked like an alleyway.

Wyatt released a silent breath. Now Brenna was no longer in sight, there was no excuse to not get back to what he was supposed to be doing. He had three days' worth of work to catch up on. With a last lingering look at the alleyway, he turned away from the window.

Hettie tapped on her phone before glancing across at Wyatt. 'Brenna says thanks for playing along and she hopes the rest of your stay is matchmaker free.'

Hettie had been right. Brenna's message was an obvious goodbye. 'I'm guessing if I accepted Taite's dinner invitation, she wouldn't be there.'

'Sorry, no. While you'd be safe from prying eyes at Glenwood Station, someone would have to collect you. The quilting club has an enthusiastic and extensive spy network.'

Wyatt took a novel off the shelf to hide his restlessness. 'What's your plan?'

He had no doubt Hettie had one. Her eyes shone.

'Can you play pool?'

'I did as a kid.'

Even though he'd been underage, there'd been some remote pubs where he'd play pool to earn money for food.

'How about Taite and I bring Brenna to The Bushranger for dinner tonight? She can't resist the lure of the pool table.'

He looked up from the book. 'We'll be seen together.'

'The entire town knows how competitive Brenna is. Even the most optimistic matchmaker will rule out anything happening between you while she has a pool cue in her hand.'

He returned the novel to the shelf. He'd no idea, even after reading the back cover, what the story was about. 'I don't usually do things like this.'

'I wouldn't be helping if you did.' Hettie smiled. 'Roy also wouldn't have introduced you to Elsie if you weren't to be trusted.'

After they'd exchanged numbers and stepped outside, Hettie gave him a wave before strolling away. Wyatt searched the main street for any familiar faces. When he was certain he wouldn't be ambushed, he headed to the pub.

He knocked on the door marked *Private* and a smiling Elsie ushered him inside.

'That was an exciting morning smoko run,' the uni student said as he passed her the donuts. 'I've never seen Mrs Moore move like she did when she and Vernette dashed into the candle shop after Brenna.'

Wyatt thought his groan had been silent until Elsie giggled.

'As for the way those two sneaky old ladies then walked *ever* so slowly past the bakery … Poor Brenna had no idea you were inside.'

Wyatt quirked a brow as Elsie took a large bite of her donut. She had his number and had texted to ask him to get her another one. 'A little warning would have been nice.'

Elsie grinned, a dimple forming in her cheek. 'And spoil all the fun? I don't think so. People watching through the front window beats doing my marketing assessment any day.'

Wyatt sat the other bakery bags on the table. He had no idea what it was like to have a younger sister but ever since Roy had invited him to dinner last night, Elsie seemed to have adopted him. By dessert she was teasing him and by breakfast she was stealing his toast. It didn't matter that he rarely laughed, she'd just pat his arm and say how much her grandfather liked him and how that made him family.

But there was something beneath all her chatter and curiosity that he couldn't quite decipher. Every so often she'd glance between him and Roy with what almost looked like relief. He'd also caught Dave, Roy's son who ran the pub, giving him an intent look whenever Roy chuckled at something Wyatt said.

Patty wasn't the only one to no longer be with Roy. Elsie had said her mother had died when she was a teenager, so it had become just the three of them. Perhaps what he was sensing was the strong bonds of a close-knit family, something he had no experience with.

Paper rustled as Elsie took out another donut. 'These are so yum. You should try one.'

Wyatt smiled as he walked over to the desk. 'Maybe later. I've an apple slice with my name on it.'

Elsie had been kind enough to lend him her computer to work on. When he went to touch the screen to wake up the laptop, Elsie *tsked* from beside him.

'Wyatt … it's not a touchscreen, remember? I'm a poor student. I don't have your fancy city tech.'

She reached past him to tap on the keyboard and a spinning wheel filled the screen. The website he needed still hadn't loaded.

Elsie sighed. 'Bundilla doesn't exactly have the fastest internet. Here.' She offered him the bag she held. 'Donuts make everything better.'

Touched by her gesture, he shook his head. 'Thanks, I'll survive.'

Between Roy and Elsie's warm acceptance and his hyperawareness of Brenna, his usual detachment seemed to have lost its edge. He should be alone in his room working yet here he was choosing to be around people and eating sugar-loaded baking.

Roy entered the room carrying two boxes. His gruff expression gave way to amusement. 'Wyatt, I heard you caused a traffic jam.'

When Wyatt looked at Elsie, she lifted her hands. 'I never said a word. My generation posts pictures. Grandpa over there is old school. There wouldn't be a whisper in town that doesn't reach his ears.'

Roy winked. 'A good publican never gets involved in other people's business but still likes to know what's happening.' He placed the boxes on the table and shot Wyatt a grin. 'These came for you while you were out becoming front page news.'

Elsie handed Roy the bakery bag that contained his lamington before checking her phone after a message whooshed in. 'I always say this, but Trent's worth his weight in donuts.'

Roy nodded. 'What animal has he rescued this time?'

Elsie held up her mobile. 'A huge draft horse.'

Wyatt's hands stilled on the box he was opening. 'Draft horse?'

Elsie came over so Wyatt could see the picture. 'Trent's the local vet and he sends me details of the animals who need a home so we can ask around. Brenna usually takes the horses, but I think she's still working with the two donkeys from the previous rescue.'

Wyatt thought he'd hidden how much the sight of the large but too thin Shire horse had affected him. Then he glanced up and saw Roy studying him. Despite knowing he'd reveal too much, Wyatt looked at the photo again.

The draft horses his grandfather had bred were as much a part of his memories as the kindness and love of his grandparents. The horses had taught him so much. Patience. Vulnerability. Strength. To see one emaciated, eyes dull and in need of care unsettled his already volatile emotions.

'You'd give a horse like this a worthy home, son,' Roy said, voice quiet.

'I live in the city.'

Roy shrugged. 'What's in those boxes tells me you can work anywhere. All you need is the right farm. Put a caretaker or manager on, and you'd be free to come and go.'

Wyatt stared once more at the picture, his chest tight. He knew what it was like to not belong anywhere. To rescue this Shire horse would be a way of honouring his grandparents. How they'd weathered the early rough months and not given up on him, he'd never know. It would also be a means of following his grandmother's advice to always pay it forward.

Roy spoke again. 'There's a local farm … it has a house and a cottage, stables and cattle yards. The owner needs a buyer urgently. He'll sell his stock but otherwise wants to walk away so it will be fully furnished. All you'll have to do is move in.'

The muscle that worked in Wyatt's cheek must have given Roy all the answers he needed.

'I'll be back,' Roy said over his shoulder, 'with a phone number.'

Conscious of Elsie's attention and that he was losing the battle to keep his feelings in check, Wyatt busied himself with unpacking a box.

He was the first to admit he'd financially overcompensated for having no money as a child, so he could afford a farm. After the trek he'd made the decision to have horses in his life. Then there was Mia and baby Emily … having a place where Emily could grow up surrounded by animals was something Nick would have liked. He pushed aside the whisper that said buying land around Bundilla would also guarantee he'd see Brenna.

He lifted out the first of the two laptops and passed it to Elsie. 'I hope this makes uni a little easier.'

Confusion creased her brow. 'What are you talking about?'

'You said your old one is glitchy and you lost an assignment the other day.'

Elsie made no move to take the computer. 'I can't accept this.'

'Elsie … I owe your grandfather a debt I'll never be able to repay.'

He hadn't realised how close his emotions hovered to the surface until his voice rasped.

Elsie examined his face. Then her smile grew. 'It's really mine?'

He nodded as she took hold of the laptop. 'And it has a touchscreen.'

She ran her hand over the silver surface and then moved to give him a hug. 'Thank you.'

Just like when Roy embraced him yesterday, Wyatt stood unyielding and uncertain.

Elsie tightened her hold. 'Wyatt, I'm not letting you go until you hug me back.'

He put his arms around her and was rewarded with a grin when after a few seconds she pulled away. 'See, that wasn't too hard. I'll make a hugger out of you yet.'

Roy returned to glance between Wyatt and Elsie, who clutched the laptop as though it were gold-plated and covered in diamonds. With a pointed look at Wyatt, Roy placed a piece of paper with a name and phone number on the table.

Wyatt frowned before picking up the note and, without reading it, slid it deep into his jeans pocket. Despite Roy's arguments for buying a farm and his need to help the draft horse, there was one key issue. His country boy days were a part of his past. A past he'd firmly left behind and had zero intention of revisiting.

CHAPTER 9

'No way,' Brenna said with her best glower. 'I'd rather make a soufflé than go to the pub for dinner.'

To emphasise her point, she planted both hands on her hips. She needed all the bravado she could muster with Hettie and Taite looking at her from where they sat in their living room. Brenna had stayed for a coffee after she and Hettie had returned from town with Bundy. They'd found the kelpie asleep in the sun beside Hettie's car when they'd finished lunch.

'Bren …' Taite started to say in the same patient and soothing tone he used whenever settling a spooked horse.

She shot him her never-fail glare. Taite stopped.

Hettie masked a smile and Brenna returned her focus to her old friend. As sweet as the redhead was, Hettie could never be underestimated. Somehow, she always seemed to get her own way.

'Hettie, it's immaterial that Wyatt won't be at dinner. We'll be under the same roof. The Bushranger isn't big enough for the two of us, even before I had a matchmaking bullseye on my back.'

When Hettie didn't say anything and just kept giving her a serene stare, Brenna narrowed her gaze. Hettie's expression didn't change.

'I'm not going,' Brenna repeated.

'I didn't expect you to.'

Brenna took her hands off her hips. 'It's settled then.'

'It is. I only asked as I thought you'd like to play pool. Wyatt apparently plays. I'm no expert but I'd say he'd know his way around a pool table.'

Brenna ground her teeth. Of course Hettie knew exactly what to say to make her rethink her decision. And of course her adrenaline was already surging at the thought of playing Wyatt. Judging by his horse riding, she'd no doubt he'd be a formidable opponent, even if he hadn't held a pool cue in years.

'Wyatt's just had three days off. He'd be in his room working, not hanging out downstairs.'

'I'm sure he'd be working,' Hettie said. 'But I did get the impression when we had a quick chat in the bookshop that he'd be playing pool tonight.'

Brenna gave a frown so Hettie and Taite wouldn't think she was a total pushover. 'Okay, I'll go, but only for a quick dinner and if Wyatt is around, *one* game of pool.'

Hettie left the lounge to give her a hug. 'I'll make a booking and Taite can chauffeur us in at six.'

As Brenna left Taite's stone cottage to walk to the main homestead, she realised two things. One, Bundy had left with her which meant he was still planning to stay at the main house. And two, the prospect of seeing Wyatt left her feeling unaccountably rattled.

The first issue was straightforward to deal with. She shook her finger at the kelpie as he trotted beside her. 'I mean it about no funny business. And I'm not getting dressed up for dinner.'

Bundy wagged his tail.

The second issue wasn't so easy to address. She was under no illusions that her path wouldn't cross with Wyatt's tonight. Bundilla wasn't called a small town for nothing.

It had been bad enough that when she'd seen him that morning, she'd been thrown off balance. Every mortifying moment of her meeting with Wyatt continued to replay in her head frame by frame. What were the quilting ladies thinking? A man like Wyatt wouldn't look twice at an unsophisticated country girl like her. No one in their right mind could possibly consider them a suitable match.

As for her own thoughts, she was sticking to her non-negotiable rules. She and Wyatt would never work. Which was why there was no logical reason to feel even a little unsettled at the prospect of being around him tonight.

By now she and Bundy had reached the front garden gate. Instead of following the path to the homestead, she turned right to head to the stables. She'd make an early start on her jobs so she could be ready for dinner at six. At least then she'd be too busy to think about a man with flint-grey eyes who rode with such skill and masculine grace.

In keeping with what she'd said to Bundy, when Brenna opened the door of Taite's four-wheel drive to step onto the footpath outside The Bushranger, she was wearing her farm clothes. Admittedly they weren't the ones she'd been in earlier. After mucking out the stables, she'd showered and chosen her most faded cotton pink shirt and worn jeans. If any matchmaker saw her, it would be obvious she hadn't dressed to impress. The only thing she had on that was remotely respectable was a silver necklace and locket that her mother had given her.

She closed the car door and stared at the iconic pub. The building had always intrigued her. Over the years there'd been countless stories about how the pub had earned its name after being held up by bushrangers. There even was a long-held rumour that loot stolen from a gold escort coach could still be hidden inside.

As a child she hadn't ever been allowed on the premises. Like anything she'd been told she couldn't do, such as ride her pony with a lead rope and halter, she'd taken it as a personal challenge. When her teenage self had finally snuck through the pub's back door to see the legendary shrapnel marks on the wall from the long-ago gun fight, she hadn't been disappointed.

She slid her hands into her jeans pockets. But what had been a letdown was when she'd made it to the front bar. She'd always associated the pub with her father's rare laughter as he'd come home in a jovial mood. But when she'd peered around the doorway, the bar wasn't the happy place she'd envisioned. Instead it had smelled of beer, and two red-faced men had shouted and pushed each other before a fight broke out. She'd taken refuge in the quiet of the pool room and that's when she'd discovered the true magic of The Bushranger.

Taite touched her shoulder. 'All set?'

'I am. If Wyatt's free to play pool, he'd better bring his A game.'

When Taite cast her a sideways look, Brenna turned away. Her stomach was as tangled as Ebony's muddy mane. Just as well Taite would have no idea how uncertain she felt.

She led the way inside and past the doorway to the front bar. After all these years the strong waft of beer hadn't changed. She glanced inside to see Arthur, her neighbour, sitting by himself at a table. He half turned his head and that was enough to glimpse the distaste on his craggy face.

She continued into the dining room. When she couldn't see any quilting club members seated at the tables, she let out a silent breath. She needed all her wits about her. Whatever happened tonight, she couldn't be distracted. She had to keep her unbeaten pool winning record.

Too late Brenna caught sight of a blonde woman dressed in a vibrant purple dress, her smile gleeful as she hurried towards her from the beer garden. Even though Cynthia was now with Dan and no longer officially a town matchmaker, old habits were hard to break.

Behind her, Taite chuckled. It was all right for him, he was no longer single. Before she could glare over her shoulder at her twin, Cynthia enveloped her in a cloud of strong perfume.

'*Brenna.*'

'Cynthia.'

Cynthia didn't appear to register Brenna's resigned tone. After what seemed like an eternity, her exuberant hold on Brenna loosened. 'This is unexpected.'

Brenna opened her mouth. But before she could voice a blunt response, Hettie's soft touch on her arm had her reining in her irritation. She settled for a mild, 'Is it?'

Cynthia's head bobbed and her red-framed glasses slid down her nose. 'You've already been to town once today. I didn't think you'd be in for another week.'

Taite covered a snort with a cough.

Brenna replied through clenched teeth. 'I don't keep track of when I come in.'

'I should hope not. As I said to Vernette, you have better things to do, like running your treks. A little birdie told me you just spent three whole days with Wyatt, who just happens to be staying here.'

Before Brenna could shoot back an answer, Hettie spoke. 'I hate to interrupt, Cynthia, but I believe Dan has your meals.'

Cynthia turned to wave gaily towards her date, Dan, as he sat two plates filled with hamburgers and chips onto their table.

'So he does.' Cynthia's attention homed back in on Brenna. 'This has been such a nice chat. We need to catch up again soon. We have so much to talk about.'

Brenna didn't trust herself with a verbal reply so she arched a brow instead. Nonplussed, Cynthia beamed a high-wattage smile. After waggling her fingers in the air, she headed for her seat.

'I knew this was a terrible idea,' Brenna muttered as she followed Hettie and Taite to their table, which was thankfully on the other side of the room.

'It could have been worse,' Taite said as he sat between Brenna and Hettie. 'The old Cynthia would have grabbed your hand, asked Roy for Wyatt's room number and marched you upstairs.'

Brenna grimaced as she reached for the menu. This was true. She pushed aside all thoughts of Wyatt to concentrate on choosing what would be her only meal in town this week. Until he left she would be stuck eating her own cooking.

Despite the numerous looks Cynthia threw her way, Brenna enjoyed her fish and chips. When it came time to order dessert, she pushed back her chair. The sooner she knew whether or not Wyatt was available for a game of pool, the sooner her nervous system could switch off high alert.

'I'll go and warm up. If there's no sign of Wyatt, we can leave whenever you finish dessert.'

Careful not to make eye contact with Cynthia, Brenna left the dining room. She took a shortcut to the pool room past the office so she wouldn't have to pass through the front bar. Elsie gave her a grin from where she sat behind the desk typing on a laptop.

'Hi, Brenna. Did Trent contact you about the draft horse?'

'He did. He's hopeful Murphy might have a home, so I'll have him for the short term. New computer?'

'It's from Wyatt.'

Brenna hid her surprise. 'That was very kind of him.'

'It was. I'm sure he'll think twice about giving me anything again, though. He wasn't so sure about me hugging him.'

Brenna smiled. Elsie was renowned for her openness and warmth. 'You don't happen to know if he's downstairs, do you?'

'He was but I'm not sure if he still is.'

When the pub phone beside her rang, Elsie sent Brenna an apologetic smile before answering.

Deep in thought, Brenna continued on her way. Thanks to the trek she knew Wyatt looked out for others, but there was no way Roy would allow a stranger to buy his granddaughter a present, let alone something as significant as a laptop. He was fiercely protective of Elsie and his family.

She pushed open the door into the pool room and found it empty. At the sight of the familiar rectangle of green and the pool cues lined up on the back wall, her tension ebbed. Just like being around horses, playing pool took her into another place.

Her love of the game had started after her mother had been diagnosed with a brain tumour. She'd been at boarding school and had struggled to find an outlet for her distress and pain. Playing pool in the recreation centre had enabled her to block out the real world by narrowing her focus to a single white ball. There'd also been something cathartic about whacking a solid object.

But when she was at home, while she had her horses and Taite, there had been occasions when she'd felt overwhelmed. Even though she'd been underage, she would sneak into the pool room at the pub. Roy had always caught her but whenever he'd escorted her out he'd give her a bag of her favourite salt and vinegar chips.

She took down the pool cue she always used and chalked the end. She then busied herself with setting up eight balls across the table. She'd just sent the first ball flying into the end pocket when the door to the front bar creaked open. Her senses knew it was Wyatt before she saw him. She'd caught the faint drift of sandalwood.

Just like on the day they met, when his eyes found hers, she felt the impact as a physical response. Beneath her shirt sleeves, goosebumps rippled along her arms.

'Brenna.'

She gave him a curt nod. 'Wyatt.'

He'd only been in Bundilla a handful of days but he'd already lost his crisp city edges. His dark hair was tousled, jaw stubbled and the blue cotton shirt he wore was untucked like many of the locals. 'Hettie mentioned you play pool.'

'I do, but it's been a while.'

She'd forgotten how much she liked the deep timbre of his voice.

'I'll go easy on you.'

His lips briefly curved before he went to collect a pool cue and drag chalk over the end.

Needing something to focus on besides the bizarre feeling that she'd possibly missed him, she racked the balls into a triangle. 'How's Mia?'

'Emily's teething so she's sleep deprived, but otherwise she's had a better week.'

'I'm glad.'

She indicated that he take the first shot. He did so. The way he made the break confirmed he was no slouch despite not having played for years. Further small talk soon wasn't necessary. Her excitement built as Wyatt challenged her skills and tactical thinking. She couldn't remember when she'd played such a fast-paced game, let alone had the feeling she mightn't win.

When the momentum subtly slowed, the suspicion took hold that it was actually Wyatt going easy on *her*. After she sent her eight ball hurtling into her chosen pocket, the knowledge she'd won didn't bring any satisfaction.

She straightened and set a hand on her hip. 'That wasn't a fair game. You let me win.'

'Not at all.'

His calm reply didn't mollify her scepticism or satisfy her competitive side.

'Okay. Let's play again.'

He shook his head and replaced his pool cue on the wall.

'Wyatt.' Her firm tone conveyed her offer was non-negotiable. 'This is my last trip to town while you're here.'

He stopped in front of her, expression unyielding.

She tilted her head so he could see her face and how serious she was. 'It's now or never.'

His gaze coasted over her features, and it had to be a trick of the light, but his eyes seemed to darken.

She held his stare. If he refused, she would be the one at a disadvantage. Even if she had legitimately won, which she doubted, the question would linger in her mind over which of them was the better player.

She didn't realise Roy had joined them until she heard the crinkle of a chip packet to her left. 'Young lady … do I need to check your ID?'

It was over a decade ago that she'd been underage, but Roy still insisted on asking for her ID and she in turn sweetly sassed him.

'Do you have your glasses? The print on my driver's licence is small. I'd hate for you to strain your eyes.'

She didn't miss the amused lift of Wyatt's mouth.

Roy gave an exaggerated sigh. 'Your brother has never given me any trouble, but you …'

'You'd miss me if I followed the rules. Roy, your city-boy guest here let me win and is refusing to have a rematch before he leaves.'

Roy passed Brenna a packet of salt and vinegar chips. 'You might need these.' He turned to Wyatt. 'You haven't told her, have you.'

As inscrutable as Wyatt's expression was, it was as though shutters descended to conceal what little emotion had been visible.

Roy gave another chuckle. 'You'll have plenty of opportunity to play Wyatt again.' Roy waved between them, his grin widening. 'Brenna … meet your new neighbour.'

CHAPTER 10

Wyatt was certain he was witnessing a once-in-a-lifetime event. The sight of Brenna lost for words even had Roy lift his brows.

Except Brenna wasn't the only person who had been caught unawares by the old publican's announcement. The neighbour bombshell was news to Wyatt too. He shot Roy a narrow-eyed glance, which he ignored.

When Roy had gone through the details about Strathdale he hadn't once mentioned that it shared a fence line with Glenwood Station. None of the maps he'd consulted had listed the adjacent property names. And even the GPS directions for the two farms showed no location link as their front gates had to be on different roads.

As for the property inspection, things had happened so quickly he hadn't undertaken one. Wyatt didn't trust many people, but he did trust Roy. So he'd been satisfied when Roy had vouched for

Arthur, saying that the photos and videos he'd provided were a true representation of the property.

Brenna's mouth shut as she quickly rallied. Wyatt could almost hear the snap of her whip-smart brain.

'Roy … how would Wyatt know about Arthur's place, let alone that it was for sale?'

'I told him.' Roy's tone was the gentlest Wyatt had ever heard him use. 'Brenna, Arthur was never going to sell Strathdale to you. A city developer was giving him a counter offer next week that he was going to accept.'

'Let me guess … the developer wanted to cut up Strathdale into hobby farms.'

Roy nodded. 'Wyatt doesn't look so bad now, does he?'

The tense lines of Brenna's expression didn't ease as she went to add her pool cue to the row on the far wall.

When she returned, Roy continued. 'If it helps, Wyatt paid far more than the market value which will increase the worth of your place.'

When Wyatt threw Roy another look, the publican grinned. 'Son, you could afford it and Arthur needs the money. He has a health battle which won't be cheap.'

For the first time since Roy's announcement, Brenna met Wyatt's gaze. 'What will you use it for? A weekender?'

'That's the plan. Mia's excited about staying and loves the idea of Emily having animals.' He folded his arms against a sudden feeling of vulnerability. 'I'd also like to breed draft horses, like my grandfather did.'

'Trent's rescue horse … so he does have a home?'

'He will. Arthur has agreed to a quick settlement. I'm planning to return in a month.'

'Autumn will be here by then. Arthur's place is supposedly stuck in the sixties with only one fireplace, so I'd be stocking up on thermals. There'll be no more walking around with your shirt unbuttoned.'

She stilled, as though regretting her words, before spinning on her boot heel. 'When you are here, *neighbour*,' she tossed back as she headed for the door, 'we need to have a rematch and don't even think about not playing to win.'

The challenge in her tone was unmistakable.

Wyatt hadn't realised he was still staring at the doorway Brenna had disappeared through until Roy cleared his throat.

'Son, you're going to need these too.' He handed Wyatt a packet of salt and vinegar chips. 'It's no surprise you don't remember, but you've met Brenna before, back when you were first here.'

Wyatt's denial was quick. 'I haven't.' He didn't want to think of a young Brenna meeting the kid he'd been.

Roy nodded at the scar on Wyatt's hand. 'When Patty took you to the doctor, Brenna was there. She no doubt would have had her hair in braids and been wearing cowgirl boots. Some things never change. Patty said she came over to you. Patty didn't hear what she said but it looked like she sassed you before giving you her chips.'

Wyatt stared unseeingly at the pool table as faded pictures crystallised into the image of a girl with white blonde hair, big blue eyes and knobbly knees. Even then Brenna had left an impression on him. He'd thought about her kindness in giving him her chips, and what she'd said, long after he'd forgotten he'd ever been in Bundilla.

'She asked me if my hand hurt. I said no. She rolled her eyes and said something like "you're such a boy". I must have frowned so she said, "You know boys can cry. My mum said they can and she knows everything." She shoved her chips into my good hand and went back to her seat.'

He scraped a palm over his face as if the action would erase the memories. What he didn't say was that when Brenna had returned to her mother, they'd said something to each other before the woman had given Wyatt a smile. The woman's expression had been so tender and caring it had unleashed his grief at losing his own mother. He'd had to squeeze his eyes shut to stop his tears. When Patty had put an arm around him, he'd been embarrassed and angry at being so demonstrative and weak.

'Wyatt.' Roy's voice was quiet. 'Brenna was a child. She wouldn't remember either. But if she did, it wouldn't be a problem. Your past … you'll never be free, unless you talk about it.'

'It's behind me.'

'Who we are is the sum of our experiences.'

Wyatt didn't reply. Between grieving for Nick, struggling to support Mia, and Brenna always being on his mind, he had no emotional bandwidth to revisit his childhood, even if he wanted to. No good would come from unleashing his demons.

Roy clasped his shoulder. 'A word of advice … don't let Brenna win again. Once you've lost her respect, let alone her trust, you won't get it back. You're not the only one with things you'd rather forget.'

At his sharp look, Roy gave a smug grin. 'So, it bothers you that your new neighbour has things to work through, yet it's fine for your past to sit there unresolved. Living next door to each other will be good for the both of you.'

Still appearing pleased with himself, Roy left the pool room.

Wyatt remained where he was. While Brenna and the old publican still appeared to be at loggerheads, concern had threaded Roy's voice when he'd talked about Brenna having things she'd rather forget. He hadn't missed how Roy had given her the same affectionate look he gave Elsie when she'd left the room.

The vibration of his phone in his shirt pocket had him exiting via the door Brenna had walked through. He had a company to run. When he passed Elsie, who was on the phone taking a dinner reservation, he placed the packet of chips on the desk beside her. She blew him a kiss as he continued upstairs to his room. But once there, he found himself in no mood to return to work. He opened the French doors and stepped onto the veranda that overlooked the main street.

Beyond the buildings the distant rugged peaks were etched against the violet and pink evening sky. A cool breeze blew over his skin, triggering a yearning to be on horseback in the high country. He closed his eyes to temper the strength of his longing. There was no doubt that being in the mountains had changed him.

Instead of waking at dawn and working until late, he was behind on his to-do list. Usually content with being alone, he'd had more personal conversations over the past four days than he'd had in four months. As for what was happening in the stock market, he'd never not had his finger on the financial pulse. Just as well that after Nick's death he'd structured things so he could step away from his private equity firm and all would be business as usual.

He sunk onto a nearby lounge and stretched his legs out before him. Only a slight twinge in his muscles reminded him he'd spent three days in a saddle. He linked his hands behind his head to ease his tension. He'd never felt so disorientated, not even when he'd wake as a child in a strange room in another nameless town. It was as though the person he'd shaped himself into to erase his past had cracked to reveal who he'd always been.

His attention remained on the darkening mountains. The streetlights below emitted a soft glow. Roy, and now Brenna, and even the town in front of him all were a direct link to everything he'd fought to escape. Yet not only had he bought a farm to tie him to Bundilla, he still meant what he'd said to Hettie. He did want to see Brenna again. As for Roy's comment about Brenna's past, this only intensified his need to help her. Both feelings were things he was no closer to understanding.

Maybe on a subconscious level, he'd known she'd been the girl in the doctor's waiting room. Or perhaps it was because her defensive response when he'd startled her on the trek was something he understood. Whatever the reason, if he added in attraction to her blonde beauty and admiration for her spirit and honesty, he was drawn to her in a way he hadn't thought possible.

He lowered his arms and flexed his tight shoulders. But he didn't need rationality to tell him that such a connection had no place in his life. Brenna needed someone, even more so in light of Roy's comment, who would be good for her. He didn't let people get close to him let alone do relationships or emotional intimacy. Numbers and making money were all that he knew. He was barely able to support his best friend's widow who he'd promised to look out for. Brenna deserved to be with someone who would always be there for her.

All he could hope for was that in the month until he returned, his real-world common sense would kick in. His reaction to Brenna would simply be a by-product of his internal instability. Surely when he next saw her, the curve of her bottom lip wouldn't sabotage his thoughts and her smile wouldn't make the day seem a little brighter.

He pushed himself to his feet and went inside to where he'd set up his new laptop on the small desk. He needed the oblivion of work to blank out how when they'd been playing pool all he could smell was roses and all he could focus on was the way Brenna's faded denim jeans hugged her curves.

He'd only answered two emails when a text from Elsie came in on his phone.

Want dinner? I'm here by myself.

Wyatt's first instinct was to say he had reports to read. But he was hungry. He hadn't had anything to eat since his ill-fated bakery run. Solitude also wasn't proving as soothing as it usually did. He typed out a message.

Be there in five.

A few minutes later, he knocked on the door marked *Private*. Elsie greeted him with her usual impish grin. 'I thought you'd be hungry after your epic pool battle.'

On the table behind her, Wyatt could see a jug of water and two plates piled with lasagne.

He followed her inside. 'Brenna wants a rematch.'

Elsie chuckled. 'The young fellas who push each other out of the way to play her wish they could be so lucky.'

Wyatt couldn't stop his frown as they each took a seat.

Elsie continued. 'Brenna never does anything without a reason. If you'd won she'd be a gracious loser so she obviously thinks you went easy on her. Which I can see you doing.'

He stopped pouring water into Elsie's glass to stare at her. Since when had he become so easy to read?

Elsie grinned. 'Don't look so shocked. You might act like a tough guy but you're really just a cinnamon roll.'

He finished filling Elsie's water glass. He wasn't sure whether to be insulted or impressed. He'd been called many things but never something so innocuous, let alone sweet.

'I saw your face when I showed you Trent's picture of the draft horse. And then there's the fact you bought Arthur's farm.'

'Which I apparently paid top dollar for.'

'That's my grandfather … always looking out for everyone. How do you think I know when someone is all gooey on the inside? My grandfather can break up a fight with one look, but he has the biggest, softest heart.'

'I am not *gooey*.'

Elsie's lips twitched. 'You are *so* gooey, city boy.' Her expression grew solemn. 'But you also wear a no-trespassing sign. Can I ask what the debt is you owe my grandfather? When I asked him, he just said he knew you when you were young.'

Wyatt hesitated. There was something in Elsie's earnest expression that suggested she needed the answer for a reason besides curiosity. Even though he never talked about himself, he'd give her an abbreviated version.

'I stayed here years ago with my father.'

'How old were you?' Elsie had rested her fork on her plate.

'Ten.'

Her brow creased as though she were calculating something in her head. 'I don't suppose you remember if my grandparents had a Jack Russell.'

'They did. She used to come into my room to sleep.'

'Her name was Opal.' Elsie swallowed. 'They bought her for my … brother.'

Wyatt too placed his fork on his plate. Sadness now pinched Elsie's face. 'I didn't realise you had a brother.'

'He was four years older than me. He died when he was nine. Leukemia.'

Wyatt reached out to cover Elsie's hand with his. 'I'm sorry.'

'Opal was only a puppy but would sleep in his room too. If she was fully grown, you would have been here after Scott had died. Losing him hit my parents hard, but my grandparents were particularly devastated.'

They both stayed silent as they considered the implications of what they'd revealed. Wyatt's chest tightened as he thought of Roy and Patty's pain and how him being there would have been a reminder of the grandson they'd lost. But instead of their grief consuming them, they'd gone out of their way to help him.

Elsie squeezed Wyatt's hand. 'How my grandfather acts around you … I knew there had to be more to how you'd met. Whatever time you spent together all those years ago was important to him and I'm sure to my grandmother too.'

'My childhood was … difficult. Your grandfather and grandmother were kind to me.'

Elsie smiled, her eyes overbright. 'I'm glad they were. I'm also glad you bought Strathdale. You've helped Arthur, the rescue horse plus my grandfather. He'll love having you around. Not to mention Brenna will have a neighbour who won't glower at her.'

Elsie's teasing tone had Wyatt resume eating. Silence was the best, and least incriminating, reply. There'd already been enough attention on him and Brenna tonight.

Except when Elsie spoke again, he wished he didn't have a mouthful of lasagne.

'The quilting club will be beside themselves now you'll practically be a local. You and Brenna will have the cutest babies.'

When he choked, Elsie patted his arm and handed him his glass of water.

'Don't worry, I won't help them despite how much I'm looking forward to being your chief babysitter. Your cinnamon roll secret is safe with me.'

CHAPTER 11

'This is becoming a bad habit,' Brenna muttered as she guided Outlaw to the crest of the hill that gave her a clear view over the neighbouring farm of Strathdale.

Just like yesterday, Arthur's old home looked deserted. Instead of his belligerent bulls grazing by the creek, the paddocks lay empty. The only movement was the slow spin of the windmill beside the water tank. And just like on each of the previous days when there was no sign of Wyatt, something inside her twinged. If she was being dishonest, she'd label it relief, but deep down she knew it was disappointment.

Not that she'd been stalking him over the past month, she just wanted to be prepared for whenever he made an appearance. She wasn't having a repeat of being caught flat-footed by Vernette and Mrs Moore outside the bakery. And logically she did have Murphy, Wyatt's rescue Shire horse. Not that she would be telling anyone about how often she'd ridden up this particular hill. If she ever did need to justify her actions, Murphy gave her a valid reason for having to be in the loop about Wyatt's plans.

A cold wind rippled through Outlaw's dark mane and Brenna zipped up her navy jacket. Even though she had exchanged a handful of texts with Wyatt about Murphy, he hadn't volunteered when he'd return and Brenna hadn't asked. She'd made a point of sticking to non-personal topics even when there were some things she should have mentioned. Any whiff of her and Wyatt knowing each other's business and the town matchmakers would renew their efforts to bulldoze them together.

She also regretted revealing as much of herself as she had to Wyatt on the trek. Now that she didn't have his sandalwood scent or strong jaw to distract her, it was clear how incompatible they were. Even though she had no doubt about who he was as a person—his rescuing of Murphy had shown her which of her two theories had been correct—she couldn't again be sidetracked.

There was no avoiding the reality that Wyatt only ticked one of her boxes. So, from here on in, she'd treat him like any other man who'd failed to meet her rules. Which meant she'd not give him a second thought.

Another gust of icy wind engulfed her. Over the past weeks, the warmth of summer had given way to the chill of autumn. The poplars that dotted the valley below contained a glimmer of gold amongst the green. It wouldn't be long until they lit up Glenwood Station like candle flames.

She turned Outlaw for home. She had other things to do beside fixate on Wyatt.

Now that her treks had ended, she'd gone back to training horses and running her riding school. She'd also given herself the off-season goal of sorting through her mother's and grandparents' belongings that filled the attic. She hated clutter and even though last winter Taite had organised everything into neat piles, she'd found every possible excuse to avoid dealing with the boxes and trunks. This year she was determined to not leave a single item unopened.

After her mother's death, her father's hobby of collecting vintage cars and tools, and anything else that took his fancy, turned into an obsession. When they lost him too, it had taken years to find homes for his possessions. While there was still a storeroom packed with old maps, papers and photographs, they'd proved handy. First to help Grace with information about her historic home, Crookwell Park, and then when Hettie needed to solve a long-ago local scandal. So for the moment Brenna was content to let the storeroom boxes stay.

Outlaw gave a sudden snort before he sidestepped. His head whipped around to stare at the snow gums to their left. The skin on her nape prickled as she smoothed the brumby's neck and scanned the trees. Surely wild dogs wouldn't come this far down out of the high country?

After another snort the brumby walked forwards again as though satisfied they weren't under threat. Brenna kept her attention on the surrounding bush. She'd drive the side-by-side back later to have a proper look around. She'd also let Taite and Wedge know to stay alert. While Wedge lived in town, he was often in the hills birdwatching.

When she reached the creek flats, she urged Outlaw into a canter. In front of the stables, she could see the cream figure of Waffles, Taite's young kelpie. As she rode closer, the pup barked and bounced, his paws muddy. No wonder Taite had holes the size of wombat burrows in the cottage garden. Bundy hadn't come to visit since Wyatt had left and Waffles missed his company.

But as much as she too missed the kelpie, she was in no hurry to see him. If he did turn up, the quilting club would not only see it as a sign that Wyatt would soon be here but also that they were destined for each other. The town's faith in Bundy knowing where he was needed had been surpassed by an unwavering conviction he was a master matchmaker. Brenna slowed Outlaw to a walk. A belief she was determined to prove false.

Once at the stables she unsaddled the blue roan. It took longer than usual to put the gelding in his paddock thanks to Waffles snagging the end of the lead rope. After Outlaw was where he needed to be, and Waffles had been distracted by a ball, she checked her phone to see if Wyatt had texted. He hadn't.

She left Waffles to roll in the grass and headed along the path to the main homestead. While walking she tapped on her mobile to return Clancy's call. The peony farmer was back from Western Australia where she'd been visiting Heath who was painting a mural on the side of a wheat silo.

Clancy answered after only a few rings. 'Hi.'

'Hi … so is there anything you need to tell me?'

Clancy laughed. 'No. When Heath proposes, after Rowan, you'll be the first to know.'

Not that Clancy knew, but Heath had been talking to Rowan and Grace about rings. As Rowan was Clancy's brother, Heath had been interested in what their mother's engagement ring had looked like. The diamond solitaire had been lost in the aftermath of their parents' death overseas. Grace was an expert at sourcing bespoke items so Brenna suspected she was involved in finding whatever ring Heath had in mind.

Brenna gave a smile to mask her inner dread. As thrilled as she was at the prospect of Clancy and Heath becoming engaged, she'd told Clancy last spring that she'd wear a dress as her maid of honour. A vow she was determined to fulfill, even if after two years of wearing her senior school uniform she'd never mastered the art of not tripping over in her long kilt.

When Clancy spoke again, Brenna didn't miss the seriousness of her tone. 'I'm guessing there's been no sign of a certain city boy.'

'Nothing. Why?'

'I'm hoping it doesn't mean anything, but after Bundy finished up at the school this morning, he jumped onto the back of your farm ute outside the grocery store.'

Taite and Hettie had gone into Bundilla and hadn't yet returned. 'Bundy could be coming here to play with Waffles and may very well stay with Taite and Hettie.'

'True. The thing is, Mrs Moore stopped to pat him.'

Brenna didn't hide her groan. If Mrs Moore knew Bundy was coming to Glenwood Station the news would already be all over the bush telegraph.

'Bundy being here doesn't mean Wyatt will magically appear. Besides, whenever he does, it will be like having Arthur next door, minus the shotgun and grumpy attitude. We will barely see each other.'

She ignored the memory of a grin tugging at the corners of Wyatt's mouth and how his flint-grey eyes had softened. The truth was having Wyatt as a neighbour would be nothing like sharing a boundary fence with Arthur.

'You both will be busy,' Clancy agreed. 'Wyatt mightn't get away from the city often either.'

'Exactly.' The more they talked about Wyatt, the more breathless she felt. She slowed her fast walk to a stroll. She wasn't supposed to be reacting to the prospect of having him back or giving him a second thought. But she had a question she needed answered before she ended their current conversation. 'You can't ever remember Wyatt being here before, can you?'

'No. Why?'

'I get the impression Roy already knew Wyatt. He was okay about him buying Elsie a laptop.'

'Roy's very careful about who he lets get close to his family.'

'Exactly, plus he rarely leaves town, so I doubt he'd have met Wyatt in Sydney. As for Wyatt, with his clothes and fancy car, he'd stand out in Bundilla like a fox in the snow. There's no way he could have visited before without people knowing.'

'Aubrey certainly didn't slip in and out unnoticed.'

The first time Grace's city friend Aubrey had visited Bundilla, her black lycra and power-red lipstick had got everyone talking. Not to mention Aubrey and the local vet, Trent, had been so busy proving their point to each other they'd been oblivious to everyone else around them.

'That's what I mean. There has to be a logical explanation. Thanks for telling me about Bundy. Once you're unpacked, let's go for one of Beck's death-by-chocolate brownies. My shout.'

'You're on.' Clancy paused. 'Brenna … whenever Wyatt does turn up it's going to be matchmaker bedlam.'

'It won't be out here and there's no way I'm going to town.'

'Don't underestimate the quilting club. They could visit like they did to check up on Taite and Hettie.'

Brenna reached the main homestead and stopped on the bottom veranda step. 'They won't if I padlock the front gate.'

Clancy laughed. They both knew she was serious. 'As long as I have a key to get in. Wyatt had better put a lock on his as well.'

'Don't worry, Taite has a box full of padlocks.'

Last winter they'd had a trespasser. Then this summer there'd been an increasing number of incidents of rural theft.

'I'll look forward to our coffee. See you soon.'

Brenna ended the call and climbed the steps. The idea of a gate padlock held more appeal than it should. Except before her parents had put in a cattle grid, she and Taite had been in a constant battle over whose turn it had been to get out in the cold or heat to open the front gate. Besides, she didn't need any lock for emotional protection. As much as she hadn't exactly been prepared for how Wyatt had affected her when they'd met, she'd had almost a month to regroup.

Once inside she took off her boots in the hallway and headed for the kitchen. Though in many ways she was a tomboy, she loved the colour pink and it filled her home. She wasn't sure why it appealed so much, it just made her feel calm and happy. She flicked on the pale pink electric kettle.

With a cup of steaming tea in her hands, on a whim she went into her office. Despite what she'd said to Clancy about Bundy only coming to play with Waffles, there was a chance he was here because of Wyatt. If everything was on track with the sale of Arthur's farm, Wyatt should take over ownership this week.

She plonked her mug on a coaster and sat in her chair. While she was certain that she knew who the real Wyatt was, it was going to bug her about him and Roy possibly knowing each other. She didn't want to be caught unawares, even by a small surprise.

She typed on her keyboard. After putting in several internet searches about Wyatt and Roy, and Wyatt and Bundilla, there remained no hits about anything that linked them. She then put in Elsie's and Wyatt's names. Elsie was at university and while she was studying marketing, who was to say that Wyatt wasn't a lecturer? Finance and marketing could overlap. Nothing popped up.

She delved a little deeper into Wyatt's business profile. While his university in Sydney was mentioned, she could find nothing about where he'd grown up or gone to school. It was as though anything before his university days had been erased. She examined a photo of Wyatt standing beside a blond-haired man. The caption identified his companion as Nick. While Wyatt wasn't smiling, he was as relaxed as she'd ever seen him. No wonder Nick's death had hit him hard.

Realising that she was staring at the photo, she shut her laptop lid and shot to her feet. This was ridiculous. She was not spending another moment thinking about a man she could have no future with.

Her mug of tea again in her hand, she made her way to the rear of the house and up the attic steps. Once inside the large roof space, she settled herself on the chair she'd positioned on a floral rug. In front of her was a battered trunk that she'd dragged out from the corner on an earlier visit. Whatever was in there had to be as solid as bricks. Most likely the trunk contained more of her mother's photo albums and family history research.

She prised open the latch. She'd enjoyed seeing pictures of her mother when she was young and the faces of the grandparents she'd loved. The family history volumes from the previous trunk were downstairs sitting in her office waiting to be read on a rainy day. If the forecast was accurate and the wet summer turned into a damp autumn, she'd have plenty of chances to go through them soon.

Except instead of the trunk lid lifting easily, it kept falling back into place. Before she could find something to wedge it open, Taite called her name.

She moved to the attic doorway. 'I'm in here.'

A tan-and-black kelpie bounded up the steps.

'I'm happy to see you too,' she said to Bundy with a laugh as his tail thumped against her legs. 'Is it too much to hope you've come to stay with Taite?'

Her twin appeared and she waited for him to climb the stairs.

'Rowan called from Tumut.' Taite stopped on the landing, his tone light but eyes serious. 'A fancy four-wheel drive took the turn to Bundilla. He says he might be wrong, but he's pretty certain our new neighbour's back in town.'

CHAPTER 12

Wyatt's journey along his new driveway could only be described as off-road adventuring. Roy's description of Strathdale being a little run-down due to Arthur's poor health was a slight understatement.

Wyatt grimaced as he slowed and had no choice but to hit another pothole that was so deep it could swallow a wallaby. He bounced in his seat, thankful his four-wheel drive had more ground clearance than his city car. Otherwise it wouldn't only be his wheel rims taking another beating.

He'd been right about his farm being on a different road to Brenna and Taite's place. He'd passed Glenwood Station's distinctive arch of rusted farm machinery before turning onto the gravel road that led to Strathdale. He glanced in his rear-view mirror at the front gate he'd had to drag open. The corner post had tilted so much that frayed blue baling twine had been used to lengthen the chain. As for his mailbox, it had once been a fridge. The door was now missing and a bird's nest filled the top shelf.

He could add getting a new mailbox and gate to his to-do list, along with having the driveway graded.

When he finally made it to the farmhouse, he crawled to a stop at the carport. There was no way he'd park beneath the shelter. The drunken lean of the tin roof suggested all it would take was a puff of wind and the structure would collapse.

He turned off the engine and stared through the grimy side window at his new home that looked like it hadn't been painted this century. If anyone had said a month ago he'd have bought a farm on impulse, he would have told them it was an impossibility. There was a reason why he'd been successful at making money. Every share purchase, company acquisition and business investment had been based on numbers, logic and strategy.

He unclipped his seatbelt. But instead of his out-of-character purchase making him feel off kilter, he almost felt … excited. A feeling that was as foreign as the silence that surrounded him. No car horns honked, no traffic sounded, and no sirens wailed.

Wyatt left the driver's seat and breathed deeply. When he'd been here four weeks ago the breeze had been warm and infused with peppermint from the peppermint gums. Now it was brisk and carried the scent of woodsmoke. Wisps of white cloud draped the surrounding granite peaks and a far-off eagle glided in graceful circles. The depth of his longing to be on horseback and riding in the high country had his shoulders tense. He also couldn't see the mountains and not think of Brenna.

He fought the urge to look to his right to where the country girl's home would be visible through the trees. Any thoughts about when he'd see her would only take him down a rabbit hole he might never reemerge from. Whatever clarity he'd hoped to find back in the city had been non-existent. It hadn't mattered whether he'd been awake or asleep, Brenna had constantly been on his mind.

But what had changed was the strength of his certainty that he wasn't the right person for her, no matter how much the town matchmakers thought otherwise. He mightn't be privy to the details of Brenna's past, but he did know she'd already been through enough. While his desire to help her still ran deep, his gut told him he was the worst possible person for the job. She needed someone who was as emotionally competent and together as she was. He could no more complicate Brenna's life than he could let her down or fail her.

He rolled his shoulders before taking the overgrown path that cut through what had once been a garden. Between being neighbours and caring for Murphy, it was inevitable that his and Brenna's lives would intersect. But there could be nothing more between them. He had to do what he did best and bury his emotions. It shouldn't then be a problem to keep a tight hold on his attraction.

His steps slowed as he neared the front of the house. According to the paperwork, the original home had been a cottage situated closer to the creek. Past a cluster of sheds, he glimpsed a small stone building surrounded by weeds. Roy had warned him that Arthur had sold his stock and literally walked out so there would be some mess left behind. *Mess* might be an optimistic description if the scrap metal strewn in the nearby knee-high grass was any indication.

His boots clattered on the veranda steps as he dug a key out of his jeans pocket. Except before he could unlock the front door, his phone rang. Roy's name lit up the screen.

Wyatt smiled as he answered. 'Roy.'

'Just calling to check that city car of yours still has four wheels. I'm sure I saw one rolling into town after you passed through.'

Wyatt chuckled. 'All four wheels are present and accounted for. Besides, I took the back road. I didn't want to advertise I've returned.'

'Just as well you at least let me know of your plans. It took two ute loads to clear that front veranda so you wouldn't take one look and leave.'

Wyatt surveyed the neatly swept floorboards beside him that were at odds with the unkept garden and driveway. 'Thank you.'

'If I had a key I'd have started inside, but I thought you'd need something to do.'

Roy knew he never sat still. But there was an underlying snugness to the old publican's words that warned Wyatt he wasn't going to like where their chat was heading. 'Because …'

'Let's just say the upside is you won't have to go to the bakery for morning smoko.'

Wyatt rubbed at his brow. The news had to be out that he was back. There was only one town where he'd stopped. 'Someone saw me getting fuel in Tumut, didn't they?'

'Mrs Brown was there having breakfast with her granddaughter.'

When Wyatt remained silent, Roy chuckled. 'Your welcome-back food deliveries so far include scones, pikelets, banana bread … and Elsie has just come in with a sponge cake from Vernette.'

'Roy …' Wyatt stopped as he heard the clink of china before Elsie said, 'I saw how big that slice was.'

Roy's reply to his granddaughter was muffled as he chewed. 'Sugar and cream hasn't killed me yet. Wyatt … forget what I said about the cake, it'll be gone by the time you show up.'

He couldn't hear Elsie's exact words but her exasperated tone indicated she hadn't finished scolding her grandfather.

'It could be worse,' Roy said. 'All this food could be home delivered. But not even the quilting club would be game enough to take on that driveway of yours.'

Wyatt made a mental note to push grading his driveway down his to-do list.

Roy spoke through another mouthful of cake. 'Seen your pool-playing neighbour yet?'

'No.'

Despite the brevity of Wyatt's response, Roy didn't take the hint to change the topic. 'Brenna's done such a fabulous job with Murphy. You'll notice a big change.'

'From the pictures he looks like a different horse.'

'He would, even though he still has a fear of being floated. It might be an idea to put a gate in between you and Brenna so he can walk between the two farms.' Roy paused as Elsie murmured something in the background. 'Elsie says if I have another piece of cake, I'll be the one walking.' Roy gave a dramatic sigh. 'All right, Wyatt can have the rest.'

Wyatt couldn't help but laugh. Even being on the periphery of Roy and Elsie's family orbit made him feel like he belonged. His mirth ebbed. Except there was a reason why his city house resembled a hotel and not a home. He didn't allow himself to become attached to anywhere or anyone. He'd only end up leaving.

Roy's voice sounded again. 'Even if I do have to share Vernette's baking, it's great to have you back, son.'

'It's good to be here.' Wyatt surprised himself by not only saying such words but genuinely meaning them. 'I'll be in to see you and Elsie soon.'

He ended the call. To avoid thinking about what he'd revealed, he unlocked the heavy front door and pushed it open. He registered the musty smell first, followed by the sheer volume of the house's contents. No wonder Arthur hadn't sent through many interior photos.

Piles of boots, magazines and newspapers were stacked along the hallway, many in danger of toppling over. Whatever room existed at the end of the hall was chocked so full of furniture that to a minimalist like himself it looked uninhabitable. As for the walls, he'd never seen so many photographs or prints crammed together in haphazard rows.

When the rumble of a powerful engine broke the silence, Wyatt let the door swing shut. He retraced his steps along the path and lifted a hand in greeting as Taite came to a stop beside his four-wheel drive.

Taite left his ute with a broad grin. 'Welcome back.'

Wyatt shook his outstretched hand. 'News travels fast.'

Taite laughed. 'Trust me, it does. A mate, Rowan, saw you leaving Tumut.' Taite's face sobered. 'It's no secret my sister wanted this place, so I've come to clear the air and to say there's no hard feelings. She's happy the buyer wasn't a developer.'

'Did Brenna want the land for her horses?'

'That was part of it, but she was also after the farmhouse. She thinks Hettie and I should have the homestead.'

Brenna's unselfishness at thinking about Taite and Hettie's future deepened his respect for her.

'If she just saw what I did, she mightn't have been so keen to buy Strathdale.'

'That bad? I don't suppose I can take a look? When Brenna and I were kids we'd have given a year's worth of pocket money just to peer through the window.'

'Be my guest.'

They walked side by side around to the front veranda. When Wyatt swung the door wide open, they both stared.

Taite rubbed at his chin. 'There goes Brenna's childhood theory that Arthur had a pet bunyip. Even a rat would have trouble fitting.' He paused. 'Wyatt … don't let Brenna see inside until it's been emptied.'

At Wyatt's quick glance, Taite shrugged. 'As much as Arthur and my father disliked each other, they had something in common—clutter. When my father died, it was a massive job to clean out his sheds. Brenna insisted on doing the bulk of the work herself and spent weeks doing so instead of sleeping. Now she's a stickler for having things neat and orderly.'

Wyatt nodded and kept his thoughts to himself. Brenna would have been grieving but after her clenched-fist reaction to him on the trek, her insomnia could have been caused by something else. If anyone knew closing your eyes didn't always guarantee peace, it was him.

Taite shot him a sideways look. 'Here long?'

'A week, maybe more.'

'One thing's for sure, you can't stay here. Brenna would agree. She has a wing of empty guest rooms.'

'Thanks but Roy's booked me in.'

'No worries.' They turned away from the house to walk back to Taite's ute. 'Your dinner invitation still stands, you know. Call in whenever it suits to see Murphy and Co.'

'Co?'

'I take it you haven't been talking to my sister?'

Wyatt slowly shook his head. He'd been careful to match Brenna's brief and infrequent businesslike texts. He hadn't wanted to cross the line she'd established between them. Brenna or Trent must have found him some more draft horses. He'd mentioned he'd like some companions for Murphy.

When they reached the carport, Taite faced Wyatt. 'Fancy a coffee? There's no time like the present for my sister to do some explaining.'

If he'd been in the city, Wyatt would have given a polite refusal. But he did need caffeine and he wanted to see Murphy. And perhaps once he saw Brenna, he could fully focus on what he'd come there to do. There was the slim possibility she'd no longer have any impact on him.

'Thanks. I would.'

'Jump in. At least if my ute falls to pieces on the way out, Joe the mechanic would already have the spare parts.'

Wyatt returned Taite's smile as he opened the passenger side door. After having to wait days for his new wheel rim he could imagine the delay should his city four-wheel drive need another thing fixed.

Despite the driveway's teeth-rattling bumps and jolts, Wyatt found himself relaxing as he and Taite discussed their mutual love of turbo engines.

Once they'd driven beneath Glenwood Station's archway and past the life-sized metal sculptures of a deer and a brumby mare and foal, it wasn't long until Taite parked outside a small stone cottage.

A blue birdhouse hung in a tree in the front garden and two pots of white and purple flowers sat either side of the doorway. A patch of the lawn was strewn with balls, a sock and what looked like a leather gardening glove that had been chewed by puppy teeth.

'If we're quick,' Taite said as he undid his seatbelt, 'we can make it inside before Waffles turns up. He's probably in the stables with Brenna.'

Except after they'd walked through the front door and the smell of fresh baking wrapped around him, it became obvious Waffles wasn't in the stables. And neither was Brenna. The country girl was sitting on the living room sofa, the cream puppy asleep on her lap. Her wide gaze flew to meet Wyatt's.

Any hope that she wouldn't affect him dissipated. His memories over the past month hadn't done justice to the symmetry of her fine features or the force of her pale blue stare. Her blonde hair seemed longer as it fell loose around her shoulders. As for the full curve of her bottom lip …

Just like on the morning they met, his internal switches tripped. Brenna wasn't only someone who made him acutely aware of his weaknesses, she tested him on multiple levels. So much for his trademark detachment. His heartbeat slammed against his ribs and it took two attempts before he could look away from her mouth.

'Brenna.'

His greeting was more clipped than usual.

She gave him a curt nod. 'Wyatt.'

The look she then speared her twin with was razor-sharp.

Hettie's calm voice sounded. 'Wyatt … what perfect timing. Tea or coffee?'

'A coffee would be great.'

Bundy came to sit in front of him and Wyatt ruffled the kelpie's neck. The cream puppy leaped off Brenna's lap and bounded over. Before Waffles' teeth could latch onto the bottom of Wyatt's jeans, Taite scooped him into his arms.

'No, you don't. I'm sure there's a gumboot buried somewhere that you haven't totally destroyed.'

'More tea?' Hettie asked Brenna as Taite headed outside with a squirming and wriggling Waffles.

Brenna shook her head. 'I'd better get back to work.'

She didn't glance at Wyatt as she came to her feet.

'If you're heading to the stables,' Taite said to Brenna when he returned, 'now might be a good time for Wyatt to meet Murphy and—'

'*Taite.*' Brenna's tone was long-suffering. She took a moment to turn to look at Wyatt. 'I have a surprise for you.' While her expression appeared composed there was a pinch of tension around her eyes. 'It's probably wise to have your coffee first.'

Taite's deep chuckle rumbled. 'Wyatt, I'd recommend seeing your surprise now. You'll be needing a coffee *afterwards*.'

CHAPTER 13

One minute Brenna was sitting with the warm weight of a sleeping Waffles on her lap as she vented to Hettie about Wyatt being back, and the next she was walking over to the stables with the man who vexed her.

She didn't dare assess Bundy's expression as he trotted beside them. His wagging tail made it all too apparent how pleased he was to have Wyatt there. As for how she felt, she wasn't backpedalling on her intention to treat Wyatt as just another guy there was zero chance of her being with, even if she was working on not giving him a second thought. And even if he still smelled of sandalwood and her fingertips itched to feel the rasp of the stubble across his jaw.

He was the same, and yet different. She'd thought the grooves beside his mouth had lessened, but when he stopped to allow her to walk through the doorway before him, they were more deeply etched than ever. He again wore city clothes that likely cost as much as her winter hay bill. Yet his jeans were faded as though he'd had them for years and despite the chill the sleeves of his half-zip black woollen jumper were casually pushed up. Here was another male, like Taite, who seemed impervious to the weather.

She cast a quick glance over her shoulder at Taite's cottage that she'd give anything to still be inside. As for her so-called loyal twin, not only had he engineered this current excursion, he hadn't accompanied them. His excuse that he had a phone call to make was rubbish. She'd later check his phone and if there was no call, she'd make him cook her dinner for a week.

Hettie had offered to accompany them but it had been Wyatt who said he wouldn't be long. He must have noticed Hettie's slight limp from when she'd tripped in the garden thanks to Waffles' puppy excavations.

Feeling Wyatt's gaze on her, she turned her head. It had been a month, so maybe, just maybe, she wouldn't react when their eyes connected. At least when he'd arrived, she'd been too stunned to feel anything. But when their gazes caught, her stomach did the normal tumble. She hoped Wyatt put her slight misstep down to a dip in the track.

She lifted her chin and broke the silence. 'How have you been? Busy?'

Everyone was always busy and loved to talk about how flat out they were. Such a question was her secret weapon at book club where she was notorious for saying the wrong thing and breaking the unwritten rule not to say that a book sucked.

'No more than usual.'

She ground her teeth, both at his reply as well as the way his deep voice caressed her skin like a physical touch. Trust Wyatt to be the one person her never-fail question didn't work on. He was about as communicative as the echidna she'd met on her morning ride.

Strain stretched between them before Wyatt asked, 'How about you?'

'Let's just say …' He was about to find out just how busy she'd been since he left. 'I've had lots on.'

She increased her pace so she could lead him inside the stables. While the front door was open, the far one was closed. How Wyatt reacted to what she said next was going to determine whether or not she opened the second door.

She stopped at the end of the stables. Bundy sat beside her. Major hung his head out of his stall and for once didn't demand extra treats. It was as though he too wanted a front row seat to Wyatt's reaction.

'So,' she started, only to pause when Wyatt left a body space between them. While she appreciated the personal distance, his action left her feeling uncertain. Whenever they'd talked on the trek, he'd been close enough for her to see the steel blue amongst the grey of his eyes.

She continued, tone crisp. 'Murphy hasn't been my only new rescue. Midge arrived the day before. As you know, Murphy doesn't float well so was unsettled his first night. I still don't know how Midge got into his paddock, I suspect she opened the gate, but she was with him the next morning. The two are now inseparable.'

'I'm more than happy to adopt Midge too. Murphy needs a companion.'

'I was hoping you'd say that but I won't hold you to it just yet. You see … Midge isn't a draft horse and she comes as a package deal.'

'Package deal?'

'Yes.' Brenna turned to slide open the stable door.

Outside in the yard to their right stood a Shire draft horse. Black with a white blaze, deep shoulders and standing at least seventeen hands high, Murphy was an imposing figure. Beside him was a piebald miniature pony that didn't come close to reaching his chest. Then behind them, in what looked like a blue plastic clam, swum a large white goose.

Wyatt blinked. 'A mini pony and a … goose.'

'Yes. His name's Merlin. And no, I didn't name him or Midge.'

Brenna held her breath while Wyatt's attention flickered between the two horses and the goose. His face remained impossible to read.

'This is quite the surprise,' he said, voice expressionless.

'I won't be separating Midge and Merlin.'

The firmness of her words had Wyatt turn to study her.

She spoke again. 'I understand if you only want Murphy, but we will need to find him some other friends soon as he's rather attached to these two.'

She still had no clue as to what Wyatt was thinking. He had taken on Murphy but adopting a mini pony, let alone a goose, might be too far outside his comfort zone. And if it was, it was no problem. The unlikely duo were right in her wheelhouse. Well, they would be once Merlin stopped hissing at her.

As if privy to her thoughts, Wyatt spoke. 'Merlin … is he friendly?'

'The short answer is no. But he's only protecting Midge and Murphy. The long answer is once he trusts you, he'll be better than a guard dog.'

A smile tugged at Wyatt's lips. 'I like Merlin already.'

Merlin eyeballed them and left his temporary pond to flap his wings before heading over to Midge. He draped his head over her shoulder almost like he was giving her a hug. Murphy lowered his nose to sniff at the goose.

Brenna's heart melted. None of the three's lives had been easy but now they had each other. If only Murphy ended up living next door, he wouldn't be far away. She'd make sure they had plenty of opportunities to see each other.

Wyatt gave no indication he was about to move. He was out of the stables and striding towards the paddock before Brenna realised he was gone. No wonder Taite had said he wanted Wyatt on his rugby team. Wyatt was light on his feet. Brenna shared a look with Bundy. The next few minutes would decide everything.

As Merlin always did when anyone approached, he snaked out his head and hissed. His meaning was clear. Stay away. Except Wyatt kept walking over to the fence.

When Merlin rushed at him, Brenna pressed her lips together to prevent herself from warning Wyatt to be careful. She wasn't supposed to be revealing her softer side. Even Bundy seemed on edge, his ears pricked forwards. An enraged Merlin could easily fly over the wire. She knew firsthand that denim didn't exactly stop the sting of a goose bite or the thwack of a hard wing. But then Merlin stopped, and Wyatt and the goose stared at each other.

After several long seconds, Merlin straightened his neck, lifted his wings and with a honk spun around to return to Midge and Murphy.

Brenna released a silent breath. She could add goose-whisperer to her theory about there being so much more to Wyatt than what he allowed people to see.

Midge was the first of the horses to approach Wyatt. Her long black forelock covering one eye, she trotted over to the fence on dainty hooves. Murphy watched the mini pony. Despite his size, he'd take his cue on how to react to their new visitor from the more confident Midge. Merlin glared but otherwise didn't come any closer.

Wyatt scratched the mini pony's tiny nose. When he spoke softly, Midge whickered. Wyatt called Murphy's name and the gentle giant cautiously walked over. Brenna couldn't hear what Wyatt said but after Wyatt touched his neck and the horse leaned in closer, a lump wedged in her throat.

Murphy didn't trust easily, but with Wyatt the neglected Shire horse felt safe. It was as though Wyatt felt a similar way. Even though she could only see his profile, his smile appeared genuine and the rigid line of his back had relaxed.

Brenna turned to Bundy who sat beside her. 'Maybe I was the one who needed that coffee first. This is all a bit too much for me.'

She busied herself with retying a piece of blue baling twine hanging from the fence. She couldn't allow the image of Wyatt bonding with Midge and Murphy to override all the reasons why she and Wyatt would never be a match. Whoever she did end up with had to love animals as much as she did.

'A package deal works,' Wyatt said, when after a last pat to the draft horse and mini pony he walked over to Brenna. 'I'd also owe you agistment money for Midge.'

'No, you don't.'

She set off towards the stables. For some reason further proof of Wyatt's innate decency left her feeling irritated. She wasn't changing her dating rules no matter how many gold stars Wyatt kept accumulating. It was enough that he was paying for Murphy to stay. She didn't expect financial reparation for the rescue work she did. Even if Trent had been adamant that she be paid and had told Wyatt a weekly rate higher than what she'd normally charge.

'I insist.' Wyatt's taut reply brooked no argument.

Brenna shook her head before she slid the stable door shut behind them. Such a tone might work in the city, but it wouldn't here. Once she'd made up her mind, even Taite knew when to concede defeat. Besides, now Wyatt had seen his surprises, she had other more important things to discuss.

'Our pool rematch,' she said, getting straight to the point. 'I can meet you at the pub any night.'

'No.'

'*No?*'

Wyatt's gaze shifted to her mouth and then to her eyes with such speed she wasn't sure she hadn't imagined it. 'I don't play pool with people I owe money to.'

She set her shoulders. She'd been right about him not letting her call the shots. 'You don't owe me money. You didn't know Midge existed before today.'

'Now I do.'

'Well, I don't do backdated agistment for horses and geese who have been my guests. Besides, I make provision for rescue horses in my business plan.'

'What about rescue geese?'

There'd been a hint of humour in his words.

'They're not exactly in there … yet.'

'Which means I need to pay for Merlin's … board and lodging.'

She failed to hide a smile as they strolled out of the stables. She wasn't sure of the exact terminology for geese agistment but board and lodging worked.

'Okay. The cost for Merlin will be a dollar a week. I'd appreciate the four dollars in my account overnight so we can play pool from tomorrow.'

Amusement lightened Wyatt's eyes to a smoky grey. 'Are you sure there shouldn't be some zeros after the four?'

'Nope. And if you try to add some or include extra for Midge, I'll keep adopting pets for you. I'm sure you've got room for at least four dogs, three cats, two alpacas and a ferret.'

Wyatt's chuckle shouldn't make her feel so pleased she'd made him laugh.

There was one further thing they needed to discuss before they reached the fork in the path where she'd continue towards the homestead.

'Now … if we bump into each other in town, we need to walk in the opposite direction. The quilting ladies won't have abandoned their matchmaking plans.'

He nodded. 'Apparently there's baked goods waiting for me at the pub.'

'Already?' She grimaced. 'We're never going to have any peace.'

'Roy seemed quite pleased, especially after Vernette's sponge cake arrived.'

'I'm sure he did. Her sponge cakes are legendary. She uses some sort of secret ingredient and is always winning first place at the local show.' Brenna cast him a quick look. 'Roy seems to have taken a shine to you.'

'I haven't noticed. Have there been any more wild dog visits?'

Her steps slowed. Whenever Taite wanted to change the subject, he too answered a question with a question. Her suspicion grew into a certainty that there had to be more to Wyatt and Roy's relationship than a recent friendship.

'Not that we know of.' She returned to the topic he'd sidestepped. 'It's almost like you and Roy knew each other before. Roy doesn't just let anyone buy his granddaughter a new laptop.'

They came to where the track branched into two paths.

Wyatt stopped. She thought he wasn't going to reply and then he slipped his hands into his jeans pockets. 'It's a long story from a long time ago.'

His low reply echoed what she'd said last month about her relationship with Roy. She had been right. They had known each other. And if he had been here a long time ago, perhaps as a child, that would explain why no one else in town remembered him. Wyatt had mentioned his childhood on the trek, but it had to be a part of his past that he'd rather forget, otherwise he'd have given her a more specific answer.

She lifted her hand to touch his arm. It mattered more than it should that he could still be paying a price for things he wouldn't have had any control over as a kid. But before her fingertips could brush his bare forearm, she lowered her hand. Wyatt might have offered her support while they were on the trek, but they weren't friends. Nor was he a man who would be comfortable with her trespassing into his emotional space.

A belief confirmed when a muscle worked in his jaw. 'Thanks for everything you've done for Murphy and my two surprises.'

'They're welcome to stay for as long as you need.'

When Wyatt gave her a nod and strode away towards the cottage, Bundy accompanying him, she couldn't help but call out, 'Don't forget about our pool rematch.'

She had an inexplicable urge to prolong their contact.

Wyatt looked over his shoulder with a half smile. 'You can count on it.'

His answer made her heart light as she strolled home. To combat the need to return to the cottage and have a second cup of tea just so she would be around Wyatt, Brenna climbed the steps to the attic. The trunk she'd opened wouldn't unpack itself.

She made herself comfortable in the chair and lifted the trunk lid. When it again wouldn't stay in place, she used a small piece of wood to prop it open. Just as she'd hoped, the trunk contained more family albums and journals.

When the contents had been sorted into neat groups beside her, she stretched to ease the twinge in her lower back. A tear in the corner of the lining on the underside of the lid caught her eye. There seemed to be a small cavity. She tested the weight of the lid. Something wasn't right. It felt heavier in the middle than the edges.

She snapped a photo of the lining to document what she was about to do, then went downstairs in search of a knife and to wash her hands. If there was a hidden compartment, she didn't want to damage whatever she might find in there.

Once seated, she scored a short line around the inner edge of the lid. When the lining sagged she continued slicing until she could slip her hand inside. Her fingertips brushed against paper. Taking care, she eased out a bundle of yellowed letters and newspaper clippings secured with a blue ribbon.

When she reached further into the hollow, her fingers encountered metal. After cutting away a little more of the lining, she manoeuvred out a thin tarnished tin. Her brow furrowed as it took several attempts to carefully prise open the top.

All breath left her lungs. Nestled in a bed of once-white fabric were gold coins stamped with a crown and the words *one sovereign*.

CHAPTER 14

'Another scone?' Hettie asked Wyatt from where she sat beside Taite on the lounge.

Outside in the cottage garden, growling sounded as Bundy and Waffles play-wrestled.

Wyatt placed his fresh mug of coffee onto the low table in front of him. 'Thanks. I will.'

He added a third scone to his plate. His stomach hadn't been impressed that he'd only made a quick stop for fuel on the drive from Sydney. As it turned out, his efforts, and hunger, had been in vain. The bush telegraph had still known he was back.

He piled fresh cream and jam onto the still oven-warm scone. After his two surprises, he did need coffee. But not for the reason Taite would have suspected.

If Nick had been here, he'd have laughed himself hoarse over Wyatt being the owner of a mini pony and a goose. Wyatt hadn't even had a pot plant to care for. Except he couldn't bring himself to separate Midge and Merlin from Murphy. They all were in need of a home. When Emily grew older, she was going to adore cute little Midge.

Wyatt took a swallow of coffee. No, it wasn't his new charges who had left him in need of caffeine, but the woman who had introduced him to them.

When it came to Brenna, he could no more shut off his emotions or cool his attraction than he could power down his overactive brain. As uncomfortable as he was with failure, he needed to admit that he'd never succeed in suppressing how she made him feel. Her beauty and strength stirred something in him that he couldn't quite name.

But her perceptiveness in realising that he and Roy knew each other was a red flag. He couldn't have her unravelling his past. As for how her hand had lifted when he'd mentioned it being a long story, there was no excuse for almost taking a step towards her to feel her touch or how hard it had been to walk away.

He had to remember that he wouldn't ever be the man she'd need to help her through whatever it was Roy said she had to overcome.

'Taite?' Hettie asked. 'Another scone?'

When there was no response, Wyatt glanced up to find Taite staring out the cottage window. It didn't seem like Taite to not answer his fiancée. His and Hettie's deep connection was obvious. He'd be lying if he didn't admit that the way they looked at each other made him feel as though he was missing out on something important.

Hettie turned to rest her hand on Taite's shoulder. 'Taite?'

He looked away from the window. 'Sorry, I was—'

Taite's phone began to ring from his shirtfront pocket and he scooped it out. He didn't even check the screen to see who the caller was before he pressed the mobile to his ear.

He spoke straight away. 'Brenna … everything okay?'

From what Wyatt knew of twins, Taite's preoccupation almost suggested that he knew something was wrong before Brenna had called.

'You what?' Taite said. 'Okay, I'm coming over.'

He returned his phone to his pocket. 'Brenna's apparently discovered something in an old trunk.' He glanced at Wyatt. 'Fancy a drive? Whatever she's found hasn't got her making any sense.'

'Sure.'

Once outside, Bundy and Waffles sped ahead as they raced each other to the dual cab farm ute. When Wyatt went to open the back-seat door Hettie shook her head with a soft laugh.

'Wyatt, you sit in the front. Trust me, as cute as Waffles is you don't want him on your lap.'

After Bundy jumped onto the trayback, Hettie settled the young kelpie close beside her in the back seat. He remained quiet for all of three seconds. Then excited puppy whines were followed by Waffles' wet nose on Wyatt's neck. Once Taite pulled up at Brenna's garden gate, it was all Hettie could do to hold hyperactive Waffles in place. As soon as she set him on the ground, he charged off after Bundy.

Wyatt accompanied Hettie and Taite up the veranda steps of the single-storey homestead. He couldn't hide his interest as he walked through the front door and along the hallway, noting how feminine the renovated interior was. In what had to be the living room he passed pink floral cushions on the leather lounge that sat between two dusty pink wingback armchairs. When they reached the kitchen, all the appliances were pale pink.

Hettie smiled. 'No guesses as to what Brenna's favourite colour is.'

He shouldn't be surprised. He'd only ever seen her wear shirts in various shades of pink. As fuss-free as she was, her love of the colour hinted at the softness he'd glimpsed beneath her straight-shooting exterior.

'I'm coming,' Brenna called from somewhere deep in the house before she appeared carrying a large trunk.

When Wyatt moved to help her, Hettie gently grabbed his arm to stop him. It was clear Brenna didn't like to accept assistance.

'One day, my sister will ask for help,' Taite said, voice quiet. 'And I'll be so shocked I'll just stand there.'

'Everything's in the living room,' Brenna said as she deftly manoeuvred the trunk through the doorway to their left.

They followed her into a large room. A wooden table that looked handmade had one end covered in letters and newspapers. From their yellow colouring and what faded print he could see, they appeared to be very old.

'Brenna ...' Hettie said, tone awed. 'This newspaper clipping's dated 1862.'

'I know, and the couple of letters I've seen are from then too.' Brenna sat the trunk beside an antique cedar sideboard. 'They were in a secret compartment in the trunk lid.'

'No way,' Hettie breathed.

Brenna nodded with an excited grin.

'These are all about bushrangers.' Taite bent to take a closer look at the clippings. 'And stolen gold.'

Brenna's eyes danced as she reached for a narrow tin sitting on the table. When her attention flicked to Wyatt, her vitality travelled through him like the current from his grandfather's electric fence.

'You won't believe what's in here.' Brenna slowly opened the lid.

A stunned silence filled the room as they all took in the gold.

Brenna eased out a sovereign and flipped it over. *1861* was stamped on the back along with an image of Queen Victoria.

Hettie's eyes widened. 'You're right, I can't believe this. To think these have been hidden in the trunk for over a hundred and fifty years.'

Brenna placed the tin on the table. 'It can't be a coincidence that the newspaper clippings and gold are together.'

Wyatt nodded towards the article closest to him. 'This one talks about a gold escort coach being robbed. A combination of gold and money were taken.'

Wyatt continued reading. The bushranger gang sounded organised and resourceful with a wealth of local knowledge. They'd found the perfect combination of rocks and a river crossing to make their heist a success. The large rocks had provided a hiding place and the crossing had slowed the coach. No one had been killed in the shootout, but a young constable had been wounded.

Taite had his phone in his hand and was tapping on the screen. 'According to this history website not all of the loot was found.'

Hettie pointed to an article on the top left of the table. 'This mentions the siege at the pub. It happened a month after the coach robbery and apparently the same Miller gang were involved.'

Wyatt went to take a read. When he'd stayed at the pub as a child, he'd been fascinated when Roy had explained that the dents in the walls had been gouged from bullet shrapnel.

Brenna waved a hand over the pile of letters that seemed to have been forgotten about. 'If stolen gold wasn't interesting enough, then there's these.'

Hettie inclined her head towards the faded blue bow. 'Let me guess, they're love letters.'

'I've only looked at two, but so far yes. I've taken a picture of the couple I've opened so we won't need to keep handling them. I'll get my laptop.'

When Brenna rushed from the room, Wyatt made sure his focus stayed on the trunk contents. He couldn't have Taite pick up on how hyperaware he was of his twin. He was still coming to terms with how deep the need had been to feel her fingertips brush his bare skin.

Brenna returned and set up her computer on the table. Hettie pulled up a chair beside Brenna, while Wyatt moved with Taite to stand behind the girls. An image of a letter written in neat lines filled the screen.

Brenna pointed to the initials at the top and bottom. 'There's no names, just *Dearest C* and *Your loving A*.'

Wyatt scanned the elegant, flowing handwriting. The words used, the warm tone and the description of having to stay behind while the men took the cattle to the high country for the summer confirmed that whoever A was, she was a woman.

Brenna flipped to the second letter. 'This is from C.'

Wyatt cast a quick eye over the less than graceful scrawl and the shorter sentences. Again the contents pointed to the author's gender, in this case a man.

Hettie leaned forwards in her chair to take a closer look at the laptop screen. 'This gives me a bad feeling. For the letters to be hidden, the relationship must have been too. And seeing as we have letters from both A and C, someone must have returned the ones they received or retrieved their own.'

Brenna's shoulders moved in a sigh. 'That's what I was thinking. Add in the sovereigns and newspaper clippings and my first theory is that C could have been a bushranger.'

'With any luck,' Taite said, 'there'll be some more clues in the other letters. From this second one it's obvious C broke in horses and had a favourite chestnut.'

Brenna nodded. 'Look at the line where he describes the chestnut as being fleet of foot. Bushrangers used to steal racehorses so they could outrun the police. If C was involved in anything shady, he'd want a fast horse.'

At Taite's chuckle, Brenna turned to him, her eyebrows raised. 'What?'

'I thought you hated history at school.'

'It wasn't as bad as Latin and anything about horses I remembered. Otherwise I pretty much slept through every class except for … actually, there was no subject that didn't send me to sleep. They were all boring.'

Hettie smiled. 'This could take a while. I'll put the kettle on.'

Taite turned to Wyatt, his eyes questioning.

'If I'm not in the way,' Wyatt responded, 'I'd like to stay.'

It was barely perceptible, but Brenna seemed to still before she came to her feet. 'I'll wash my hands so I can touch the rest of the letters.'

Taite gestured towards the table and Wyatt chose a seat that positioned him the furthest away from Brenna. Standing behind her had already filled his lungs with the fragrance of roses.

Brenna settled herself back into her chair and after taking the top letter off the pile, carefully opened it. She photographed the two pages and uploaded the images to the laptop. Everyone fell silent while they read what A had written to C.

Hettie returned carrying a tray loaded with a teapot covered in a pink tea cosy and four mugs. After making sure everyone had a cup of tea, she collected a notebook and pen from a drawer in the sideboard. She sat and took notes about anything on the laptop that might help identify who A and C could be.

Wyatt spoke into the quiet. 'While nothing is said outright, A mainly writes about a new foal, and there's a definite sense of worry, almost fear.'

He felt rather than saw Brenna's quick look.

Hettie nodded. 'I agree. The writing has changed. The lines slope as though this letter had to be written in a hurry. Here ...' Hettie used her pen to point at a faint smudge at the bottom. 'After A promises that when C returns they will be together, this has to be a tear.'

'C being away further fits in with him possibly being a bushranger,' Brenna said before taking photos of the next letter.

New images appeared on the screen. A simple note from A to C saying that she was thinking of him was accompanied by a black and white drawing.

'She was a talented artist,' Wyatt commented as they all took in the detailed sketch of a large boulder, gum trees and what appeared to be the edge of a clearing.

'Maybe this is where they used to meet?' Brenna said, peering at the screen. 'This letter is dated two months before the previous one.'

'I agree. Wherever this place is, it's significant,' Hettie said.

Taite rubbed at his chin. 'Assuming that the location is local, there's granite boulders everywhere which will make it difficult to narrow down.'

Brenna tilted her head. 'The top of the rock has a slight groove almost like an apple. An indent like that would deepen after a century and a half of erosion.'

Brenna and Taite looked at each other as though they knew what the other was thinking.

Taite gave a nod. 'It's Platypus Hollow. The old miner's hut would have been in the clearing. With the letters being found in a trunk in our attic, it's logical to assume either C or A lived or worked here.'

Taite typed on the laptop keyboard to bring up an aerial view of Glenwood Station and the valley surrounding it. He pointed to an irregular grey circle.

'This is the boulder. Even today you can see there are no access roads anywhere nearby. If this is our lovers' meeting spot, they would have to be able to get here without being seen and in a short amount of time.'

'They could have both lived at Glenwood Station,' Hettie said, head nodding. 'One might have been a family member and another an employee.'

Brenna's pensive gaze found Wyatt. 'Or,' she said, 'it was something more than social status keeping them apart.'

Wyatt understood where Brenna was going with her train of thought. 'Like a feud between neighbours.'

Taite let out a low whistle. 'There had to have been bad blood between the two families even back then. Arthur would yell over the fence that we hadn't been welcome on his land for generations and he wasn't about to break with tradition.'

'Which means,' Wyatt said, 'that unless there were other dwellings at this end of the valley, the only place apart from here that the other letter writer could be from is Strathdale.'

Hettie's expression turned dreamy. 'I knew there was a romance tangled up in the feud somewhere. It's such a perfect scenario … two neighbours overcoming the impossible to fall for each other.'

Hettie had gazed at the hand-drawn picture that lay on the table while she'd spoken; her comment didn't possess any hidden meaning. Even knowing this, Wyatt couldn't stop himself from glancing at Brenna. Unlike the two star-crossed lovers, he and Brenna weren't destined to be together.

Brenna half turned her head. Their eyes connected for a heartbeat and then each looked away.

CHAPTER 15

'Okay, I want an update,' Clancy said, not making any move to tuck into her death-by-chocolate brownie the waitress had delivered. 'A *full* update.'

Brenna inwardly groaned. Clancy had more on her mind than love letters and gold sovereigns. They were yet to catch up after Wyatt had arrived in Bundilla.

'That might take the rest of the day,' she said, attempting to keep her voice light.

It wasn't that she didn't want to discuss Wyatt. It was just she didn't know how to explain how he made her feel to herself, let alone to someone else. One of the reasons she'd come to Bundilla was because he'd texted to ask if it was okay to see Murphy, Midge and Merlin that morning. She never backed away from anything, or anyone, but avoiding Wyatt was a definite bonus of making an early trip to town.

Clancy smiled. 'Just as well I ordered an extra large hot chocolate.'

As if on cue, the waitress returned with two jumbo-sized mugs.

Clancy wrapped her hands around the white porcelain with a contented sigh. 'As much as I like summer, hot chocolate doesn't taste the same in the heat.'

Brenna turned and reached for the crocheted pink, white and green blanket draped over her chair. They'd chosen an outdoor table at The Book Nook Café so they could chat in private. She tucked the small rug over her knees. There was a reason why they were the only customers sitting outside; the chilly autumn wind felt like it had blown straight off the mountain peaks.

'So …' Clancy said after a mouthful of brownie.

Brenna started with the easiest thing to talk about: the contents of the hidden trunk compartment.

'As I messaged last night, we've read the letters and found no proof about who A and C could be.'

Hettie had been right about there being a lot of correspondence. It had been late afternoon when Wyatt had finally left and she could fully focus on the letters.

'Are you still thinking one lived at Glenwood Station and the other at Strathdale?'

'Yes, and my theory about C being a bushranger still stands. It was C who gave A the sovereigns which were apparently to start their new life. If they were hidden in our attic that makes it A who possibly lived there.'

'It's so sad. They were obviously never able to use the money. If C was a bushranger, do you think he was either caught or killed?'

'I'm not sure. A newspaper article listed the gang members and there was a Charlie. Kathy has given me some bushranger books.'

Kathy was the local studies officer at the library and an expert on all things Bundilla.

'Lovers sometimes use pet names so his name mightn't even start with C. There's also the possibility that he might not have been known to the police, so he'd never publicly be associated with the gang.'

'True. As for who A could be, I'm going to look through our family history notebooks. But it could be that A only worked there and wasn't any relation to us.'

'If you need a hand, let me know.'

'Thanks.' Brenna paused to sip her hot chocolate. The longer she could put off talking about Wyatt the better. 'I went to see Mabel to keep her in the loop.'

Mabel was the local journalist and although she was relatively new to Bundilla, the town had been quick to claim her as one of its own. Kind and generous, Mabel never hesitated to help wherever she could. She ran Bundy's social media pages and was on multiple committees.

'She must have been excited. She loves a mystery. Can I see the picture of the sovereigns again?'

Brenna brought up the image and passed her phone to Clancy.

'They almost don't seem real.'

'I'm surprised the police didn't ask me to bring them in. They said they'd look into the legality of who owns them, but as they were found on my property the most likely outcome is that they're mine. With coins of this age they believe it's highly unlikely someone would lodge an ownership claim.'

Clancy's eyes rounded. 'Do you think there's any more in your attic?'

'If there are they're well hidden. I've checked every trunk.'

Clancy handed Brenna her phone. 'You know where there could be more …'

Brenna slowly nodded. 'Strathdale. If our theory is right, there could be some gold or letters there. Taite said the place looks like it hasn't been touched in decades.'

She took a bite of brownie to hide that any mention of the farm made her think of Wyatt. And when she did, the troublesome whirlpool in her stomach swirled.

Clancy considered her over the top of her mug. 'Speaking of Strathdale … how did it go seeing Wyatt?'

Brenna chose her words carefully to hide just how much Wyatt continued to rattle her. 'Let's just say, for however long he's here, I'm not going to town. Not only is Bundy staying with me but Wyatt is in at the pub, so every man, woman and quilting club member will know he's back.'

'I shouldn't laugh,' Clancy said with a grin. 'But you're right. You might need that padlock on your front gate. The quilting club will be out to visit before you know it.'

'That won't be the only padlock we'll need. Roy suggested putting in a side gate on the boundary fence for Murphy. If I didn't know Roy better, I'd say he was in cahoots with the quilting ladies.'

Clancy shuddered. 'Now that would be terrifying. No one would be safe. But Murphy will appreciate being able to walk to his new home.' Her tone turned teasing. 'A side gate could also end up being well used.'

Brenna didn't smile. 'That's what I'm afraid of. Taite and Wyatt are already best buddies so will always be over visiting each other.'

She didn't realise she stared into her hot chocolate until Clancy reached over to touch her hand. 'This isn't like you. You take everything in your stride.'

'I'm just … frustrated.'

Clancy waited for Brenna to elaborate.

'Wyatt and I are not compatible so why does he affect me like he does? It's as though I become a different person and one I don't like. I never do well with uncertainty.'

'Your brain's telling you Wyatt isn't right, but the part of you that proves everyone wrong when they say you can't do something argues otherwise.'

'So how I feel is some sort of weird rebellion thing?'

'Not at all. When it came to rebellion, you were never uncertain, only determined. Remember how Heath had to get your ute out of the river after you were grounded for sassing your dad?'

'Taite could stay out all night and yet I still had a curfew, so I snuck out to celebrate Taite winning the rugby final. There was too much water in the causeway for my old red ute.'

'I can't believe your dad wasn't mad.'

Brenna took a mouthful of hot chocolate, waiting for the pain to pass. She'd dealt with almost every aspect of losing her parents, but the knowledge that she hadn't been enough to keep her father engaged with life after her mother died still haunted her.

That night, instead of being furious that she'd disobeyed him and could have been hurt, he'd given her his cold, almost indifferent glare. Then he'd gone back into the shed filled with objects he cared about more than her. Even to this day she could remember the slam of the steel door and the intensity of the silence that followed.

'Brenna.' Clancy's voice was soft. 'Wyatt might not be a good match on paper but there's something about him that sets him apart from anyone else you've met. Whatever that is, it could end up counting for more than what boxes he ticks. It'll be hard with the spotlight on you, but when it's just the two of you perhaps try to get to know him better. Maybe then you won't feel so uncertain.'

Brenna chewed on her bottom lip. 'I could go over this afternoon. I really want to see inside Arthur's house.'

'You could take something as a neighbourly housewarming gift.'

When Brenna arched a brow, Clancy grinned. 'I'm not suggesting you bake. You could take some of Beck's brownies from here.'

'True.' She broke off some brownie. 'Who knows when Wyatt will be back, and if there's something over there that leads to discovering more about A and C, then two sets of eyes will be better than one.'

'Exactly.' Clancy lowered her voice and spoke behind her hand. 'Vernette's driving past. I've no idea if she can lip read from such a distance but I wouldn't be surprised.'

Brenna turned to see a familiar white sedan travelling at the pace of a spring turtle. She gave a cheery wave to the driver before facing Clancy and gulping down her hot chocolate. They both knew they had about five minutes before Vernette pulled over and came to speak to them. They'd hugged each other and had gone their separate ways in under four.

As she strode away from the café, Brenna realised she'd forgotten to stock up on Beck's brownies. She texted Hettie to see if she'd been baking as otherwise she'd have to risk heading to the liquor store for a bottle of red wine. Seeing as she usually bought beer, which was mostly to bribe Taite with, the news of her wine purchase would no doubt travel around town with the speed of a grass fire. Then there would be no question about who the local gossips would think she was buying the wine for. Unfortunately they would be correct.

When Hettie's reply arrived saying that she'd just taken a batch of orange and poppyseed muffins out of the oven, Brenna gave a sigh of relief and changed direction to cross the main street. Now Vernette had seen her, she needed to leave town as fast as she could.

Clancy's advice played on Brenna's mind as she drove home. Perhaps being around Wyatt was the key to unscrambling her confusion. The more proof she had that they weren't compatible, the easier it would be to see him as simply a neighbour.

She collected the container of muffins Hettie had left on the cottage kitchen bench before bouncing her way along Wyatt's driveway. Bundy raced to greet her. Hettie had texted earlier to say that the kelpie had gone back with Wyatt after his morning visit.

'My lips are sealed that you're over here,' she said as she left the driver's seat to scratch behind Bundy's ears. 'Those meddlesome quilting ladies can't ever know that you're hanging out with Wyatt.'

The kelpie accompanied her along the uneven path that led around the side of the house. Despite the overgrown state of the garden, the front veranda was spotless. After sucking in a quick breath, Brenna knocked and called out, 'Anyone home?'

Footsteps sounded before Wyatt appeared. He stepped outside and shut the door behind him. There was something about the careful action that suggested it had been deliberate. While his mouth curved in a smile, his eyes were guarded as he gave her a nod.

'Brenna.'

His subdued tone added to the impression that he possibly wasn't pleased to see her.

Bundy tilted his head as he watched them.

'Happy housewarming.' She held out the muffins. 'Thanks to the quilting club you won't be short of morning smoko, but these come without any magical matchmaking ingredients.'

'Thank you.'

While his words were sincere as he accepted the muffins, he made no move to step aside so she could enter the house.

She looked past Wyatt at the closed door. As much as she was already regretting coming, this wasn't going to be a wasted trip. She hadn't driven along his bone-jarring driveway for nothing. She had a lifetime of curiosity about Arthur's home to assuage.

She spoke again. 'Now's when you invite me in and show me around.'

Wyatt lifted a hand to clasp the back of his neck. He wore a simple charcoal-grey T-shirt with jeans and both were smudged with dust. The soft cotton lifted a fraction to reveal a strip of tanned abs above his leather belt. As he rubbed at his nape his biceps curled.

Brenna's awkwardness morphed into an intense awareness. The need to slip her hands beneath Wyatt's T-shirt and smooth her palms over his warm skin was as distracting as it was disconcerting. Her mild attraction criteria shot to the top of her list. She'd never felt such a physical pull towards anyone. She could barely keep her attention on Wyatt's face.

'Brenna … the house is a mess.' Expression serious, Wyatt lowered his arm. 'Taite said it wouldn't be a good idea for you to see inside until it's been emptied.'

'Did he now?'

While she appreciated her twin looking out for her, she had always faced things head-on. She knew she had an issue with clutter and that she had unresolved grief about her father to deal with. She just refused to allow such things to hold her back.

'Your father was apparently a collector.'

'That's one way of putting it.' She snuck a quick glance to her left. If the tidy veranda was any indication, the house couldn't be that bad. 'I'd still like to see inside.'

Wyatt studied her before stepping aside to open the door. 'Okay then.' He smiled. 'Come in. Allow me to show you around.'

She blamed having never been on the receiving end of Wyatt's full smile for not moving. Relaxed and at ease, his hard edges had receded, giving her a glimpse of the man he could have been had his childhood treated him differently.

Realising she was staring, she said a hurried, 'Thank you.'

She looked at Bundy to check if he wanted to go in first. The kelpie wagged his tail before turning, nose to the ground, and disappearing into the garden.

Conscious of Wyatt's attention on her, she strode through the doorway, head high. She was prepared for whatever she found. She made it to the end of the hallway, then came to an abrupt stop. The stale smell hit her and then the sheer claustrophobic enormity of how full and dark the house was. No wonder Bundy had elected to stay outside.

To her right had to be some sort of living room but it looked more like a man cave on steroids. An open box of dismantled torches sat on the coffee table beside machinery parts and tools. Masculine mess, including letters, junk mail and used cups, covered every flat surface.

She closed her eyes against the onslaught of memories. Cleaning out her father's sheds had almost destroyed her. Every item she'd touched had been a tangible reminder of his abandonment. He'd rejected the children who needed him in favour of inanimate objects that couldn't love him back.

'Brenna.'

Wyatt's fingers wrapped around hers. Before she realised what she was doing, her hand curled into his.

'It's okay,' he said. 'You don't have to go any further.'

Her eyes flew open. It was the compassion and gentleness in his tone more than his words that pulled her from the past. Wyatt's care, even if it wasn't personal, triggered a need that winded her with its intensity. It was as though her strength melted and she had the insane urge to feel his arms around her. She was so tired of proving to herself she didn't need anyone.

She eased her hand free. But nothing good came from showing weakness, no matter how emotionally exhausted she was. She looked at the living room chaos and angled her chin. She was not leaving. Her scars might be invisible, but they were a constant reminder to never relinquish power over her life, and that included her fears.

CHAPTER 16

There were very few things from his childhood that Wyatt would label as silver linings. One would be his love of books. He still had a tattered copy of a story about a steam train that his mother had read to him. Another would be that no matter what was going on inside him, on the outside he could always appear emotionless. And right now, he'd never been more appreciative of his ability to hide his thoughts.

He hadn't only miscalculated; he'd made a mistake. He should never have touched the woman standing stiff and still beside him in the Strathdale farmhouse. There was no excuse for allowing Brenna's vulnerability to undermine his control. It didn't matter that her fingers had curved around his. After her reaction on the trek when he'd startled her, he shouldn't have intruded into her personal space.

He also shouldn't have allowed the physical contact between them to stir needs he'd deluded himself into thinking he'd never have. When it came to Brenna it was a competition between his feelings and his testosterone as to which proved the hardest to repress. His grip tightened on the container of muffins he held and he slid his other hand into his jeans pocket. He didn't quite trust himself not to reach for her.

'I'm fine to go further.' Brenna's voice was quiet but steady.

He was again reminded of her emotional intelligence as well as the contrast between her appearance and who she was. As slender and fragile as her fingers had felt, the calluses on her palms proved that only a fool would underestimate her. She was far more than fine bones and a beautiful face.

He nodded. 'At the end of the hall, turn left into the office.'

He hoped the half-cleared room wouldn't make her feel so overwhelmed. Without another word, Brenna carefully made her way down the hallway. As she walked, she didn't glance through the open doorways into the other rooms. He followed, making a brief detour to the kitchen to leave the muffins on the bench.

When Brenna stepped inside the office, her hands unclenched. While the floorboards were dusty, they were visible, and the walls were bare. Removalist boxes were positioned in a neat row. One was for rubbish, another for charity items, and the final box for anything he wanted to keep. He moved to open the window to let in fresh air as Brenna went to scan the shelves on a crowded bookshelf.

'Do you really collect old books?' she asked.

He understood her suspicion. On the day they'd been caught outside the bakery by the town matchmakers, his comment may have seemed like a throwaway line. Normally it never bothered him what people thought, but it mattered that Brenna knew he'd been speaking the truth.

'I do.'

She turned to stare at him as though trying to see everything he kept buried before tilting her head to read the book spines. 'Rowan and Grace have a historic house they're restoring with a huge library. I'm sure they'd be interested in any books you don't want.' She straightened to look at the antique desk beside her. 'Plus any furniture. I can give you Rowan's number?'

'Thanks.'

Brenna went over to the desk. 'Is it okay if I take a look inside? After yesterday, I've got gold on the brain. If this is where C lived, there could be something hidden here as well.'

At his nod, she opened and shut every drawer before looking under the desk and tapping at the wood. As she did so cobwebs caught in her loose hair. He crossed his arms to stop himself from brushing the clump away.

Hands on her hips, she surveyed the room, a slight indent in her forehead. Apart from the desk, the bookshelves and other cupboards were relatively modern. If any more gold or letters were to be found, they wouldn't be in this room.

'We could take a look in the attic?' he said.

Excitement kindled in her eyes. 'Great idea.'

He led the way through the maze of rooms to the attic steps. Brenna waited below while he went to the landing to open the door and switch on the light. The bare globe cast a weak glow. With only a slight hesitation, Brenna climbed the stairs. A scurry sounded in a far corner as a rat made himself scarce.

She gave Wyatt a brief grin. 'You sure you don't want to adopt the three cats, two alpacas and one ferret I could find for you?'

The darkness within him that had followed Nick's death ebbed a fraction. Now Nick was gone, nobody really spoke to him in such a teasing way. He guessed in the workplace he wasn't thought to possess a sense of humour.

'I already have three cats. There's a mother and two kittens in the hay shed.'

'Let me guess, the mum's ginger. We had a ginger kitten in our shed last summer and I always wondered where she went. Her sister is still with us. I think her favourite pastime is jumping out to scare poor Waffles.'

As if she suddenly realised they were smiling at each other, Brenna glanced around. When she spied a pile of trunks covered in decades of dust, she went to walk towards them. As space was limited Wyatt took a step back to allow her to pass. When her hip and shoulder brushed him, she hesitated and then kept moving.

Not looking at her, he strode over to another collection of trunks deep in the shadows. His heart hammered. So much for his reputation for being cool under pressure. Brenna didn't only fire up the synapses in his brain, she torched his boundaries. Just as well he was staying in the pub. He'd be needing a cold beer to decompress from her visit whenever he made it into town.

Neither of them broke the silence as they set about searching for hidden compartments. When he saw Brenna struggle to lift a large box to reach the trunks below, he went to help. She shot him a warning look and he masked a smile. Now that Roy had reminded him of his first meeting with Brenna, he could see shades of the girl she'd been.

She stood to the side to indicate that they'd work together. The top of the box hit him about mid-chest, while on Brenna it was closer to shoulder height. She always projected so much self-sufficiency it was easy to forget how petite she was.

They shifted the box onto a nearby table and after a nod of thanks Brenna bent to open the trunk. As well as the cobwebs in her hair, a smudge now marked her cheek. Even covered in dust, she made his blood thrum like no designer-dressed city girl could.

He knew she'd noticed his gaze lingering when she lifted a hand to her jaw. 'Is there something on my face?'

It would be all too easy to cup her cheek and smooth his thumb over her skin. 'Just some dirt.'

She made no attempt to wipe her face clean. Instead, she lowered her hand and swung away. 'I don't do dresses and heels, let alone neat and tidy.'

While her tone was crisp, what he could see of her profile as she rummaged around in the trunk appeared uncertain.

'I'd take dust and cobwebs over neat and tidy any day.'

She straightened, her expression sceptical. Even though he'd worn his oldest clothes, he imagined he still looked like he belonged in the city.

He spoke again. 'It's who I really am.' He stopped before he revealed too much.

Her eyes searched his. She must have found what she was looking for because she slowly nodded and relaxed.

He went to move away when she said, voice quiet, 'I've a group in tomorrow morning, but if you wanted a ride in the afternoon we could go to Platypus Hollow. I'd like to see how far it is from here in case this is where C lived.'

It was his turn to nod before heading to his section of the attic, glad of the physical space. Two days ago he and Brenna had been exchanging impersonal texts. Yesterday she seemed underwhelmed to see him. Now she'd offered to spend time together. Her gesture wasn't anything other than her being neighbourly so there was no reason to feel even a degree of relief.

Except Elsie had been right. He wasn't as tough on the inside as he appeared. Not that this exactly made him a cinnamon roll, but if this afternoon with Brenna had shown him anything it was that he was nowhere near to restoring emotional order.

For the next thirty minutes, while he and Brenna remained in the attic and then when he walked her and Bundy to her four-wheel drive, he kept his thoughts on what he'd come to Bundilla to do. Then on the rainy trip into town he returned his most urgent work calls.

It wasn't until he'd had a shower and knocked on the door marked *Private* that he remembered he hadn't had any of the muffins Brenna had brought, nor had he eaten since breakfast.

When Elsie opened the door and he caught the rich aroma of whatever she'd cooked for dinner, his stomach grumbled.

Elsie grinned. 'It's your lucky day. I made a double batch of beef stroganoff.'

Since he'd checked in, Roy and Elsie had made it clear he was to stay as a friend and not as a guest. Elsie had insisted he join them for whatever meals he was around for.

She moved aside so he could walk through the doorway. 'Thanks to more special deliveries, I didn't have to make anything for dessert.'

At Wyatt's groan she chuckled. 'From a marketing perspective the quilting ladies are on brand. Your arrival took them by surprise yesterday so there was no theme, but today it must be hearts.'

Wyatt came to a sudden stop when he saw the array of baked goods covering the kitchen bench. From heart-shaped cookies and cakes to cupcakes with love-heart icing, it was as though Valentine's Day had come early.

Roy entered the kitchen and made a beeline for a plate of vanilla cookies. With a smile, he nabbed the closest biscuit and had taken a bite before Elsie could react.

'You'll spoil your dinner,' she scolded as she went to remove the plate. 'Don't think I don't know how many cupcakes you've eaten.'

Wyatt couldn't resist swiping a cookie as Elsie passed by on her way to put them in the cupboard.

'*Wyatt.*'

Her disapproving tone was ruined by her laughter.

Roy and Wyatt finished their contraband before helping Elsie set the table for dinner. They were soon seated and tucking into the beef stroganoff. It wasn't just the delicious home-cooked meal that warmed Wyatt but the unfamiliar feeling of being at ease in his surroundings.

Talk turned from Wyatt's first full day cleaning up the Strathdale farmhouse to the likelihood of finding any more letters or gold.

'I have my fingers crossed for you,' Elsie said. 'If the letters stopped with the lovers still being apart, their story isn't finished. We can only hope there's more stashed somewhere.' She paused, expression thoughtful. 'Actually, I wonder if some could be here.'

'Here?' Wyatt took another mouthful of stroganoff.

Roy nodded. 'There's a few different stories about why the bushrangers held up the pub. One version is that the Miller gang who robbed the gold escort coach split their spoils. Some of the members were tracked to the caves down south. While none were arrested, their share was found. Then supposedly others came here for a drink and to hide their loot.'

'So, one belief is that the gang held up the pub to get their gold back?' Wyatt asked.

'There was talk about a double-cross, so the exact location of the stash wasn't known. Apparently everyone was ordered into the front room so the pub could be searched.'

'The story then goes,' Elsie piped up, 'that the siege ended in a gun fight because a local, Earl Ramsey, unlocked a door for the police to enter.'

'One bushranger was shot but escaped,' Roy continued, 'and gold sovereigns were left behind. While this was officially believed to be the missing loot from the gold escort, rumours persisted that it was only a small portion.'

'As for the unofficial version passed down by previous pub owners,' Elsie added, eyes bright, 'the siege wasn't about gold at all … but a woman.'

CHAPTER 17

'Outlaw, *really*?' Brenna sighed as the brumby flung his head high and, ears flickering, stared out across the paddock behind the stables. 'Not you too.'

Somehow the blue roan knew that Wyatt was putting in a gate on the boundary fence with Taite. It was bad enough that her twin had a bromance going with him. Now all Outlaw and Bundy wanted to do was be around Wyatt. The kelpie might have stayed the night with her but he'd disappeared as soon as he'd heard Taite start the side-by-side engine to head next door.

She stopped brushing Outlaw and placed a hand on his shoulder. Beneath her palm she could feel the quiver of his excitement. Usually the brumby would lower his head and fall asleep whenever she groomed him. But this morning he was having trouble staying still.

'Relax, buddy. You'll see Wyatt after lunch.'

She went back to brushing the gelding.

She needed to heed her own advice. After how she'd reacted to Wyatt yesterday afternoon, it was obvious her awareness of him hadn't waned in their month apart. If anything, it had intensified. She blanked out how anchored she'd felt when his hand had found hers and how deep the need had been to stop and fit herself against him when their bodies had brushed in the attic.

As for asking him to go for a ride, what had she been thinking? Even though Wyatt seemed genuine when he said he wasn't a stuffy city boy, she shouldn't have made the offer. It was just that she'd remembered the longing on his face when he'd looked at Outlaw on the day he arrived. The brumby would also enjoy going into the high country with Wyatt.

She gave Outlaw a final brush as the blue roan again shifted and gazed out towards the boundary fence. She made sure she didn't look in a similar direction. Somehow, she had to renew her efforts to push Wyatt off the centre stage of her thoughts. Otherwise she'd end up as smitten as the brumby.

She untied Outlaw and led him towards his paddock. Her morning riding clients would soon be here. She had a group of four booked in for a two-hour trail ride. As she and Outlaw walked by, Murphy and Midge lifted their heads from where they grazed.

She'd been up early but Wyatt had beaten her to see the pair. They'd been munching on their breakfast plus both were mud-free despite the overnight rain. Merlin sat plonked in the middle of the run-off that had pooled in the paddock corner. His new pond hadn't improved his mood. As soon as he saw Brenna, he gave her a honk followed by a hiss.

Once back in the stables, the sound of a closing car door let Brenna know her riders were here. Carmen and her friends had been out on several occasions and their visits were always filled with laughter and chatter. Carmen's mother, Mrs Walters, might be in the quilting club but thankfully there was no sign of the matchmaking mantle being passed to the next generation.

Except as Brenna reached the front stable door and caught sight of the four figures, it wasn't Carmen and her usual friends. Mrs Walters, along with Vernette, Mrs Moore and Mrs Brown were making a beeline straight for her. Brenna forced herself to keep walking and reminded herself of her non-swearing policy. Clancy had been right in saying the quilting club would be out to check on her and Wyatt. She'd mistakenly thought they'd have kept their curiosity in check until Taite's sculpture fundraising event on tomorrow.

All four women gave her a cheery wave. It was as though they'd raided their daughters' and granddaughters' wardrobes and were dressed to be an extra on a modern-day *The Man From Snowy River* movie set. Each quilting club member wore jeans and a western shirt with either a vest or jumper. Mrs Walters had a red bandana tied around her neck and Mrs Moore had on a wide-brimmed hat. Except instead of boots, they wore their usual sensible thick-soled shoes.

Vernette reached her first. 'A very good morning to you, Brenna. Bundy not with you?'

'No.' She didn't elaborate. The quilting club members did not need to know that he was with Wyatt. 'Carmen couldn't make it?'

Mrs Walters stopped beside Vernette. 'She sends her apologies. When she called last night to say she was sick it seemed such a shame to cancel.' Mrs Walters' smile grew. 'So, here we are.'

'Yes, here you all are.'

Brenna couldn't quite keep the wry note out of her reply. The four ladies were busy looking around as though she had Wyatt stashed somewhere. At least they hadn't really come to ride. Mrs Moore held a container filled with what looked like jam drops. She'd be a little worried about putting the group even on her quietest horses. At least three of them had health issues that could affect their balance and mobility.

'Cuppa?' Brenna asked.

'I'd love one,' Mrs Brown said with obvious relief. Major had hung his chestnut head over his stall door and she'd been shooting him nervous glances.

Brenna led the way to the kitchenette. Once everyone was seated and she'd filled their hot drink requests, she too sat at the table. Mrs Moore offered her a jam drop and she took the closest one. She didn't dare acknowledge that the strawberry jam centre was in the shape of a heart.

'Fancy a tour in the gator?' she asked after her first bite.

If the weather turned bad and it wasn't possible to ride, she often took her clients on a farm tour in the six-seater side-by-side. Thankfully Taite had taken the two-seater. As much as she knew the group had come to see if anything was going on between her and Wyatt, she felt bad they'd gone to the trouble of dressing up. They might prefer to stay in the warmth of the stables and quiz her about her new neighbour but she'd offer them a little taste of adventure. She'd make sure they stayed away from the fence where Taite and Wyatt would be working.

Vernette clapped her hands. 'What a fabulous idea. How about we drive over to see Wyatt?'

'I'm sorry, that won't be possible. The side-by-side isn't registered to drive on the road.'

Mrs Moore reached over to pat Brenna's hand. 'That's all right, dear. We can just go in the paddock next door to Wyatt's place. Who knows, it might be our lucky day and we catch sight of him.'

Brenna dipped into her emergency supply of patience. 'With all the rain, that paddock's rather muddy. How about we take a look at Taite's deer? There's some adorable fawns.'

For a second she thought she had them onboard as no one spoke and then Vernette smiled. 'Now Rowan's with Grace, he's turned into such a talkative young man. When we saw him in town before we left, he was quite happy to stop and chat. Before he always had somewhere else to be.'

Brenna nodded, already not liking where this conversation was going. Thanks to her ongoing single status, it was now her turn to do everything possible to avoid the quilting club's machinations.

Mrs Moore took over the conversation. 'And when we asked if he'd met your new neighbour, he said that he hadn't but would later on today after Wyatt finished putting in the new gate with Taite.'

'It will be so much easier for Murphy now he can just walk between your farms,' Mrs Brown piped up, tone innocent.

Brenna mentally counted to ten. There were two ways she could play this. Hold her ground and not take the quilting ladies anywhere near Wyatt and deal with the consequences, or take them to see him and prove there was no potential for any relationship between them. The sooner they understood this the better.

She reached for another jam drop. 'Are you sure you want to drive through the mud? It could get messy and slippery.'

'Oh yes, dear,' Vernette said, nonplussed. 'We're sure, very sure.'

While all four ladies gulped their tea and coffee as though they were trying to set a world record, Brenna fired off a warning text to Taite.

They left the kitchenette and went outside to where the side-by-side was parked beneath the stable overhang. Brenna helped each lady into the low farm vehicle. She handed them a small pink polar fleece blanket to tuck over their knees and made sure everyone wore their seatbelts.

Mrs Walters gave her a smile from the front passenger seat as Brenna slid behind the steering wheel. 'You're so like your mother, always taking care of others.'

'Be careful, Moira,' she said with a wink. 'I've a don't-mess-with-me reputation to uphold.'

Everyone laughed.

Brenna resisted the impulse to find something urgent to do in the stables. She was prepared for anything but had a bad feeling about taking her passengers to meet Wyatt. There was far too much mischief in the expressions surrounding her. With a silent sigh she started the engine.

As she'd warned, mud flicked up to hit the underside of the gator and the track proved slick in places. But as much as the tyres spun, the buzz of anticipation around her didn't wane. Going off the four quilting club ladies' delighted exclamations, they were having a marvellous visit.

'We should do this more often,' Vernette said as water sprayed beside them when they drove through a deep puddle.

Brenna thought it best not to reply.

All too soon the fence line came into view. As did the two men who were lifting an ornate gate into place. Bundy sat on the gator trayback, supervising.

Taite lifted an arm in greeting. Despite the chill in the air, he and Wyatt had discarded their coats and were dressed in half-button shirts, jeans and boots. Wyatt must have visited the local workwear shop, as unlike Taite's blue shirt, his wasn't creased or ripped. Both had whiskered jaws and wind-tousled hair.

She pulled to a stop. The white flash of Wyatt's smile seemed to temporarily rob the quilting ladies of all thought. Then suddenly there was a scramble to unclip their seatbelts. Brenna waited in her seat and examined the high-country peaks while Taite and Wyatt helped everyone out. What she wouldn't give to be up there right now.

While Taite made the introductions, she went to pat Bundy. Apart from a fleeting glance at Wyatt, where she'd discovered his gaze on her, she was determined to ignore him. The seasoned matchmakers would soon see there wasn't anything between them, especially not sparks that could be fanned into something more.

She turned her face into the wind to strip away an incriminating wash of heat. Now wasn't the best time to remember how she had responded to the curl of his biceps yesterday. It also wasn't fitting to sneak another glance to check out how hot he looked in his country clothes.

Bundy pushed his nose into her hand, which was her cue to pay attention to the conversation around her.

When the quilting ladies laughed at something Wyatt said, she clenched her jaw. Of course he'd be witty and charming instead of silent and reserved. So much for supposedly foiling any matchmaking plots.

'It was our pleasure to deliver all those welcome goodies,' Mrs Brown said with a definite titter.

'Thank you again.' Wyatt gave a full smile that Brenna had taken weeks to receive and took his phone out from his jeans pocket. 'So, this is Midge and Merlin.' He angled his screen to show the group a picture of Murphy standing with the goose and mini pony.

'Brenna, you were such a gem to find them for Wyatt,' Mrs Moore cooed. 'Merlin looks like a sweetheart.'

It was no surprise Mrs Moore called Merlin sweet despite his beady-eyed glare. Mrs Moore had a precious flock of ever-expanding geese.

'I found them for *Murphy*,' Brenna clarified.

Taite did a poor job of hiding his grin. She threw him a look that said he'd better behave himself. If there ever was an occasion that required the twintuition that they didn't share, it was now. It would have been very handy for him to know what she was thinking. She couldn't have him encouraging the quilting ladies.

'That's a lovely gate, Taite,' Mrs Walters said.

The group nodded as they all took in the beauty of the ornate metal swirls. Brenna knew she was biased but what her twin could create out of rusted metal scraps was breathtaking.

'I had this sitting there and it seemed a shame to put in a regular gate,' he said.

'I agree,' said Vernette. 'It's symbolic of a new era between the two properties.'

'That's one way of looking at it,' Brenna said smoothly, not wanting to encourage any speculation about what form a new era might take. 'Another way is that it's very practical to have a gate here.' She paused to adopt her bossy trekking tone. They had tarried long enough. She needed to get the quilting club members away from Wyatt before her bad feeling turned into a premonition. 'Now we've had our first stop, let's keep going on our tour.'

Vernette rubbed her knee. 'My old bones might need a few more minutes. The drive here was rather … bouncy.'

Vernette had shown no discomfort when she'd marched over to stand by Wyatt's side.

Taite chuckled. 'Your tour guide might want to avoid the puddles. I thought for sure you'd be bogged.'

Brenna frowned. She hadn't deliberately tried to sabotage the journey across the paddock. There was just a lot of water and mud. She'd never put the elderly ladies in harm's way. She also didn't want Wyatt to think she was the type of person who would do so.

'I have an impeccable driving record, thank you very much. I can't remember when I was last bogged and I've never crashed.' Too late she realised what she'd said. Her secrets could never come to light. She hastily added, 'Well, except for that time when my ute was written off.'

As steady as she'd kept her voice, she knew her damage control hadn't been fast enough. Taite turned to look at her, a deep furrow in his brow. As for Wyatt, she didn't know how he'd picked up on her tension, or maybe he'd noticed Taite's reaction, but his eyes narrowed.

'That's right, dear,' Vernette said. 'Didn't you break your collarbone?'

'I did. I had to wear that ridiculous sling and couldn't ride.' She summoned a smile. She needed to change the topic plus get away from Taite and Wyatt. Both were watching her too closely. 'So, ladies, how about a photo with Bundy for his social media pages? You all look fabulous dressed up.'

Vernette eagerly reached for Wyatt's arm while the other ladies arranged themselves around the two men. Bundy went to sit at the front of the group.

Brenna snapped some shots on her phone. Once finished she waved towards the side-by-side. 'All aboard.'

Except none of the quilting members moved.

Vernette dipped her hand in her vest pocket. 'I'd like to take a photo too … of the three of you. This is *such* a historic moment.'

Brenna looked skywards. She knew a matchmaking ploy when she saw one.

Vernette pinned Brenna with her best schoolteacher stare. 'Over you go.'

Head high, Brenna avoided the space between Taite and Wyatt and went to her brother's far side. As his arm slid around her shoulders, he whispered in her ear, 'No crashes? What was that about?'

'Nothing. Just my bad memory.'

Her attention flickered to Wyatt. The intensity hadn't left his eyes. It was as though his astute gaze could see all the things she'd vowed to keep concealed.

Vernette lifted her phone and Brenna pasted on her most amenable expression. She'd hated lying to Taite four years ago and loathed it even more now. But he could never know the truth. He already carried more than his fair share of the burdens life had thrown at them.

It might have been her ute that had been totalled, but she hadn't been the person driving. More than that, she hadn't been a willing passenger.

CHAPTER 18

Wyatt swung into Outlaw's saddle. Even before he'd slid the toes of his boots into the stirrups, he felt as though something off kilter within him had realigned. He should never have left it so long to bring horses back into his life.

Outlaw danced sideways and he ran a hand over the gelding's smooth neck. Wyatt was just as restless to get going. Except Waffles had zoomed into the stables like a mini tornado and Brenna and Bundy had left to return the kelpie to Taite's cottage. Brenna's mare, Ebony, was tied to the nearby hitching post. The swish of her black tail made it clear to Outlaw that he wasn't to get any ideas about being the lead horse just because he had a rider on his back.

Wyatt turned the brumby to ride over to Murphy and Midge. The Shire horse ambled towards the fence to greet them while Midge trotted to keep up. Merlin glared from where he sat beside a pool of water. Wyatt couldn't help but grin. Earlier that morning the goose had waddled over to accept some watermelon. As if realising he'd ruined his antisocial image, he then quickly reverted to his normal disdainful self.

When the three horses touched noses, tiny Midge gave a squeal. What she lacked in height she made up for in sass. The look she gave him from under her long forelock whenever he'd run out of apple never failed to make him smile. Whenever Murphy appeared nervous, the mini pony would go to his side and the huge Shire horse would calm down.

When Murphy and Midge gazed past him, Wyatt didn't need to turn to confirm that Brenna had returned. The current of awareness that ran through him had already told him she was in the stables. He took a second to mask his thoughts.

The sense that something significant had taken place that morning by the new gate deepened. Brenna's fleeting look of distress before she'd made light of having crashed her ute refused to leave him. Taite hadn't been looking at his sister when she'd spoken, he'd been patting Bundy. But somehow he'd known, without seeing her face, that something had thrown her more than simply having a bad memory.

As close as Brenna and Taite were, his suspicion grew that she hadn't shared all of her past with her twin. He wasn't sure how he knew that what had happened earlier was connected to her reaction to him on the trek, he just had a feeling. And his childhood had taught him to trust his gut.

Brenna rode over, Bundy by her side. 'Sorry about Waffles holding us up. Are you in a rush to get back?'

'Not at all. The rats in the kitchen need time to move out.'

She gave a brief smile before tucking her windblown hair behind her ear. While she'd worn a wide-brimmed hat on the trek, today her head was bare.

'Sorry about this morning.' She cast him a grimace as they rode along the laneway that skirted the main horse paddock. 'I underestimated the quilting club's persistence.'

'There's no need to apologise. They didn't stay long.'

'It would have been long enough to hatch more devious plans. Please tell me you aren't still getting daily deliveries?'

'Let's just say yesterday I learned that cakes can come in the shape of hearts. Then today, well, who knew there were so many shades of pink?'

Brenna briefly closed her eyes. Neither of them stated the obvious that pink was her favourite colour. 'Surely the quilting club will run out of energy soon.'

'If they don't, I might need to go for a run with your brother up that road Rowan called Coronary Hill. I've never eaten so many cupcakes in my life.'

Instead of smiling, Brenna worried her bottom lip as she looked to where Bundy walked between the horses. 'At least Bundy has the sense to realise the futility of trying to turn us into a couple. He hasn't done anything to bring us together.'

As much as Wyatt agreed with her, a sense of disquiet seeped through him. He didn't have a tight enough grip on his feelings yet to contemplate the reality of another man one day having Brenna in his life. To distract himself, he focused on a pair of grey donkeys down by the creek.

'Elsie mentioned you had taken on some rescue donkeys?'

As smooth as he'd intended his small talk to sound, his words were strained.

She nodded. 'I'm going to miss them when they go to their new home near Tumut. A farmer's been losing cattle to wild dogs so they're becoming guardian animals.' She turned to look at him. 'I'm glad you met Rowan earlier. He's a great guy.'

'He is. He left with a ute full of books and will be back for more.'

The conversation lapsed as they entered the adjacent paddock and followed the boundary fence along to the new gate.

Once through, Brenna looked around, her blue eyes alive with curiosity. 'I never thought I'd see the day when I'd be riding on Strathdale.'

'You and Taite are welcome anytime.'

'Thanks.' She slowed Ebony so the horses walked alongside each other. 'I've no idea if we can get to Platypus Hollow from here but it's worth a try.' She pointed to a notch in the ridge to their right. 'That's our landmark. Once Taite's sculpture fundraiser is over tomorrow I'll keep going through the family journals to see if there's anything about our mysterious couple.'

'I'm guessing I should make myself scarce for the exhibition?'

'It's for a worthy cause, the local school wants to train more story dogs like Bundy, but it would be wise. There'll be an abundance of stealthy quilting club members.'

His shudder made Brenna smile before she turned Ebony to follow an animal trail.

Wyatt settled into the saddle. A cool breeze washed over his skin and he filled his lungs with the fresh mountain air. The call of a currawong faded, replaced by the creak of saddle leather and the steady clop of the horses' hooves. In front of him Brenna's shoulders loosened as though she too was responding to the natural beauty around them. Water gurgled as they approached the creek before rocks clattered as the horses waded through the crystal-clear water.

They headed for a rusted gate and then continued deeper into the bush. Every so often Brenna would lift her head to check where the ridge landmark was and then adjust their path. Even though the landscape would have changed since the long-ago lovers had met in the clearing, the ride had so far been straightforward. There was a natural break in the gum trees that created a meandering line along the gentle rise of a gully.

When the weathered contours of grey granite appeared through the timber, Wyatt experienced a tightening in his stomach. If C had travelled this way, then at this point he'd know he'd be close to seeing A. Wyatt forced his attention off Brenna's straight back and the fall of her tousled blonde hair.

He never planned on being in anything but a casual relationship so wasn't about to question what he'd do to be with someone. But if he had been C, then even the steep ridge towering beside him wouldn't have kept him from the woman he loved.

Once out of the trees, Brenna halted Ebony and held up a picture of A's drawing on her phone to match it to the view.

'Assuming this sketch was drawn from memory and shows what A usually saw, she couldn't have approached Platypus Hollow from this direction.'

Brenna walked Ebony to the other side of the boulder. When she compared the drawing to the landscape in front of them, her satisfied smile let him know it was a close fit.

She turned to look over her shoulder. 'This has to be the way A would have ridden to meet C.'

Wyatt too turned. The track behind him that wound its way through the grass tussocks was the one they'd taken on the first day of the trek and led directly to the stables. 'That means whoever A was, she had to be from Glenwood Station.'

Deep in their own thoughts, they took the bridle trail to the clearing where the old miner's hut once stood. Unlike when

Wyatt had last arrived and the sky had been storm-dark, today Platypus Hollow was bathed in the golden glow of late-afternoon sunshine.

Brenna rode beneath the pitched roof of the large shed and dismounted. 'We could have a cuppa?'

He left his saddle and secured Outlaw to the hitching rail. 'I'll light the fire.'

He waited for Brenna to shake her head but after a moment she nodded before going to a small cupboard to take out two mugs.

It wasn't long until flames flickered, embers glowed and steam swirled from their billy tea. Bundy sat nearby, his nose resting on his paws as he slept.

'How's Mia?' Brenna asked.

'In a much better place. Emily's sleeping through the night, which helps.'

A month ago he hadn't ever thought he'd speak such words. But while Mia's grief, and his own, was still very real and at times overwhelming, they were coming to accept that Nick was gone. Brenna's advice that what worked one day to help Mia mightn't the next had led him to develop a variety of strategies. Failure was only ever a wrong word away, but even when he didn't quite know what to say he no longer felt as though he was making such a mess of things.

Brenna sipped at her tea and as she gazed around, the softness in her eyes became tinged with sadness. Just like on their first trip here, he had the impression that this place was important to her.

'Did you come here as a child?'

He thought she wouldn't answer and then she said, voice hushed, 'It was our favourite place to camp and have picnics as kids. The summer after we lost our mother, Taite and I built this shed. Our mother made us promise that even though she wouldn't be with us, we would keep making new memories.'

Wyatt took a mouthful of tea to quell his need to reach over and take Brenna's hand. He'd already ignored common sense to comfort her in the farmhouse and Brenna had been the one to break contact.

She wrapped both hands around her mug. 'When I visit by myself, it still feels as though she's here with me.'

'I know the feeling. After we lost my grandfather, my grandmother and I would sit in the stables so we could feel closer to him.' Wyatt stared off into the distance. 'One morning, a week after he'd gone, I found her there … I thought she'd fallen asleep, but her heart had given out.'

'I'm so sorry. It would have been difficult to lose them both, let alone so quickly.'

He only nodded. Even now, years later, the loss felt raw and brutal.

'You said you'd lived with your grandparents as a teenager?'

'I did.' As uncomfortable as it was to talk about his history, he would if it somehow helped the woman watching him, her gaze unblinking, to face hers. 'They died after I turned eighteen. When my uncle sold the farm, I'd finished school so moved to the city to work and study.'

'On your own?'

'Yes.'

'That must have been hard as well.'

He finished his tea. Temporary homes, hunger and exhaustion were his childhood norms.

Brenna's attention stayed on him. When a splash sounded from over at the creek, she gestured for him to stand. Bundy opened one eye and then returned to his nap.

'We have to be really quiet,' Brenna whispered as she and Wyatt left the shed.

Together they walked past the lone poplar and through the smooth-trunked candle barks to the creek. Brenna lightly touched his arm as she pointed to a ripple of concentric circles close to the bank. Bubbles floated before a brown body with a large bill emerged. The platypus hovered before ducking out of sight and causing another splash.

When Brenna glanced at Wyatt, he returned her smile. The simplicity of the moment and a feeling of being complete had him wishing for things he could never have. He broke eye contact and turned away. He could no more give his feelings free rein than he could allow his past to taint Brenna's life.

He and Brenna turned to retrace their steps. As they'd done on the way over to the creek, they avoided the muddy area that skirted a wombat hole. Except one second Brenna was walking alongside him and the next she'd sunk thigh deep in the ground as a section of the tunnel caved in.

'No way,' she groaned as she leaned back to stop herself from falling forwards.

Wyatt moved in as close as he could. The ground beneath him, while wet, appeared stable.

'Need a hand?'

She blew hair out of her eyes and twisted to assess how deeply she was wedged in the burrow. 'Probably.'

He extended his arm and her hand clasped his. Just like at the farmhouse, he felt her fragility and strength. And just like then, her touch made him feel the opposite of detached.

'On the count of three,' he said.

She shook her head and slipped her hand free. 'I'm in too far. I'll pull you over.' Frustration flashed in her eyes. 'I need to get myself out.'

'Brenna … you're the most independent person I've ever met. But sometimes we all need help.'

If it hadn't been for a teacher in a remote outback school putting the pieces together, he could never have left his father on his own.

Brenna sighed and lifted her arms. 'Can you come closer? We'll need two hands for leverage.'

'Sure.' He leaned over, making sure he let her know what he was about to do. 'But if I hold onto your waist …' Her raised arms caused her jacket to ride higher and his palms wrapped around the indent of her waist. 'And you grab my arms, we'll get the best momentum.'

For a second she didn't move and then her fingers curved around his biceps. Even beneath the thick wool of his navy jumper he could feel the imprint of her grasp.

'After three?' she asked, voice quiet.

He nodded. 'One, two, three …'

In a single fluid motion, he pulled her free and set her on solid ground. Their bodies aligned, her jacket touching his chest. The heat of her skin warmed his hands through her cotton shirt and he breathed in the fragrance of roses. A flood of need caused him to still, waiting for when Brenna's grip would loosen and she'd move away. Except she stayed where she was.

The world narrowed. There was no past or future, just the woman staring at him, her pale blue eyes intent and serious.

'I should let you go.' His tone was as rough as the gravel in the nearby creek bed.

'And I should step back.' Even as she spoke, her grip on his arms tightened and she seemed to move closer.

He bent to brush his lips over her hair. 'I'm not right for you.'

'I know.' Her hands swept up to slide around his neck. 'But I'm not exactly thinking about what boxes you don't tick.'

'Boxes?' He pulled her close, his mouth tracing the fine line of her jaw.

'So many boxes.'

Her words were a husky whisper across his lips.

Brenna was everything he shouldn't want or yearn for. But even knowing this wasn't enough to stop him. He framed her face and slowly lowered his head to give her time to pull away if she was having second thoughts. As right as this felt for him, he couldn't assume she felt the same way. She stayed where she was.

Their mouths met and her lips parted. Every degree of logic and common sense fled. Brenna was the light of dawn on a winter horizon and the warmth of a spreading sunrise. She was the compass that centred him in a world that had no direction. He tilted her head to deepen their kiss.

When they broke apart, their unsteady breaths punctuated the silence. He threaded his fingers into the silken weight of her hair to stop himself from again seeking her mouth. One kiss would never satisfy his need for her, but he'd already tempted fate enough. A feeling she shared if the widening of her eyes was any indication.

Her hands lowered to rest on his chest, but she didn't push him away. 'That can't happen again.'

He touched a thumb to her bottom lip, not ready to let her go. 'Those boxes have to be ticked.'

'They do.' Her fingers curled into his jumper. 'Neighbours?'

As much as he was no good for her, he needed to be more than that. 'Friends?'

Her attention fixed on his mouth, then she dipped her head in agreement before taking a step away. His arms dropped from around her, cold air replacing the warmth of her body.

As she turned to walk away, he didn't immediately follow. He dragged in a breath and forced his mind to focus. But as his thoughts cleared, there remained an inescapable reality.

After having his hands tangled in Brenna's hair and her lips on his, seeing her as just a neighbour, let alone a friend, would be impossible.

CHAPTER 19

Today wasn't the day to correct her bad baking record.

Brenna wiped her flour-dusted hands down the front of her pink apron. Not only did the kitchen smell like smoke and she'd ruined her favourite oven mitt, but she'd melted the end of a plastic cutting board.

She opened the oven door with a frown and slid in the tray of chocolate chip cookies. She already had a hunch they weren't going to end up looking like the picture on the recipe. They were more like golf balls than soft domes of dough.

But she wasn't giving up. Nor was she calling her master-chef twin for help, even though there had been flames. She wasn't having him ask what was wrong. There were some things he didn't need to know about—such as yesterday's kiss. She was not discussing how Wyatt's touch had awoken every nerve ending she owned or how desperate she'd been to slide her hands beneath his shirt. She could barely admit such things to herself.

Needing something to keep her mind busy, she opened her mother's recipe book to the never-fail chocolate slice. Normally she'd work through whatever was bothering her in the stables. But being in her happy place hadn't given her any answers about how to deal with her attraction to Wyatt, nor about why he thought he wasn't right for her.

She'd also usually talk to Hettie or Clancy. But last night Hettie had been busy helping set up for the sculpture exhibition on today. Then this morning she'd been stringing fairy lights in the garden. Meanwhile Clancy was back in Western Australia seeing Heath while he finished his current silo project.

She sighed as she reread the recipe. She had to do whatever it took to pull herself together before Taite's event opened in a couple of hours and the quilting club ladies arrived. Even if it meant baking a chocolate slice that Waffles, who ate everything, wouldn't touch.

After a small episode of butter exploding in the microwave and a larger problem of burning the melted chocolate, Brenna scraped what she hoped was an edible mixture into a pan. Just to be sure, she added extra sugar.

She'd taken out the chocolate chip cookies and put in the slice when she realised Hettie was standing at the doorway. The redhead's eyes widened as her gaze swept around the kitchen.

Brenna plonked the hot cookie tray onto the bench that resembled a war zone. Hettie quickly grabbed a tea towel and moved the tray onto the nearby sink. Brenna had a vague memory of being told not to put anything too hot directly onto the pale grey stone.

They both stared at the biscuits, which were flat and had merged together to fill the tray.

'I was going for the cookie pizza idea,' Brenna said, words wry.

Hettie took a butter knife and carefully separated the cookies. 'They smell delicious,' she said, tone diplomatic.

'Shall we try one?' They both looked at each other before Brenna added, 'I'll go first.'

She picked up an oven-warm cookie and nibbled the edge. Sure, it was hard and dry, but the chocolate made it palatable.

'It's not quite Michelin star quality, but I'd eat them.'

Hettie selected a cookie and took a small bite. Brenna filled a water glass and passed it to her as she tried not to choke.

'I think,' Brenna said, frowning at the mess that covered nearly every surface of the kitchen, 'I might have forgotten to put the sugar in. That's what I was supposed to be doing when the oven mitt somehow ended up on the hot plate.'

Hettie set her glass and uneaten cookie on the sink. 'I'm sure your chocolate slice will be fine.' She turned to face Brenna. 'Something happen on your ride with Wyatt?'

'Can't I bake without a reason?'

Hettie bit back a grin. 'No.'

Brenna switched on the kettle. 'This might take a while.'

Hettie took two mugs from the cupboard. 'I've plenty of time. The sisters are here helping.'

Millicent and Beatrice were identical twins and a mainstay of any Bundilla fundraising event. As much as she was often on the receiving end of a raised brow from either of the older women during book club, they at least never dabbled in matchmaking.

Once their coffees had been made, Brenna took off her apron. She and Hettie headed for the living room where they could curl up on the sofa. Brenna sat a rose-pink velvet cushion on her lap and plucked at the tassels.

'So …' Hettie said, voice gentle.

'So … this attraction is going to be the death of me.'

'You kissed Wyatt.'

'Should I find it disturbing you don't sound surprised?'

Hettie laughed softly. 'You already said you're attracted to him, plus he isn't exactly ignoring you.'

Brenna's fingers stilled. 'What do you mean?'

'The obvious thing, kissing involves two people, plus he watches you when you're not looking.'

'It's probably because he's thinking *I can't believe she said that* or wondering if I own a single shirt that's not pink.' She paused. 'We might have kissed but he himself said he's not right for me. The only explanation I can think of is that he believes the whole city–country thing won't work. City girls would be more his thing.'

'I'm not so sure of that. He's single, isn't he?'

'He says he does fine on his own.'

Hettie lifted her mug but not before Brenna saw a smile in her eyes. 'Point proven. That's not a conversation people have with each other if there's zero interest.'

'He was only saying what I said.'

'Taite likes him.'

Brenna groaned. 'Why will no one believe me when I say Wyatt and I could never be together? He meets none of my criteria.'

'Except for looking good on a horse.'

'I've taken that off,' Brenna grumbled. 'And I've added another one. I can't be with anyone who kisses like Wyatt does. I'd get no work done.'

Even now her senses still remembered the heat and strength in his touch and how hard it had been to commit to being friends.

Neighbours she could handle. But friends meant hanging out together and already her hormones were demanding a repeat lip-lock.

'Does that mean you'll stop getting to know him?'

Clancy's advice to spend time with Wyatt to see if her uncertainty about him changed had worked. She did feel like she knew him better.

The trouble was the knowledge only increased her confusion. She more than ever felt like a different person around him. For a start, the normal her would have found a way out of the wombat hole herself. Secondly, she'd never before had a problem with letting go of a man's biceps, no matter how firm they'd felt.

'We agreed to be neighbours, and friends. Both means we'll be seeing each other. But I'll be making sure that's all we are. He's just too …' She pulled a face as she searched for the correct word.

'Wrong,' Hettie suggested.

While that was the word that fit logically, it didn't encapsulate how she felt. 'Too *much*. Too good-looking. Too strong. Too astute. I need someone who won't challenge me.'

'Considering your favourite word at school was *bored*, a little challenge might not be a bad thing.'

'I've mellowed in my old age.'

Hettie smiled. 'Wyatt's different to the guys you're used to. But he's also decent. There's nothing wrong with being attracted to him. If anyone's worth breaking your rules for, it could be him.'

Brenna picked up her coffee mug. She'd rather wear acrylic nails and eyelash extensions than ditch her rules. Not that Hettie knew but after everything she'd been put through by a man she'd believed to be unassuming, being challenged was the one thing she didn't need. She had to be in charge of her life.

Hettie reached over to squeeze her hand. 'Your slice smells ready. We can try a piece and I'll help you clean the kitchen. Who knows how many quilting ladies will pop over pretending they need a cuppa so they can talk about Wyatt?'

The sculpture fundraising event had only been open ten minutes before a knock rattled Brenna's front door. Hettie had been right. She was about to be inundated with wily nannas harbouring hidden agendas.

Looping a hair tie around her side braid, which draped over her front pocket, she strode along the hallway. She'd changed into a clean pink shirt and her best going-to-town jeans. The sun was out and the sky cloudless so she wouldn't need a jacket or vest.

For her sanity, and to give her one less Wyatt thing to think about, she needed the matchmakers to back off. So, her mission for this afternoon was to defuse as many plots as she could. Starting now. She threw open the front door. But there weren't any smiling elderly ladies on her veranda.

Instead, Wyatt stood there with Bundy, looking more gorgeous than any man had a right to. Hair tousled, jaw stubbled, she had difficulty remembering that he was a city boy. Conscious of the line of cars coming in along the driveway, she grabbed his arm and hauled him inside.

As soon as the front door swung shut behind him, she released her grip. She led the way along the hallway into the kitchen, too irritated to feel any awkwardness after their kiss. Wyatt and Bundy being at her house, in full view of anyone, wasn't in any way amusing.

She turned and folded her arms. 'None of the quilting club ladies better have seen you two.'

Instead of replying, Wyatt lifted his phone. He tapped on his screen to show her a photo. Initially she wasn't sure what she was looking at and then her mouth fell open. She took the phone, barely registering the brush of their fingers. She enlarged the image. What looked like old letters were spread out across the surface of a small table.

From their compressed appearance something had to have been sitting on top. A thin green ribbon, which once would have been around the letters, had been tied into a bow and placed at the bottom right corner.

She raised her eyes to Wyatt's. What she'd thought were steel-blue flecks in the grey were now a warmer hue.

'Where did you find them?'

'In a washstand.'

'Have you read any?'

'I'm waiting for you.'

Warmth filled her at his thoughtfulness. 'Right … I'll be—'

A knock sounded on her front door, then Vernette's voice called out, 'Brenna, dear, are you home? A cuppa would be nice before I walk through the garden.'

Brenna thrust Wyatt's phone into his hand. 'Follow me.' She strode towards the back door. 'Please tell me you didn't drive.'

She stopped at the doorway, waiting for his answer.

'What type of neighbour do you think I am?' His gaze travelled over her face, slowing when it reached her mouth. 'I used the side gate.'

Distracted by the way the blue flecks in his irises had darkened, she forgot about Vernette. Another knock hammered on the front door.

'Well, *neighbour*, don't get seen or waylaid. As soon as I can escape, I'll come over.'

He gave her a nod. Not waiting to see him and Bundy leave, she sprinted towards the front of the homestead.

At the door, she took a second to slow her breathing and to calm her nerves, which she wasn't sure were solely from being about to face Vernette. Wyatt's appearance had thrown her more than she liked. It seemed that even the parameters they had put in place around how they interacted weren't enough to insulate her from the way he made her feel.

For the second time that day, she flung open the door.

'Vernette.' She quickly tempered her smile. Vernette's expression had sharpened. 'Sorry I took so long, I was looking at something on the phone.'

The fact that it was Wyatt's phone wasn't relevant.

Vernette peered past her into the hallway. 'Are you here by yourself?'

'Yes.' She stepped out and shut the door behind her. 'I was just coming to see who's arrived.' She waved as she saw Ruth from the candle shop leave her parked car.

She tucked her arm in Vernette's. 'You mentioned a cuppa? The bunting around the coffee van looks so pretty. How about we make the most of the sun and have one outside?'

The vintage van would already have a queue forming and Vernette would be sure to find someone to talk to. Brenna could then slip away. If she could just make it to the stables, she could ride Ebony bareback over to Wyatt's. The building would block her from the view of any exhibition visitors.

Vernette glanced at the closed front door. 'Nothing goes better with a cuppa than people watching. Maybe we'll spot a certain nice young man who smells of sandalwood.'

Brenna adopted her best smile. 'Wyatt very kindly made a donation, but he isn't able to pop over.'

'That's a shame, but the fact you've been talking is music to an old lady's ears.'

Brenna thought it prudent to not reply. She kept a firm grip on Vernette's elbow to help her down the veranda steps, willing the heat out of her cheeks. After yesterday she and Wyatt had done more than talk.

As Brenna hoped, when they crossed the lawn towards a sculpture of an eagle, Vernette stopped to chat to a former student of hers. Children's laughter floated on the breeze as four youngsters raced each other around a scrap metal bull that had a live kookaburra perched on its head. The smell of sausages and onions wafted from the barbecue tent set up near the garden entrance.

Brenna's phone vibrated and she checked her screen. When she noticed Vernette taking a sneaky sideways glance, she angled her mobile so the message wouldn't be visible. The text was from Wyatt.

Operation Make It Home Unscathed was a success.

She hid a smile as she typed.

Operation Make It To The Stables was a failure.

Need backup?

She might have accepted his help to get out of the wombat hole, but she wasn't making a habit of relying on someone other than herself.

As if.

His laughing emoji shouldn't have made her feel almost carefree. He wasn't a man she could relax around. Yesterday had shown her what happened when she forgot why she lived her life the way she did. Her rules were in place to keep her safe. It wasn't an option to break them. He knew as well as she did that they weren't right for each other.

She sent a SOS text to Hettie and returned her phone to her shirt pocket. When her mobile rang, she scooped it out, expression innocent, and mouthed the words, 'I have to take this,' knowing Vernette could lip read. Then, phone against her ear, she filled Hettie in as she marched through the crowd avoiding all eye contact. She ended her call and entered the stables, making sure to close the door behind her. Mission accomplished.

Except as she headed to the tack room to grab Ebony's bridle, her pace slowed. She had a sneaking suspicion that the quickening of her pulse wasn't entirely from the prospect of reading the new letters. Despite all her self-talk, a part of her was eager to see Wyatt.

CHAPTER 20

In his city world Wyatt's phone was never far from his hand. It was an indispensable component of how he ran his private equity firm. But he'd never let it govern his life.

He switched his mobile off when he needed to focus and hadn't missed not being connected when he'd been on the trek. Yet ever since Brenna had texted, all he could think about was when he'd hear from her again.

He took what would have been his third look at his phone in five minutes. Muttering under his breath, he snatched up a bag of rubbish that was only half full and left the bedroom he'd been sorting through. It was either leave or check his phone again. Bundy followed.

Wyatt didn't need to see his reflection in the hallstand mirror as he strode by to realise he was scowling. So much for his self-discipline and ability to tune out disruptions. It wasn't as though

Brenna was coming for a personal visit. She was only rushing over to see the letters.

She hadn't exactly been pleased to find him and Bundy on her doorstep earlier. Her surprise had quickly turned to horror as she'd glanced past him in case anyone had noticed their arrival. He'd known he'd be cutting it fine with the sculpture exhibition opening, but the side-by-side he'd found in the shed had been slow to start. He had made sure that he and Bundy wouldn't be seen heading to Brenna's house after he'd parked out of sight beside the stables.

He walked outside and added the rubbish to the large skip. In hindsight he should have messaged Brenna about the letters. He shouldn't have overruled his caution and given in to the need to see her reaction. Even more so after their kiss, he had to adhere to their friends and neighbours agreement.

He flexed his shoulders and went to return to the house. Instead of accompanying him, Bundy dashed through the overgrown garden towards the side garden gate. Wyatt looked across to the neighbouring paddocks. Not that he could see anything through the trees, but Brenna had to be on her way. As he set off after Bundy to open the gate, he erased all emotion from his face.

Bundy's tail wagged as she appeared riding Ebony without a saddle. Wyatt watched as the pair cantered over. As much as Brenna believed she didn't compare to sophisticated city girls, she possessed a natural grace and elegance. When she lifted her arm in a wave, he returned the gesture. Now wasn't the time to analyse the warmth that flowed through him.

She greeted him with a smile as she slid off Ebony's back. Wisps of hair framed her face from where they'd escaped her braid. While she wore her usual pink shirt and jeans, today her shirt was fitted and tucked into dark denim jeans that mapped her slender curves. Where the top two of her shirt buttons were undone, he caught a glimpse of smooth skin and a silver chain.

'Sorry, I couldn't get away sooner.' Brenna bent to pat Bundy. 'I'd also better not stay long. I wouldn't put it past Vernette to sweet talk Rowan into driving her over if she suspects this is where I've bolted to.'

He wouldn't put anything past Vernette either. What he didn't need right now was the seasoned matchmaker witnessing him acting about as cool as a winter bonfire. When Brenna led Ebony through the gate he used the seconds she wasn't looking at him to nail down his attraction.

'Need some baling twine?' he asked as they made their way to the stables.

Brenna would understand that he was checking if Ebony was right to go in the yards or if she needed to be tied up outside. The sugar-rich green grass inside the fence perimeter wouldn't be suitable for a horse prone to laminitis.

'Ebony will be fine. She doesn't have any history of founder.'

Once in the yards, Brenna removed Ebony's bridle and the mare dropped her head to eat.

Conscious that Brenna had to return next door as soon as she could, Wyatt turned to head towards the house.

Brenna fell into step beside him. 'I can't believe you found more letters.'

'I was lucky. A washstand in the attic had been damaged by a roof leak. When I lifted the marble to see if the wood could be salvaged, I found a hidden compartment. Thankfully the water hadn't reached what was inside.'

He reached for the front door and Brenna sailed through, followed by Bundy. Unlike on her last visit, there was no hesitation as she strode along the hallway. His own steps dragged. Brenna hadn't even been in the farmhouse five minutes and already her energy made the house feel like a home.

'Second door on the right,' he said.

Brenna entered the living room and went straight to the washstand standing in the middle of the empty space. She stared at the letters filling the rectangular wooden frame before taking out her phone and snapping photos.

'I don't suppose you have a laptop handy?' she asked.

'I do.'

Her smile had him swing around to head for the kitchen to collect his computer before the memory of how soft her lips were had his gaze lock on her mouth. He returned and busied himself setting up his laptop on the built-in bar top. While he did so, Brenna went to wash her hands so she could handle the letters. Bundy stretched out by the window to snooze in a patch of sunshine.

Brenna took the first letter from the top row in the washstand and sat it on the bar. Carefully she pried open the yellowed paper and separated each page. She stepped back while Wyatt took pictures and uploaded them to his laptop.

'So,' Brenna said as she examined the neat and fluid handwriting. 'This letter is from A to C and is dated 1861, so almost a year before the others. And seeing as these letters were stored here, it looks like we were right about Strathdale being C's home.'

Wyatt nodded. 'The language is also more formal. It's as though they're just starting to get to know each other. Instead of dearest C, it's dear C. And when A signs off it's plain yours, not your loving A.'

Brenna's lips pursed as she concentrated. 'It seems as though they met when A was out riding and her horse went lame. C came to her rescue, and she's writing to say thank you.' Brenna paused. 'Look at the second paragraph. If we assume C was a member of the family who lived here, which makes him Arthur's distant relative, this could be referring to the feud between the two farms.'

Wyatt's gaze skimmed over the words that indicated the couple had to be careful not to be caught corresponding as five of A's father's cows had gone missing and he blamed C's family. 'I agree.'

Brenna's fingers followed a line of handwriting on the screen. 'Here … A says she hopes C will keep writing to her despite how her father and uncle treated his brother when they found him on their land.'

'Things obviously deteriorated quickly.'

'And then never improved. No wonder C and A had to hide their relationship from their families.'

'Next page?'

At Brenna's nod, Wyatt brought up the second image.

They both remained silent as they read. The letter contained no more personal information, just references to how A filled her day.

Working together, they opened, photographed and read through the next three letters. All were again from A to C.

Wyatt pointed to a section on the fifth letter. 'Here's a possible bushranger connection. A apologises for the things her father and uncle said. She tries to reassure C she doesn't think he's a bushranger, despite the rumours circulating in town.'

Brenna sighed. 'For A's sake I hope C wasn't a gang member, but the gold could suggest otherwise.'

They read the final three letters, the last two of which were only a page long. What was obvious in the tone and the endearments

A now used was that the couple had found a way to meet and had grown closer.

Brenna took a step away from the laptop, her expression pensive. 'These provide precious background information, but we still don't have any names. At least we know C and A are from the two neighbouring farms. My ancestor will hopefully be easy to identify; she'll be in my family tree. As for who C is, this won't be so straightforward to figure out. I'll start with the names of Arthur's parents and work my way back from there.'

Wyatt stayed silent. He hadn't realised how comfortable he'd been having Brenna in his space. Now she'd moved away to refold the letters he felt strangely disconnected. He'd spent his life forming as few attachments as possible and being satisfied with his own company. Yet in that moment, he could almost swear he felt lonely.

She sent him a sideways glance. 'Thanks again for waiting to read these with me. I'd better head home. I'll keep you updated on anything I find in my research.'

'Shall I bring the letters over tomorrow so they can be added to the others?'

She nodded and bent to ruffle Bundy's neck. 'No need for either of you to come see me out. I've taken up enough of your day.'

With a quick smile and a last look at the letters, she was gone.

As Wyatt frowned at the empty doorway, Bundy came to his side. He scratched behind the kelpie's ears. 'It's just the two of us again.'

With the house feeling too quiet, Wyatt went to collect his phone from where he'd left it in the bedroom. When he saw he had a missed video call from Mia, he rang her back.

He thought she wouldn't answer but then her face filled the screen.

'Sorry,' she said as she moved the camera to show a smiling Emily in her arms. 'As innocent and clean as Little Miss looks, five minutes ago I was wearing her lunch over my dress.'

He too had been on the receiving end of baby Emily's sensitive stomach. He mightn't have had any experience with children, let alone infants, but he did what he could to help Mia take care of Emily. Even if that meant having a change of shirt in his office and navigating his way around the baby section of a pharmacy.

Emily gurgled and sucked on her fist. Her eyes, so like Nick's, stared back at him. It had only been four days since he'd last seen her but she looked bigger.

'She's grown.' He didn't hide the softness in his voice.

While shadows were smudged beneath Mia's eyes and her brunette hair was in a haphazard ponytail, her smile was content. 'She has.'

Wyatt didn't reply as they both gazed at Emily. As much as they each missed Nick, his mirror-image daughter had helped fill the void within them.

Mia cleared her throat before she studied Wyatt. 'You okay?'

'Yes.'

'You sure?'

Nick had met Mia in their last year of university and from then on she'd also been a part of Wyatt's life. As much as he supported Mia and didn't expect anything in return, it was as though she'd taken on Nick's role of checking in with him. Despite sleep deprivation and what she called baby brain, Mia's lawyer instincts remained well-honed.

'Wyatt,' Mia prompted. 'Something's up.'

'It's nothing. Emily still sleeping through?'

'You know deflection won't work. Neither will your poker face. Nick used to say that whenever you looked like that, your mind was in overdrive.'

'You've got more important things to think about.'

'This is about your new neighbour, isn't it?'

When he frowned, Mia laughed quietly. 'Your glower is wasted. Don't forget I've seen you with baby powder on your face.' She paused, her expression sobering. 'Wyatt ... I made a promise to Nick. A promise you're not going to like. But I'm to make sure you don't spend the rest of your life alone.'

'I do more than fine on my own.'

'Tell me about it. You have no idea how many cocktails I've had to buy over the years for girls to drown their sorrows in.'

'There hasn't been that many.'

'They were the ones you *didn't* go out with. So ... this Brenna ...' Mia stopped to settle Emily closer as the baby's eyes fluttered and then closed.

'Friend and neighbour.'

He'd assumed the brief response would end the conservation. He was wrong.

'You don't do friends.'

He thought about the people he'd met since arriving in the mountains. 'As it turns out ... I do.'

'That's so good to hear. I'd like to meet them. Back to Brenna ... would Nick like her?'

When he stripped all expression from his face, Mia's lips quirked. 'Wyatt, stop trying so hard to be nonchalant. I've known you too long. The way you said friend and neighbour was a giveaway, plus the order you said it in. As soon as I put Emily to bed I'm looking this Brenna up online. Her trekking business must have a webpage.'

Wyatt rubbed at his jaw. 'Yes.' Mia wasn't making an idle threat. 'Nick would like her.'

'Why?'

'I'm not under cross-examination.'

'No but you've piqued my interest and I need to get answers in the next five minutes before Emily decides she's hungry.'

'Our first meeting, Brenna kicked me off the trek.'

Mia lifted a hand to hide her amusement. 'I'm a fan already. What did you do?'

He hesitated. 'I was on the phone.'

'I'm so sorry. That would have been with me. I should never have kept talking for so long. Brenna obviously reconsidered.'

'She did.'

'And now you're friends and neighbours.' There was no teasing in Mia's tone now.

'Yes and …'

'*And* … Wyatt, I'm on a time limit here.'

'Don't laugh too loudly or you'll wake Emily. The town matchmakers have us in their sights. Every day I receive a delivery of baked goods, with themes such as hearts or the colour pink.'

Mia made no attempt to stifle her mirth. 'Heart-shaped cakes and biscuits?' she managed between chuckles.

He slowly nodded.

'I am so coming to stay when Emily can travel.' Mia lowered her voice as Emily stirred. 'Wyatt, as clever as that brain of yours is, don't let it stop you from being happy. Brenna has to be someone important if you've let her get close to you, even as a friend.'

Emily's eyes snapped open. Whatever Mia would have gone on to say was drowned out by a loud and hungry cry.

Mia gave him an apologetic smile before ending the call.

Wyatt stared at the blank screen. Theoretically Mia's words made sense. But the reality was no matter how important Brenna might be to him, there could be nothing further between them. Even if Nick had been determined to end Wyatt's bachelor ways and had passed on the baton to Mia.

He knew his limitations. He wasn't relationship material and he definitely couldn't start something with someone who he wasn't right for and would only end up failing. No matter how much he'd wanted to slip the band off Brenna's thick blonde braid so her heavy hair slid over her shoulders. And no matter how much a rising sense of regret refused to leave him.

CHAPTER 21

The ache in her lower back had Brenna stretching in the dining room chair. After she'd said goodbye to the last of the sculpture exhibition visitors and had finished her stable jobs, she'd put a cushion on the seat to make the chair more comfortable. She'd had a hunch she would be there for a while, and she had been right.

In front of her on the table were the family history journals. So far she'd been through three. She'd made notes and had drawn diagrams of family trees, but the details were so convoluted her head was ready to blow a fuse.

She pushed back her chair. Through the large window in front of her she saw that evening shadows had settled over the valley. Thanks to autumn's arrival the days were getting shorter. She went to pull the curtains shut before heading to her bedroom for a jumper and ugg boots.

Instead of returning to the dining room to open another journal, she made a detour via the kitchen. She should have dinner otherwise her patience would wear rather thin. Her gaze settled on her phone that sat charging on the bench.

She didn't need help so much as someone to talk through what wasn't making sense in her family tree. Before she could question the wisdom of what she was about to do, she picked up her mobile and called Wyatt's number. Bundy hadn't yet come over to spend the night, so Wyatt had to still be at Strathdale. It was also natural, after reading the letters together, that she'd discuss the journals with him.

Despite her logic, her nerves twisted as she waited for him to answer.

After another ring, the deep timbre of his voice sounded. 'Brenna.'

'Hi.' For a split second she felt like a gauche teenager. What was it about Wyatt that made her forget she was well past her teenage crush years? Not that she actually had a word for how she felt about him. Jaw clenched, she continued, 'I'm guessing you're next door as there's no sign of Bundy.'

'Yes, Bundy's with me. Mike came to grade the driveway and we've been talking. I know Bundy usually comes over himself but it's late. I can drop him round on my way past?'

'Thanks. Actually, would you like a coffee? A few things have popped up in the family history journals.'

'I'd love one.'

She looked at the clock on the kitchen stove even as her stomach rumbled.

'If I promise not to burn anything, will you stay for dinner? You must be hungry, and I'll feel rude eating if you're not. I was just going to throw some steaks on the barbecue.'

Her mother had always invited extras for meals, so she didn't second-guess asking Wyatt to dinner until after she'd made the offer. She hoped he wouldn't think she was straying over either the friends' or neighbours' line. In the city he'd have to have women taking advantage of any opportunity to be around him.

'If it's no trouble, dinner would be great. I've found a wine cupboard … I could bring a bottle?'

'Either red or white would be lovely.' Then, feeling the return of her awkwardness at how this almost felt like a date, she wrapped up their phone call. 'See you whenever you can get here.'

She placed her phone on the bench and went to prepare a salad. Instead of setting the small kitchen table, which she would have done had it been Hettie or Clancy coming, she decided to eat at the larger table where the journals were. The more physical space between her and Wyatt the more she could concentrate on why he was there.

After reading today's letters she was even more invested in the star-crossed lovers. Arthur's hostility had been so ingrained she could imagine how difficult it would have been for a relationship to grow in the face of such neighbourly animosity.

So far, they'd also only uncovered the beginning and middle of the couple's story and not the end. Maybe it was her need to always know whether her so-called theories were correct, or maybe it stemmed from everything she'd been through in her life, but she hated not having closure. She had to find out what had happened to A and C.

With the salad in the fridge, she then took out two steaks, which she seasoned and left on the bench to warm to room temperature. As much as she loathed following recipes—she was too impatient to read every step—she had no problems using a barbecue. Tonight she was determined there'd not be a whiff of smoke or trace of charcoal. Even if she was without an oven mitt thanks to yesterday's baking mishaps. She went to put Bundy's favourite dog biscuits in his bowl.

As prepared as she was, when footsteps rang on the veranda, she couldn't suppress a twinge of nerves mixed with anticipation. She opened the door and mentally ordered her body to behave. As much as she couldn't forget her kiss with Wyatt, it wouldn't ever be on the menu again.

Even though she'd seen him that morning, her stomach did its usual tumble. His navy half-zip jumper emphasised the breadth of his shoulders and deepened the blue flecks in his grey eyes. In one hand was a bottle and beneath his arm a box. Bundy sat beside him.

'I went with a red,' Wyatt said with a half smile as he passed her the wine.

'Thanks.' She stepped back to let him inside. The whisper of contact between their fingers was enough to flood her face with warmth.

She met Bundy's amber gaze. As obvious as the quilting club's intentions were, perhaps she should be paying more attention to the kelpie. He didn't seem to be doing anything to push her and Wyatt together, yet he continued to divide his time between them. He'd better not be waiting for the perfect matchmaking opportunity. Maybe when he went to be a story dog in town next Thursday he would go on to stay with someone else.

She followed Wyatt and Bundy into the kitchen. Wyatt placed the box on the bench and took out a clear plastic bag in which she could see the letters.

'I'm not sure if you'd like any of these,' he said, with a nod at the box. 'But you're welcome to them.'

She moved closer to peer inside at the pink teacups and plates and what looked like a pink lamp base. There were also two large glass vases. She glanced at the crystal vase by the sink that had been her mother's and which she always kept full of flowers. Wyatt must have noticed it on a previous visit.

Touched by his thoughtfulness, she took out a fine bone china teacup the colour of a pale rose petal.

'Thank you.' Then fearing her words were a little too breathless she said in a more controlled voice, 'Who knew bachelor Arthur had such pretty things hidden amongst his macho mess.'

Wyatt smiled, his gaze lingering on her face before he turned away. 'What can I do to help with dinner?'

'You could pour the wine. Glasses are in the top cupboard to your left.'

She'd just taken the cover off the steaks when her phone rang. A photo of an unimpressed Taite flashed up on the screen with the label *Old Twin*. She looked apologetically at Wyatt. 'Sorry, it's my brother.'

Wyatt picked up the barbecue utensils and she gestured towards the side door.

She answered the call. 'Hi. What's up?'

'Hettie's cooked roast chicken if you wanted to come for dinner.'

Taite sounded like he was in the side-by-side so would still be packing up after the exhibition. His offer wasn't unusual. She often ate over at the cottage. But what was off was his timing, plus he normally would have texted and not called. From the fancy lights of Wyatt's four-wheel drive it would have been obvious who she had visiting. 'Are you checking up on me?'

Taite chuckled. 'Why would I do that?'

'Because you saw Wyatt drive in. And,' she lowered her voice, 'before you get any ideas, he's just dropping Bundy off and we're discussing the attic journals.'

'As if I'd get any ideas.' Her brother's innocent tone didn't fool her. 'Wyatt's also welcome for dinner.'

Brenna briefly closed her eyes. She should have known where this conversation was heading. 'Wyatt's eating here.'

'Brenna—'

'Don't say it. I've got everything under control. It's salad and a barbecue. There's no fire risk *and* it's just a meal between neighbours.'

'I wasn't going to say a thing.' She would have believed him if his tone wasn't so amused. 'Do you need dessert?'

'No.' She lowered her voice to a whisper so Wyatt couldn't hear her through the open kitchen door. 'This *isn't* a date.'

'Too bad.' The honk of the side-by-side's horn came from outside. 'I've left you an apple pie at your front door. You can thank me later.'

Before she could reply, and she wasn't exactly going to say thank you, Taite ended the call. Outside, the gator engine faded as he sped away. Brenna ground her teeth.

Wyatt and Bundy re-entered the kitchen.

'Was that Taite leaving?' Wyatt asked.

She gave what she hoped passed as a calm smile. 'Let's just say we have an apple pie for dessert courtesy of a stealthy food-delivery driver.'

For the remainder of the time it took for the steaks to cook and then for her and Wyatt to seat themselves at the dining room table and enjoy their meal, Brenna found herself growing more and more relaxed. She could add feeling at ease around Wyatt to all the ways in which he was too much. She couldn't remember when she'd laughed so often even when on a proper date. Usually with someone she was still getting to know she kept her defences firmly in place.

With their dessert bowls empty and a coffee in front of them, talk turned to the journals.

'So,' she said, sliding the notebook towards where Wyatt sat at the end of the table. 'This is my family tree that my mother put together. A would have to be on my mother's side, as Glenwood Station has always been in her family. But the only relation with a name that starts with an A is on my dad's side.'

'Maybe A worked here?' Wyatt paused to study the family names and birth dates. 'You sure do have lots of twins in the branch on the left.'

'Taite and I are fraternal twins, so it's genetic. My mother was a twin and so was my grandmother.'

Brenna stared at the notebook page. 'The problem is that for the 1860s another branch of the family lived here. From my mother's notes there was no one to leave Glenwood Station to so it went to a distant relative from California, which was my great-great-grandmother.'

'So the feud started with ancestors you were only remotely related to?'

At her nod, Wyatt reached for the closest journal that was labelled *Glenwood Station History*. 'Fingers crossed your mother found some information about the family members who were here before your great-great-grandparents.'

'That's what I'm hoping.' Brenna took the next journal in the pile. 'Are you sure you haven't had enough of all this?'

'I'd rather be here than face what's waiting for me at the pub. Apparently the theme of today's deliveries is kisses. Elsie says I have a huge cake with a topper that says "kiss me at midnight" and cupcakes with crosses on them.'

Brenna stayed silent. She didn't know whether to laugh or be horrified. There was no way the quilting club could know they had kissed.

As if reading her thoughts, Wyatt spoke, voice low. 'Brenna, it's okay. They have no idea what is and isn't happening between us.'

If only she could share Wyatt's certainty. She was already unbalanced enough whenever in his company. After their kiss she didn't trust herself to not look at him in such a way as to make it obvious that they'd shared an up-close-and-personal moment. This wasn't the quilting club's first matchmaking rodeo. They were experienced at identifying even a flicker of chemistry. When it came to Wyatt, her attraction was at an inferno level.

'I've seen the quilting ladies in action. They always seem to know.'

'There's no way they could. Neither of us would have said anything to anyone.'

'Ah, I have. To Hettie, but she wouldn't have even told Taite.'

When Wyatt glanced out the window, Brenna asked, 'What are you thinking?'

Even though Wyatt didn't appear deep in thought, she knew him well enough to sense he was. 'Roy. Last night he asked if I'd seen you. I said we'd gone for a ride.'

For Roy's suspicions to be triggered, Wyatt must have given some sort of sign that something had happened between them. She only hoped it wasn't him appearing as though he'd regretted whatever it was.

'Roy's a master at reading people. I also wouldn't put it past him to have Vernette on speed dial. She's probably bribed him with sponge cakes.'

Wyatt's gaze drifted over her mouth. 'On the off chance the kiss theme wasn't a coincidence, we both know that any future matchmaking efforts will be in vain.'

'Exactly.' Brenna smoothed open her journal, hoping her voice sounded more normal to Wyatt than it did to her own ears. As imperfect a match as they were, the thought of someone else being Wyatt's perfect partner left her feeling uneasy. 'Let's see if there's anything in here about who my great-great-grandparents inherited Glenwood Station from.'

Wyatt too opened his journal. The amicable silence was only broken by Bundy's quiet snores from where he slept on the floral rug.

Brenna snuck a quick look at Wyatt. He'd already turned a page. As she watched he flipped over another.

'Are you even reading?'

'I am. I usually have reports to go through.'

Brenna glanced back at her own journal to hide how much she was enjoying having him there. Of course he was a speed reader. There wasn't anything he couldn't do.

When the hand he was using to turn the pages stilled, she glanced up. 'What have you found?'

His eyes narrowed. 'What makes you think I've found something?'

'You stopped turning the pages.'

'Remind me never to play you at poker.'

She smiled sweetly. 'I don't play poker, only pool. You'd better work on your game face for our rematch.'

The corner of his mouth lifted. 'You're right. I have found something.'

He slid the journal around and tapped on a line that contained a row of three names. Her first thought was that all the siblings' names started with A. The second was that they were girls. And the third was that the middle sister, Alice, had passed away unmarried.

She didn't try to temper her excitement. 'Alice could be who we've been looking for?'

Without waiting for a reply, she checked the dates. They matched.

The three sisters were born in the 1840s and had passed away by the 1880s. Alice had died unmarried in 1863 aged nineteen. The last letter had been dated 1862. Maybe that was why the couple couldn't spend the gold sovereigns on their new life together. Their relationship had ended in tragedy.

She read the information on the other two sisters. None had had any descendants. This had to be the generation when Glenwood Station had passed to her branch of the family.

Wyatt leaned over to flip the page. 'There are usually photographs in the following section.'

Brenna's breath caught as she stared at the grainy black-and-white headshot of a young woman with dark hair, large eyes and a heart-shaped face. The label confirmed the image was of Alice. No wonder C had fallen in love with his neighbour.

'She's beautiful.'

'She really is.'

It was only hours after Wyatt had left and Brenna was lying in bed, her mind hazy with sleep, that she realised when Wyatt had replied, his gaze hadn't been on Alice's picture but on her.

CHAPTER 22

'So,' Elsie said, voice teasing, 'I wonder what delicious goodies will arrive today.'

Wyatt pre-emptively covered his breakfast with his hand as Elsie walked past on the way to the fridge. Even though she was still munching on the first slice of toast she'd stolen from off his plate, it hadn't stopped her yesterday from swiping a second piece. Her excuse was that she had uni exams and didn't have time for breakfast.

'I have no idea. Did you get your practice essay done for this afternoon's exam?'

'No,' she said with a dramatic sigh as she eyed off his protected toast.

He lifted his hand and passed her the plate. 'Will this help?'

A dimple indented her cheek. 'It will but not as much as donuts.'

He gave a solemn nod. He'd learned this week that study food was a serious topic. He'd do a bakery run before heading out to Strathdale. 'Cinnamon or chocolate or both?'

Elsie appeared to think even though each of them already knew her answer. 'Both.'

Roy's chuckle sounded from the kitchen doorway. 'Well, the wait is over.' He held up a plate covered in foil. 'Today's quilting club delivery theme is …' He whipped off the cover.

Wyatt came straight to his feet. 'I'm out of here. I've got donuts to buy.'

Elsie laughed so hard, she wiped tears from her eyes. 'Look, Wyatt, those little pink baby booties on the top of the cupcakes are so cute.'

He had no words for a reply. He placed his coffee mug in the dishwasher and gave a still giggling Elsie and a grinning Roy a nod before making a hasty exit.

'Don't forget I'm going to be your chief babysitter,' Elsie called out before the door closed.

Wyatt dragged both hands through his hair as he walked along the hallway. The trouble was his thoughts were a step ahead of the quilting club. After seeing Emily on the video call yesterday, he'd found himself missing the warm weight of her in his arms and her sweet baby smell. He'd never wanted a family but the arguments as to why didn't seem to hold as much weight as they once did. Another day of clearing out Strathdale's clutter didn't seem so bad compared to being surrounded by baby-themed food that had him questioning whether or not work was enough to fill his life.

After making some business calls and doing a donut run for Elsie, Wyatt left town. He stared through the windscreen at the low clouds clustered around the mountain peaks and let the beauty dissolve his tension. Every drive the view changed. The golden tint of the poplars alongside the road had deepened, while trees flamed red in farmhouse gardens.

He slowed as the paddock filled with black Angus cattle and calves came into view. Today he counted three new additions. A group of energetic calves splashed their way across the run-off from an overflowing dam. Next week it would be a struggle to adjust to the bland daily commute to his city office.

He turned through his front gate, gravel crunching beneath his tyres as he drove along his now smooth driveway. With any luck the news that the road into his farm had been graded wouldn't reach the local grapevine. He didn't need any personal baking deliveries from eagle-eyed quilting ladies with only one thing on their meddling minds.

While he still believed yesterday's theme was a coincidence, he couldn't be sure Roy hadn't seen something in his behaviour the previous night. He was the first to admit he would have seemed distracted. He couldn't stop reliving his and Brenna's kiss or revisiting how having her in his arms smoothed all his jagged edges.

Today it was more important than ever that he conceal his attraction and feelings for Brenna. Taite had texted to see if he was free to help move his sculptures. As much as he and Taite respected each other, when it came to Brenna, Taite was fiercely protective. He'd never want anything but the best for his sister. From Taite's perspective, not only did Wyatt come from a different world, he was a workaholic.

Wyatt parked and headed for the side-by-side in the shed. As he drove over to Glenwood Station, the valley opened up in front of him. A curl of smoke drifted from Taite's cottage chimney and beside the creek a herd of horses lingered. When he pulled up at Taite's front garden gate, Waffles sprinted after Bundy who carried a stick in his mouth. The young kelpie's exuberant yips made Wyatt smile.

Taite appeared from a nearby shed. If he'd been bothered by Wyatt having dinner with Brenna last night it didn't show in his easy grin.

'You survived having my sister cook for you?'

'I did. No tea towels were harmed. Thank you for the apple pie.'

Taite chuckled. 'No worries. Thanks for helping Brenna. She was very excited to discover that A stood for Alice. She's now on a mission to find out who C was and has roped Hettie into working on Arthur's family tree with her.'

'If anyone can discover C's identity, Brenna can.'

'When she gets set on something, she can't be swayed.' Taite paused, his eyes serious, to consider Wyatt. 'Which can be both good and bad.' Then, his grin back in place, Taite waved a hand towards the sculptures that dotted the lawn. 'Ready to do this?'

'Sure.'

For the next two hours Brenna's name didn't come up again. With the help of the tractor and a truck, the heavy sculptures were collected and relocated to beside Taite's workshop. Every sculpture had a new home and would soon be on their way out of the mountains, some overseas. Wyatt ran his hand over the neck of a rearing brumby which would sit at the entryway of a distillery. After seeing what Taite could do with rusted machinery and old tools, he'd never think of such items as scrap metal again.

Taite came to his side. 'I'd offer you a beer but it's a bit early. How about a coffee?'

Wyatt nodded and followed Taite into the nearby shed that served as his workshop. Bundy and Waffles raced inside to wrestle on the rug in front of the enclosed fire. Orange flames flickered behind the glass and warmth radiated from the cosy corner.

Taite flicked on the kettle and indicated for Wyatt to take a seat in one of the three comfy chairs. As he did so Wyatt recognised the plastic crates filled with rusted metal on his left. He'd cleaned out one bay of the machinery shed and had brought Taite anything he thought he might use.

Taite spooned ground coffee into two mugs. 'Thanks for the plough discs. They're hard to find as they've become popular for fire pits.'

'There's more. Just let me know when you've reached your threshold.'

Taite chuckled. 'When it comes to rusted metal, I can never have enough.' He handed Wyatt his coffee. 'I pretty much spend winter in here and by spring Brenna's warning me not to pinch parts off things that still work.'

Taite settled himself into the chair next to Wyatt. 'Is there anything you'd like me to make? It's the least I can do after all the metal you're sending my way.'

'Actually, Strathdale needs a new front gate. It seems a shame to put in a regular steel one.'

'Consider it done. I'll take some measurements and we can chat about a design. You still leaving Thursday?'

'That's the plan. Even though I'll need at least another week to finish clearing out everything. The house will eventually need renovating but Grace has offered to style whatever rooms I'll end up using.'

'Rowan mentioned Grace's thrilled with the books and furniture he's been bringing over.'

Wyatt took a mouthful of coffee. Taite's intent gaze hadn't left him. The deer farmer looked like a man with something on his mind. He hoped whatever it was didn't involve his sister.

It wasn't to be his lucky day.

'So … Brenna?'

Wyatt didn't pretend to misunderstand his unspoken question or deny that it needed to be asked. Even if Hettie hadn't mentioned their conversation about him wanting to see Brenna, Taite had to have noticed Wyatt's hyperfocus on his twin.

'Friends and neighbours.'

Taite's brow quirked. 'That sounds like a job description. Mutually agreed?'

'It is. I don't tick Brenna's boxes. And I'm the first to admit that I'm not right for her.'

'Has she mentioned what these boxes actually are?'

Wyatt shook his head.

Taite's expression grew thoughtful. 'Saturday afternoon. What happened?'

It was Wyatt's turn to study Taite. Hettie knew the exact details so had she told Taite then he'd know for sure what had gone on between him and Brenna. It was as though Taite had been tuned into his sister's feelings.

'The day I arrived, when Brenna found the letters and sovereigns, you knew something was going on with her before she called, didn't you?'

Taite's eyes narrowed. 'This is just between us. Brenna and I have never done the whole twintuition thing, least of all admitted to it. She's always wanted to be her own person. But yes, I can pick up on her emotions if her feelings are strong enough.' Pain flashed across his eyes. 'Not that she will open up even when I know something's happened.'

As Wyatt had suspected on the trek, Taite sensed that something had darkened Brenna's past, but she'd never revealed what it was.

Wyatt answered Taite's previous question. 'A kiss happened. But it can't happen again. We don't … suit.'

He made sure his expression didn't alter even though the thought of never holding Brenna again left him feeling hollow.

Taite stayed silent, then he scraped a hand over his chin. 'I don't say this lightly … Wyatt, you're a good bloke. Why don't you think you and Brenna are a match?'

'I don't exactly have the best relationship track record. I'm also an emotional work in progress.'

Taite gave a wry smile. 'Aren't we all.'

'Maybe … but I wouldn't be able to be there for Brenna in the way she deserves. The last thing I'd ever want to do is fail her.'

His jaw clenched. He hadn't meant his words to sound so deep or hoarse.

'I get it. I spent years thinking the same thing about Hettie. All I can say is, life has a way of turning everything we believe on its head.'

'I don't doubt it. If that happens, you have my word, I'll always do the right thing by Brenna.'

Taite leaned over to clink his coffee mug against Wyatt's. 'Which is why you tick every box I have for her.' He winked. 'Except for one.'

'Which is?'

'You are yet to try her baking and keep a straight face when she asks how bad it is.'

'That might be a box best left unticked.'

Taite chuckled. 'Believe me, it is.'

Wyatt finished his coffee. He'd be a fool to think about his compatibility with Brenna in any context, even a jovial one. Especially with Taite's speculative gaze still on him.

Bundy and Waffles had stopped wrestling and were stretched out in front of the fire. When Bundy lifted his head and stared towards the door, tail wagging, it was a sign they were about to have company.

Instead of a knock sounding, the shed door flew open.

'No surprise Brenna's childhood nickname was Whirlwind,' Taite muttered.

Brenna's boots rang on the concrete floor as she strode inside, her phone in her hand. The dogs ran to meet her and she lavished them with affection. Even knowing Taite was sitting beside him, Wyatt couldn't look away.

An oversized navy jacket covered her pink work shirt, and her faded jeans had a rip across the knee. Her cheeks were flushed from the cold, and her hair was plaited into a loose braid that his hands itched to unravel. By the creek her hair had slipped through his fingers like warm silk.

Her eyes briefly met Wyatt's before she turned her attention to Taite. 'I wondered where you two were.'

She flopped into the spare chair. Waffles took it as an invitation to jump onto her lap. As she stroked his cream back, his puppy eyes closed. Just like on the first day they'd met, Wyatt saw the warmth and softness beneath Brenna's no-nonsense exterior.

'Coffee?' Taite asked.

'This is just a quick stop. Hettie and I've only found two generations of Arthur's family tree. It's taking forever. I don't think I've sat still this long for years.'

Taite turned his obvious chuckle into a cough. 'Make that never.'

Brenna smiled her saccharine smile. 'At least Hettie doesn't have to stay with me when Julie's cutting my hair.'

'That doesn't count,' Taite grumbled. 'Hair salons are not like the pub. You have to get in and out as fast as possible. Besides, Grace has to sit with Rowan too.'

When both sets of blue eyes turned to him, seeking his opinion, Wyatt grinned. 'Don't look at me. I have someone come to my office so I can work.'

Brenna frowned. 'That's wrong on so many levels.' Her brow cleared as she held up her phone. 'Trent sent a message. He's been trying to get hold of you.'

'My phone's in my car.'

'Why?' Surprise coloured her voice.

'I was helping Taite.' He remembered the desperation with which Dean had stared at Brenna's mobile on the trek. 'I might be a city boy but I'm not surgically attached to my phone. To be honest, I'd rather use it as little as possible.'

In his peripheral vision, Wyatt thought he saw Taite mimic ticking an imaginary box before he asked, 'Do you like viral videos of deceptively sweet goats?'

'I can't say I've seen any.'

'I wish I could say the same.' Taite shuddered. 'My kind and loving sister over there has a bucketload she can show you. She too would rather leave her phone at home but she has found it serves a purpose … I happen to not be a fan of tiny goats called Rebel who blink their big innocent eyes even while they're plotting to trip you over.'

Wyatt couldn't hide his amusement. Taite was a mountain of muscle, with a will as strong as his sister's. Whoever Rebel was, the goat definitely had him rattled.

Waffles left Brenna's lap, and expression mischievous, Brenna raised her phone towards her brother. She went to tap on the screen as if to show him a video.

Taite scowled. 'I've got the slow cooker on with a lamb casserole ...'

Brenna appeared to think about his proposition before touching the screen. When she lifted her phone, it showed a picture of a draft horse. Taite visibly relaxed.

Brenna blew him a kiss. 'Dinner invitation still stand?'

'If you leave your phone at home.' Taite glanced at Wyatt. 'You're welcome too.'

'Thanks, but I promised to help Elsie study for her accounting exam.' Brenna passed him her phone. He studied the blurry image of a bay horse that looked to be a Clydesdale. 'Is this why Trent's been wanting to reach me?'

'Yes.' Brenna leaned in close to look at the picture and he caught the fragrance of roses. 'Her name's Belle. She's due to foal soon. Her owner had a fall and is in aged care and his daughter isn't horsey. He wants the mare to go to a loving home.'

Wyatt felt the same deep pull to help the draft horse as he had with Murphy. He didn't hesitate. 'Where is she? I can hire a horse float to get her this afternoon.'

'She's already on her way. If she was too much for you to take on, I would have.'

It was only when Taite cleared his throat that Wyatt realised that not only were he and Brenna smiling at each other but their bodies were almost touching. Brenna must have realised the same thing because she quickly sat back in her seat. When he handed her the phone, she came straight to her feet.

'Right. I've got Arthur's family tree to wrangle.'

Then, without another look at either him or Taite, she left.

Taite again gestured as if ticking an imaginary box. But while the deer farmer wore a broad grin, Wyatt didn't miss the gravity in his eyes.

CHAPTER 23

'Bundy, stop looking so pleased with yourself,' Brenna said after she finished her breakfast porridge by taking an oversized mouthful. 'I'm not in a rush to catch Wyatt when he comes to see Murphy and Co. I've got things to do before Belle arrives.'

When the kelpie didn't stop staring at her, head tilted, she moved to put some bread in the pale pink toaster. He'd already had a slice of peanut butter toast, so she'd give him another to distract him. While Bundy crunched on his extra breakfast she went to change out of her flamingo-pink pyjamas into work clothes.

Usually she braided her hair, but this morning's braid didn't work. It was either crooked or didn't sit flat. Maybe she should stop putting off seeing Julie at the hair salon. Her hair was so long it reached between her shoulder blades. Not that she would ever admit it to Taite, but she too had trouble sitting still in Julie's chair.

With a sigh she left her hair loose and pulled on a pink beanie. *If* she did bump into Wyatt then she wouldn't look like she'd just gotten out of bed.

She left the warmth of the house and went outside into the crisp autumn morning. It had rained overnight and the green lawn glistened. White wings flashed as cockatoos screeched and swooped low over the creek. When an icy breeze brushed over her, she pulled her beanie lower. As warm as the days could be, winter was on its way.

Usually the walk to the stables filled her with contentment but the restlessness that she'd experienced yesterday morning continued to churn inside her. She blamed it on not knowing who C was and being no closer to discovering what had happened to the young couple. It wasn't because with every day that passed she was becoming used to seeing Wyatt and he'd soon be returning to the city.

It took a second to register that her phone was ringing from within her jacket pocket. Clancy was still away seeing Heath and it wouldn't be long until the flower farmer rang to say that she had exciting news.

Except the caller wasn't Clancy but Wyatt. Brenna squashed a rush of happiness. This wasn't a personal call; Wyatt would be contacting her about Belle.

'Morning,' he said when she answered.

'Morning.' She blamed a shiver on the cold and not on hearing his voice. 'You sound like you're still in that show-pony car of yours.'

'Let's just say I left town later than usual.'

'Do I want to ask …' She paused as she thought she heard a goose honk. He had to be passing Mrs Moore's place on the way out of Bundilla. 'About today's baked goods theme?'

'No theme. There haven't been any cake deliveries.'

'Finally. The grocery store must have run out of flour and sugar.' This time there was no missing the honk of an irritated goose. 'Wyatt, where are you?'

'Almost at your front gate. Brenna … there was still a delivery, just not of food.'

She sighed. 'You have a goose onboard, don't you?'

'I do. Her name's Angel and she's far from it if these last twenty minutes have been any indication. According to the card that came with her, she will walk on a lead. Except I'm not sure how I'll get close enough to get the pink bow off her neck to put on her harness.'

'Those sneaky conniving nannas,' Brenna breathed. 'They've sent out a girlfriend for Merlin.'

'It would be funny if I wasn't now deaf.'

Brenna was saved a reply as Angel honked. Very loudly.

'I'll see you soon,' Wyatt managed before ending the call.

Brenna looked down at Bundy. 'Did you know about this?'

The kelpie wagged his tail.

After a look at the sky, in the vain hope that the sight of the white wisps of cloud set against the airbrushed blue would calm her, she went to prepare for Angel's arrival.

When Wyatt's fancy high-powered engine rumbled, Brenna dusted off her hands on her jeans and went outside.

Wyatt left the driver's seat with a grimace. 'That was *the* longest trip.'

Brenna couldn't stifle her laughter. 'I'm sure Angel honks like the proper little lady Mrs Moore would have raised her to be.'

As if on cue, Angel honked. It was not at all ladylike. In fact, it was even more indignant and irate than the sounds Merlin made.

Expression pained, Wyatt bent to pat Bundy. 'Welcome to my world.'

Wyatt moved to open the back of his four-wheel drive. Angel hissed as he carefully lifted out the portable crate. Brenna noticed

Bundy kept as far away as possible from the goose as they walked to the stables.

Once inside, she opened the half door into the stall where she'd laid fresh straw for Belle's bedding. 'If we let Angel out here we can get the bow off, harness on, and walk her down to introduce her to Merlin.'

Wyatt stopped in the doorway. 'We?'

'Yes, Mr Goose Whisperer. I've seen how Merlin tucks himself under your arm for a cuddle while you feed him treats.'

She wasn't going to add how the gander still glared at her.

Wyatt shared a look with Bundy before the kelpie turned and trotted away. With a sigh, Wyatt continued inside and placed the crate on the ground.

Brenna picked up a container of pellets. 'I'll distract her while you work your magic.'

Angel surprisingly cooperated as long as she had food. When her bow was off and her harness and lead on, she waddled towards the door. Wyatt bent to take a photo of the two of them.

'Wyatt Killion, did you just take a selfie with a goose?'

He tapped his nose. 'It's our secret. My reputation would be ruined. It's for Mia.'

Brenna's delight at seeing this new lighter and almost carefree side of Wyatt ebbed. She busied herself with closing the crate.

Wyatt had said he was single a month ago; that didn't mean he still was. By the creek, he'd been upfront about not being right for her. Maybe it wasn't because he was from the city after all. Maybe it was because he was developing feelings for Mia. It would be understandable. Their support for each other through the aftermath of Nick's death could set a firm foundation for any relationship.

As for him kissing her, perhaps that was commonplace where he came from. Dating, let alone the chemistry she experienced whenever around Wyatt, wasn't exactly something she had a tonne of experience with. If Wyatt and Mia were drawing closer, she should be happy for them. It would certainly make her life much easier. The day couldn't come soon enough when she'd be off the quilting club's hitlist. But instead of relief, an inexplicable sense of loss had her take a moment before facing Wyatt.

'We all good to go?' he asked.

She forced a smile. 'Absolutely. Let's go and make cranky Merlin happy.'

With Wyatt holding Angel's lead, they left the stables. As soon as Merlin realised there was another goose, he flapped his wings and sped towards the fence. Angel waddled faster.

Murphy raised his head from where he grazed to watch while little Midge whinnied in welcome.

'Aw, this actually is quite adorable,' Brenna said as she walked ahead to unlatch the paddock gate.

When she was sure Merlin wouldn't dash through, she opened the gate wide enough for Wyatt and Angel to enter. Bundy stayed with Brenna outside. Wyatt took off Angel's harness. Their tail feathers wagging, the two geese approached each other, squawking and chattering. Brenna snapped a picture to show Mrs Moore that Angel approved of her gander beau.

'Well, at least this part of the quilting club's matchmaking plan was a success,' Brenna said as the two geese headed over to the blue clam to swim.

Even though she felt Wyatt's attention on her, she didn't meet his gaze. She couldn't have him see that a part of her now wasn't at all averse to the thought of being his match. When it came to Wyatt, her hormones had always been a lost cause. No good would now come from her having feelings that were impossible to reel in and would never amount to anything.

Wyatt fell into step beside her as they strolled over to the stables.

'Belle's agistment,' he said. 'Shall I double Murphy's amount? And for Angel put in an extra dollar?'

Brenna risked a sideways glance to assess his level of resolve. His stubbled jaw was set.

'There's new terms. Zero dollars.'

'Let me guess, if I don't accept them you'll follow through on your threat to get me four dogs, three cats, two alpacas and a ferret? The first three I'm okay about, but I'm sure the ferret will have a better forever home with someone else.'

Her lips twitched. 'What's wrong with ferrets? They'll evict all your attic rats.'

'Maybe I feel the same about ferrets as Taite does tiny goats.'

She stopped. She didn't think anything would terrify Wyatt. 'Really?'

He grinned. 'No. So there's no need to look for any funny ferret videos.'

Realising that she was staring, she walked again. She'd never known anyone's irises to change as much as his did. When relaxed, Wyatt's eyes went from flint to a smoky grey.

She refocused on their conversation. 'Instead of agistment money, can Taite and I possibly grow lucerne on your river flats?'

'Yes.'

'You don't want to think about it?'

'No. You need hay, so it makes sense to bale your own. Arthur's hay baler is still in the shed so you're welcome to use it. I should have offered you use of the river flats earlier.'

'Thank you.'

She wasn't going to dwell on why her voice was a little husky. Hettie was right. Wyatt was decent as well as generous and thoughtful.

When tyres crunched on gravel and the rattle of metal sounded, Bundy left Wyatt's side to run ahead. Trent and Belle were here. Brenna and Wyatt followed the kelpie through the stables to where Trent had parked. The float he towed was larger than he usually used to accommodate Belle's extra height and weight.

The local vet left his white four-wheel drive with a smile. 'Nice to finally meet you, Wyatt,' he said, with an accompanying handshake.

'Likewise.'

Trent went to give Brenna a hug. 'How's my favourite horse rescuer?'

She returned his embrace. They were firm friends. He'd aided and abetted her in several schemes, such as pairing Taite with an untrainable brumby to help him emotionally connect after losing their parents.

When she pulled away, she caught Wyatt watching them, a hard glint in his eyes. But the emotion disappeared before Brenna could put a name to it.

'All ready for the Bundilla Cup?' Trent asked.

'Not at all.' This was a familiar conversation. The annual town bush festival would soon be on and the pinnacle event was a race around a gruelling mountain course. 'You know I don't enter.'

She'd never gone into her reasons about why she refused to participate.

'Now might be the year. Those young fellas in the pub are getting very cocky about winning.'

She shook her head, tamping down the urge to test her mettle against the confident, and increasingly vocal, group of young farmers.

'How's Aubrey?' she asked as she led the way over to the horse float.

The city girl had moved to Bundilla to be with Trent at the start of last summer.

'Plotting. Frank beat her at chess.'

Frank, a retired judge, was Grace and Rowan's neighbour. His and Aubrey's chess battles were legendary.

'There'll be no peace until she evens the score.'

'Tell me about it.'

Despite Trent's words, his grin was so adoring, Brenna felt a twinge of envy. Not for the first time, she wished she could be loved in the same way that Trent did Aubrey.

Lost in thought, she hadn't realised that Trent and Wyatt were staring at her. She blinked. 'Sorry. What did I miss?'

Trent gave her an odd look. 'I was just saying that as Belle's an older mother, she'll have to be monitored closely. You'll do that anyway, but any worries, give me a call.'

Brenna only nodded. Wyatt's assessing gaze hadn't left her face.

When Trent went to open the side float door, Wyatt asked, voice low, 'Everything okay?'

'Yes.'

To avoid any further questions she went to lower the back of the float. Wyatt came to help. Once the ramp was down, they moved out of the way. Bundy came to stand beside them.

It was obvious from how Belle's stomach had dropped that she would soon foal. Brenna was relieved to see that the mare's bay coat was shiny and her large plate-sized hooves were neatly trimmed. She was in good condition and had been well cared for.

She glanced at Wyatt, needing to see his reaction. While his profile was inscrutable, his eyes were fixed on Belle. As the draft horse edged backwards Brenna glimpsed splashes of white on her mahogany brown side. She sensed Wyatt stiffen and stole another look at him. Just like when he'd stared at Outlaw on the first day of the trek, it was as though his jaw was carved from stone.

Belle had slowly been backing out when she suddenly stopped to turn her head. She then gave a high-pitched neigh before she reared. Beside Brenna, Wyatt said something she couldn't catch as Belle swung around, pulling Trent with her. Brenna's breath caught when she saw where the mare was looking.

'Let her go,' she yelled to Trent.

Thankful that the vet trusted her enough to know what she was doing, he did so. Without the pull of the lead rope, Belle was free to turn on the ramp. Her massive hooves clattered as she leaped out of the float. Lead rope flying, she headed for Wyatt. Except he was no longer next to Brenna.

In three strides his hand was on Belle's neck and her head was over his shoulder.

All Brenna could hear was the thrum of blood in her ears and the beat of her heart.

Brow furrowed, Trent came to her side. 'What just happened?'

Brenna found her voice. 'Wyatt's grandfather bred draft horses. Belle has to be one of them. She'd only have been young, but she clearly remembers Wyatt. Trent … her eyes … when she saw him.' Brenna fanned her face. 'I'm a little teary.'

He draped an arm around her shoulders. 'You don't get teary.'

Brenna committed the raw emotion in Wyatt's face to memory as he spoke softly to the mare. Such a look had shot to the top of her checklist. She wanted a man who could care so deeply about a horse that his soul would never forget them. 'It appears as though I do now.'

CHAPTER 24

'Has she always been called Belle?'

Brenna's quiet question sounded from the stall doorway. She'd returned to the stables after saying goodbye to Trent.

Wyatt didn't look up as he ran a brush over Belle's bay coat while she ate from a hay net. He'd spent so long being a closed book he didn't feel comfortable revealing how he felt.

When he was certain his voice would sound casual, he spoke. 'My grandfather called her Mirabella. Over the years it must have changed to Bella and then just Belle.'

'Mirabella's such a lovely name.'

'It is. She pretty much was a miracle. Her mother died and we hand-raised her.'

'Were you there when Belle was born?'

He gave a single nod. He and his grandfather had stayed up all night trying to save her dam. Apart from the day his grandparents had arrived to collect him, it was the only other time he'd seen tears in his grandfather's eyes. 'The photo you showed me was blurry. I had no idea it was Belle.'

'She hasn't forgotten you.'

As if knowing what Brenna had said, Belle turned her head to look at him. He stroked the white blaze on her nose. 'I tried to find her.'

Brenna stayed silent as though understanding that he needed to get a tighter grip on how he was feeling before he continued. He went back to brushing Belle before speaking.

'After my grandparents died, my uncle agreed to let me stay on until he found a buyer for the farm if I looked after the horses. I was left a small amount of money for university but intended to use it to keep Mirabella and another mare, Honey. I'd found a place to agist them. I went to Sydney to sit a scholarship exam and when I came home my uncle had sold the horses.'

'Wyatt, that's horrible.'

'There was nothing I could do. My grandfather talked about changing his will the week before so Mirabella and Honey would be mine, but he never made it to town to see the solicitor.'

'You wouldn't have even been able to say goodbye.'

His hand holding the brush stilled at the empathy in Brenna's words. He wasn't going to elaborate that his childhood was littered with unsaid goodbyes. 'No.'

'Would Honey still be alive?'

He shook his head. 'She would be thirty by now.'

'I'm even gladder then that you and Belle have found each other again. And in ten days there will be a baby Belle.'

Wyatt smoothed his hand over the rounded contour of Belle's stomach. 'Trent said she's had foals before so everything should be fine, but I have to be here.'

'Of course.'

He risked a glance at Brenna. 'You told Trent to let the lead rope go.'

'Belle recognised you and could have slipped and hurt herself in her rush to leave the float.' Her eyes searched his. 'And I knew you knew who she was.'

He looked at Belle. He wasn't going to ask how Brenna had known. His out-of-control feelings would have been plastered all over his face. If he needed any further proof about why he wouldn't be right for Brenna, this was it. His ability to be there for her would be compromised by the work he needed to do on himself. He could no more regulate his emotions about seeing Belle than he could rewind the clock so he'd be working with his grandfather in the horse yards.

'Coffee?' Brenna asked.

'Thanks but I'm good.'

When he next glanced at the stall door, Brenna was gone.

Belle gave a quiet whicker. 'Yes, I know. I'm still working on being more laid-back.'

Even as a yearling Belle had been calm and gentle. She'd follow him around and when he'd had a bad day she'd hang her head over his shoulder just as she'd done earlier. He groomed her until his arm ached, relishing that a part of his past he'd thought lost had been returned to him.

When he was done, he scratched the spot she'd always liked on her neck. 'I have to go away for a few days but will see you as soon as I can, okay?'

After a last pat, he let himself out of the stall. When china clinked from the kitchenette, Wyatt hesitated before going to find Brenna.

The truth was he'd been on edge even before he saw the white markings on Belle's side and realised who she was. His days of feeling numb seemed a lifetime ago. When Trent had given Brenna a warm hug, something had unravelled deep inside him. He'd never had a problem seeing the women he casually dated on another man's arm. It had only been Brenna asking about the woman Trent was involved with that had dissolved the tension gripping his shoulders.

He walked into the kitchenette. Brenna gave him a smile from where she was pouring milk into her mug.

'Belle all settled?'

'She is. I'll head over to Strathdale to finish a few jobs before I leave for Sydney tonight.'

Brenna carefully sat the milk bottle on the bench. 'Sydney?'

'I was planning to stay a couple more days but if I'm to be here when Belle foals, I have to head back. There are some work meetings I can't miss and Mia needs help taking Emily to a medical appointment.'

Brenna returned the milk to the fridge, and he lost sight of her expression. 'Is there anything you'd like done over at Strathdale while you're away?'

'There is, if that's okay. The kittens in the shed, they've become pets. There's cat food in the kitchen.'

She faced him, her features unreadable. 'I'm starting to think you're a big softie.'

'You sound like Elsie. According to her, I'm a cinnamon roll.'

'Well, you did take that selfie with Angel.'

'I did.'

Now was the opportune moment to leave. He'd proven to himself that he could, unlike earlier, contain his emotions. He'd also stuck to the friends and neighbour brief. But he couldn't make his feet move. Tomorrow he'd be far from Brenna and the mountains.

'Good luck with Arthur's family tree,' he found himself saying.

'I'll need it.' Her gaze searched his. 'Will you be okay? Belle … must bring back memories.'

'I'll be fine. See you hopefully Monday.'

He let his eyes hold hers for as long as he dared before she could see just how far he was from fine.

He released a taut breath as he strode from the stables, Bundy by his side. Every step he took tightened the band constricting his chest. As much as he hated to leave Belle, if he did he'd be here when she needed him. As for Brenna, putting space between them would be wise. Maybe then he'd be able to think about something other than pulling her hard against him and sliding his hands into her hair.

On the drive to Strathdale he called his PA to rearrange his schedule and concentrated on directing his focus towards work. Except when he arrived, a restless energy had him heading to the wood pile. He wasn't in the mood for being trapped in a musty room sorting through another box of torch parts.

After answering a text from Taite asking if he could come over and measure the front gate, Wyatt shrugged off his khaki coat. Arthur had left some logs to be split for the winter fire. Wyatt had managed to get the chainsaw started so had added the fallen branches in the garden to the pile.

As Bundy ran off down to the creek, Wyatt draped his coat over the small stack of wood he'd already split. Next winter he'd invest in a log splitter, but right now using an axe suited his mood perfectly. He took hold of the handle and, after placing a log on a flat stump, swung. The slice of steel into the wood and the loud crack had his tension receding. He lined up another log and soon lost track of time.

The chug of a side-by-side engine had him pause. Taite was heading over. He went back to chopping wood. Intent on what he was doing, he didn't look up when the gator stopped close by. When he did, he saw it wasn't Taite sitting in the driver's seat but Brenna, who looked across at him with a frown.

He swung the axe to divide the log in front of him before straightening. As Brenna walked over, he rested the axe beside where his jacket hung.

Her gaze flickered over his face, then his navy shirt, before lingering on his biceps. 'Wyatt, what are you doing? And don't say chopping wood.'

He finally registered just how high the stack of split logs was. He'd cut more than enough for winter.

He passed a hand around the base of his neck. 'Taite get held up?'

'No, I offered to measure the gate as I wanted to pass on a message from Trent. I wasn't sure when you'd see your texts since you were leaving.' Her hands planted themselves on her hips. 'And don't answer my question with a question to avoid the subject.'

Even bossy and demanding, Brenna was more than beautiful. She no longer wore her pink beanie and her loose hair lifted in the breeze. He was certain that she'd come to check on him. She'd known he hadn't spoken the truth in the kitchenette. While this should have made him feel vulnerable and exposed, it instead made him feel seen.

'Wyatt.'

Her firm tone told him she'd not let the matter drop no matter how much he deflected her questions. But he could still delay answering to give himself a chance to order his thoughts. 'It's a long story.'

'It just so happens …' She moved to roll out a block of wood to use as a seat then pinned him with a stare. 'I have a long time to hear it.'

He took a seat as well and folded his arms.

She gave him a small smile. 'Do I need to remind you that I have an uncommunicative brother? My patience is unrivalled.'

'Unrivalled?'

'So much so I'll win Merlin over one day.'

Wyatt uncrossed his arms and picked up a small sliver of wood. If he was going to do this, he'd need something to look at other than Brenna. While words would explain why he needed to chop a year's worth of firewood, he couldn't reveal the accompanying emotions.

'Belle wasn't the only important part of my life that I never got to say goodbye to.'

'Your grandparents?'

He nodded, staring at the small piece of wood he flipped between his fingers. 'And my mother. She died when I was five. Her car rolled on a wet road.'

'Wyatt ... that would have been devastating.'

'It was.' His voice hardened. 'Not that my father thought so. He was an indolent and selfish drunk. My mother's parents offered to raise me, but my father refused. He only kept me because the government money he'd receive for my upbringing would fund his benders.'

Wyatt glanced up to assess Brenna's reaction. Anger had fired in her eyes. The strength of her reaction soothed him.

'It took seven years for my grandparents to find me. During that time I missed more school than I attended, learned bullies only listened to fists, and that if I wanted to eat I had to win at cards or pool.'

'Wyatt ...' Brenna's voice was so gentle and compassionate, he had to look away before he could speak.

'I don't remember the outback town, but when I was twelve I came to school with a bruise on my chin. My father never hit me but I wasn't always fast enough to dodge what he threw my way when he lashed out. The teacher asked the usual questions and I told the usual lies. But she didn't believe me. She took me into her office, sat at her computer and wanted to know about my extended family and what I remembered about them. Which wasn't a lot.'

'Your grandparents … she found them?'

'She did. There was an online article about a draft horse ploughing competition and a photo of my grandfather. She called them. It was a fourteen-hour drive to where I was. My grandparents were there in the morning.'

'They sound like very special people.'

'They were. So much so, they made sure I said goodbye to my father. I never saw him again. He's buried somewhere in Queensland.'

Brenna pressed her lips shut as if to stop herself from saying something.

'As cliché as it sounds, the six years with my grandparents changed my life. They provided me with more than a stable home. They gave me self-worth and the reassurance that I was my own person and wouldn't turn into my father. My grandmother tutored me so I could catch up in school and I learned to find peace while working with my grandfather and his horses.'

He stopped to stare at the wood still in his hand.

'Then life changed again,' Brenna said softly.

'Yeah. I became a city boy.'

'When you moved around with your father, is that how you met Roy? He would have been managing The Bushranger back then.'

Wyatt glanced up. As whip smart as Brenna was, he couldn't have her remembering he was the boy she'd met with the injured hand.

His moment of weakness when hot tears had burned his eyes wasn't something he'd been proud of.

'Roy caught me working in the kitchen to cover the beer my father was downing. He let us stay for a few weeks until my father woke me at dawn one day and said we had to leave.'

'You didn't get to say goodbye to Roy either.'

'Or Patty.' He tossed away the sliver of wood. He'd survived. He'd told Brenna about his past. 'So that's the long story. You were right, seeing Belle did bring back memories that I had to work through.' He came to his feet. 'But now, not only will I not be able to move my arms tomorrow, I've got enough wood to survive a blizzard.'

Brenna stood. As light as he'd made his words, her eyes remained sombre.

'Wyatt.' She took a step towards him. 'Can I give you a hug?' She paused, looking uncertain. 'Just as a friend and neighbour.'

'Sure.' He forced himself to smile. She was still a body length away and he already knew touching her was asking for trouble. 'Brenna Lancaster, I'm starting to think you're a big softie.'

As he'd hoped, his parroting of her earlier words chased the shadows from her expression.

He lifted his arms and she closed the distance between them. Just like at the creek, holding her filled his senses and made him feel things he hadn't thought he was capable of.

'I'm sorry your childhood was so rough,' she said, words muffled. 'And you've been through so much.'

He tightened his arms around her, breathed in her rose fragrance and rested his chin on the top of her silken head.

'But,' she continued, 'that doesn't mean I'll start taking selfies with disagreeable geese no matter how cute they are. Only one of us is a cinnamon roll.'

CHAPTER 25

The first day without Wyatt stretched on forever.

Not even being in her happy place teaching adorable kids to ride was enough to stop Brenna from thinking about him. A sense of feeling incomplete, which was as irrational as it was deep, refused to leave her, as did her worry. As much as he had seemed okay when she'd left him yesterday, she knew seeing Belle and revealing what he had would trigger painful memories.

The second day of not having Wyatt next door was a Thursday. As Bundy needed to be in town to be a story dog, she called Grace and arranged to meet at the café. Despite their two-hour-long coffee, thoughts of Wyatt continued to preoccupy her. It didn't help that Bundy wasn't sitting by her four-wheel drive after he'd finished at the local school. The trip home without the kelpie only magnified Wyatt's absence.

The third day was wet and miserable. Brenna had no choice but to stay inside. She tackled her bookwork and when that made her cross-eyed, she resorted to cleaning out another trunk in the attic.

By the fourth day, which was a Saturday, she'd had enough. She gave herself an ultimatum. *Move on.* Wyatt wasn't relationship material. There was no excuse for moping around, let alone missing his smile and rare laughter. She made dinner plans with Mabel. After she finished doing some research at home, they'd meet at the pub and then Brenna planned to play pool with whoever would take her on. She was long overdue whacking something solid.

Her tough love worked. Not only could she focus long enough to trace Arthur's family history back another two generations, but after she did so, thoughts of Wyatt finally emptied from her head. Excitement thrumming in her chest, she stared at the name of the second son that appeared on her laptop screen. Could C stand for Clement Douglas?

She scrolled to see when he was born as well as the year of his death. March 6 1863. The date appeared familiar. She opened the file containing Alice's death certificate and sucked in a stunned breath. It was as though she were looking at Clement's details. The date Alice died matched his, as did the cause of death plus the location. Alice and Clement had both drowned in the Tumut River on the same day.

This couldn't be a coincidence. Clement had to be Alice's beloved C. Heart heavy, she double-checked every detail of Clement's information before leaving to get ready to meet Mabel.

Once on the way to town, Brenna snuck a glance at her phone where it sat on the passenger seat. Wyatt hadn't messaged today, and especially after she'd texted to say she'd found the other half of their star-crossed couple. He'd replied straight away when she'd sent him photos of Belle and the ginger kittens in the hay shed. And also when she'd passed on the news that she'd gone to Strathdale to tell him the day he left. News she'd thought he needed to hear as it involved both the draft horses that had been part of his life with his grandparents.

Trent had called the daughter of Belle's previous owner, who'd filled in the mare's backstory. The Clydesdale had been with her father for at least eight years and had been an aged care therapy horse. Before then she'd lived on a farm near Tamworth where she'd been with another draft horse who had been bought with her. The older horse had since passed away. The information was enough to reassure Wyatt that Honey and Belle had never been separated.

Brenna tapped her thumbs on the steering wheel. As for the reason why she'd forgotten to tell Wyatt what Trent had discovered when she'd gone next door, her heart still ached for everything Wyatt had to endure as a child. She hadn't needed the stack of firewood beside him to tell her that he was upset. The bleak cast of his expression and the sheer force of his axe swing had been proof enough.

As worried as she'd been about him, she'd still registered the shift and flex of his torso beneath his navy shirt. She'd been right in thinking that no city boy she'd ever met had been built like he was.

She flicked the indicator before turning onto the road that would lead her over the historic wooden bridge. As much as she knew how those firm and sculpted muscles felt beneath her palms, she was *not* adding such a criterion to her potential partner list. It didn't matter that at this rate she'd end up looking for a man she wasn't attracted to and who didn't know which end of an axe to use, the important thing was he'd let her remain in charge of her life.

For the rest of the drive, she refused to glance at her phone or listen to the whispered doubts that now Wyatt was in the city and around Mia maybe his Bundilla life was no longer important. She found a park outside The Bushranger and without checking her appearance, left her four-wheel drive. The only concession she'd made to meeting Mabel for dinner was to put her hair in a high ponytail instead of a braid. Mabel was so stylish she needed to at least brush the hay out of her hair.

The knowledge that Wyatt wasn't at the pub and that all eyes wouldn't be on her left her feeling relaxed as she pushed open the front door. The smell of beer wafted over as she passed the front bar. A group of young farmers turned to stare.

When a tall blond gave her a smirk and gestured towards the door to the pool room, she slowed her steps to nod that she'd meet him in the pool room after she'd eaten. She wasn't fussy about who she played. As the group's attention lingered, she shot them her customary glower. A redhead she hadn't seen before continued to give her the once-over, so she swung around to stand in the doorway, hand on her hip. The group suddenly picked up their beers as though they needed a drink, all except for the redhead.

She wasn't exactly sure what the young farmer beside the redhead muttered, but she thought he said, 'If you want to wear your beer, keep on looking.'

The redhead glanced around the table and when he saw everyone else studying their drinks, he swivelled on his seat so he no longer faced her. With a brief smile, she continued on. The group was just bored. She was way too old for any of them.

She strode into the dining room and after a quick scan verified that, unlike on her last visit, Cynthia wasn't lurking in the beer garden. Mabel gave her a wave from a table tucked in the far corner. The local journalist looked as put together as usual. Her glossy brunette hair was pin-straight and her tailored white linen dress spotless.

When Brenna approached, Mabel got up to give Brenna her trademark warm hug. It was no surprise Mabel, unlike Brenna, was a favourite of grumpy old Roy.

'It's been ages since I've last seen you,' Mabel said.

'Being in the quilting club's crosshairs has turned me into a hermit.'

Mabel gave a soft laugh. 'At least with Wyatt away you can come and go as you please without Vernette ambushing you.'

'You have no idea how much I've missed having a pub meal. I've exhausted my very limited dinner repertoire.'

She took a seat, not voicing her thoughts that the quilting club's focus would eventually turn to single Mabel. But with her sister having left her husband to relocate to Bundilla, the town knew Soph was Mabel's priority. Mabel didn't talk much about her life before coming to town but Brenna's instincts told her there was a man behind Mabel's move. Despite her ever-present smile, her eyes could fill with sadness whenever around the town's recent couples.

After perusing the menu, they went to order their food and drinks. Once they were again seated, talk turned to Brenna's most recent discovery.

'So,' Mabel said, leaning forwards in her chair. 'Tell me who C is. I've been trying to put it together all afternoon.'

'Drumroll, please … C stands for Clement Douglas, Arthur's great-great-uncle on his father's side. It took a while to find him. Arthur might have been an only child and had no children, but some of his ancestors had huge families.'

'It's so sad to think that the feud prevented Alice and Clement from being together.'

'I know. And instead of leaving to start a new life, they died here … on the same day.'

Mabel's expression grew solemn. 'There's a story there. Have you been able to look at the digitised database of old newspapers to find out what happened?'

'Not yet. My theory is there either was an accident or a flood.'

Mabel nodded as the buzzer on their table flashed red. Their hamburgers were ready.

Once they'd collected their meals, they resumed their conversation.

'Just so I have this straight ...' Mabel said after her first mouthful. 'Alice and Clement were neighbours and in a clandestine relationship from at least 1861. They met at Platypus Hollow in the miner's hut. By 1862 they were apart but had somehow amassed a fortune in gold sovereigns to start a new life together.'

'Then by 1863, Clement was back in Bundilla.'

Mabel took a sip of wine. 'The bushranger articles found with the sovereigns suggest a connection.'

'They do. But there wasn't anything I could find tying Clement to the Miller gang. His older brother and cousin were members, though.'

'There has to be a bushranger link even if it's not obvious. Is there anything you'd like me to look into?'

Usually Brenna would have said she had it covered. She still had some family history journals to go through, but excitement shone in Mabel's eyes. She'd let Wyatt help her enough to question that maybe she didn't have to do everything on her own.

'If you want, maybe you could look into the bushranger gang. I've used Kathy's books but there'd be more information online.'

'I'd love to. After Roy telling Wyatt that the pub siege was over a woman and not stolen gold, I'm curious. I'm sure Soph would like to help as well.'

'The more we know about them the better.'

She didn't add that with Soph still settling into her new life in Bundilla, aiding her journalist sister with research could be a welcome distraction.

As they finished their hamburgers the conversation turned to dessert and the upcoming bush festival. All too soon, Mabel gave Brenna a farewell hug before leaving to attend a committee meeting.

Brenna took the shortcut past the office to the pool room. Last visit Elsie had been behind the desk, but tonight it was Roy. When he caught sight of her, his grey brows pulled together as he came to his feet.

'Do you have ID on you, young lady?'

Brenna shot him her too-sweet smile. 'I do.'

She opened her phone case to take out her very first driver's licence which she kept for this purpose. She held it up for him to see.

'Looks familiar.' Amusement softened his gruff tone.

'It should. I've been showing it to you for over ten years.' She turned to look at the picture. 'What was my eighteen-year-old self thinking getting a pixie cut?'

Roy chuckled but when she glanced at him his expression was deadpan. 'The same thing you were thinking when you went to dinner with Roger's young bloke.'

That was a date best forgotten and another thing her eighteen-year-old self hadn't thought through. She'd only gone out with Will because their parents were friends and he'd had dark hair and nice cheekbones. 'Don't remind me. I had no idea he was high and would have driven with him to meet Taite.'

Roy had refused to let her leave in Will's ute and had organised for a female member of his staff to drop her off at the party where her brother was. Roy's high-handedness had angered her as much as it had Will when Roy had called his dad to collect him. She'd already had her own father telling her what she could and couldn't do. It was only later she found out Will's bloodshot eyes weren't from hay fever as he'd claimed.

When Roy didn't reply, just folded his arms, Brenna spoke. 'I owe you a long overdue thank you.'

'You're welcome.' He studied her for a second before adding, 'Still not entering the Bundilla Cup this year?'

'No.'

'You'd win even if you were riding backwards.'

'I'm not entering.'

'It's because of your father, isn't it?'

She pressed her lips together, fighting her memories as well as her reaction. Her father was a topic she didn't discuss.

When she stayed silent, the old publican unfolded his arms, his hard gaze softening. 'There's no doubt who you get your stubbornness from. You are so much like your mother.'

Brenna's hand lifted to her neck to feel her mother's locket. Her questionable decisions were not the only things to have happened when she was eighteen. She'd lost the mother who'd been her best friend.

'How do you know she was stubborn?' She thought back to her childhood and could find no memory of Roy and her mother being anything but casual acquaintances. 'Only my father ever came in here.'

'I knew her.' The lines deepened on Roy's face. 'She was once very much a part of my family. She was engaged to my younger brother, Tony, who we lost in a motorbike accident.'

Brenna blinked. She knew very little about her mother's life before she'd married her father. She would have remembered if her mother had mentioned loving another man.

'I'm so sorry. I had no idea.'

'Tony wasn't someone your mother talked about. They were high school sweethearts and his death affected her deeply. It took years before she was ready for another relationship.' Roy rubbed at his chin. 'I liked your father, but he wasn't an easy man.'

Roy wasn't saying anything that wasn't common knowledge. Even before her mother had died, her father had been a stern and complicated figure.

'Why are you telling me all of this?'

'Because even though your father never knew Tony, he was jealous of him. When he lost your mother, for some reason in his mind he thought they were together again and this made him angry.' Roy sighed. 'Brenna … we both know your father was harder on you than Taite. And the reason for that was because you reminded him of your mother.'

'He told you this?'

Roy slowly nodded.

'So he was angry at me too?'

'I'm sorry. As much as he loved you, he was.'

She lifted her hand to press her fingers against her tight temple. Her own anguish and rage at losing her mother had eventually dulled into resigned acceptance. But her father's had morphed into cold indifference. While he had treated Taite in a similar fashion, she'd always sensed she was the one who could never do anything right.

Roy spoke again. 'When you entered the Bundilla Cup in memory of your mother, I was so proud of you.' As she frowned and lowered her hand in disbelief, he chuckled. Their relationship had always been combative. 'I promised your mother to look out for you. In those early days, when you were mad at me, the spark would return to your eyes.'

Roy's expression sobered. 'Instead of coming to support you and watch you ride, your father went to some machinery auction.'

'He told me he'd be there.'

It had been the start of his absence in her and Taite's life. Soon it would be their birthdays that he'd miss.

'When he didn't show, you pulled your entry and didn't ride. I found you in the pool room.'

Her throat tightened. She was again that grieving eighteen-year-old fighting tears at having lost her joyous mother months before, feeling so unloved and worthless her heart had felt physically crushed. When she'd asked her father why he hadn't come to the race, he'd shrugged and said he had better things to do.

She forced herself to speak. 'It was the only time you never asked to see my ID. You also gave me two packets of salt and vinegar chips instead of one.'

'Ride in the Bundilla Cup for your mother. Don't keep paying the price for the choices your father made. No one, not even you, could have stopped him from living in a world that wasn't always based on reality.'

Touched by the sincerity in Roy's words, she said, 'I'll … think about it.'

Roy gave her a nod before moving to open a cupboard. Inside was a large box of salt and vinegar chips. 'In case you're wondering, Elsie calls this the *Brenna Stash*.'

She swallowed. After all these years Roy was still honouring his promise to her mother.

He handed her a packet of her favourite chips. 'You'll be needing these.' She didn't stop to question why. She wasn't used to seeing a twinkle in Roy's steely gaze. 'Now go and take those young fellas' egos down a peg.'

She hesitated and then stepped forwards to give the old publican a hug. 'Thank you.'

Not wanting him to see how soft her heart really was, she strode towards the pool room. The sound of a ball hitting the pool table edge told her one of the young farmers was warming up. She pushed the door open.

Smoky-grey eyes caught hers. The overhead light glinted on dark hair and she caught a hint of sandalwood.

She ground her teeth.

Wily Vernette was the least of her matchmaking problems. No wonder Roy had given her the chips. They were to soothe her ire that he'd neglected to mention one very important fact.

Her new neighbour was back.

CHAPTER 26

It was official. The woman staring at him, chin angled, from across the pool room was Wyatt's blind spot.

Just because he'd had no respite from the way she filled his thoughts didn't mean he had to leave Sydney a day early. Just because he'd seen her park outside the pub didn't mean he needed to see her that night instead of the next morning. And most of all, just because Roy said there was a group of young farmers lining up to play Brenna in pool didn't mean he had to turn into a neanderthal and get to the pool room first.

Nothing that he'd done made sense. And yet as his and Brenna's eyes connected, everything that had felt out of kilter since he'd left settled back into place.

'Wyatt.'

There was no missing her unimpressed tone or the irritation in her eyes. All things that were familiar since the day they'd met. But what was different was he'd glimpsed another emotion that could have been hurt.

'Brenna.'

'I like to be prepared.' Her words were brusque. 'And I can't be if I don't know where you are. Belle could go into labour any day.'

'I apologise that my being here is a surprise.' He planted the end of his pool cue on the floor to stop himself from moving towards her. 'I wasn't supposed to leave until late tomorrow. I sent you a text but I should have done so earlier before I lost reception.'

Without taking her attention off his face, she took her phone out of her jeans pocket. Her gaze flicked to the screen and then to him. The tense line of her mouth eased.

'I didn't read your message because my phone was on silent while I was having dinner with Mabel.' She returned her mobile to her pocket. 'Bundy hasn't turned up, so if he doesn't know you're in town the quilting club will be none the wiser. You should be spared from any morning deliveries.' She headed for the row of pool cues on the far wall. 'Finally, we can have that rematch.'

The straight line of her shoulders said she meant business and that it wasn't the time to talk about who C was or how Belle was going. Unlike their last match, he also had to play to win. Roy had warned him that if he lost Brenna's trust, he wouldn't get it back.

Except as she reached for a cue and her long blonde ponytail dipped down her back, his focus wasn't on playing pool. Dressed in a faded navy rugby top and jeans, she made him feel and want things that no woman ever had.

She chalked the end of her cue. 'I'll do a quick warm-up.'

He took advantage of her lining up a row of balls to blank out her rose scent and put his game face on.

She bent over, her hand on the pool table and cue in position, readying to take her first shot, when the door behind her opened. A young farmer entered. Oblivious to Wyatt standing to the side, his attention zeroed in on where Brenna's rugby top had lifted. Wyatt's grip on the pool cue tightened. The man wasn't exactly looking at where Brenna's phone sat in the back pocket of her jeans that fit her like a second skin.

Wyatt cleared his throat and shot the man a death stare that Nick had joked was cold enough to freeze a summer heatwave. Realising Wyatt was there, the young farmer's jaw slackened before he slunk back into the front bar. Busy sending the final ball into the corner pocket, Brenna hadn't appeared to notice they'd had company.

Wyatt racked the balls into a triangle. 'I broke last game, it's your turn.'

Even to his own ears his voice sounded gruff.

Brenna cast him a quick look before shooting the white cue ball along the green felt. Wyatt forced himself to concentrate and keep up with Brenna's skill and the sharpness of her tactical brain.

It was only when there were a handful of balls left on the pool table that he detected a shift in her energy. An impression confirmed soon after when he sent the eight ball into the middle pocket to win.

She gave him a calm smile followed by a slight bow. 'That was worth the wait. Well done.'

He arched a brow.

She ignored him to walk over and return her cue to the back wall.

He followed. As he added his cue to the neat row, he bent to rasp near her ear, 'You went easy on me.'

She inclined her head so his breath ruffled the fine hair at her temple. 'Did I?'

'I want a rematch.'

'Well, city boy, you can't always get what you want.'

He gave a low chuckle. Life had been dull over the past few days without her sweetness and sass. He threaded his hand through the heavy silk of her ponytail.

'I missed you.'

'I missed you too.'

'Is that a yes to a rematch?'

She turned to face him, her ponytail sliding through his fingers. Even though their bodies remained close, without his hand threaded in her hair, she felt too far away. He curved a palm over her right hip. She didn't move to put space between them.

'That's a maybe. I'll have to check my busy game schedule.'

Thoughts of the group of young farmers all too willing to play her had him scowling at the door to the front bar.

'Is that right?' His words were a low growl.

'I'll try to fit you in. But don't worry …' She ran her fingertips over his clean-shaven jaw. 'You're the only one I break my pool-cue rule for.'

'Pool-cue rule?'

'Anyone who gets closer than that gets a well-placed elbow.'

The relief that slid through him shouldn't have been as powerful as it was. His hold firmed on her hip and she swayed towards him. His head dipped only for the door to the front bar to open and then quickly close as though someone had entered but changed their mind.

Brenna blinked and took a step back. He let his hand drop away from her warmth.

Colour washed her cheeks, but her voice was steady as she said, 'So, that's a win apiece.'

'It is. I'll look forward to our rematch.'

'Our *maybe* rematch.' She moved to collect the packet of chips she'd left on a chair and lifted a hand in farewell. 'See you tomorrow. Try to be inconspicuous. The grocery store hasn't restocked yet so they aren't ready for another quilting club baking blitz.'

Wyatt watched her go, his mouth dry. Brenna bypassed his walls so effortlessly. If he wasn't careful, the country girl would dismantle every boundary he'd built to hide who he was. It didn't matter how successful he'd become, he'd always be the son of a dishonest drunk.

While Brenna knew his story, there also was a difference between knowing his past and being personally involved. He couldn't have her remembering that he was the dishevelled and broken boy in the doctor's waiting room. If she did, he'd feel like that was all he could ever be.

He dragged a hand over his face. As for his admission that he'd missed her, that was yet more proof he made questionable decisions whenever around Brenna. Her reply that she had missed him too didn't mean anything, nor did the fact that they'd almost shared another kiss. Friends could still miss each other and neither of them had denied the intensity of the chemistry that sparked between them.

From now on he had to apply the discipline and commitment of his business world to his personal life. He'd seen Brenna now so could get back to focusing on why he'd returned. He had a farm to get under control, a manager to find plus he needed to be there for when Belle had her foal. He couldn't have anything happen to her like it had to her dam.

Intending to head to his room, he instead found himself taking the turn towards the pub's private living quarters. He was yet to say hello to Elsie.

He knocked on the door. It swung open and when Elsie saw him, her smile dimpled.

'Wyatt.' She rushed forwards and he lifted his arms to receive her hug.

Her grin widened as she pulled away. 'See, I told you I'd turn you into a hugger.'

Not waiting for an answer, she pulled him into the kitchen. 'Have you eaten?'

When he shook his head, she fussed around serving him up a plate of beef cannelloni. He helped where he could and tried to get a word in when he couldn't. His city home had felt quiet without having Elsie's constant chatter. He still had a lot to learn about fulfilling the big brother role Elsie had assigned to him. For her part, having Elsie act as a pseudo little sister filled a void in his life he hadn't thought existed.

When Elsie was finally seated across from him, he ate while they discussed her latest exam and upcoming semester break plans. When he offered her his beachside house, she squealed, her fingers flying across her phone as she told her friends they had a place to stay.

After she insisted on him having seconds, she cast him a teasing grin. 'I'm glad you're back. It's been very boring without any daily deliveries. I'm sure Grandpa has been having sugar withdrawal symptoms.'

'I'm hoping the quilting club would have lost interest by now.'

Elsie laughed so much she spluttered and had to reach for her water. 'Wyatt, don't hold your breath. You have more of a chance of seeing Brenna in a dress than that ever happening.'

His frown only made her chuckle more. 'Besides, I'd be devastated if they did. I'm so invested in you and Brenna being together I've bought a chief babysitter T-shirt.'

At his dubious expression, she patted his hand. 'Jokes aside, you're perfect for Brenna.'

'Elsie … I'm not.'

'Pfft. You're a cinnamon roll … and she's a tiramisu. You don't get any more compatible than that. She has layers. As Grandpa says, it will take someone strong but understanding to get through them all.'

'I'd be no good for her.' He put his fork down. He was no longer hungry. 'Emotions and I have a love-hate relationship.'

Elsie considered him before replying. 'A month ago a local girl was here with an out-of-towner. When Kristy went to leave, the guy grabbed her arm. Before my dad could get over there, Brenna was in the guy's face. No surprise he let her size fool him into thinking she wouldn't be a problem. He let Kristy go and said he'd take her hot blonde friend home. When he went to touch Brenna, no one heard what she said, but he left.'

Elsie stopped to glance to where Wyatt held his glass, his grip white-knuckled. Brenna having put herself in a vulnerable situation, even though he had no doubt she could handle herself, left him on edge. There was still so much he didn't know, and might never know, about her history. So much for helping Brenna. He carefully erased his expression. He was already failing her. He'd been the only one to address his past.

'Wyatt … don't do that. Don't shut down.' Elsie reached for his hand. 'And especially don't shut me out. We're family.'

He slowly nodded. 'I'll try.'

Elsie seemed happy with his hoarse reply. 'Thank you.'

She squeezed his fingers. 'I didn't tell you about Brenna to worry you but to show you that she doesn't need anyone to fight her battles, just like you don't. But like her, you are careful about who you let get close. If anyone can understand each other, it's the two of you.'

He wished he shared Elsie's optimism. 'It's not just me saying we're not a match. Brenna herself says I don't tick any of her boxes.'

'Do you even look in a mirror? You rescue horses and have turned into a hugger. Wyatt, you tick all the boxes for almost every woman in Bundilla, married and unmarried, and that includes Brenna.' Elsie's eyes twinkled. 'I hope my chief babysitter T-shirt arrives soon. Now you're back things are going to get interesting around here very fast.'

CHAPTER 27

It wasn't unusual for Brenna to wake at dawn. It was as though her body was attuned to the early morning birdsong which acted as an alarm clock. What was odd was that instead of leaping out of bed, ready to start her day, she stayed where she was.

She rubbed at her gritty eyes. The reason for remaining beneath her warm covers had nothing to do with the autumn chill and everything to do with the man who'd arrived in Bundilla yesterday. She'd mistakenly thought that now Wyatt was here her preoccupation with him would wane. She couldn't be more wrong.

His comment that he'd missed her played on a continuous loop in her head. Had he meant it as a friend? With his fingers tangled in her hair, it hadn't felt like he had. She was sure that he'd been close to kissing her. But that could have just been a misinterpretation of their banter and her own wishful thinking. She couldn't get physically close to him without wanting to feel his mouth on hers.

Her sigh echoed in the shadowed room. She needed to talk to Hettie. She wasn't getting anything done, like finding out more about Alice and Clement. It wasn't simply the strength of her attraction that made Wyatt unforgettable, but now that she understood more about his childhood she respected and admired the man he'd become. It took immense strength and courage to overcome all that he had.

She flipped back the covers and shivered as the cold air hit her bare arms and feet. There wasn't a horse she couldn't ride but when it came to relationships she was a novice. She'd never been interested in anyone enough for it to matter whether or not their casual dates progressed to anything more. It didn't help she'd never grown out of her teenage partiality to dark hair and sculpted cheekbones.

She'd soon discovered she wasn't the only one to like such traits as they were usually accompanied by an inflated ego. Wyatt, who hands down had the most gorgeous combination of both she'd ever seen, was the only man who wasn't arrogant. Tough and intimidating, yes. But self-absorbed and egotistical, no.

She shrugged on her dressing gown and thrust her feet into her ugg boots. She didn't have any horse-riding lessons until after lunch. She'd have breakfast, make an early start on her jobs and find Hettie to have a cuppa and a chat.

Hours later, when the mist had lifted and Brenna had returned from the stables to have a hot shower, she added laundry to her morning to-do list. Hettie had a radio interview over the phone for her photography book and afterwards they'd meet up at Taite's home gym for a workout. Just as she did whenever she went on a washing frenzy, Brenna threw everything she could find into the machine. It wasn't until she went to look for gym clothes that she realised she had nothing suitable to wear. Not that she and Hettie ever did anything too strenuous, they were usually too busy talking, but she couldn't exercise in jeans.

After finding a pair of black leggings at the bottom of a drawer, she settled for a neon pink crop top. The only person she'd be seeing was Hettie. She threw on a large jacket and filled a water bottle before leaving to jog over to the shed midway between the house and cottage. Unlike her, Taite took his fitness seriously and his home gym had more equipment than the regular one in town.

The country music drifting from the shed told her Hettie was already inside. Brenna pushed open the door and stepped out of the wind.

Hettie smiled from where she used the treadmill, her red hair in a practical top knot. 'Let me guess … you've been washing.'

'What I wouldn't give for some trackies and an oversized T-shirt. I knew there was a reason why I don't wear this top.' She tried to tug the snug pink material higher. 'I can hardly breathe.'

'Just as well you don't go out in public dressed like that. You'll have people driving off the road.'

'Very funny.' Brenna looked down at her too-obvious cleavage. The chocolate brownies that she'd treat herself to whenever in town had obviously gone somewhere. 'I'll leave Aubrey to wear her lycra down the main street. She can pull it off.'

Brenna removed her jacket and after placing her phone on a chair, bundled the coat on top. She went over to the exercise bike beside the treadmill. Taite had given up moving the two machines apart as Brenna and Hettie always shifted them back so they could talk.

'Any word from Clancy?' Hettie asked as Brenna programmed the bike.

'No, but Heath has to propose soon.' Brenna used the band she'd worn on her wrist to put her hair into a messy bun.

'How are you feeling now your new neighbour's back?'

Brenna had called Hettie on the drive home from the pub last night to fill her in about Wyatt having returned.

'I'm in a pickle. What you said before about Wyatt being someone to ditch my rules for … there's no point thinking about such a thing if Wyatt still believes he's not right for me. I need to know where he stands.'

'Brenna … he kissed you. He said he missed you. Those rules need to go.'

Brenna frowned across at Hettie. Usually her advice was gentle, measured and reassuring. 'That's something I would have said.'

'Exactly.'

'I'm not sure if I can.'

'You can. There's nothing you can't do. You're fearless.'

'I was. Before Wyatt rocked up looking so gorgeous I swear I forgot my name, and he apologised as he patted Bundy, who'd become his best friend. If that wasn't enough, he sat on Sonny as though giving a masterclass on how to look good on a horse.'

Amusement shone in Hettie's blue eyes. 'You're grumbling about Wyatt being good-looking, having integrity and being an expert horseman?'

'I'm grumbling about him putting me into a spin and not knowing what to do. I'm always prepared for anything.'

The ring of Hettie's phone stopped her from making a reply. She picked it up from where it sat on the treadmill console. 'Hi.'

Brenna didn't need Hettie to say anything more to know that it was Taite calling. The softness and love in her voice made Brenna's heart ache. A loneliness she'd always denied seeped through her.

She slowed and stopped the bike. A sedate workout wasn't going to burn her energy or take the edge off her restlessness. She'd need to go for a ride.

'Yes, she's here.' Hettie glanced across at her. 'Why?' She turned to look at the door. 'Okay.'

A loud knock sounded.

Brenna headed for the door. Taite had to be on the other side. She flung it open, ready for the lecture her twin would give her. Yet again she hadn't answered her phone when he was trying to track her down. Technically she did have it with her, even if it was on silent and under her coat.

But it wasn't Taite's broad shoulders blocking out the daylight.

She registered two things. One, crop tops weren't designed to be worn when it was cold. The chilly breeze rushed over the gap of skin left bare between the top and her leggings. And two, no matter how cool the wind was, when Wyatt's gaze raked over her and his eyes darkened, she felt as warm as campfire embers.

She took what she'd planned to be a calming breath. Instead the action only caused her chest to push against the pink lycra. She gritted her teeth. Next trip to town, she was donating this top to charity.

If she didn't know better she'd have said Wyatt's usual control seemed strained. A muscle worked in his jaw.

'Belle's in labour.'

His taut words provided an explanation for his tension and galvanised Brenna into action.

She spun around, saying over her shoulder, 'I'll be right there.'

She didn't think twice about Wyatt's eyes tracking her as she grabbed her jacket and phone. He understandably would be worried about Belle having her foal after losing her dam. Then she glanced at Hettie. Her old school friend wore what could only be described as a satisfied smile as she looked between the two of them. From the corner of her eye, she saw Wyatt pass a hand around the base of his neck before moving out of the doorway to wait for her.

When Brenna shrugged on her coat, Hettie came over to fix her messy bun, which had listed to the side.

Once done, Hettie pulled her close for a hug. 'For the record, you need another condition, like having a man look at you like Wyatt just did.'

'He's only worried about Belle.' Brenna kept her voice quiet so Wyatt wouldn't hear. 'That's why he looks a little distracted.'

'*A little.*' Hettie chuckled. 'That was distracted with a capital D. It was also the answer to where Wyatt stands and your green light to breaking all your rules.'

Brenna frowned as she zipped up her jacket as high as it could go. 'What about Mia?'

'Trust me, he wasn't thinking about Mia.' Hettie reached out to unzip Brenna's jacket so a hint of cleavage showed. She gave her a gentle push. 'Go and break some rules.'

'I'm going to deliver a foal,' Brenna said in a fierce whisper. 'And I'll freeze with my jacket not done up.'

Hettie just gave her a serene smile and waved her off.

When she was at the door and far enough away from Hettie, she tugged the zip upwards. As she stepped outside, she was so focused on the task and thinking about Hettie's words she tripped on the uneven step. She pitched forwards. Wyatt's arm wrapped around her waist, steadying her.

Through the thick layers of her jacket she could feel the strength in his hold and the ease with which he supported her. All she could breathe in was sandalwood and all she could think about was that in another second she'd be turning towards him. And if that happened there was no way she could predict where her hands would go. Her palms heated at the thought of touching him again.

She snapped herself upright and moved away. His arm dropped from around her.

'Thanks,' she said, not risking a glance at Wyatt let alone turning to look at Hettie. 'And that's exactly why I don't wear heels. I can't walk in anything but boots.'

Bundy ran over to her. It had been almost a week since the kelpie had been at Glenwood Station. Even though his visit would only encourage the town matchmakers, she was glad to see him. She bent to scratch behind his ears. She needed a moment. The icy breeze wouldn't be quite enough to strip the warm flush from her cheeks.

'Bundy was asleep in the sun beside my car,' Wyatt said from where he stood at least two body lengths away.

'I wondered when he'd turn up.' She ruffled the kelpie's neck before setting off towards the stables and pressing her phone to her ear as she called Trent.

Belle had to be her priority, not her conflicted thoughts about the man who maintained distance between them as they walked. She had everything crossed all would go well with Belle foaling, but she didn't want to leave anything to chance.

She entered the stables to the sound of Belle's huge hoof pawing the floor. There was no doubt the Clydesdale was in the beginning stage of labour. Brenna had given Belle the largest stall so there would be plenty of room for her to move. She'd also put Major in his paddock to stop the old chestnut either wanting treats or complaining he wasn't getting enough attention.

After they'd opened the half door, Wyatt went to stroke the mare's nose while Brenna assessed her. The Clydesdale's neck felt warm and damp and her tail gave an agitated swish.

Brenna smoothed Belle's shoulder as she took in Wyatt's tense profile. 'I'll just get what we need and be right back. Wyatt … Belle's done this before. She'll be okay.'

Wyatt didn't look at her as he nodded.

Brenna sped to the house to change into her work clothes, braid her hair and collect everything they'd need for what could be a long day and possibly evening. She then called her little riding school clients who were all too happy to reschedule their after-lunch lessons knowing that when they'd next visit there'd be a foal. As an afternoon storm was predicted and lessons would likely have had to be postponed anyway, Belle going into labour proved to be perfect timing.

With a bag of snacks and extra blankets to add to the ones already in the stable's apartment, Brenna headed back. Wyatt had closed both stable doors and she walked into the warmth. In front of Belle's stall he'd positioned two camp chairs and a bale of hay that doubled as a table and footrest. Nearby, Bundy lay on a saddle cloth, fast asleep. A faint floral perfume had her look around. Hettie must have put flowers in the kitchenette again.

When Wyatt left Belle's stall, she gave him a smile as she crossed the stables. At the kitchen door she came to an abrupt stop. There wasn't a single vase of flowers on the bench. Instead multiple glass jars decorated with pink ribbons were filled with pink flowers, everything from roses to daisies to carnations.

Conscious of Wyatt standing behind her, she turned. 'Is this what I think it is?'

'The quilting club have changed tack. As devastated as Roy is at not having any more sponge cakes, I thought you'd like today's deliveries. Elsie already has dibs on whatever tomorrow's will be.'

'I do.' She tried to hide how much his consideration moved her. 'I especially love the roses.'

'I thought you might.'

'Coffee?' she asked, entering the kitchen. The deep timbre of his voice hadn't lost any of its ability to feather over her skin like a physical touch.

'Thanks,' Wyatt said from the doorway. 'I can make it.'

She shook her head as she went over to the coffee machine. 'I've got it.'

Caffeine probably wasn't the best idea, she was jittery enough around Wyatt, but she needed to keep busy. It would be just them alone for the rest of the day. Even after Belle foaled, the mother and baby would need to be watched closely.

She emerged with two mugs of steaming coffee and headed to where Wyatt was sitting in a camp chair. He accepted his hot drink with a brief smile.

Brenna sat down and racked her brain for something to say. She was back to being awkward around him. Hettie had to be wrong. Someone like Wyatt couldn't be interested in someone like her. She was the total opposite of the women he'd date. It didn't help that he'd positioned their chairs so close together their shoulders almost brushed.

As much as she needed to monitor Belle, she was aware of every move and gesture that Wyatt made. Needing a diversion, she took a sip of scalding coffee.

Wyatt's phone vibrated.

'If you've work to do,' she said, trying to hide her hope that he'd have something urgent to attend to, 'Belle will be okay.'

The irony wasn't lost on her. The day Wyatt arrived she'd wanted him off his phone. Now here she was wishing that he'd have a call to make. Having an empty chair beside her, even if for a few minutes, would give her blood pressure a chance to subside.

'Work can wait.' He angled his mobile to show Brenna the new image that had come through. 'It's Mia. Emily's got her first tooth.'

Brenna stared at the photo. Emily was the most adorable baby and Mia was stunning. Her sleek brown hair was curled into soft waves and her thick-lashed eyes were a green-flecked hazel. Brenna stopped her hand from checking if any hair had escaped her hastily plaited braid.

'Emily's too cute.'

'She is.'

There was no missing the affection in his tone. A hollowness that chilled her far more than the earlier cold wind swept through her. She had to know if Wyatt's feelings for Mia ran deeper than friendship. If they did, that was the only answer she needed about whether or not to break her rules.

'Mia's beautiful.'

'When Nick met her, he was lost for words, which didn't happen often. Nick made her promise to be open to finding someone after he was gone. When she's ready, I might need to enlist the quilting club's help.'

Brenna kept her attention off Wyatt. She couldn't let him see how much it mattered that his willingness to help Mia possibly find happiness again flagged that he didn't see her as anything but a friend. 'They would be in their element.'

Her relief quickly turned to confusion. If there wasn't anything more between Wyatt and Mia, then why did he think he wasn't right for her? She was no closer to knowing the reasons behind what he'd said after their kiss by the creek.

'It's Nick's birthday on Wednesday,' Wyatt said, voice quiet. 'I'll head to Sydney to spend the day with Mia and Emily.'

He reached out to pluck a small yellow leaf from her hair. She'd walked under the wisteria on the way to the stables.

'Those young fellas at the pub, do they tick any of your boxes?' Wyatt's hand hovered near her cheek.

She blamed caffeine for the acceleration of her heartbeat and the desperation to feel his fingertips trail across her skin.

'Not in a million years. Besides, I don't have boxes anymore. I've simplified things.'

His arm slowly lowered but his eyes never left hers. 'How so?'

She kept her reply light to hide her increasing breathlessness. 'That will remain one of life's eternal mysteries.'

She came to her feet. She'd never describe herself as reckless, but she'd just done away with her checklist. A rush of uncertainty followed. Her rules were in place to keep her safe and without them she felt exposed and vulnerable.

She didn't realise she was rubbing at the collarbone that had shattered along with her life until Wyatt's sharp gaze zeroed in on her hand.

CHAPTER 28

It had been less than twenty-four hours since Wyatt had returned to the mountains and already he felt like he had emotional whiplash.

Just like on his previous visits, his inner chaos had nothing to do with his grief and everything to do with the woman staring at him with wide blue eyes. Even though Brenna was no longer touching her collarbone and had masked her unease, she didn't fool him. Her action had been significant.

He hadn't forgotten Taite's shocked reaction when she said she'd never crashed a car. Brenna would never lie. She also simply hadn't forgotten she'd written off her ute or sustained an injury. She was full of secrets. Secrets he hoped she might eventually feel comfortable to share with him.

Except that time obviously wasn't now. She wouldn't even look in his direction. With her body angled away from him, she bent to reach for his empty coffee cup before turning to head into the kitchen.

As for her simplifying her box system, what did that mean? An unfamiliar feeling that he could only describe as hope stirred. Was there a chance he could be a match? If so, why didn't his conscience shut down the idea like it usually did? The caution in Brenna's voice when they'd talked about Mia had prompted him to clarify that there was nothing other than friendship between them. Normally it didn't matter if a woman thought him unavailable.

He tunnelled a hand through his hair. If the high emotion of the previous ten minutes wasn't enough, he was still recovering from having the shed door fly open to reveal Brenna in leggings and a crop top that exposed more smooth skin than it concealed. As slender as she was, her work clothes hid full feminine curves.

He'd been powerless to hide a punch of deep need. A fact Hettie hadn't missed. She'd sent him a sympathetic smile when Brenna had turned to grab her coat. As for when Brenna had tripped and for a brief moment there'd been contact between them, his control had only been tested further.

A rustle of straw had him come to his feet. Today had to be all about Belle and not the country girl who sent him into a tailspin. For the next hour and a half he did what he could to ease Belle's discomfort. When the mare lay on the ground and didn't get up, he returned to his chair. As much as Belle trusted him, in this second phase he wanted to disturb her as little as possible.

Brenna approached to place a container of muffins on the hay bale in front of him.

'Don't worry, I didn't make them,' she said, tone cheerful.

She appeared to have moved on from their earlier conversation. They hadn't again discussed anything personal and their small talk had stuck to neutral topics. As much as this enabled him to keep his attention on what was happening with Belle, he was under no illusion that his thoughts wouldn't return to Brenna once he had nothing to distract him.

She took a seat and grimaced as Belle arched her neck to weather a strong contraction. 'I hope it's not long now.'

Wyatt ground his teeth as Belle's sides heaved. While the mare rested between contractions, she had to be getting tired.

'Wyatt.' Brenna's fingers touched his fisted hand. 'She's doing really well. I'm sure the foal's feet will present soon.'

When the Clydesdale pushed again, Brenna's prediction proved true. The tips of two hooves appeared.

'There you go,' Brenna said, a smile in her voice. 'The heels are facing the ground, so the foal is in the right position.'

Instead of reassuring Wyatt, the knowledge that Belle's foal could soon be here ratcheted up his tension. Things still could, and did, go wrong. Despite his grandfather's experience and a local vet's expertise, Belle's dam hadn't survived the difficult hours that followed her own feet presenting.

After what felt like an eternity, Belle pushed. More of the foal's feet came into view, along with a small nose nestled between the tiny hooves. Wyatt clenched his jaw. He was going to be grey by the time this foal arrived. When Brenna settled lower in her camp chair, her shoulder rested against his in a silent show of support. He didn't move away.

'It should only take one more push,' Brenna said, words calm.

Belle rested for longer than usual and then her head lifted. Her stomach rippled and finally the foal slipped free. When it didn't move, Wyatt went to stand.

Brenna's hand gripped his. 'Give it a few more seconds.'

He started counting. If there was no movement by ten, he was going into the stall. He got to nine and the foal twitched. His relief was short-lived. The foal began to thrash its head, but the membrane covering its nose wouldn't break to allow it to breathe.

Beside him, Brenna tensed and released his hand. 'They're going to need a little help.'

He was already out of his chair. Moving quietly, he went to free the foal. Belle lumbered to her feet and approached to lick the foal's chocolate-brown coat.

Wyatt returned to his seat so Belle and her baby could bond.

'The miracle of life,' Brenna said, her words little more than a whisper. 'It never gets old.'

When he didn't reply, she glanced at him. 'All good?'

He gave a stiff nod.

He thought she was going to touch him again but she instead stood up. 'I'd better make a start on my jobs. I'm certain Major doesn't stop rolling until every bit of him is covered in mud.'

Wyatt glanced out the stable window. He'd lost track of time. The once blue sky was now a moody grey and the mountain peaks were invisible in the heavy cloud.

'Need a hand?'

She shook her head, but the relaxed gesture told him it wasn't an automatic no and that she had been open to him helping. 'You stay and enjoy watching Belle and her beautiful baby. The foal needs to be standing within one hour, drinking within two and the afterbirth has to pass within three.'

He nodded. His grandfather used to say the same thing.

In between doing the feed runs to her various herds of horses, and brushing the mud off Major, who was literally covered from his neck to his tail, Brenna checked on Belle. Wyatt didn't tire of watching the tenderness in Brenna's expression whenever she looked at the mare and her little filly.

After he was certain the foal, who was on her feet and feeding, had settled, Wyatt left his chair to stretch. The predicated rain had come and gone and early evening shadows drifted over the valley beyond the stables. The hiss of the coffee machine confirmed Brenna was in the kitchen.

When he entered, she was pouring milk into a stainless-steel jug. She didn't look up. He stopped inside the doorway. Unlike on the trek, he didn't again want to approach her unawares.

'Brenna.'

She spun around, milk sloshing in the bottle. While her arm didn't rise like before, her eyes blazed and her shoulders squared. As quickly as her fight response took hold, it ebbed. The agitated rise and fall of her chest gentled.

He shoved his hands in his jeans pockets to stop himself from reaching for her. Already the uncertainty and regret that pinched her face had given way to an embarrassed flush. She carefully sat the milk on the bench.

'This is like deja vu.' She folded her arms. 'Except you told me you were there, and the room is fully lit.'

'Are you okay?'

Her chin tilted. 'Would you believe me if I said this doesn't usually happen when I'm surprised?'

'If you believe me when I say I'm here if you want to talk.'

'I'm fine.'

'So I'm not going to find you chopping enough wood for two winters?'

'Never.' Her lips briefly curved. 'One, I use a chainsaw and two, that's not my preferred form of stress relief.'

'Which would be going for a hell-for-leather ride on that mare of yours.'

'True.' She hesitated, her eyes skimming over his face as though she were making a decision. 'This isn't just a long story. It's a very long story.'

'I'll be here for however long it is.'

Still, she studied him. Then she swung around to pick up the milk. 'We're both going to need another coffee.'

With their mugs filled, they took their seats in the camp chairs. Belle whickered softly as she nuzzled her filly, who lay curled up asleep at her feet.

'She's such a lovely mumma.' Brenna's words were even despite her white-knuckled grip on her mug.

'She is.'

Brenna took a sip of coffee and after a long moment spoke. 'No one knows, not even Hettie and Clancy, and especially not Taite. We'd just lost our father.' Her lips twisted with bitterness. 'Plus I was the one who stuffed up.'

'Brenna …'

'Don't say it. Taite was all I had left; I had to protect him even if he would have been there for me. This was my mess to deal with.' She stared at the far wall. 'Losing Mum and then Dad … I wasn't my usual self. I studied my business degree part time online, but I still had to go to Wagga Wagga for residential schools. I met Neil there. He was a city boy, softly spoken and conscientious. I was in such a brain fog I didn't question why I kept bumping into him in my favourite café, or at the library and pub. He never made a move on me and had actually been helpful keeping guys away.'

When Brenna stopped to put her unfinished mug of coffee on the floor, her hand shook. Wyatt linked her fingers with his. She stilled and then her hand clasped his.

'Things began disappearing from my room, nothing major, just some earrings, a scarf and a belt. Then Neil started resenting me hanging out with my friends. The normal me would have kicked him to the kerb, but the lost me was just trying to make it through each day.'

Wyatt's thumb brushed across the back of her hand.

'It was a Friday night and Neil wasn't happy I was going out even though it was someone's birthday. When he turned up at the pub, I knew something was wrong but didn't have the energy to trust my instincts. He bought a birthday round. I never left my drink unattended or accepted one from strangers, but when Neil handed me my glass, I thought nothing of it.'

Wyatt locked down his anger. He knew where this was going but didn't want to do anything to interrupt Brenna from telling her story.

'When my brain felt fuzzy, I realised Neil had spiked my drink. I tried to tell my friends, but my words slurred. They trusted him like I had. He took my keys and promised to drive me home. In the car park when I resisted, he simply picked me up. I was in and out of consciousness but knew we were leaving town. He kept saying I'd work out soon enough I was his. He'd waited long enough.'

When Brenna paused as if to choose her words, Wyatt lifted their hands and pressed his mouth to her knuckles.

Her voice hardened. 'I wasn't scared so much as furious. I knew I couldn't let him take me wherever we were going and managed to unclick my seatbelt. Then I leaned over and reefed on the handbrake. I remember the screech of tyres and the car sliding but passed out before we hit the tree.'

As careful as Wyatt was to hide his thoughts, Brenna must have sensed his fury and his fear. She gave him a quick look.

'A good Samaritan stopped. He had a daughter my age and somehow I muttered enough for him to know what was going on. He made sure the police knew I wasn't there of my free will. The driver's side took the brunt of the hit. Neil had to be cut out but I escaped with a broken collarbone and concussion. Hospital blood tests showed I had GHB in my system.'

'I hope this is heading where it should go, because otherwise I'll be needing Neil's last name.'

'It is and even if it wasn't, I would have dealt with him years ago. A local girl had been an earlier target and when she came to see me in hospital, we joined forces. The court case to convict Neil was brutal but it was worth it when he was sentenced. I went to visit him in prison. I was back to my normal self and will never forget his kangaroo-in-the-headlights expression when the penny dropped that I wasn't the weak and fragile person he'd believed me to be. He'll never bother me, or anyone else, again.'

Brenna turned to face Wyatt. 'So, when you startle me, I'm not scared. I'm angry and most of all at myself. Neil took me for a fool.'

'You were grieving and are far from a fool. My grandmother used to say that the world needs more kindness, especially in the way we treat ourselves.'

'She was a wise woman.'

Despite Brenna's words, her expression remained dubious. It would take time to process all that she'd revealed, especially as she hadn't talked about what had happened before.

Giving in to the need to touch her, Wyatt tucked the hair that had fallen over Brenna's cheek behind her ear. 'Thank you for telling me your long story.'

Her gaze lowered to his mouth. When footsteps sounded outside, she pulled her hand free as the stable door slid open.

Taite and a reed-thin older man entered along with Bundy and Waffles. The tense jut to Taite's jaw let Wyatt know he'd sensed his twin's turmoil. Wyatt gave him a subtle nod to say Brenna was okay.

After Bundy and Waffles had their obligatory pats, Brenna made the introductions. 'Wyatt, this is Wedge. Wedge … Wyatt.'

When the conversation turned to the new foal, Wyatt didn't miss the way Wedge's suspicious glare remained on him. He knew better than to judge someone; he'd been judged enough as a child. But the broken capillaries in Wedge's cheeks were all too familiar. As sober as the elderly man seemed, he guessed he hadn't always been that way. He hoped that Wedge's drinking days hadn't coincided with when his father had been in town.

Wyatt forced himself to listen to Taite as the deer farmer hooked an arm around Brenna's shoulder and said, 'I think a celebratory dinner at the cottage is in order.'

Wyatt gave a small shake of his head. 'I'll stay to watch Belle.' The mare wasn't right to be left as her placenta hadn't yet passed.

'I'll keep you company,' Wedge said, taking the seat Brenna had vacated.

Brenna nodded. 'I'm sure Hettie won't mind making two meals to go.'

When Brenna hesitated, even knowing that Wedge and Taite were watching, Wyatt met her gaze to double-check she really was okay. Her blue eyes held his before she turned to leave.

Wyatt waited until the stable door closed before sitting beside Wedge. He knew what was coming. Wedge had stared at the scar on his hand.

'Brenna, Taite and Hettie are like family to me,' Wedge ground out, without any pretence at small talk. 'You had better not be like your old man.'

'I'm not.'

Wedge scoffed. 'Alcohol mightn't be your poison, but something must be. Drugs? Gambling?'

'Work.' Even as Wyatt spoke his phone vibrated in his jeans pocket.

Wedge grunted. 'Roy may sing your praises, but I'm not so easily bluffed. I've been out of town, otherwise we'd have had this little talk sooner. Want to know how I remember you? You have your father's eyes. In all my years of drinking I've never seen a man so eager to shirk his parental responsibilities.' Open hostility burned in Wedge's rheumy gaze. 'I'm not named after an eagle for nothing. Just in case the apple doesn't fall far from the tree, I'll be watching you, especially when you're around Brenna.'

CHAPTER 29

'There can't be a more adorable sight,' Brenna said, her cheeks aching from smiling.

Belle and her filly, who Wyatt had named Cora after his grandmother, were outside in the morning sun. Cora frolicked in the warmth, all lanky legs and big, long-lashed eyes. A kookaburra landed on a nearby fence post as if to watch.

Wedge chuckled from where he stood beside Brenna by the paddock gate. 'You haven't seen a baby cockatiel.'

Wedge was an avid birdwatcher. He'd turned his life around last winter and was now a frequent visitor to Glenwood Station. If he wasn't helping out, he'd take his binoculars and disappear into the hills. He'd been away attending a birding festival. Hettie had discovered there was such a thing and they'd all chipped in to make sure Wedge attended. It was hard to imagine the animated man beside her was once the surly grump who would sit on the bench outside the pub.

Wedge lifted a gnarled hand to his head. 'They have these little mohawks. Next spring keep a lookout in that dead tree up near the creek where you're determined to break your neck. They always nest there.'

She glanced sideways and saw his grin before he continued. 'Don't worry, your secret's safe with me. If Taite knew you had your own Bundilla Cup course that any grown man would think twice about attempting, he'd put one of his high deer fences around it and weld the gate shut.'

Brenna didn't laugh. She wasn't sure what Taite would actually do but he wouldn't be happy at her riding such a challenging route. The fact that she, or whatever horse she'd been on, had never come to any harm wouldn't appease him. He'd take one look at the near vertical slope and the size of the fallen trees she jumped and deem the circuit too dangerous.

She turned to face Wedge. 'Ebony loves going round there even more than I do. It's not so much a secret … it's just if Taite knew he'd disapprove.'

Sympathy replaced the amusement on Wedge's face. 'I saw you ride it about a month ago. After I remembered to breathe, I realised you hadn't stopped smiling.' Wedge's voice gentled. 'Roy said he'd spoken to you about this year's cup. Are you going to show those young fellas how to ride?'

Brenna looked back at Cora as the foal gave a tiny buck. 'Possibly.'

The Bundilla Cup hadn't exactly been on her mind. There were so many other thoughts tangled in her head. But after talking to Wyatt last night about Neil, it was as though a huge knot had loosened. She now felt like she had the room to unravel the other threads that were tightly twisted together. But that didn't mean she would enter the race. Her deep-seated feelings about not being enough for her father hadn't lost any of their power to wound her.

'Compared to your course,' Wedge said, drawing her attention back to him, 'the actual cup will feel like you're at pony camp.'

'We'll see.' She changed the subject. 'You're here early.'

His expression grew serious. 'There's something I need to keep a close eye on.'

No doubt there were some birds that Wedge wanted to make sure were coping with the wet weather. After the rainy summer and autumn, the dam was close to overflowing and the creek swollen. She gazed at the clouds hovering over the high-country peaks. And there would be more rain coming. Despite the sunshine it was due to storm that afternoon.

On the valley edge, a flock of cockatoos suddenly took flight. Light glinted off their white wings, and the wind carried their screeching calls. Brenna scanned the low hills. Something had upset the birds.

She glanced at Wedge who tracked the cockatoos as they roosted in another tree. 'Before you left, you didn't see any sign of wild dogs, did you? Sometimes I get a feeling that I'm being watched when out riding. Outlaw and Ebony get skittish when I take the trail to billy button ridge.'

Concern deepened the creases on his face. 'No, but that's not to say they aren't around. I'll keep a look out.' Wedge's bushy grey brows drew together. 'Here comes trouble.'

At first Brenna thought Waffles had bolted across to the stables from the cottage, then the sound of a side-by-side came from the laneway that ran alongside the horse paddock. Wyatt was on his way over and would soon be here.

'Wyatt's trouble?'

Wedge scowled. 'I'm not proud of it, but I was a drinking buddy of his father.'

'Wyatt mentioned he visited Bundilla as a child.'

They both watched as Wyatt, with Bundy on the back, drove through the gate.

'Wyatt has his father's eyes and that way of looking straight through you.'

Wedge didn't need to add that he hoped this was all Wyatt shared with his father. Wedge staying in the stables long after she'd brought dinner over last night now made sense. He'd only left when Wyatt had.

Wyatt gave them a wave before he turned to head towards Murphy and Midge's paddock. Only Brenna waved in return.

The Shire horse and mini pony trotted to meet him while the two geese left the large corner puddle to waddle over. It was a morning ritual that Wyatt would feed them all apples. The quilting ladies might have stripped the grocery store shelves of flour and sugar, but she was pretty sure Wyatt was their best apple customer.

'Wyatt isn't like his father.'

'Are you sure of that? His father was a charmer too. He'd sweet-talk people into getting what he wanted and then leave town before they'd discover he was full of nothing but empty promises.'

Wyatt parked the side-by-side and went to pat Murphy and Midge.

'Wyatt isn't exactly charming; not like some of the silver-tongued city boys I've had on my treks. If anything, he doesn't say much at all.'

Wedge glowered as Wyatt bent to feed the geese slivers of apple. 'I hope I'm misjudging him, but his father wasn't a good man. You and Wyatt looked very cosy in the stables. I don't want you to get hurt.'

'You know me … I'm the least likely person to get hurt and the most likely to wallop someone if they're out of line.'

The tense set to Wedge's mouth didn't relax. 'Just be careful. If Wyatt is anything like his father, one day he'll be here and the next he'll be gone.'

Brenna stayed quiet as Wyatt and Bundy drove towards them. When Wyatt turned off the engine, Bundy leaped off the back and raced over for a pat.

'Morning,' Wyatt said as he approached.

Even without Wedge's warning, she would have picked up on the tension between the two men. They exchanged a look that while polite on Wyatt's end, could only be called a glare on Wedge's.

Wyatt stopped beside Brenna and looked over to where Cora gave another tiny buck. 'Someone's enjoying the sunshine.'

Belle lifted her head and gave a quiet whicker before ambling over to see Wyatt. He scratched the Clydesdale's neck and gave her the apple he'd saved.

Brenna snuck a sideways glance at Wedge. The depth of the bond between the mare and Wyatt was unmistakable. The older man's unimpressed glower said Wyatt wasn't even close to dispelling his suspicions.

Belle moved away to graze and Wyatt stared out over the high-country peaks. While his face was unreadable, she could feel his yearning and restlessness. He hadn't been on horseback since their jaunt to Platypus Hollow.

'I'm heading out for a ride,' she said, speaking before common sense could stop her. 'You're welcome to join me.'

Conscious of Wedge's disapproval, she waited for Wyatt to answer.

'Thanks.' He didn't look at her. 'I'd like that.'

Wedge grunted. 'You could always go out past the cockatiel nesting tree.' Brenna then heard him mutter, 'That course of yours will sort out any lily-livered city boy.'

She had been thinking of taking Wyatt around her circuit. Except her reasons weren't to do with proving he didn't belong in the country. Outlaw had ridden the course as much as Ebony and the brumby would enjoy having Wyatt take him round. She'd only ever completed the route on her own so it would be a challenge to have Wyatt to compete against.

'I think I will.'

Wedge's frown turned into a smirk. 'Better buckle up, Wyatt.'

Wedge stayed by Brenna's side while they brought in Ebony and Outlaw. Once she and Wyatt were in their saddles, Wedge waved them off. Bundy loped ahead, leading the way past the deer-filled paddocks.

Brenna glanced across to where Wyatt rode alongside her. 'Wedge doesn't like many people.'

'I'd be worried if he did like me after meeting my father. He's right to be protective of you.'

He met her raised brow with a smile. 'Not that you need anyone to protect you, it's just he cares about you so wants the best for you.'

'Nice answer.'

She relaxed into the saddle. Galahs trilled as they flew overhead and the breeze rippled in the grass tussocks lining the track. She unzipped her navy jacket, enjoying the warmth. It wouldn't be long until the first autumn snowfall dusted the mountain peaks.

She broke the companionable silence between her and Wyatt. 'Dare I ask if there were any more deliveries?'

The corner of his mouth lifted. 'Today's flower theme was white. Elsie has been sending photos all morning of where she's put the arrangements.'

Brenna smiled. Elsie loved flowers almost as much as donuts.

'So what's this course we're riding that Wedge is hoping I'll come a cropper on?' Wyatt asked.

'The day Belle arrived Trent mentioned the Bundilla Cup …'

'Which you don't enter?'

'I won't bore you with why, but I've made my own course so I don't feel like I'm missing out.'

Wyatt slanted her a serious look. 'You wouldn't bore me.'

She shook her head, both at his unspoken words he'd be there for her as well as at her need to talk to him. 'It's not important. The circuit is a little hairy, so it's fine if you'd rather ride somewhere else.'

She'd already divulged enough about her past. There was no way she'd open the vault that contained her unresolved feelings and grief about her father. As understanding as Wyatt had been yesterday, her embarrassment lingered. It didn't matter that she'd not been herself four years ago, she should have seen Neil for who he was. Today it was important to be her usual in-control self. She didn't want Wyatt to think any less of her.

'Does Taite know about this hairy course?'

'Nope and it's going to stay that way. He'd only worry.'

As they approached what looked like a sheer drop, Wyatt threw her a frown. 'If this is where we're riding, Taite wouldn't worry, he'd have a heart attack.'

'Haven't you seen *The Man from Snowy River*? This is nothing. It's not that steep.'

Wyatt stopped Outlaw at the crest of the hill. 'I think our definitions of *steep* differ. Where do we go next?'

She pointed out the landmarks they'd be using to navigate their way through the wide gully once they reached the bottom.

When she'd finished, Wyatt didn't immediately speak. 'Let me get this straight. There's a fallen tree that Midge can't see over that we have to jump, a creek that basically is in flood, and low tree branches that you suggest I avoid if I want to keep my teeth?'

She grinned. 'Exactly. It is safe, it's just not sensible. I also promise not to go easy on you.'

Wyatt's deep chuckle made the sun feel warmer and the day brighter.

'After three?' she asked.

They shortened their reins. Already Ebony was prancing and Outlaw sidestepping. Together they counted and on three the horses exploded forwards, Bundy close behind. When they plunged down the slope, Brenna leaned back in her saddle. She shot Wyatt a glance. His grin flashed white. As soon as the steep descent gentled, Wyatt leaned over Outlaw's neck and the brumby edged away. Ebony tossed her head and Brenna allowed the mare to lengthen her stride to close the distance between them.

It was then as though they rode in tandem as they flew around the circuit, hooves pounding, dirt flying and Brenna's soul soaring. They thundered neck-to-neck past the old tree Wedge had mentioned that marked the finishing line. Her heart feeling like it filled her chest, and her adrenaline merging with a swell of emotion, she slowed Ebony. She could spend a lifetime riding beside Wyatt.

Too late she registered a pale flash in her peripheral vision. Ebony spooked and by the time she'd settled the mare, Wyatt had set off with Bundy after a muddy dog. She followed.

'She's wearing a collar,' Wyatt called over his shoulder. 'And is injured.'

Wyatt's words confirmed her own first impressions. This was no feral wild dog, otherwise she would have been more aggressive and Bundy wouldn't be chasing her at a measured pace as though he were running after Waffles. If the dog continued on in the direction she was heading she would reach the end of the gully. A large boulder would then make escape difficult.

The dog slowed, her limp becoming more noticeable as she favoured her front right leg. As if realising the way was blocked, the dog swung around to face them. Expression fearful, she held her right paw off the ground. Bundy stopped nearby, his tail wagging.

Brenna halted Ebony beside Outlaw. Now she was closer she saw that beneath the mud the dog was a champagne gold colour and her collar was a faded pink. With her white markings and bone structure, she appeared to be a border collie.

'Do you happen to have any food on you?' Wyatt asked quietly.

Brenna dipped her hand in her coat pocket to take out a small plastic bag. 'Horse biscuits. I make them myself out of oats so they'll be okay for a dog.' Instead of giving him the bag, she spoke. 'Are you sure this is a good idea?'

Wyatt nodded as he dismounted. 'If she was a threat Bundy wouldn't be where he is.'

Brenna looked over to see Bundy and the dog touching noses. She passed Wyatt the biscuits and in return he handed her Outlaw's reins.

As Wyatt slowly approached, the dog's first instinct was to retreat but then she returned to Bundy's side. The kelpie obviously made her feel safe. When Wyatt reached the pair, he asked Bundy to sit and offered him some biscuit. The kelpie did so and ate the small piece. When Wyatt outstretched his hand towards the border collie and her muscles tensed, Brenna was sure she would bolt.

But then, she didn't know what it was Wyatt said, or if it was just his sense of calm, the dog sat and accepted the treat. Wyatt smiled and fed her another biscuit. When he was finished, she edged forwards. He carefully reached out and when the dog dipped her head as if wanting his touch, he ruffled her neck.

Brenna swallowed. Wyatt didn't just have a special way with geese and horses but dogs as well. Except it wasn't only animals that his empathy and patience worked on. They had worked on her too. Wedge's warning to be careful had come too late. As much as she tried to be prepared for any eventuality, she hadn't been prepared for Wyatt.

Since that first day on the trek, even though he'd been so wrong for her, he'd thawed the ice that encased her heart. Now seeing Wyatt win over the frightened dog, the final protective piece fell away. She could no longer deny the reason why he affected her like he did and why she'd been the opposite of her usual confident self. She loved him.

But with such an admission came vulnerability. She'd never expected to feel so completely or so deeply about someone. She was so far out of her area of expertise, she had no idea what to do. There was no clear path forwards or way to prepare herself for what might or might not happen between them. Wyatt could very well still think he wasn't right for her. Then there was the whole city versus country reality. They came from different worlds.

She looked away from where the dog leaned against Wyatt's leg, gazing at him with trusting eyes. She had no doubt she stared at Wyatt in the same way, a way that left her open to hurt and disappointment. She'd told him she'd simplified her boxes. Her sole requirement had been to not end up with someone the quilting club approved of. A stubborn part of her refused to go along with any matchmaking plan.

But now, after admitting to herself how she felt about Wyatt, the criterion should have been to not fall for someone who had the potential to break her heart.

CHAPTER 30

'Let's see if you have a microchip,' Trent said, tone gentle as he waved a portable scanner over his new patient's neck.

Wyatt smoothed a hand along the border collie's back to keep her still on the table in the stables. When a chip registered, the border collie started at the loud beep. The dog was so thin he could feel the jut of her bones beneath her matted coat as well as the quiver of her fear. As uncertain as she'd been when Taite had arrived in the side-by-side to collect her, and then when Trent had tended to her lacerated paw, she'd stayed calm as long as he'd been close by.

'What happens now?' he asked, already not wanting to hear the answer. Just because the border collie had bonded with him didn't mean she'd become a part of his life. Her owners would be searching for her.

'I'll look up the contact details and make some calls. I'll let you know as soon as I find anything.'

Even though Wyatt felt the intensity of Brenna's stare, he didn't turn his head to where she stood next to him. Wedge had been waiting for them in the stables and his glower hadn't changed. Taite too was looking between him and Brenna more than usual. Which wasn't a surprise as on the ride back she'd been too quiet.

When he'd checked in with her, she'd said she had a few things to think about. He knew from when he'd told Brenna about his childhood how exposed he'd felt, and she'd only just opened up about what had happened to her when she'd been away from the mountains. He'd made sure to ride alongside her on the journey home.

Brenna moved to stroke the border collie's shoulder. 'We're happy to keep her for as long as she needs to stay.'

'Thanks.' Trent smiled at Bundy. 'I'm sure my favourite patient will help keep her company.'

The vet nodded towards the bandages, pain relief and antibiotics that he'd left on the nearby bench. 'Any problems, give me a call. I'd usually put on a cone collar, but she's scared enough and hasn't shown any sign of wanting to lick her paw.'

With a farewell wave, Trent accompanied Taite outside.

'Right.' Wyatt wrapped his arms around the dog. 'Let's get you off this table.'

He lifted the border collie down. Bundy padded over and the pair wagged their tails at each other. The sight dispersed some of the tension within him. Technically there was no further need for him to be there. The border collie would be in safe hands with Brenna and Bundy.

Except the strength of his need to stay surprised him. Not only did he want to make sure the dog was settled, he couldn't shake the feeling that something wasn't right with Brenna.

'Wyatt, she'll be okay.' Brenna took a step closer towards him.

Another thing he wasn't used to was having someone be in tune with what he was thinking. He kept his expression from changing. If he wasn't careful, Brenna would realise that when it came to her, his thoughts had never been neighbourly.

'I'll just do a day trip tomorrow to see Mia.'

'That's a big drive.'

He shrugged as the border collie came over to him for another pat. 'That way I can be back.'

'In case you need to say goodbye?'

He only nodded. Wedge continued to scowl in his direction and Brenna's pale blue gaze was too perceptive. As much as she knew about his past, he was still learning to be comfortable with someone knowing as much about him as she did.

Brenna continued to speak. 'I'll come. I can help drive. After all the rain, detours will make the trip longer. I'll find something to do while you're at Mia's.'

'Brenna—'

'Don't give me that look.' She cut off his polite refusal even though the city would have to be the last place she'd want to go. She glanced at Wedge. 'And you too.'

'It's too much of an imposition to ask.' Wyatt folded his arms.

'I agree,' Wedge said, tone disapproving. 'You hate it when there's even a traffic jam here.'

'I'll survive. It will be good for me. I've barely left Bundilla in … years.'

Wyatt uncrossed his arms. Had Wedge not been there, he would have reached for her. What Brenna was really saying was after what she'd been through, she hadn't wanted to leave the security of her home.

'Are you sure?'

'I am.'

If looks could maim he was certain Wedge had just dismembered him.

'Mia has been wanting to meet you so she wouldn't hear of you not coming for lunch.'

Wyatt gave the border collie a final rub behind her ears to reassure her that he would return. Brenna moved to place a comforting hand on the dog's head so she wouldn't follow him out of the stables. With a nod at Wedge, Wyatt left.

As he stepped outside, the icy rasp of the wind across his skin couldn't stop the warmth spreading through him. As much as he'd be missing Nick tomorrow, if there was anyone he'd want to spend the day with, it would be Brenna.

The dull grey start to what would have been Nick's birthday matched Wyatt's mood when he pulled up outside Brenna's front garden and parked alongside a battered white Hilux. Even the sweet perfume that drifted from the flowers on the back seat failed to soothe him. He'd already spoken to Mia twice and they'd both admitted that getting through today was going to be harder than they'd anticipated.

The noise of the engine faded but Wyatt didn't leave his seat. He stared at Wedge's Hilux. It wasn't only grief making him feel on edge. The old local had seen straight through him to the lost boy he'd been. Even though his grandparents had assured him he wouldn't turn into his father, Wedge's doubts provided a stark reality check. He could never be the man Brenna deserved or needed. He scrubbed a hand over his clean-shaven chin. He might again be dressed in tailored city clothes and occupy a world vastly different to his childhood, but he couldn't lose sight of Wedge's reminder about his past.

Bundy and the border collie dashed down the veranda steps. Their guest no longer limped and her coat was now free from dirt and tangles. He left his four-wheel drive to greet the dogs. Footsteps sounded and he glanced up to see Brenna and Wedge.

Brenna's blonde hair fell in loose waves down her back. He wasn't the only one to have altered his appearance. Instead of her usual farm clothes, Brenna wore a long tan wool coat tied at her waist, along with black jeans and pale pink cowgirl boots. As she turned he noticed the light application of makeup that made her eyes appear a startling blue, her cheekbones sharper and her lips fuller.

'Morning.' She briefly glanced at him before she checked the contents of her leather tote bag.

'Morning.'

Wedge shot him a scowl that would have curdled milk. He hadn't missed how Wyatt had been so busy taking in how stunning Brenna looked that he'd been slow to reply.

He gave Wedge a nod before opening the passenger door.

'That massive bouquet had better not be from the quilting ladies,' Brenna said from the veranda. 'It would have cost a fortune. I already feel bad about the money they've spent on their baking.'

'It's for Mia. This was today's delivery.' He reached in to remove a box that contained jars filled with red roses, dahlias and geraniums.

Brenna groaned. 'Of course, the flowers are all red. They'd better go to Hettie and Taite who I swear celebrate Valentine's Day every day.'

Wyatt carried the box up the stairs and set it on the ground beside the door.

Brenna turned to kiss Wedge's cheek. 'Thanks for looking after everyone. See you tonight. Don't forget Hettie said to come over for dinner.'

The old man flashed Brenna a grin. 'I won't.'

His faded gaze locked with Wyatt's, the warning clear.

Wyatt and Brenna bid the dogs farewell before Wyatt asked quietly, 'Would you like to drive?'

'I would. Thanks.' She cast him a serious glance. 'Not because I don't feel safe with you behind the wheel. I do. I just know the shortcuts.'

He slid into the passenger seat while Brenna walked around to the other side. Brenna saying she felt comfortable with him driving calmed the chaos within. She gave him a smile as she started the engine.

True to her word, Brenna drove along gravel roads he had no idea existed and avoided others that were closed due to minor flooding. Instead of taking the scenic route through the mountains, they headed west to the highway that would deliver them straight to Sydney. After the mountains had faded into the horizon behind them, they crossed a bridge strewn with golden leaves to stop at a small town for something to eat.

Once back in the four-wheel drive, with Wyatt now driving, Brenna's phone rang.

She took a few seconds to answer as she finished her chocolate caramel slice from the local bakery. 'Hi, Mabel.'

Wyatt relaxed his hold on the steering wheel at the confirmation the call wasn't from Trent. It wouldn't be long until the vet would ring to tell them that he'd heard from the border collie's owners. Wyatt was already dreading saying goodbye.

'You have?' Brenna said. 'That's wonderful. I'm with Wyatt so I'll put you on speaker.' She tapped the screen.

'Hi, Wyatt. So …' Excitement bubbled in the journalist's voice. 'Soph and I went through the digitised newspaper database. We thought we'd hit a dead end but then we struck gold.'

Brenna grinned. 'After seeing those sovereigns, I'm very partial to gold.'

Mabel laughed. 'Don't say that too loudly or guess what colour your next flower delivery will be.'

Brenna threw Wyatt a pained grimace.

He smiled. As much as he wouldn't admit it, seeing what theme the town matchmakers had come up with for that day had become part of his morning routine.

Mabel spoke again. 'Does the name Earl Ramsey sound familiar?'

'Wasn't he the man in the siege who unlocked the pub door to let the police in?'

'He was. Soph found a journal written by his sister, Victoria. Except Earl wasn't the upstanding local he appeared to be. He was rather taken with Victoria's best friend, who just happened to be … Alice.'

'No way,' Brenna said, holding her phone closer.

'We still have the bulk of the journal to read, a single entry goes for pages, but I wanted to give you a quick update. Alice had told Victoria about Clement and there were numerous references to Victoria trying to defuse her brother's anger at Alice rejecting him. Then, after Earl followed Alice and saw her meet up with Clement, Victoria's entries became about stopping her brother from breaking them up.'

'Earl sounds toxic,' Brenna said, her expression concerned.

'He was. When Clement went away, Earl ingratiated himself with Alice's family so much they believed an engagement was imminent.'

'That could be when the first lot of letters ended,' Wyatt said. 'Did the journal say where Clement went?'

'No but I'm thinking gold prospecting as Victoria said he went to strike it rich so he could be with Alice. After he'd left, Victoria wrote that her brother had become obsessed with having Alice.'

Wyatt gave Brenna a quick look which she returned with a small nod to say she was okay and that the parallel with her past wasn't triggering.

Mabel went on, 'Victoria describes several incidents between Earl and Clement, but in this last entry she mentions the pub siege. The hold-up was about the gold escort loot, but also Alice. So, the rumour passed down by the old publicans was true.'

'Let me guess,' Wyatt said. 'For Earl to let the police in, he was hoping Clement would be associated with the gang like his brother and cousin were, and then Earl would appear to be the better choice for Alice.'

'He wasn't just hoping … he'd taken stolen gold, which Victoria believes he blackmailed someone in the gang to get hold of, to plant in Clement's saddlebag. She told Alice, who then rode to find Clement's brother and cousin. That's why the gang went to the pub, to help Clement and to retrieve the gold. They obviously achieved their first goal but not the second as the gold was left behind and recovered by the police.'

Brenna frowned. 'Do we know what happened to this Earl?'

'I'll look up his death certificate and report back.'

'Thank you and please pass on our thanks to Soph. We can't wait to hear what you discover next.'

Mabel wished Wyatt and Brenna safe travels before ending the call.

Wyatt concentrated on the busy highway filled with trucks and impatient drivers. He'd been prepared for his emotions to be all over the place today. Relationships had never been on his radar and one with Brenna was especially off limits. But her inclusion of him in her parting comments magnified a longing he didn't have a name for.

Soon the lush paddocks and infrequent houses gave way to grey concrete and neat suburban streets. The blast of car horns and the roar of engines replaced the trill of galahs and rosellas. Once relaxed and at ease, Brenna now sat stiff and silent, her hands twisted in her lap.

She shuddered as they crawled along in a line of cars. 'Give me the mountains any day.'

'We're turning off soon. You'll like where Mia and Emily live. Nick made sure their family home was in a leafy area where they'd have space and privacy.'

As he'd hoped, once they'd left the congested highway and the streetscape became softened by green leaves, the tight line of Brenna's shoulders lowered. He parked outside a large house with an established garden dotted with touches of russet autumn colour.

Brenna stared through the side window. 'Are you sure I won't intrude? We passed a coffee shop … I could wait there.'

An unexpected vulnerability edged her words. Like yesterday he had a sense that something was wrong. As much as Brenna appeared at ease in his company, she'd spent more time looking away from him today than at him.

'Brenna …'

Her eyes met his, her expression guarded.

The urge to reassure her trumped the mental warning to not touch her. He lifted his hand and ran the back of his fingers over her cheek.

'Mia's really excited to meet you. She wants to hear about how you kicked me off the trek.'

'The unfiltered country girl version?'

He forced his arm to lower. Her skin was as soft as silk and the pink on her lips made it a constant struggle to keep his attention away from her mouth. 'She'd be disappointed with anything less.'

'Really?'

'Just be yourself.'

She slowly nodded.

Shoulders tight, he reached for his seatbelt. In another three seconds he'd be crossing every friend and neighbour line there was by tilting her chin and kissing her.

They left the four-wheel drive and went through the garden gate. They were only midway along the sandstone path when the front door opened. Dressed in a flowing blue dress, Mia waved at them. While her eyes were red-rimmed, her smile was warm.

She walked down the steps to pull Brenna close for a hug. 'It's lovely to meet you. I hope the drive wasn't too boring with Wyatt being on his phone working.'

Brenna shook her head and gave a quick grin. 'I was the only one to take a call.'

Mia's fine brows rose as she accepted the flowers Wyatt handed her. When she hugged him, she said in a teasing tone so only he could hear, 'Not a single work call, huh? I wonder why?'

Once inside Wyatt headed straight for the light and airy kitchen where he could hear cooing and rattling. Emily lay on her back on a mat as she used her feet and hands to grab and kick at the toys dangling on the play gym.

Wyatt scooped her up, relishing her squeals and laughter. He kissed the top of her downy head before tucking her into the crook of his arm.

Mia chuckled. 'Wyatt, for such a tough guy you're already putty in those chubby little hands. Just wait until Emily learns to give you puppy dog eyes, you'll have no chance.'

Brenna came over to meet Emily but stopped a short distance away, giving Mia an apologetic glance. 'I'm more used to foals than babies.'

The five-month-old turned to stare at Brenna. Wyatt felt Emily's weight shift as she reached out an arm towards her. Brenna edged closer.

'Watch your hair,' Mia warned. 'She won't be able to resist grabbing it.'

Brenna lifted her hand close to Emily's, who wrapped her tiny fingers around Brenna's thumb. Wyatt's whole world narrowed to the baby and woman smiling at each other.

His hypervigilance vanished. All he could focus on was the beauty and tenderness in Brenna's expression. All he could hear was the pounding of his heart. And all he could think was that he'd been such a fool.

He'd been blind to what really mattered. Nick had known all along what was important. It wasn't work or money. It was love. And that was what he felt for Brenna.

There was no other explanation for the yearnings that had surfaced since he'd met her. He wanted to share his life with someone. He wanted a home and a family. And the only person he wanted these things with was Brenna. He wanted her to look at their children the same way she did baby Emily.

His mouth dried. But wanting and having were two different beasts. Wedge was right to think he'd be no good for Brenna. Not because of any similarities to his father, but because losing Nick had exposed parts of himself that were lacking and in need of work. He'd been so driven to escape his past and achieve his career goals, he'd been oblivious to the importance of feelings and human connection.

He shifted Emily higher in his arms and avoided Mia's eyes. Mia was staring at him as though she knew how hard he'd fallen for Brenna and how out of his depth he was.

As much as he loved Brenna, he refused to be selfish like his father and put himself first. After knowing her history, now more than ever, Brenna needed someone emotionally stable and present. Two things he was no closer to becoming. Brenna's needs were all that mattered. His jaw locked, setting off a dull ache. Even if that meant he could never tell her how he felt or how desperate he was to spend his future by her side.

CHAPTER 31

The first thud of a hard hoof hitting wood vaguely registered as Brenna finished mucking out Belle and Cora's stall. The mare and foal were outside making the most of the brief appearance of the morning sun.

The second and very loud whack on a stall door had her straightening with a sigh.

'Major,' she said, voice loud. 'You will be next. You know you'll only roll in the mud then want to come inside because it's cold.'

The old chestnut snorted.

Brenna filled Belle's hay net with fresh hay. It wasn't Major's fault he was still in the stables and tetchy. She couldn't get her mind off Wyatt and onto what she was supposed to be doing. By now she'd usually have finished Major's stall, but she was going in slow motion. Just as well her morning clients had cancelled due to their farm road being impassable after the overnight rain. Thankfully Taite had needed to go to town so had taken Bundy to the school for his story dog duties.

As she opened Major's half door, he gave her an unimpressed side eye before sauntering out. Once he was in his paddock and the gate double latched so he wouldn't open it himself, Brenna busied herself cleaning his stall. Despite her best intentions, her thoughts returned to Wyatt.

If she wasn't already head over heels for him, after seeing him with baby Emily yesterday she'd have lost her heart again. She couldn't believe she'd ever considered him aloof and detached. He'd been attentive, caring and hands-on. Despite the gravity of the day, he'd made Mia laugh. When they'd shared stories about Nick, he'd listened and encouraged Mia to talk. If only Wedge could have seen how Wyatt had made the visit about everyone else but himself, then his worries about Wyatt being like his father would have been assuaged.

Realising she was standing in the middle of Major's stall doing nothing but staring at a cobweb in the corner, she rubbed at her temple. The problem was, as much as she'd enjoyed her day trip with Wyatt, she was no closer to working out what to do about her feelings for him. If anything, her uncertainty had intensified.

She felt tongue-tied and couldn't stare at him for too long lest she give away her thoughts. If she were her normal straightforward and confident self, she'd just ask him if he still believed that he was wrong for her. But she was discovering that when deep emotions were involved it wasn't so easy to be fearless. The stakes were too high. If all she could be to him was a friend and neighbour, that was far better than causing any awkwardness between them, let alone having him leave her life.

The visit to the city had reinforced that such a place was not for her. If a miracle happened and Wyatt did return her feelings, where they lived was a serious hurdle to any potential future. It was almost impossible to see a way they could make a long-distance relationship work or merge their two very different lives.

An indignant whinny warned her Major was wanting to return to the warmth of his stall. Reading herself the riot act, she worked without stopping until she was done. Once the grumpy chestnut was in his five-star accommodation, Brenna went to make herself a cup of tea.

She flicked the kettle on. When her phone chimed, she leaned against the bench and accepted the video call.

'Hi, Clance.' Behind the flower farmer Brenna recognised the white arches of a familiar farmhouse conservatory. 'Are you at Ashcroft?'

'Yes, we arrived last night.'

Clancy moved to the side and Heath's face appeared.

Brenna grinned. 'MacBride, you exist. And you're not covered in paint like when I last saw you. Welcome back.'

'It's nice to be home.'

She'd known Heath and Clancy all her life. She'd also become used to seeing their joy and their arms wrapped around each other. But there was an extra radiance in their smiles and Clancy's expressive grey gaze looked suspiciously bright.

'Clancy Parker, show me your left hand.'

Even before Clancy raised her arm, Brenna knew Heath had finally proposed. They'd exchanged a glance filled with such love, Brenna's eyes misted.

Light sparkled from the solitaire diamond ring on Clancy's slim finger.

Brenna blew them a kiss. 'Congratulations. You've made my morning. I'm so thrilled for you.'

'Thank you.' Happiness lilted in Clancy's words.

Brenna focused on Heath. 'Please tell me you didn't propose at the top of a cherry picker?'

As Heath spent most of his painting life on a boom lift, it was a running joke he'd ask Clancy to marry him in one.

'You'll be pleased to know I proposed in the stables.'

Brenna gave him a thumbs up. The stables at Clancy's historic farm were more than a place for her horses. Ashcroft had been her family home and held many poignant memories of her parents. They had loved Heath and had faith, even when he'd left Bundilla, that he'd find his way back to their daughter.

Clancy's eyes shone. 'We were supposed to go for a ride. I thought Heath had gone to saddle the horses. When I got there the stables were full of flowers and candles. Then I saw the chocolates and champagne.'

Brenna's chest ached at the sweetness of Heath's gesture. He knew Clancy so well and had to have planned this for weeks.

Heath's tone turned teasing. 'So, Brenna, you know what this means.'

She groaned. 'I do. My tripping-over-in-a-dress days are about to start again.'

Heath chuckled while Clancy's expression softened. 'As my maid of honour you can wear a pantsuit.'

'It's your special day. I said I would wear a dress and I will. Now, do you have a date in mind?'

Clancy shook her head. 'Maybe late spring? It just depends on how the season goes with my peonies.'

During spring Clancy would be busy cutting her fabulous flowers. 'Whenever it will be, I'm here for whatever you need me to do.' Brenna blew them a second kiss. 'Now you'd better get busy calling everyone. Once the bush telegraph gets wind of your engagement it will go into a frenzy.'

Clancy waved and Heath flashed her a grin before the call ended.

Brenna's mind buzzed with ideas about how to incorporate Clancy's palomino, Ash, into the celebrations. Heath's kelpie and Clancy's two golden retrievers would have to be involved as well as Bundy. She took out her phone to search for inspiration. She was only onto her second website about horse wreaths when the stable door opened.

Hettie's voice called out, 'I just got off the phone with Clancy and Heath … such exciting news.'

'It is.' Brenna stuck her head through the kitchenette doorway. 'Their wedding is going to be absolutely beautiful.'

She bit her lip to silence her fears that in a dress she'd be clumsy and awkward and stand out like a trout in a goldfish pond.

'Don't look so worried,' Hettie said as she stopped in front of her. 'Whatever you wear as maid of honour, you will be stunning.'

Hettie knew of her aversion to dresses as well as her promise to wear one for Clancy.

At Brenna's grimace, Hettie's gaze turned thoughtful. 'I have an idea … you're not going to like it … but this morning let's look for a practice dress.'

Before Brenna could back into the kitchenette, Hettie's gentle fingers clasped her wrist.

Brenna didn't know whether to frown or shake her head, so she did both. 'As thrilled as I am about Clancy and Heath's news, I need at least a week to psych myself up to even try one on.'

Hettie smiled as she tugged at Brenna's hand. 'Come on. We're both free for the next couple of hours. The sooner you have a practice dress, the more relaxed you'll be. You can complain the whole way to town.'

'Should I be worried that bossy tone sounds like me?'

Hettie gave her a sideways grin as they walked towards the stable door. 'I've learned from the best. Besides, after you're my maid of honour, I have no doubt Grace will want you in her bridal party next. Now Heath has proposed, you watch, Rowan will ask Grace. You'll be a dress-wearing expert by your own wedding.'

Brenna stopped. She'd been so concerned with finding someone, she'd never given her own wedding a thought, other than that a voluminous white dress would be her worst nightmare. She was only just coming to terms with loving Wyatt. Thinking any further beyond what to do about her feelings terrified her.

Hettie gave her a hug. 'Just breathe. If anyone is meant to be together it's you and Wyatt.' Hettie paused, her smile soft. 'And before you say that's hogwash, I've always known what he's meant to you even if you haven't always admitted it to yourself.'

There was no point disputing Hettie's words. Her old school friend knew her as well as she did herself.

Hettie tucked her arm in hers. 'Now, Miss Maid of Honour, let's go shopping.'

After a quick shower, all too soon Brenna found herself in the town's dress shop. A place she'd previously avoided as though it would give her equine influenza. The owner, Nancy, gave her a wide-eyed look before Hettie took charge.

After Hettie had handed Brenna three pink dresses and practically pushed her into the fitting room, Hettie said through the closed door, 'I want to see *every* dress, so no pretending to try them on. Oh, and you'll need this. I grabbed it while you were in the shower.'

Hettie opened the door to pass Brenna a familiar rose-pink bra that she rarely wore and bought on impulse before burying it in her bedroom drawer.

'You can't wear those hideous sports bras under a dress. I should have burned them at boarding school.'

'Yes, I can—'

Hettie shut the door on her protests.

'This is worse than any matchmaking,' she grumbled.

'I can hear you.'

Brenna stripped off her farm shirt and jeans. 'That had better be the back of that long pink dress as if it's the front, I won't be decent.'

Hettie laughed. 'It's the back.'

Brenna mentally ran through half her list of venting words as she struggled to put on the first dress. 'Okay, I'll come out, but only if there's no one around.'

'Taite's walked in, but otherwise the shop's empty.'

Brenna drew a deep breath that only popped the top button on the dress that barely did up around her chest and opened the fitting room door. As she walked out, despite wearing flat cowgirl boots, she stumbled in the full skirt.

As she righted herself, Hettie whistled while Taite's mouth fell open.

He covered his eyes with his hand. 'That's a no from me. I do not need to see that my twin has cleavage.'

Hettie grinned. 'I am so burning those sports bras. But yes, I don't think Bundilla is quite ready for Brenna the tomboy to become Brenna the runway lingerie model. I'll find the dress in the next size.'

Cheeks hot, Brenna disappeared into the fitting room. This had been the worst idea ever.

Her mobile rang and when she saw Wyatt's name she answered. At that point she was so desperate for an interruption she would have taken a call from Vernette.

'Hi,' she answered, hoping her voice wasn't too surly.

'Is everything okay?'

'It would be if I was a girly girl who didn't mind being imprisoned in a fitting room full of dresses. Please tell me there's some emergency I need to deal with.'

'No emergency.' Brenna could hear the smile in Wyatt's voice. 'But there's something odd going on with the quilting club. There were no morning deliveries.'

'You're kidding.'

Brenna didn't know whether to be relieved or rattled. The thought that the town matriarchs may have given up on her and Wyatt made her stomach plummet. Maybe this was a sign that she shouldn't do anything about her feelings.

'I'm not. Roy might miss the sponge cakes but Elsie has been enjoying the flowers.'

'I'm sure they're still plotting something.'

'We'll see.' Brenna couldn't work out from his neutral tone whether he'd be pleased or displeased if the deliveries continued. 'Trent called. The border collie's owners have responded to his messages. Her name's Tilly.'

'Tilly suits her.' Strain had deepened Wyatt's voice. He'd bonded with the border collie as much as the dog had with him. 'What's her story?'

'She's been missing for over two months and has travelled a long way from home. They were glad to hear she's been found but they live in town and she was always escaping. They're also expecting their first child so asked Trent about surrendering her to a rescue organisation. They said she needs somewhere with more space and owners who won't be as busy.'

'Wyatt ...'

She didn't need to put into words her offer to look after Tilly until Wyatt was in a position to keep her.

'I've already asked so much of you. I'm working on being here for longer than a week, but it's not going to happen soon.'

Her fingers found the silver chain of her mother's locket as she pushed aside the loss at not always having him next door.

'It's no trouble. I'd like to help. I've got used to having Bundy around and Waffles needs a friend.'

Silence.

Then Wyatt spoke, voice low. 'Thank you. I really appreciate your kindness.'

She closed her eyes and kept her reply light to hide how much his words moved her. 'I'll enjoy having Tilly when you aren't here. She's a sweetheart.'

Hettie knocked on the door before opening it and thrusting inside more dresses.

Brenna groaned. 'I'd better go before I drown under all these clothes. Hettie just gave me more things to try on.'

He chuckled. 'Good luck.'

For the next hour, Brenna gritted her teeth as she worked her way through Hettie's selections. Taite sat in a chair with a coffee looking drained.

When he gave a long-suffering sigh as Brenna appeared wearing a sleeveless sheath dress that made her skin itch, she put her hands on her hips. 'Hey, I'm the one doing it tough here. You hate clothes shopping as much as I do.'

Taite averted his eyes from the bodice that was again too fitted. 'Roy's going to ban you from playing pool if you turn up at the pub looking like that. He'll be breaking up fights all night.'

Brenna gave him a withering look. As if that would happen. She accepted another dress from Hettie. This one was sewn out of pink-and-white gingham. With its long loose sleeves, high neckline, belted waist and knee-length skirt, it looked as practical as a dress could be. As soon as she slipped it over her head and the fabric floated into place, she knew it would be bearable to wear. She walked out and twirled without tripping.

Taite gave a relieved nod. 'That's my pick.'

'Mine too,' Hettie said with a satisfied smile.

When she went to return to the fitting room to change into her usual clothes, Hettie caught her arm. 'No time like the present to practise.'

Brenna narrowed her eyes. She wondered why Hettie had taken her farm clothes. She'd thought it had been to give her more space in the change room. She now realised it was so she had no choice but to wear the new dress in public. No doubt Hettie would, in her sweet but determined way, talk her into going to the café for a brownie.

Taite slid his wallet into his shirt pocket after paying Nancy for the dress. 'Wedge texted. There's a bad storm coming.'

Even though the last thing they needed was rain—there'd been low-level flooding on the drive into town—the storm's arrival provided Brenna with a timely excuse to leave. Baby Cora would have never experienced a storm before, and she wanted to be there for her.

'I have to go,' she said before striding as fast as she could towards the door.

To her surprise Hettie didn't try to stop her. Instead she called after her, 'I'll head home with Taite seeing as Bundy hasn't finished at the school yet.'

Brenna stopped to turn and wave before hightailing it outside. To her relief she reached her four-wheel drive without causing anyone to veer off the main street at the sight of her in something other than jeans, though she did get two horn honks. She left town in a hurry.

Wedge had been right to send Taite the weather warning. The closer she drove to Glenwood Station, the darker the sky grew and the stronger the wind became. Leaves scooted across the road, cockatoos screeched as they sought shelter and stock stood with their rumps against the approaching storm.

As she passed beneath the iron archway, intermittent raindrops splattered the windscreen. Only a short while later, the drops had multiplied into a steady pitter-patter as she parked beneath the carport. Hettie still had the jacket she'd worn to town, but she'd be fine to make it the short distance to the stables.

Except Brenna had only made it halfway when the leaden sky burst open. Within seconds she was drenched. Water soaked the thin material of her dress, dripped from her loose hair and slid into the tops of her boots. She muttered increasingly colourful words under her breath as the wet fabric clung to her legs, making it difficult to walk without face-planting. It wasn't her gruelling Bundilla Cup course that was a safety hazard and would see her ending up in hospital but this dress.

She reached the awning of the stables and dragged the hair plastered across her face away so she could at least see. Water slid down her back like a trail of icy fingers. She could add being useless in a downpour to the litany of things she hated about wearing dresses. Thunder rumbled as she opened the stable door and squelched inside. She came to a sudden stop.

Instead of being greeted by anxious whinnies and horses peering over the half stall doors, the stables seemed empty and quiet. Even old Major wasn't in sight. Despite the determination of the wind to lift the roof eaves and the hammer of the heavy rain, everything felt peaceful.

Brenna took a step back. She could only hope Wedge was the reason why all appeared calm. If Wyatt were here, she needed to make a hasty exit. She wasn't sure what was worse: him seeing her in a dress or her looking like a drowned rat. She took another silent step backwards.

Then a familiar set of shoulders filled the doorway of Belle's stall and Wyatt stared straight at her.

CHAPTER 32

Even though Wyatt hadn't heard anyone enter the stables, when Belle's ears flickered towards the door, he guessed they had a visitor.

It wouldn't be Wedge. The old local had popped in earlier with Tilly and Waffles. As soon as he'd seen Wyatt checking on the horses, he'd left. Which meant Brenna had returned. Except when he caught sight of the country girl standing stock-still midway across the stables, it wasn't a Brenna he'd seen before.

Not only did she wear a dress but the wet material was practically transparent. He snapped his gaze away from the outline of the pink lace cupping curves no longer hidden by her farm shirts. Brenna was already shooting him a self-conscious frown. Now wasn't the time for his testosterone to forget that Brenna's needs had to come first, no matter how deeply he loved her or how much he was attracted to her.

He left Belle's stall. 'So, you made it out of the fitting room in one piece.'

He kept his words casual.

Brenna rubbed her arms. 'Don't get me started on how torturous this morning was.'

He stopped a body length away, telling himself not to even think about pulling her close to warm her. 'Would you like a towel? I'm sure I saw some in the kitchenette cupboard.'

'There's no point, I'm drenched. I'll head off for a shower in a second.'

When her teeth clattered, he tugged off his navy half-zip woollen jumper and draped it over her shoulders.

'Thanks.' Her fingers buried themselves in the thick wool as she pulled it tight around her. 'Cora okay?'

'She hasn't been worried at all. Major was a little spooked but he calmed down when he realised I had apples.'

She nodded before tipping her head to the side and scrunching her hair. When she squeezed, water streamed into the puddle forming around her boots.

His jumper slid down on her shoulders and he reached out to tug it higher. Her skin felt ice-cold and she shivered against his fingertips. Without thought, he curved his palm around her nape to share his warmth. When she didn't move, he swept his thumb across the delicate hollow of her collarbone to smooth away the droplets beaded there.

'Are you sure you don't want a towel?'

She shook her head, her eyes searching his.

When she swayed towards him, he took her in his arms. Her palms rested against his chest, seeking his heat. He held her, uncaring that water seeped through his shirt. When Major whinnied, Brenna didn't step back. Instead her hands slid upwards and her cold fingers stroked the bare skin at his throat.

As light as her touch was, the fine tremor that passed through her, along with her steady gaze, communicated that her action hadn't been accidental. Despite their agreement at the creek, she too wanted more.

He traced the delicate point of her chin.

'You have no idea how beautiful you are, do you?' Not even a crack of thunder could hide how hoarse his words were. 'It's been almost eight weeks …' He dipped his head to press his mouth to the side of her neck. 'I can't stop looking at you.'

'That makes two of us.' Her fingers toyed with the top button on his shirt. 'What did you mean when you said you weren't right for me? Is that the city-country thing?'

'Not at all.' His arm curved around her waist to draw her closer. Even a small space between them was too much. 'It's just … I'm not exactly a poster boy for functional relationships.'

'I've seen you with Mia and Emily. You're great with them.'

'I'd be lying if I said it hasn't been a struggle.'

'None of us are perfect.' She stretched to touch her lips to his jaw. 'That's what makes us human.'

'This simplified box system? Do I still not tick anything?'

He needed something, anything, to put the brakes on what was happening between them before they crossed a line they shouldn't.

'You tick the only box that matters.' She spoke slowly as though weighing each word. 'Being someone worth ditching my rules for.'

His control hung by the thinnest of margins, but he'd given his word to Taite that he'd do the right thing by his twin.

'Brenna … you had those rules for a reason.' His words felt and sounded as rough as weathered stone. 'I'm not the person you should discard them for. Let's get you back to the house for a hot shower.'

'I don't need a hot shower. I need you.'

The resolve and certainty in her voice was accompanied by her hands sliding into his hair. His head lowered to meet her mouth even before his self-control registered it was fighting a lost cause. When it came to Brenna, it had always been a battle he was destined to lose. His palms mapped her shape as she melted against him.

Having the woman he loved in his arms was like what he'd imagined it was to come home. All his misshapen pieces fit together, making him feel whole. His past no longer held any power or sway. There was only heat, hope and an irrefutable happiness. And Brenna seemed as lost as he was.

Cheeks flushed and eyes a vibrant blue, she pulled away to murmur, 'Bedroom … second door on the left.' She drew his head down to say close to his lips, 'And don't ask me if I'm sure, because not only is that wasting time, but I've never been so sure of anything in my life.'

Wyatt smiled against her mouth before swinging her off the ground and into his arms.

The storm had passed and the heavy drum of rain on the stable roof had become a gentle shower, but still Wyatt remained awake. His eyes might be shut as Brenna's soft breaths feathered across his throat while she slept, but he didn't want to miss a second of being with her. Life had changed too often for him to not be wary of feeling content and at peace. He needed to savour having Brenna's warmth pressed against him, and the sheets tangled around them. As much as he wanted a future with her, there was no guarantee that life wouldn't lob further curve balls at either of them.

A change in Brenna's breathing told him she was awake. Her fingers drifted through the front of his hair, followed the line of his cheekbones and touched the lashes of his closed eyes. Her head lifted from where it rested on his arm before her fingers smoothed over the scar on the back of his hand. He'd pulled the blanket up to cover her, not wanting her to feel cold, and his hand lay curved around her hip.

At the sudden intake of her breath his eyes snapped open. Her fingers had stilled to rest near his scar. Had seeing his old injury up close triggered her memories?

'Wyatt, how did you get this? Was it when you were a child?'

As hard as he fought, he couldn't stop tension from stealing into his jaw. Even if she hadn't remembered that he was the boy at the doctor's, he owed it to her to tell her the whole story even if it could change things between them.

'My father. I didn't move fast enough. And yes, I was young.'

Anger flared in her gaze. 'Just as well your father isn't around to get a piece of my mind.'

Wyatt cupped her cheek and kissed her. When he drew away, softness had returned to her expression.

'It happened here … in Bundilla.'

Her eyes widened but she didn't look surprised. 'You are that boy.' She sat up, her hand pressing the blanket to her chest. 'The boy in the doctor's.'

'I am. You told me boys could cry and gave me your chips.'

'That's right. Did you know who I was when we met?'

'To be honest I buried the memory. I was embarrassed. Roy reminded me the night he told us we'd be neighbours that we'd once seen each other as kids.'

Her brow furrowed. 'Why were you embarrassed? You were a child.'

'I'd let my emotions overwhelm me. I didn't mention it as I'd hoped you'd not remember. I don't want you to think of me as that broken boy.'

'Wyatt … that would never happen.' Her lips touched his but then she pulled away. He tried not to read too much into the action even if his gut said things had already shifted between them. While they still were side by side, her body no longer touched his. 'If anything, it just makes me respect you more.'

'Respect?'

It wasn't exactly the emotion he'd been hoping for.

'Yes, respect … and that's only the start of how I feel about you.'

If this was any other conversation, his fears would have stood down. But Brenna had spoken in a subdued tone, her eyes solemn.

She laced her fingers with his and lifted their hands to kiss his scar. 'This doesn't change how I think about you … but what it does change is how I think about me.' Colour crept into her cheeks. 'After I saw you, even though my mother said you weren't a local boy, I looked everywhere for you. And the trouble is … I have a feeling I've never stopped.'

He brushed his thumb across her hand, trying to understand what she was saying and why looking for him was a problem. But Brenna didn't give him any opportunity to ask for clarification.

She eased her fingers free to rub her forehead. 'I think … before we go any further with this …' She waved between them. 'It would be wise to make sure we're both in the right place. And I have some things to process. I understand if asking for some space is too much.'

Instead of speaking, he leaned over to cradle the back of her head and seek her mouth. Even though Brenna returned the tenderness of his kiss, he could feel her tension in the tightness of her shoulders.

When they drew apart, he said, voice a low rasp, 'I'm not going anywhere. I'll be here, waiting.'

As a child Wyatt was used to days feeling like they'd never end. But as an adult, he'd filled them with work so they never seemed long enough. Ever since he'd spent Thursday afternoon in the stables with Brenna, time had dragged. The reality was less than forty-eight hours had passed.

Apart from seeing Brenna on Ebony yesterday, when she'd given him a nod, their paths hadn't crossed. Brenna was avoiding him. While he was certain she wouldn't have mentioned what had happened between them to Wedge, the old man had taken great delight in telling him that Brenna was preparing for the Bundilla Cup and Wyatt wasn't to bother her.

So he made sure he didn't stay like he usually did whenever he visited Belle, Cora and Murphy and Co. He also settled for texting Brenna instead of calling. For the second morning in a row, there hadn't been any quilting club deliveries. He refused to see this as an omen that he and Brenna had no future together.

He slid his phone out of his jeans pocket to see if there was any reply to his earlier message wishing her good luck for the cup today. All around him the bush festival was in full swing. Whips cracked to his right while over in the arena horses and riders participated in a stock handling challenge. Despite the overcast day, spectators were rugged up in coats and huddled together in camp chairs and on the showground stands. A smaller crowd had gathered around a shed where blacksmiths were competing in a horse-shoeing event.

The breeze carried the aroma of lamb and gravy rolls from the food trucks while the vintage coffee van could barely be seen thanks to the queue for hot drinks. He could do with a coffee too except he had a country girl to find first.

When he'd confirmed there was still no reply from Brenna, he returned his phone to his pocket. As much as Brenna's needs were a priority and as much as he understood her needing space to work through things, he couldn't shake a sense of dread. He used to get the same feeling as a child whenever he'd begin to feel settled somewhere but knew that soon his father would wake him and they'd leave.

He headed for the area beyond the arena jam-packed with trucks and horse floats. If Brenna had arrived, she had to be there somewhere. He'd only walked three paces when he heard his name being called. He turned to see a corrugated iron pavilion with quilts hanging inside. A group of ladies were gathered at the entrance staring at him.

Vernette waved gaily. 'Wyatt.'

He changed direction to head over. The quilting club had spent time and money on him and Brenna. He needed to thank them again for everything they'd done.

Mrs Moore stepped forwards to give him a hug. Then the other ladies, some he'd never met, followed. In the space of five minutes, he hugged more people than he had in his entire life.

Vernette patted his arm. 'Brenna's so lucky. Elsie said you'd become a hugger.'

He rubbed at the stubble on his jaw. As well-meaning as the matchmakers were, they couldn't have an inkling that things had developed between him and Brenna. If there was to be any chance for their connection to grow into something more, it had to remain private. 'Brenna and I are not together.'

Technically it was the truth.

'Oh, pish posh,' Vernette said, her eyes sparkling behind her glasses as though she knew exactly what had happened in the stables. Which she couldn't. 'The two of you are so well suited.'

Wyatt raised a brow towards a group of young fellows he recognised from the pub. With their swagger, hats pulled low and muddy boots, by anyone's definition they were more of a fit for Brenna than he could ever be.

Vernette chuckled. 'Those young fellows had no hope.'

'We're all thrilled Brenna's finally going to ride in the cup,' Mrs Moore piped up. 'When she wins, we hope there'll be a congratulatory kiss.'

Wyatt kept his expression deadpan. He was sure one elderly lady just waggled her grey brows at him. 'I've no doubt she'll win and I'm sure there will be many people lining up to kiss and congratulate her.' He looked around the group of ladies. 'I'd best keep moving, I just wanted to thank you for the flowers.'

'You're very welcome.' Vernette gave him a beaming smile. 'And don't think we've forgotten about you and Brenna. We're just up to phase two.'

'Phase two?'

'Yes, dear, the consolidation phase. It won't be long now until phase three.'

Wyatt knew he shouldn't ask, but he still did. 'Which is?'

'The celebratory phase. That's why there've been no more deliveries; we've been getting ready for our favourite stage.'

Wyatt could hold his nerve when the stock market was in a freefall but right then he felt the urge to retreat. Every pair of quilting club eyes held an anticipatory gleam.

He gave a nod. 'Ladies … enjoy the festival.'

As he walked away, his phone vibrated as messages whooshed in. The first one was from Brenna thanking him and saying she'd see him after the race. The second was from Taite letting him know that he and Rowan had saved him a seat in the stands to watch the cup. After he checked to see if they wanted a coffee, he went to line up in the drinks queue before weaving his way through the crowds to join them.

When Brenna rode up to the starting line on Ebony, Wyatt had difficulty focusing on what Taite and Rowan were saying. He caught something about the ute in the arena being driven by a course marshal with a photographer in the passenger seat.

Taite glanced at him. 'Wyatt, relax. This course will be a walk in the park compared to the one at home my sister thinks I don't know about.' He tapped his nose. 'There's a reason why it stays clear of branches and the fallen trees just so happen to be in a perfect position to jump. I had to make sure I moved them before a storm so the rain would wash away the tractor tyre marks.'

Wyatt leaned forwards in his seat as the starting gun sounded. From the outset of the race, it was obvious Brenna had a game plan. She held Ebony back and kept to the edge of the group. As the slower horses fell away, she maintained a steady pace. After several horses baulked at jumping the strategically placed logs, the field further thinned. Hooves pounded as the riders tackled a steep slope and then, once at the top, disappeared into the timber.

'Keep your eye on the hill to the left above the creek,' Taite said. 'Brenna should have pulled out in front by now.'

Taite's prediction proved true. Ebony's black coat shone as the mare appeared and then plunged down the almost vertical incline, no other horse beside her. Brenna had almost reached the bottom when the other riders became visible.

Taite took a picture on his phone. 'Brenna's just got to get across the creek ... they've changed the course to make it safer, but the level's higher than usual.'

Water exploded around Ebony as she surged across the fast-flowing creek. Wyatt released a tight breath when Brenna made it to the other side. She had a clear run to the finish line and there was no way another rider could catch her.

A shrill and anxious neigh from a cluster of horses on the far side of the creek cut through the crowd's chatter. The sudden silence turned into a collective gasp as a bay and chestnut collided. The chestnut stumbled, flinging its rider out of the saddle and into the water. Brenna looked over her shoulder and slowed Ebony before turning to race back and help.

While some riders had stopped, others charged forwards. Brenna cut a wide swathe to avoid them. Except when she reached the creek, a second group burst across the water. Wyatt felt Taite tense beside him. The spray kicked up by the horses' hooves would obscure the riders' visibility.

Wyatt stood to make sure he kept sight of Brenna. As if in slow motion he saw a grey horse head straight for where Brenna had halted at what should have been a safe distance away from the fallen rider. While the grey horse swerved, it was too late and its shoulder cannoned into Ebony. The mare was slammed sideways, Brenna's body snapping in the saddle.

Then, before Wyatt could see if Brenna could right herself and Ebony regain her feet, a group of horses thundered past to block his view.

CHAPTER 33

In all the years Brenna had imagined how her ride in the Bundilla Cup would go, she'd never envisioned that she'd be in an empty horse float being kissed senseless by a city boy.

When Wyatt lifted his head, his grey eyes storm-dark, she placed her hands on either side of his face.

'Wyatt, I'm okay. Really.'

He kissed her again, leaving her in no doubt about how worried he'd been.

He tugged her close and rested his chin on the top of her head. She slid her arms around him and relaxed into the warm strength of his embrace. The adrenaline rush inside her subsided.

Things had been dicey by the creek when the grey had smashed into Ebony. But she'd managed to stay in the saddle and dismount when the last of the horses had passed to help the rider in the creek. It had been the young redhead from the bar and he'd escaped with only a sprained wrist. His chestnut was uninjured, along with the bay who had also taken a hit in the collision.

While she hadn't won the cup, it was as though she had. The crowd had been just as interested in her good sportsmanship as they were the winner. The race was as exhilarating as she'd hoped, even if it hadn't been as challenging as she'd expected. She couldn't wait to enter again.

As if privy to her thoughts, Wyatt's voice growled in his chest. 'Next year I'm wrapping you in bubble wrap.'

'Next year you can ride with me.'

He pulled away to look at her. 'Deal.'

Despite his levity, Wyatt's eyes retained a haunted look that had her tighten her hold on him. Too many times in his life he'd never had a chance to say goodbye. In all of the chaos, he would have imagined the worst.

His lips touched her hair. 'I know we're still giving each other space, but after this afternoon my city life feels too far away. I should be here.'

She leaned back so she could have a clear view of his face, even if that meant him seeing her frown. 'What do you mean? You'll move to Bundilla permanently?'

'I'll step aside and let someone else run my company.'

A rush of panic had her step out of his arms. 'Wyatt, I can't let you do that.'

Instead of replying, he stared at her, his gaze fixed and assessing.

'Wyatt. *Please* don't. Just don't give up your life … for me.'

'Brenna.' His voice was quiet as he reached out to caress her jaw. 'I'd do anything for you.'

She closed her eyes to hide the emotions prickling behind her lids. She couldn't remember when she'd been so close to crying.

His mouth brushed across her eyelids. 'Talk to me.'

She leaned into him, trying to find the words to convey all that she was feeling. 'You can't just drop everything … it's too much. Mia and Emily need you and I …'

'Don't?'

His voice was as bleak as she'd ever heard it. Her eyes flew open. She placed her palm on his chest. 'I do need you … it's just that I might not be *enough*.'

His hand covered hers, holding it in place. As if understanding how much effort it took for her to find further words, he stayed silent.

'I wasn't strong enough to save my mother. I wasn't enough of anything to please my father and to keep him engaged with life. The truth is it will break me if I'm not enough for you. If you moved here, only to leave because the reality of being with me wasn't what you expected.'

'I understand.'

'Do you? Wyatt, you could have any woman you wanted. As for me … this is what I needed to process after discovering you were the boy in the doctor's … you're the only man I want. I know we were kids but I thought you were the most beautiful boy I'd ever seen. Before I even talked to you, I whispered to my mother I was going to marry you.' She reached up to touch his cheek. 'Every guy I went out with had dark hair and high cheekbones, but none of them were you. And now I've found you, if we don't work …'

He caught her fingers and placed a kiss on her wrist before threading their hands together. From the gravity in his eyes she hoped he grasped how serious she was.

Just to make sure, she spoke again. 'I'm not sure how long this will take to work through. It could be one day, one week or one month.'

'I'll wait however long you need.'

The sincerity in his words and the softness in his eyes caused her throat to ache. She loved him with a depth that was almost incomprehensible. If only she had more faith that she wouldn't end up disappointing him.

As hard as it was to do, she shook her head. 'Wyatt … I need you to promise me something.'

'Anything.'

She swallowed. What she was about to say could cost her the man she loved.

'I need you to promise not to wait for me if life shows you that you should be anywhere but here with me.'

He didn't hesitate. 'I promise.'

Then he kissed her with such care and tenderness, her heart was in danger of breaking.

When he raised his head, he tucked the hair that had come loose from her braid behind her ear. 'Let's get you and Ebony home.'

She nodded and went to walk down the ramp to collect the mare from her portable yard. Except when she heard voices and then Vernette call her name, she spun around to look for Wyatt. They couldn't be caught together by the quilting club, especially after the talk they'd just had. There was no way she could appear cool and composed when beside him.

He gave her a wink before disappearing out the door at the front side. She took a deep breath, plastered on a smile and headed outside.

Vernette, Mrs Moore and Mrs Walters were standing beside the float, their expressions jubilant. Mrs Walters held an oversized tote bag that she lowered to sit on the ground.

'Congratulations,' Mrs Moore gushed, taking hold of Brenna's arm and giving her an excited squeeze. 'That was such a great ride.'

Vernette nodded. 'Your parents would have been so proud. Especially that father of yours who was always so tough on you.'

'Thanks …' Brenna forgot what else she was going to say when all three ladies suddenly looked at something over her shoulder. She didn't dare turn lest she see Wyatt striding away. If it was him they were staring at, it would have been obvious he'd been in the float with her.

But when Mrs Wright murmured, 'They make such a lovely couple,' Brenna risked turning. Relief filled her when she saw Trent and city-girl Aubrey walking hand in hand.

'Speaking of lovely young couples,' Vernette said, her attention zeroing in on Brenna. 'We've been working on a surprise for you and Wyatt.'

Brenna hoped her frown masked the tumult inside her. 'We aren't a couple.'

Mrs Moore smirked. 'We understand it's not official and won't be until Bundy goes on to stay with someone else, but we wanted you to have this for when it is.'

Brenna's tension quickly gave way to surprise and then delight as Mrs Wright pulled a quilt out of the tote bag. Featuring a white background and intersected circles patchworked out of an assortment of pink floral material, Brenna recognised the design as a traditional wedding ring pattern. Her mother had been given a similar gift as a wedding present.

No wonder there'd been no recent deliveries; the project would have been a mammoth task to undertake. She was humbled by the quilting club's support and faith. The quilt was exactly what she would have wanted should she ever be a bride. 'I love it. Thank you so much. I don't know what to say.'

'You don't have to say anything, Brenna dear.' If Brenna didn't know better she would have said Vernette's usual sharp gaze had grown teary. 'Just live the life you deserve and the one your mother always dreamed for you.'

Mrs Wright handed Brenna the bag and after each woman gave her a hug, they strolled away. It was only after they'd left that Brenna realised not only had she accepted the quilt without a fight but in doing so she'd confirmed there was something between her and Wyatt after all.

She stared into the tote bag at the quilt that had been so lovingly made for her. For the gift to one day become a real wedding quilt, she had to somehow find the key to unlocking her emotional baggage. And not only did she not know where to start looking, she had to do so before life proved to Wyatt that his future wasn't here in the mountains with her.

As physically and mentally exhausted as Brenna felt when she arrived home, once her stable chores were done and she'd eaten the shepherd's pie Taite had left for her, the idea of having an early night held no appeal. Her overtired brain would only spin in circles thinking about Wyatt.

So she brought in an extra load of wood, lit the dining room fire and fetched her laptop, the family journals and the photograph albums from her office. Mabel had called. She and Soph had finished going through Victoria's journal and were coming out tomorrow to finally piece together Alice and Clement's life.

With a deep sigh, Brenna went to collect her mother's jewellery box. She sat it on the far end of the table so she wouldn't be tempted to lift the lid. Her emotions had already taken enough of a battering today. She couldn't yet face reading the letter inside that her mother had left for her. She had no idea what it contained, only that her mother had said Brenna would know when to open it.

With Bundy and Tilly asleep on the nearby rug, she flipped through the photo albums searching for pictures of her mother before turning on her laptop. The soft snores of the dogs and the crackle of the fire faded as she dug deeper into the circumstances surrounding Alice and Clement's death.

An old digitised newspaper article confirmed that both her theories had been true. The tragedy had been the result of an accident as well as a flood. Alice had been swept away by floodwater and Clement had jumped in to save her. Neither had survived. Despite the warmth of the room, Brenna shivered. With rain drumming on the roof and adding to the already overflowing local creeks and river, it wasn't hard to imagine the couple's fear and desperation.

'Brenna?'

Taite's voice, and then his footsteps, pulled Brenna out of her thoughts.

'In here.'

She'd missed hearing his knock, so he'd let himself inside. He entered the living room and dropped a kiss on her forehead before going to pat Bundy and Tilly.

When he sat in the chair beside Brenna, his intent blue gaze met hers. 'Can't sleep?'

She shook her head.

Taite's attention went to the pages she'd left open of the photo albums. She'd filled him in on Roy's news about her mother having loved someone besides their father.

'So this is Tony?' Taite said, examining the photo of their young mother smiling at a dark-haired man with a generous smile.

'It is. They look so happy.'

Taite studied a nearby photo of their parents on their wedding day. 'Mum looks happy here too.'

'She does. Even though she lost Tony she found love again. Taite … if anything happened to Hettie would you be able to do the same?'

The stark bleakness in his eyes gave her his answer before he replied. 'No, but Hettie wouldn't want me to live the rest of my life alone. Is this about Wyatt?'

'Yeah.' She was past the point of pretending she didn't have feelings for him. 'He was in Bundilla years ago with his father. He's the salt and vinegar boy.'

Taite's eyebrows shot skywards. He was familiar with the story of Brenna being smitten with a boy his mother had named after the chips she had given him.

Brenna spoke again. 'He's the only one I'd want … ever.'

'And you're worried you're not enough and might lose him.'

'How do you know? Actually, *don't* answer that. I don't want to know if you feel what I do.'

Taite chuckled. 'Too late. We've always denied we have this whole twintuition thing going on … but, Brenna, I do feel what you do, even if it's just an echo. That's why I came to see you on the trek, not because of any wild dog, but because I felt the way you'd reacted to Wyatt.'

She bit the inside of her cheek as she realised the full implication of what Taite had said. He'd have to have experienced the emotions she went through when dealing with Neil.

Taite reached for her hand. 'You've always been so fiercely independent. It's okay if you haven't told me everything that's happened in your life. I just hope one day you will.' She nodded without hesitation. 'But right now we need to talk about Wyatt.

I'm guessing he doesn't know you love him … I obviously don't know how he feels but when he thought you'd been hurt today … Brenna, he cares deeply for you too.'

'He said he'll leave the city to be with me. What happens if this is a mistake? Of all the things you and I have been through, I've never felt fear like this. As much as I want to be with him, I can't imagine my life without him in it. Especially if I'm … not enough and the reason why we didn't end up working.'

'Brenna … Dad was a difficult man. I didn't always feel enough for him and he was harder on you than me. We were enough, especially you. The choices he made before and after Mum died are not on us.' He tugged her close for a hug. 'You *are* more than enough for Wyatt. And if he wasn't enough for you, I wouldn't have let his tyre down after the trek.'

She pulled back. 'What?'

Taite's grin was unrepentant. 'Wyatt's wheel rim was damaged. He'd just have been able to make it back to Sydney.' Taite reached over to close the photo albums. 'Go to bed. Tomorrow's a new day and after some sleep things will appear clearer.'

When dawn did arrive, it wasn't the usual birdsong that woke Brenna but her phone going ballistic. Pushing her hair off her face, brain foggy, she scooped her mobile from off the bedside table.

The first voice message was from Taite. All traces of sleep vanished. Thanks to the torrential rain overnight, the river had burst its banks and there'd been flash flooding on the far side of town. He and Hettie were going in to help. The roads were open to their end of the valley, so he suggested she get ready to have horses arrive.

The next message was from Trent asking if she had any room for horses needing a temporary home and what medical supplies she had to treat minor injuries. She fired off a reply saying she could have as many horses as needed and that she had a fully stocked medicine cabinet.

The third message was from Wyatt saying he was heading out with Roy to a farmer whose horses were trapped by the floodwater. Now half out of bed, her fingers flew across the screen as she tapped out a message telling him to be safe.

By the time the sun had risen, Brenna had received three float loads of wet and frightened horses. Wedge arrived to help her treat the ones with cuts and abrasions. She kept Trent updated with any that would require further veterinary care. The morning passed in a flurry of activity as more displaced horses arrived. News filtered in of how fast the water had risen, of cars being washed away, buildings inundated and stock going missing. Thankfully no human lives had been lost.

Brenna was gulping her third coffee for the day—she had no idea when she'd last eaten as her hasty breakfast was hours ago—when Hettie walked into the kitchenette. She carried a thermos and container of cupcakes. Without a word, she collected a bowl from the cupboard, poured Brenna some steaming pumpkin soup and pointed to a chair.

Brenna reached for another bowl into which she emptied the rest of the soup. 'If I have to have food, you do too.'

While Hettie's skin was usually pale, today she looked ashen from exhaustion. As they both sat down to eat, Hettie cast Brenna a sombre look.

'It's such a mess out there but at least the flooding seems to have peaked.'

'It never ceases to amaze me how quickly the water can rise and then how fast it can go down.'

Hettie glanced at where Brenna's phone lay over on the bench. 'I don't suppose you've been on social media.'

'Only to check for people looking for somewhere to put their horses.'

Hettie took out her phone. 'Well, you'd better see this before it goes viral.'

She held up an image of a man riding through thigh-deep floodwater while leading another two horses. Even without recognising Wyatt's muscled back and broad shoulders beneath the wet shirt, Brenna knew it was him. The way he sat on a horse was unmistakable.

'Wyatt's okay,' Brenna quickly reassured her. 'But he's about to become the town's new favourite son. There are reporters asking who the handsome local hero is and stories are already circulating about the horses he's saved.'

Brenna sensed there was something she wasn't telling her.

'There's more, isn't there?'

Hettie nodded slowly. 'I've checked with Grace to make sure what I heard was true, and it is. Wyatt has offered the Strathdale farmhouse to a family and the cottage to an elderly couple whose homes have been damaged. He's already organised for Grace to furnish them.' Hettie paused. 'The thing is, apparently he said they could stay for as long as they needed … because he wouldn't be living there.'

The warmth of the soup failed to combat the chill that coursed through her. Hand unsteady, she set her spoon on the table and pushed her bowl away. It might be a new day, but things didn't appear clearer—they looked worse.

Wyatt's childhood had been unstable, uncertain and unpredictable. The same words could be used to describe living in a rural environment. There was no guarantee that Wyatt would always be able to say goodbye to the people and animals he cared about. Change could happen as quickly as a riverbank giving way.

Her chest tightened, making it hard to breathe. She'd made Wyatt promise not to wait for her if life showed him that he shouldn't be here in the mountains with her. The flash flooding and devastating aftermath could very well have delivered the message.

CHAPTER 34

Another saying Wyatt's grandmother had believed in was about knowing when to walk away. And Wyatt had followed this advice throughout his adult life.

Except as much as his heart told him this wasn't one of those occasions, in order to give Brenna the space she needed, perhaps this was what he had to do. She'd been so upset at the prospect of him relocating to Bundilla, he couldn't cause her any further hurt. Which was why he'd agreed to her promise.

He tunnelled a hand through his shower-damp hair as he drove along the road that would take him to Glenwood Station. While rivulets ran like small streams down gullies, this higher side of town had been spared from any flash flooding. The setting sun cast long shadows as night closed in. He'd been up since before dawn.

As tired as he was, he'd only stopped at the pub to shower and change into dry clothes. When he popped in to reassure Elsie he was fine, she'd barricaded the door and wouldn't let him out until he'd eaten. She told him that turning up to Brenna's looking like he did would only make her so worried she'd pass out. They both knew this was the last thing Brenna would do.

But Elsie's concern reminded him that he had to have his wits about him when he did see Brenna. Even though they'd touched on many things yesterday in the horse float, there was still much to say between them. While he was better at handling his emotions, yesterday he hadn't exactly been thinking straight after seeing her caught up in the race melee.

He wasn't sure exactly when he'd realised that he controlled his feelings and that they no longer controlled him. Most likely it was when he'd admitted to himself that he loved Brenna. But despite this new clarity, loving someone and having a relationship with them was breaking new ground for him. As Brenna had said, he was only human, and as such, he'd make mistakes. He just had to keep them to a minimum. Which was why he hadn't texted Brenna to let her know that he was coming out. He was certain she'd only tell him to stay in town and rest.

When he pulled up outside the stables there were horses everywhere—in yards, paddocks and even down around Taite and Hettie's cottage. Most wore rugs and all looked to be recovering after everything they'd been through.

He opened the stable door and walked into the warmth. Bundy and Tilly raced to meet him. Except only Wedge appeared from the kitchenette. He gave the older man a nod. He'd visit the homestead and if Brenna wasn't there, he'd try Taite's cottage.

But before Wyatt could leave, Wedge cleared his throat. 'Wyatt, I owe you an apology.'

He shook his head. 'One isn't necessary. My father wasn't a decent man. We both know that. I appreciate you looking out for Brenna.'

Wedge grunted. 'Fat lot of good that did. Brenna's like that tawny frogmouth owl I warned not to fall for the male who lived in the tree hollow and ate too much, but she did anyway. They're partners for life.' Wedge gave a slight smile. 'They did have adorable chicks, though.'

'I'll try not to eat too much.'

'Eat as much as you want … you proved yourself today. You're nothing like your father.'

'That means a lot. Thank you.'

Wedge waved away his words. 'Let's not get ahead of ourselves. You can thank me later, when you and Brenna have talked. Her father has a lot to answer for as to why she's reluctant to accept help, but if ever she needs some, it's now. You both do, if what they're saying about you today is true.' The older man scratched his grey whiskered chin. 'You'll find her where they spread her mother's ashes. It's the hill beside the scrolled gate on the drive in. Walk up to the snow gums, she'll be there.'

Bundy padded over to lean against Wyatt's leg.

Wedge gave a mirthless chuckle. 'See, even Bundy knows you'll need all the luck you can get.' Wedge's hard gaze softened. 'But you're the only man who has come close to keeping up with her, so I hope things work out for you both.'

Wyatt drove to the gate Wedge had described. Brenna must have walked as there was no vehicle parked anywhere along the driveway. He shrugged on a jacket. Until things were resolved between them, he wasn't sure he'd ever feel warm again. He went through the gate and followed a well-worn track up to a stand of graceful snow gums.

Brenna sat on a bench that Taite had welded out of items that must have been important to their mother. Brenna's shoulders were hunched, one hand in her coat pocket and the other on the silver chain around her neck as she stared across the valley.

Before he was close enough to say her name, Brenna's blonde head whipped around. While no smile lit up her face, there was no defensive reaction like on the trek or in the kitchenette. She slid over to make room for him. He sat, making sure their bodies didn't connect. As much as he needed to touch her, if they were to have any sort of conversation about a way forward, he had to stick to the give-each-other-space rule.

'This is a beautiful spot,' he said to break the strain.

'It is. I come here to remember my mother.' Brenna's mouth tensed as she glanced at the gap he'd left between them. 'Are you okay? I saw the photo of you in the floodwater with the horses.'

'I'm fine.'

When her expression remained unconvinced, he added, 'I'll have a few bruises from branches and fence posts but otherwise I'm in one piece.'

She turned to face him. 'What you did … you have the biggest heart and are one of the most unselfish people I know. You are the total opposite of your father.' She paused, her chin lifting. 'Hettie said you've offered the Strathdale farmhouse and cottage to some people who've lost their homes.'

He didn't immediately reply. This is what he'd needed to see Brenna about. There was only two ways their conversation could go. He'd either leave this hill with their relationship intact or without any hope they could ever be together. 'I did.'

'Does that mean you'll keep staying at the pub?'

He slowly shook his head.

She broke eye contact to look out over her mother's final resting place.

'It means …' He ran his fingers over the silken rope of her braid that fell down her back. 'I'll be staying at my new place.'

Her gaze flew to his. 'New place? The Collins' farm sold. Were you the buyer?'

'Yes. Roy really should go into selling property. I've also put an offer on the McCallums' place.'

He watched as she put it all together. The Collins' farm was at this end of the valley and on the opposite side. The McCallums' farm then linked his new farm with Strathdale.

'Why?' Her voice was little more than a whisper, making it impossible to decipher whether she was mad or pleased.

'I wanted Mia and Emily to have their own house. The extra land will mean I can rescue more horses and I've been talking to Rowan about running cattle. But most of all I bought these farms for what I hope will be our future. This is where your home is and where you're meant to be.'

When she simply stared at him, eyes wide, he spoke again. 'We agreed to give each other space and nothing has changed. I just need you to know that as soon as I was back in a saddle again, making my life in the city was no longer an option. I did promise not to wait if I thought this wasn't where I should be, but Brenna … there's nowhere else I want to be but here with you.'

When she still didn't reply, his thumb skimmed her cheek. 'Whenever you're ready, however long it takes, I'll be waiting.' He brushed his mouth over hers. 'I love you, Brenna Lancaster.'

Not expecting a response, he went to stand. He'd said all he could. He had to walk away and give Brenna the distance she'd asked for.

But suddenly Brenna's hands were in his hair and her lips were on his. He hoped that the message she was delivering wasn't that this was goodbye but that she loved him too.

When she drew away, he'd never seen her eyes such a clear crystalline blue. It was as though all the shadows had disappeared. 'Just as well because I love you too. There's no one else I'd ever want to do life with other than you.'

He stole a long and deep kiss before tracing her face. 'We can take this as slow as you need.'

Her smile mirrored the happiness that was returning life to the parts of himself that had only ever felt numb.

'What about as fast as I need? Even a day away from you is too long. Space is not all it's cracked up to be.' Her expression sobered. 'My mother lost someone before my father … and yet she had the courage to love again. I realised last night that I had to be courageous too and stop letting my fears come between us.'

She moved to take an envelope out of her jacket pocket. 'Speaking of my mother, she wrote me this letter before she died. I haven't opened it as I wanted to work things out myself, but mainly because she told me I'd know when to read it. And I want to do that now with you.' She held up the envelope so he could see the handwriting which said, *To My Darling Salt and Vinegar Girl.* 'You see, I have a feeling she mentions you. After that day in the doctor's, she named you my salt and vinegar boy.'

He lifted his arm so Brenna could nestle against him and there would be no more distance between them.

Brenna drew an unsteady breath. 'Here goes.'

She prised open the envelope and carefully unfolded the single sheet of paper. A photograph fell out of a tiny Brenna on a shaggy white pony. A man who had to be her father held her in the saddle, unmistakable pride on his face.

She touched the image. 'That was my first pony, Sprinkles.'

'Your father looks so proud.'

She took a moment to answer. 'He really does.'

She returned the picture to the envelope before positioning the letter so they could read the contents.

His arm tightened around Brenna as her mother's love for her daughter flowed from the opening line. What also became obvious was her concern for how Brenna's father could sometimes be exacting and undemonstrative. Brenna's mother had included the photo to remind Brenna that her father had always loved her and been proud of her even if he'd rarely shown it.

'See,' Brenna said, her voice husky as she pointed to a paragraph midway down the page. 'She does mention you.'

Wyatt's lips touched her temple.

Brenna, I wish you every happiness. I have faith that you will find your salt and vinegar boy. When you do, don't be afraid to not always be strong. It takes great strength to be vulnerable. All of us need people in our lives, even you. And I promise you this: if you are meant to be with that beautiful dark-haired boy you said you wanted to marry all those years ago, you will make your way back to each other.

When Brenna turned to bury her face in his neck, Wyatt held her and then brushed away her tears.

After they'd sat wrapped in each other's arms and watched the ochre sunset flare and fade on the horizon, they came to their feet. Hand in hand they strolled down the hill. The peace that had settled within Wyatt was something he thought he'd never find.

'Is that who I think it is?' Brenna said.

Sitting by his four-wheel drive was an unmistakable black-and-tan kelpie.

Wyatt chuckled. 'Is it just me or is Bundy looking rather smug?'

'He's definitely pleased with himself. Here I was waiting for him to do some big grand gesture to push us together, but all he had to do was stay with us to make sure we didn't lose our way.' Brenna grinned. 'Mind you, he won't be the only one feeling victorious. We have a special surprise from the quilting club that might still send you racing back to the city.'

Wyatt slid an arm around Brenna's waist and kissed her to leave her in no doubt that by her side in the high country was the only place he wanted to be. No matter what the wily quilting club members might have come up with to celebrate the success of their final matchmaking phase.

CHAPTER 35

'Before anyone asks,' Brenna waved her hand towards the plates of cakes and slices filling the middle of her dining room table, 'none of this came from my kitchen. Elsie's been procrastibaking.'

Taite rubbed his hands together in excitement. 'Great, I'm starving. I thought I'd have to duck home for food.'

Brenna picked up a paperclip and threw it at her twin.

Hettie covered her mouth to hide her laughter, while Mabel and her sister, Soph, swapped smiles.

Under the table, Wyatt squeezed Brenna's knee. She still couldn't believe that the city boy she'd fallen so hard for returned her feelings. After they'd come back with Bundy yesterday, Wyatt had driven to the pub to collect his bags. There was no need for him to stay anywhere but with her, even if he had access to his second farmhouse. Before everyone had turned up that afternoon to piece together Alice and Clement's story, she and Wyatt had gone to see his new farm.

Thankfully the house had been professionally cleaned and cleared of all personal possessions. Wyatt had already spoken to Grace about using her interior design magic to furnish the rooms so another family that had been displaced by the flash flood could stay. As news spread of Wyatt's generosity, his heroic status only grew.

Brenna reached for some vanilla slice before holding up a pad of paper. 'Anyone need this for notes?'

She passed around pens and then a summary of the information they'd collated so far.

'So,' Hettie said, looking up from the typed document. 'There looks to be only a few gaps to complete before we have a full timeline of Alice and Clement's relationship.'

'That's right,' Mabel said. 'Soph and I will be able to fill in some but there's some questions that we might never find the answers to.'

Brenna glanced across at Wyatt. She knew how fast he read. He'd already scanned the pages and had started on compiling what looked like a family tree. He consulted his phone and then added more names.

'I was thinking too,' Brenna said as she looked around the group. 'Once we're done, maybe we should do something to commemorate Alice and Clement's story.'

'That's a fabulous idea,' Hettie said. 'I vote for doing something out at Platypus Hollow where they used to meet.'

Multiple heads bobbed. Taite was too busy scoffing chocolate chip cookies to respond.

Brenna threw another paperclip at him which this time he caught. He sent her an easy grin. He'd come to visit last night when Wyatt had returned to the pub to pack. While Taite had told her how happy he was for her and Wyatt, she'd also felt his joy through the twintuition they now knew better than to pretend they didn't share. When she'd told him about Neil, the tightness of his hug had made her eyes well. There were now no more secrets between them.

'Shall Soph and I start with what we've found?' Mabel asked.

Everyone nodded.

'Well, the first thing is this.' Mabel held up a copy of what looked like a list written in faded handwriting. 'This is an invoice for the gold dust and nuggets that were transported by the gold escort to the Sydney mint. They were then made into sovereigns which travelled back on the same coach to the miners.' She pointed to a line near the top of the page. 'Here is Clement's name and look at the weight of his gold. He went off to strike it rich and he did.'

Taite appeared thoughtful. 'As the bushranger articles were found with the sovereigns, we just assumed that's where they came from, but I guess we were wrong.'

Mabel nodded. 'And Clement must have had more sovereigns than what Brenna found as they weren't even a quarter of what's recorded here. The bushranger articles were a red herring but perhaps Clement or Alice collected them to make sure Clement's name wasn't associated with the gang.'

'As Clement's brother and cousin were members,' Soph added, 'the articles might also have been a way for Alice or Clement to keep tabs on what was being reported about them.'

The group nodded.

Soph spoke again. 'The next thing we discovered were more revelations in Victoria's journal about Earl's vendetta against Clement. After his plan to frame Clement at the pub failed, the police received an anonymous tip-off that Clement had hidden stolen sovereigns in the miner's hut at Platypus Hollow.'

Mabel took over with the explanation. 'Victoria told Alice that Earl was behind the tip, plus had planted the gold. According to

Victoria, Alice went to the hut, found the sovereigns and hid them close by. When the police arrived and nothing was discovered, Earl was furious.'

Soph sighed. 'I wish we could say that Earl then left Alice and Clement alone, but he didn't. When we looked into his death certificate, we found that he also died in the Tumut River on the same day as Alice and Clement.'

Brenna frowned. 'That's not a coincidence.'

Mabel's expression grew sad. 'It's not. It took several primary sources to corroborate the story but what we believe happened is that before the flood, Earl went to Alice's father and asked for her hand in marriage. He gave it. But Alice refused Earl's offer and somehow it all came out about Clement. Only her mother seemed to support her. Her father and the rest of the family forbade her from seeing Clement.'

Wyatt looked up from his laptop as everyone processed the news.

Mabel went on, 'What we're thinking is that on the day of the floods, everyone went into town to help. One eyewitness account says there was an argument between Earl and Clement that turned physical. When Alice went to intervene, she somehow ended up in the river. Both men went to save her.'

'But,' said Soph, 'another version is that Earl pushed Alice. Whether that was out of anger or because he wanted to be the hero to rescue her, we'll never know. For the record, Victoria believes he did push Alice out of spite, even though she writes that she doesn't want to think ill of the dead.'

Hettie shook her head in disbelief. 'This is even more of a reason to do something in memory of Alice and Clement. It's heartbreaking that their relationship ended in such a tragic way.'

Wyatt stretched in his chair. 'Actually, I don't think it did.'

A shocked silence filled the room as all eyes turned to him.

Wyatt elaborated. 'In the summary it says that Alice and Clement's bodies were never found. Mabel and Soph, do you know if Earl's was?'

Soph answered, 'It was but the others definitely weren't.'

Brenna turned to Wyatt. 'What are you thinking?'

'Clement had more money, so he and Alice had the resources to start a new life together even without the sovereigns in the tin. They also had a reason to disappear. Thanks to the feud, Alice's family were never going to let her marry Clement. If hypothetically they did get out of the river, they left in a hurry, so that could be why their personal letters remained hidden.'

'Where would they have gone?' Mabel asked, eyes round.

'A place far from the mountains where they would have blended in,' Wyatt said. 'A place that was in a state of flux and where it wasn't uncommon for strangers to arrive with gold to spend.'

Brenna looked at the names Wyatt had written on the family tree he'd compiled. 'California. The gold rush over there would have ended but there still would've been movement between the two countries.' As the pieces fitted together, she stared at Wyatt. 'No way.'

He nodded with a smile.

Taite pulled a face. 'Can you please explain for those of us with a brain that works at a normal speed what's going on?'

Brenna pointed to a name on their family tree which she'd included in the handout. 'Our great-great-grandparents were from California. Our great-great-grandmother was supposedly a distant relation to Alice's family. But what if she was actually Alice and Clement's child? She was married so that would explain the surname difference.'

Hettie leaned forwards. 'This is so wonderful … Is there a way of proving any of this?'

Wyatt flipped the paper he'd been writing on for everyone to see. 'There is.' He gestured between Brenna and Taite. 'Fraternal twins.' He pointed to a list of names. 'This is Clement's tree. No wonder they had such large families; there are twins everywhere.' Wyatt then indicated the page that showed Brenna and Taite's family tree. 'More twins. Keep in mind that a man will carry the gene and though he won't have twins, his daughter will inherit the gene and then can.'

Brenna frowned. 'But we don't know if there were any twins in Alice's family further back than her. I didn't look into it because I thought we weren't closely connected.'

'I did.' Wyatt gestured towards the page of names he'd been working on. 'There were no twins.' He leaned forwards. 'Let's do it this way.' He ran his pen down a list. 'Alice's family. No twins. Then here, if Alice and Clement did go to California and had a family, this is where the twin gene would come in. Alice couldn't have had twins but, Brenna, your great-great-grandmother would have inherited the gene from her father, Clement. And presto … in every generation since then you can see the fraternal twin pattern.'

Taite rubbed his forehead. 'I need a beer.'

'This all makes sense,' Mabel said.

'I agree,' said Soph.

Hettie tapped her chin. 'If Alice's mother had sympathised with her, then maybe she knew that Alice and Clement hadn't died and where they'd gone. When she was a widow and fell ill, she could have concocted the story that an American relative was to inherit Glenwood Station, when really it was Alice's daughter, her granddaughter. I just wish we had more concrete proof.'

Brenna shot to her feet, her hand touching her silver chain. 'We do. Well, I hope we do.'

She returned with her mother's jewellery box and a pair of tweezers. 'It's a family tradition for mothers to pass on an heirloom locket to their daughters.' She pulled out the locket she wore over her rugby top collar to show everyone. 'Mine was given by my grandmother to my mother, then to me. It has my grandparents' pictures below the photos of my parents.' Brenna lifted the jewellery box lid to take out a second hallmarked silver locket. 'My mother then had an older locket that had been passed to her by her grandmother.'

Brenna opened the locket from the jewellery box to show everyone the old-fashioned photographs of a man and woman. 'These are our great-grandparents. Let's see if there are pictures below these.'

She carefully prised out the images to reveal a further set of photos. She then turned over the pictures she'd removed to check the names printed in tiny handwriting on the back. They were a match to her great-grandparents.

Heads nodded.

Brenna held up the images still contained in the locket. 'These are our great-great-grandparents who came over from California. So, if there are photos below theirs, they'll be of my great-great-grandmother's parents.'

Holding her breath, Brenna lifted the image. A photo was nestled underneath.

'It's Alice,' she whispered. 'But older.' She lifted the locket for everyone to see before removing her great-great-grandfather's photo to reveal a man who had to be Clement. Just to be sure she took out the image and turned it over to read the name.

She sat back in her chair with a contented smile. 'There's no doubt. Not only did Alice and Clement survive, they moved to

California. The floods were not the end of their life together, but the start.'

Hettie's eyes shone. 'I do love a romantic happily-ever-after.' She sent Brenna and Wyatt a deceptively innocent grin. 'Especially when two neighbours from once feuding farms, with a little help from a couple of geese, some prize-winning sponge cakes, a crafty quilting club and a very wise kelpie, get the message they're perfect for each other.'

EPILOGUE

The first snowfall of the season might have blanketed the mountain peaks in white, but in the small clearing at Platypus Hollow, flames danced to keep the evening chill at bay. While the twilight dulled the golden shimmer of the leaves falling from the lone poplar, the glow of fairy lights pushed back the incoming night.

Brenna placed the final strawberries on the grazing platter she'd prepared on a trestle table before catching Taite's eye. He pretended to ignore her as he took a swig of beer and angled his body towards Trent and Heath. She grinned as she stared at him, thinking of all the baking she'd make him try. Her twin threw her an alarmed glance. Now that they'd admitted to their twintuition it came in handy. With a sigh and a resigned expression, Taite came over.

She gave him a sweet smile. 'This is for the quilting club.'

Taite's eyes widened as he glanced to where a group of elderly ladies sat around a fire pit, blankets on their laps as they laughed and knitted. Vernette gave Brenna and Taite a cheery wave.

'I can't go over there.' Taite lowered his voice. 'They're knitting *booties*.'

The quilting club had suddenly become the knitting club. Not content with their matchmaking achievements, they appeared to be looking ahead to ensure that there would be a new Bundilla generation to one day pair up.

'Taite … booties are not deadly or contagious.' She patted his shoulder. 'But I would keep Hettie away. She's already put an order in for a crocheted baby blanket plus signed Elsie up to be a future chief babysitter.'

Taite's head spun around to where Hettie sat chatting to Clancy, Aubrey, Grace and Mia. The redhead blew him a kiss before snuggling a sleeping baby Emily deeper into her arms.

'I think I need to go for a run,' Taite growled.

Brenna pressed the grazing platter into his hands. 'No, you don't. You need to take this over to the quilting club and then admit to yourself you're as clucky as Hettie. I saw you both cooing over Emily when she arrived.' She gave him a not-so-subtle push. 'Now go.'

As she watched him walk away her heart swelled. Her twin was going to make the best dad and she couldn't wait for his and Hettie's little redheaded whipper snappers.

'You're not terrorising poor Taite again, are you?' Wedge asked with a chuckle as he approached.

'Me?' she said, voice innocent. 'Never.' She turned to the old birdwatcher. 'I think your binoculars are going to come in handy when he and Hettie do have kids. They'll be hard to track, either running everywhere or wanting to fly.'

'I've already checked. I'll be able to see their new house from my back garden.'

Brenna kissed his cheek. 'You're going to be the best poppy.'

Plans were in place for Wedge to move in to Strathdale when the family staying there moved out. He had no close relations and by living next door they would be able to take care of him like he took care of them.

As for Taite and Hettie's new house, they'd been riding on Strathdale and had come across a perfect spot to build not far from the boundary fence. Wyatt had offered to subdivide the land so it could be joined to Glenwood Station. Which meant that once Taite and Hettie outgrew the cottage, Brenna wouldn't need to move out of the homestead that she and Wyatt had made their home.

'I'm going to be a busy poppy, especially when you and Wyatt have those twins of yours.'

The odds were high that she would carry on the family tradition. Whether she had twins or not, any children she and Wyatt were fortunate enough to have would be hard to keep an eye on as well. They'd either be sneaking into the pub to play pool or off riding in the mountains. She'd better put a fence around her Bundilla Cup course.

The sound of metal hitting rock had her and Wedge turn. Over at the chimney that was all that remained of the old miner's hut, Rowan was using his stonemasonry skills to shape a stone he'd removed.

Brenna reached into the basket beside her for the thin rusted tin that had contained the gold sovereigns. Inside was now nestled the blue and green ribbons that had once been wrapped around Alice and Clement's letters. The tin would soon be hidden in the chimney of the place where they used to meet.

As for the stolen gold Earl had planted inside the hut, which Alice had concealed, their research hadn't uncovered any evidence of the loot ever being discovered. This would be one question that would remain unanswered.

Brenna smoothed a hand over the tin that a lifetime ago Alice and Clement would have held. Tonight was all about honouring them and celebrating new beginnings. Their letters were safely stored in the filing cabinet in the attic while the gold sovereigns had been donated to the local museum. The police had confirmed Brenna was the owner and she'd wanted them to go somewhere they'd be valued for more than their commercial worth. Wyatt had made a donation to the museum so a secure display case could be purchased.

She glanced over to where Wyatt was in conversation with Roy, Elsie, Mabel and Soph. She'd had no idea how successful Wyatt had been in the business world. To her, he'd always be her salt and vinegar boy who looked good on a horse. As for finding someone who'd let her call the shots, she now knew what she'd really wanted was a man who'd stand shoulder to shoulder with her through life.

She took the tin over to Rowan where Bundy sat close by. Tilly and Waffles were over near the quilting ladies being fed sneaky treats. Bundy had started to not come home after his story dog duties. Even though he and Tilly were inseparable, she wondered when the kelpie would go on to stay with someone else. After handing Rowan the tin, she ruffled Bundy's neck. She was certain that when he did, he'd still be a regular visitor.

Rowan gave her a grin and busied himself with measuring the tin against the cavity he'd made in the chimney. Needing a moment, Brenna drifted away into the shadows. As she gazed at the scene before her, her joy and happiness deepened. Beneath the shed that she and Taite had built in memory of their mother, all the people who were a valued and integral part of her world were congregated.

The laughter, fun and sense of family and community made her smile.

The first of the stars gleamed above and she tipped her head to stare at the vast night sky. And for all the people she loved who were no longer with her, and for those she never knew, she hoped her parents and Alice and Clement, her great-great-great-grandparents, were looking down at the festivities and smiling too.

A splash sounded in the creek that flowed behind her.

She caught the scent of sandalwood before a strong arm tucked her close to a firm chest.

'Everything okay?' Wyatt asked, his mouth against hers.

She curled her hands around his nape and answered with a kiss.

This man was still too much. What she felt for him was too much. But this no longer scared her. Just like whenever she was in the high country that had faded into the darkness of the horizon, she knew in her soul that whenever she was with Wyatt, she was home.

The platypus that had surfaced, curious about the nearby lights and sounds, dove deeper into the creek. The recent rain had turned the clear water cloudy and reshaped parts of the bank. But the platypus continued undeterred, confident in where she was going. She always knew where her burrow was because half buried in the mud near the entrance were strange round objects that shone like the summer sun.

ACKNOWLEDGEMENTS

With each book I always start off by thanking my wonderful publisher Rachael Donovan and editor-extraordinaire Julia Knapman as without fail they wrangle my ramblings into something readable. But for this new release there literally wouldn't be a book if it wasn't for their patience and kindness in enabling me to have extra time. So, my thank you for this story is extra heartfelt.

Thank you also to Annabel Adair for her fresh final-proofread eyes and to Louisa Maggio for the stunning cover that captures the setting so well.

Thank you to my writing friends, your enduring support has meant so much, as well as to my four grown-up children and husband, Luke. A little part of you all is yet again woven into my words.

Thank you to my beautiful readers for your enthusiasm, messages and willingness to read another Bundilla book. I hope you enjoy Brenna and Wyatt's story.

Finally, this is more of a dedication than a thank you, but to my mother-in-law Chloe, for whom reading was a passion that brought her joy right until the end, thank you for always looking forward to my next book. Your purple reading chair now has pride of place in our home.

Other books by

ALISSA CALLEN

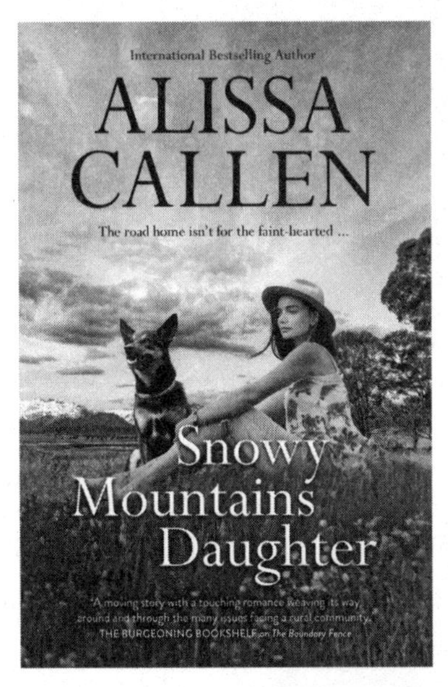

talk about it

Let's talk about books.

Join the conversation:

@harlequinaustralia

@hqanz

@harlequinaus

harpercollins.com.au/hq

If you love reading and want to know about our authors and titles, then let's talk about it.